INTRODUCING JOHN WELLINGTON'S

MARTIN FROST

T U R N I N G   P O I N T

To Romano

I would like to thank my family and friends.

Without your support, your encouragement, and your guidance this book would not have been possible.

Thank You

Turning Point

John Wellington

1

It was a Saturday, late August, 1939. Francis was first. Twenty minutes later, the girls, Emma and Anne, arrived. The sun was shining. Liverpool was leading Chelsea two goals to one with minutes left to play; it looked hopeless for Martin's team. The roast, however, was cooked to perfection, and Martin was in good spirits as he bounced around his flat.

Martin was liked by most. Outgoing and commanding. A real force of nature that, despite his shyness around women, inspired the confidence of others. Francis, on the other hand, wasn't liked by most. Maybe it was his peculiar ways. Mysteriously aloof, always talking to himself, and lost in thought in seemed. But for the height difference, Martin being nearly a foot taller than Francis, they were the spitting image of each other. People would always think they were truly blood brothers.

The two met and grew close on the sports field, rugby. Francis, despite his peculiarities, was an extraordinary athlete. Even as a first-year student, he had been the best athlete on the team. Not spectacularly built at a mere five feet eight inches. He had the muscular physique of a gladiator. A hundred and fifty pounds of muscle, which was mostly in his legs, chest, and shoulders. But he portrayed a towering unity of strength. With dark princely hair, glistening grey eyes, and a fond character that would see him do almost anything for those that captured his heart.

For better or worse, though, Francis and Martin had built a bond, a sort of union of souls that was unbreakable. A bond that engendered a feeling that to lose the other would be worse than death. Whatever came, they knew they'd be there for one another.

Anne, the redhead with green eyes, and Martin's younger sister by blood, was like the little sister to Francis and Emma, too. There was a shared note of chivalry towards Anne that was always there, hiding under the ambivalence they all preferred to project. Her wiry frame of not over five feet, and overly excitable nature, added to the vestiture of her little sister status.

Emma though, she was different. Meek and reserved, but Amazonian in appearance, with long flowing blonde hair and sky-blue eyes. Sexually attractive and beautiful through to her very soul. A beauty that was all the more mesmerising by how deeply she genuinely cared about others. But she wasn't just individually beautiful, she made the surrounding space beautiful too. She affected others and brought the beauty out of them in untold ways. With ease, and all of who she was, she made others bloom into the most beautiful of flowers. She was captivating in every way.

Emma and Martin had been doing an off and on dance of love and affection from the day they first met in Oxford. She quickly saw Martin's inner strength. Time and time again, with sensuality and caring, she would show Martin how special he was to her. Emma made Martin bloom into much more than he could ever be without her. Still, Martin was his own GPS guided by his intellect on one hand, and his deep feelings for others on the other hand. A balanced and driven person who felt that, in Emma, he had found that special something that completed him. Martin lit up when she entered his flat this day, and every time he would see her.

The four friends met at University, Oxford, and had made these gatherings a ritual over the years. However, despite Francis' misfortune, the friends had not gotten together for almost five years. To get back together again, to catch up, and to share good times was on all of their minds. For Martin, though, this day, this get together, was extra special. He had been looking forward to this day. Today was going to be the day.

At the right moment, in front of his closest friends, Martin planned to pop the question to Emma.

It was a light and delicate ring with jewels placed in the band itself. The jewels had been rescued from his grandmother's setting and stunningly reset; new jewels also added to its beauty. It was new and old, recycled, and minimalistic in a classy way. Just the way Emma would like it. A perfect one-of-a-kind jewel.

Outside, with the ever-changing British weather, the bright hue of the summer day had given way to storm clouds and softer colours of a juxtaposed palette of tranquillity. The air, that had been so still, had gained a swift movement, as if it had discovered its purpose and was raging forward to show the world.

Inside the candles, that cast soft light as the friends rejoiced, flickered every so often as the wind beat itself menacingly against the windows of Martin's cluttered, but tidy, Victoria flat in Kensington.

The girls eventually took their seat at the dinner table and continued to catch up on the happenings in each other's life. In the kitchen, Francis and Martin tended to the meal as they bantered on about the football. Francis, a staunch Liverpool fan, was elated at the misfortune of Chelsea. Neither, though, was all too pleased that, with the season drawing near, Everton looked to be in the winner's seat. For a time, the flat was ablaze with talk, banter, and laughter; not even the sudden noise of the driving rain crashing against the windows could be heard.

The boys were in their element and the girls in theirs, every so often the four of them chiming in together about the days gone by, or a funny Uni story, just like old times. Then, almost as if someone had flipped a switch in his brain, Francis was silent. He stood trancelike with his eyes towards the roast. Though it was obvious that the roast did not have his gaze. Nothing had his true gaze. He had always been a bit aloof, even in University Francis could be found walking to and fro in his dorm room from window to door and back again. His arms would be folded across his chest, and he would be talking to himself. However, this behaviour, his behaviour in the kitchen of Martin's flat, his silence, was different.

Martin looked over at the girls jabbering on at the dinner table, then back at Francis, with emphatic eyes and a flat brow before he ventured in and asked, "How have you been ... really?"

Instantly, a jolted Francis knew exactly what Martin was asking, and his eyes watered as he began to speak.

Yet he asked, "Huh, what was that?"

"How have you been?" Repeated Martin.

"Ahh ... My father? You caught me. I did it again I guess." Replied Francis.

Martin smiled. Francis smiled back. A smile, and a gesture, that Martin noticed yet again this afternoon. There was something different about Francis. Martin could feel it, see it, and was intrigued by it.

"You know it's been years since my father passed away, and I would honestly give anything and everything to have him back. There hasn't been a single day that has gone by when I do not miss him. I still to this day wonder what life would be like if he were still here." Francis said.

"We were very close, as you know. Losing him, at first, left me unravelled, unhappy, unfulfilled, unsettled, and to be fair, well on my way to hitting rock bottom. I was living a life that may have seemed a dream life for some, but one that was leaving me deeply unhappy every day.

"Then I realised I had reached the point where I knew I needed to do something. That I had nowhere else to go but up. So, I made the biggest decision of my life. I volunteered for the army." Continued Francis.

As Francis spoke, ever conscious of the girls and not wanting to get them involved, he drifted closer to Martin as his voice simmered off into a whisper. He was almost shy like in his mannerism, vulnerable, but not weak.

"That's what is so uniquely special about what seems like unbearable sadness, and complete loss of hope, seems you can't get any worse. They suddenly they get better." Replied Martin in the same whisper.

The two had been friends for a long time. They had that unbreakable bond, and a brotherly like relationship. However, in these moments of sharing, an intense chemistry developed. The likes of which neither had felt before.

"I know, that was just what I was thinking. I was scared, but needed to be happy again." Francis said as he instinctively put his hand on Martin's shoulder and looked him dead in the eye. As if to reassure Martin that he was sincere and appreciative of Martin's understanding.

Seeing that this was an important moment for Francis, Martin returned the gaze. However, he was stunned, shocked, and rattled for a moment when he did. Francis had the most alluring green eyes he'd ever seen. Martin had not noticed this about Francis before. Martin had not felt this about Francis before, either. While he had felt it about other boys, shaken it off and moved on, he had never felt this about Francis. In those moments, Martin was sexually attracted to Francis. Yet, as he had done with the other boys, Martin shook off his feelings and spoke.

"Finding happiness isn't easy. Sometimes, it's extremely difficult, hidden behind your fears, and it doesn't show itself until you have the courage and fight for it."

"But eventually, as long as we don't give up, we all find that courage. You are proof of that." Martin said before hastily forcing his way out of that awkward attraction.

"Let's eat shall we!" Martin blurted out for everyone to hear.

They were all famished.

Anne, seated to Martin's left, graced the table and silence followed as the four friends dug into perhaps the best meal they have had in a long time. The single life left little room or desire to prepare lavish meals like this one. Silence ensued long enough for the friends to devour the trapping of the splendid meal.

Then, Francis patted his lips with a napkin before gently resting it in his lap, as a slight burp passed between his lips. Emma, who was seated facing Martin, moved her hand across the table, gently touching Martin's hand along the way as she gripped a ladle. Her eyes looked into Martin's as she smiled and brought a delicious-looking pea soup into her bowl. It was as if she was bringing Martin into her at the same time. Martin saw this in Emma's movement and smiled back, a polite smile, a distant smile. His uncomfortable interaction with Francis was still playing heavily on his mind.

"Wet out there." Francis mercifully said, to liven up the room again.

The others nonchalantly nodded, with little thought.

"Looks like this is set in, we might be here for a long while." he continued.

"I can't think of a better place to be, or better people to be with." Quipped Emma.

"Agreed." The others said in unison.

Like sheep led by a Shepard they returned to their meal, with Emma taking the lead.

"How is the roast?" asked Martin.

They each looked at him one by one.

"It's lovely."

"The roast was delicious. You will have tell me your secret." Anne quipped with a smile, knowing all too well that it was she that had guided Martin in the kitchen for so many years.

"Delicious."

The compliments brought a smile to Martin's face. His smile, though, was bland. There was no emotion, no genuine joy behind his grin.

"I have something prepared for after dessert, that I hope you all like as well." He Spoke.

"What is it?" a gleeful Anne said as she grinned from ear to ear. She always seemed like the baby out of the four of them, easily amused and excited. That's how she became to be thought of as the little sister. Although, she was actually the older sibling, and only younger than Emma by a few days.

Martin's smile widened, and his spirits rose. He had crossed the threshold. Another weird encounter - the Francis thing - was behind him. Life with Emma beckoned. He got up from the table to fetch the ring. It was time; he thought.

"Does anybody remember Daniel from Uni?" Francis asked.

"Yes." was heard in reply. "He was always the life of the party."

"What of him?" "Didn't he marry Sarah, the tall brunette with the buck teeth?"

"Yes, they married after Uni." Replied Francis to make casual conversation while the three of them waited on Martin's return.

Daniel and Sarah were the topic of conversation for a while. Then they just reminisced about others that they knew in Uni.

As the conversation lulled again, Francis grabbed the ladle with his sturdy, and well-manicured, hands. The others looked on as he made himself another serving of dessert. An ambrosia custard which Emma had brought over. She was an excellent cook, but her desserts were even better.

Before Francis could take a bite, Martin, dressed in fine evening wear, as if it were New Year's Eve or something, returned with his surprise.

"Martin! What is all of this?" The ever-inquisitive Emma asked. "What going on?"

Shaking and excited, Martin walked over to Emma. He dropped to one knee. Took the ring box from his pocket. Opened it and raised it towards her. Inside, Emma could see the ring. Her eyes sparkled. She smiled. A broad smile actuated by her blushing pink cheeks. She ran her fingers through her hair, pushing it away from her eyes, which had watered. Martin's eyes caught hers as he nervously spoke.

"Emma, it's been five years since we've met, and my life has never been better. For so many reasons I love you Emma, I love you for so many reasons but most of all.

"I love you because you make me laugh when I needed it most.

"I love you because you inspire me to be a better person.

"I love you because you have dreams and you're not afraid to chase.

"I love you because of how the light shines each morning together.

"I love you because of how comfortable silence can be, with you.

"I love you because you are you.

"And most importantly, I know my life will never be complete without you beside me to share it. When I look into my heart, I see only you. If you can look into your heart and only see me, then we should spend the rest of our lives together. I love you so much that I want to be with you forever and I hope you'll say yes.

"Will you marry me?"

Everyone's heart pounded with happiness, but none more than Anne's. She was in seventh heaven. Her baby brother was getting married. She had pictured a fantasy wedding for herself, but that had not happened as yet. Might never happen as no one had caught her fancy so far. So, for now, she was happy to vicariously live out her fantasy through Emma and Martin's joyous occasion.

Francis looked at the proceedings nonchalantly, with a casual smile adorning his face.

"Say yes, say yes!" Anne said with a broadened ear to ear smile.

Emma's skin tingled, her eyes sparkled, and she started breathing quickly as she looked at Martin. She had been wishing for this day for such a long time.

As a young girl in Durham, in the North of England, Emma thought she was living in the most beautiful place on earth. On many a starry summer night, she would look to the sky and imagine her very own Prince Charming coming across the fields to sweep her off her feet. Living happily in a love filled ecstasy, they would raise their kids in Durham. But her mother saw her life differently.

From the day that Oxford began taking women, she saw her precious Emma there amongst the scholars. After all, that was what was expected within her class of society. Emma was to be a career woman. Marriage for Emma would come when it came, thought her mother.

But today was Emma's day and, in her mind's eyes, a beautiful life, being a full-time mother to her kids, awaited her and Martin in Durham.

As the sparkle in her eyes glossed over with the wet of her tears, she replied.

"Yes, with all my heart. I will marry you."

On hearing Emma's acceptance, Anne rambled on about the wedding.

"Oh my gosh!" She spoke.

"I can be your Maid of Honour.

"I will help you with all the planning.

"I can see it now.

"Everyone is happy and excited.

"You arrive at the church, a small chapel, our childhood chapel, it looks amazing with all of the wedding decoration.

"Colourful flowers, rainbow-coloured flowers, surround the church. Pink and white flower bouquets are along the aisles and at the altar. There are pink and white petals along the red carpeted aisle.

"Everyone is called up to start the wedding. Martin and Emma are a picture of happiness. It's the day they have been awaiting. Planned to perfection by me of course!

"After their vows well-wishers hug the newlyweds as they walk along the aisle. They are showered in congratulations, and the petals of flowers. It is so beautiful.

"Martin is wearing a black double-breasted jacket with wide peak lapels that show off his broad shoulders and chest. High armholes with close fitting, shorter length, sleeves give him that masculine look. Complimented by not so loose trousers that exposing more of Martin's muscular legs. He looks taller and so, so, handsome. Emma is wearing a vintage wedding dress fit for royalty a perfect Cinderel-la-Princess gown. Her dream-dress for her dream-day with her very own Prince Charming. She is the prettiest and happiest bride ever.

"The two of you are beautiful. It's a picture-perfect wed-ding." said Anne.

"Kids, a country life, in Durham, just as Emma has always dreamt, follows." Anne continued.

"Let's not get ahead of ourselves." Martin and Emma inter-jected in unison.

"Well ... okay, but I want to be a part of the planning. You two are perfect for each other." Anne said in reply.

With more talk of the future than the past, the four friends enjoyed the rest of their evening together. Martin's surprise, Emma's acceptance, and Anne's heightened excitement had put a new and refreshing light in the evening. The rain and wind even subsided, and Francis was smiling more than he had ever done since his father passed. That night, and into the days that followed, were some of the best times of the friends' lives since university. Anne even developed an eye for a young Army volunteer she thought would make a good husband.

However, with the end of summer approaching, life changed for the friends. On the first day of September, Germany marched into Poland against all expectations. Britain was thrusted into war two days later.

2

T he days brought hope. But with the nights came the blackouts - the stress, the unknown, the insomnia. Family members hunkering down in silence behind locked doors. Officers feverishly managing the command centre - ignoring each other, hoping, and praying. Clerks passing along news from the front. The Generals, the big boys, low on hope and running out of ideas. Everyone on edge wondering, "When it will start again?"

Amongst the enlisted men, the gossip was brutal. Nine merchant supply vessels had been lost to U-boats - true. Supply lines had been completely cut off - partially true. Some vessels were making their way past the U-boats. The German forces are retreating from Russia - false. The German offensive had taken a stranglehold on life in the city. The prospects for the war looked bleak.

So did the life for the four friends. It had been two years since Martin had proposed to Emma. The toll of the war had thrown the friends to different corners. They had not seen, nor spoken, to each other in the intervening years. Anne, Martin's sister, was the only one in the group still in contact with Martin. Francis was the last that they, Martin and Anne, knew was working for an intelligence arm of the government on a secret mission somewhere. Emma, they had heard, moved back to Durham, and it was rumoured that she, thinking the worst of Martin's fate, had married. Anne remained in London to support the war efforts from there while she worked with their father.

Martin, after being in battle for years, was also back in London. He had been assigned to the command centre after a tumultuous time in the European theatre. Though he was unsure which was the worst. In battle or in the command centre. In battle, he had the advantage of camaraderie, clarity, and a sense of purpose. Despite every day possibly being his last. In the command centre, nothing was clear, nothing was known. It was a mundane existence, and a toxic environment, where the allied commanders were always at each other's throat. Brits versus Yanks were dominant, but the other allies also chimed in when the battle was near to their home.

Sometimes the atmosphere was so toxic that Martin left the command centre and wandered the streets of central London - thinking, frightened, listening. Although accustomed to the darkness, brought on by the blackouts, Martin often became disoriented in the first minutes of venturing out. One clear night, in the fall of 1941, disoriented, he sat on a bench in Trafalgar Square and looked deep into the darkness. Nelson's column marked his gaze. A fifteen foot, one hundred-year-old statue that memorialised Admiral Nelson's victory in the battle of Trafalgar. A monument that stood as a reminder of the glory days of the British empire. An empire whose future looked anything but glorious to Martin these days.

As he sat, Martin's thoughts flashed here and there in rapid order. Battlecruiser HMS Hood - sunk. Heavy losses at Halfaya Pass - they are calling it "Hell-fire pass" now. He couldn't guess what will happen to Britain as the German Panzers were becoming an increasing risk, and the Luftwaffe is delivering heavy strikes - Moscow was certain to fall soon. The Russians were panicked. The possibility of negotiating peace with Nazi Germany has been ruled out. His desolation was consuming him that evening. There was also his fear of another air raid, but that night passed without the skies lighting up with German devastation.

The following day, there was a flash of optimism when news reached the command centre of the sinking of another Nazi U-boat. Two days later, the news of a wolf-pack destroying merchants' ships in the North Atlantic diminished all optimism. Wolf-packs, the name given to a group of German U-boats hunting together, were winning the Battle of the Seas.

The waiting, hoping, and prayers continued.

From a command centre beneath Whitehall, four senior officers ran military strategy for the allied forces. Three of the officers commanded the army, air force, and navy, respectively. The fourth senior officer was Sir Adrian Shaw - a battle hardened, un-killable soldier who had served in the Boer War, as well as the Great War. He had been shot in the face, through the skull, hip, leg, ankle and ear - losing one eye and one arm. Sir Adrian, a full colonel, ran a fourth division of military strategy - counter intelligence. Martin was an army, but not attached to military strategy. Marking incoming messages on a map and relaying them to the higher ups was his role in the command centre.

Hour by hour, day by day, week by week, Martin's hopes, fears, and worries grew. Then it happened. He was summoned to the office of Sir Adrian. He had a small, cramp, and dusty office. Maps of Europe, Africa, and Asia covered the wall and tracked the allies' war efforts.

"Have a seat," he ordered. Martin stepped into the office and sat in a chair next to his commanding officer - General Binney - who ran military strategy for the army. Martin felt a sense of exuberance come over him. He had longed to get into the heart of the allied offensive, and this was it he felt. His time had come, and he was ready. Sir Adrian fell into his chair and made direct eye contact with Martin. He recapped the mess they were in with the war efforts.

"As you know, Japan has started its invasion of Thailand, the Germans have Leningrad under siege, and supply lines are being attacked in the Atlantic - we are losing ground."

"Yes Sir, the German Blitzkrieg, with its rapid movement, and combined infantry and air support seems indestructible, and Rommel seems to be out manoeuvring us all the time as well."

Sir Adrian and Binney both stared at Martin with intensity as he spoke. They could see his enthusiasm and hear his knowledge. They knew they had selected the right man for the job.

"We are working closely with our allies and adjusting our tactics. Our allies can perform precision air attacks on infrastructure, and the Royal Air Force have been having success bombing sizeable areas. But the spirits of our enemy remains high, while those of our people dwindle," continued Sir Adrian.

"Yes Sir, how can I be of help to our country?" Martin replied. He was eager to get on with it. He knew what was going on with the war - he had heard it in the command centre, read it in the news, and worried about it during his walks about London.

"We are starting another offensive in Northern Africa. Taking control of Tobruk is strategic," Sir Adrian said.

"Operations Brevity and Battleaxe did not go well for us in North Africa. Are we using the same tactics on this operation?" Martin asked.

Binney spoke next. "No, I fought for a change of tactics. At first we were going to use the same tried and tested tactics. But I had to remind them that we have tried twice and failed. That our enemy knows what to do to defeat us. In the end I talked them into sending in the infantry first this time. A novel approach. Hell, we could be heading into a bit of trouble there, but if we can stop the Italians here we can put a bit of pressure on the Germans - maybe turn things around."

Sir Adrian interrupted. "General Wavell and his second - Cunningham - will be relieved of command in the Middle East. We are reorganising their forces under General Auchinleck. Lieutenant-General Ritchie will be his second in command. We will join up with the French and our other allies to begin the offensive there. We will have our best men on this one Martin. They will form our Eighth Army."

"Ritchie will begin his offensive in Libya in route to Tobruk. The Eighth will send in their infantry, to establish footing, then quickly take out the Axis armoured forces. It's called Operation Crusader, and, well, we need a strong commanding officer to lead a battalion of our men. We want you to lead them," Sir Adrian said.

They sat for a moment in the dusty and gloomy silence of Sir Adrian's office, the three allowing the gravity of the moment to settle. Finally, Martin asked, "When do you need my answer Sir?"

"Thirty-six hours. You will get the details of the transport Sunday morning, and will have to leave right away for the ship. The plan is to have you meet up with the Eighth in Algiers."

"But it's your choice Martin. We know what you went through in Dunkirk, so if you need more time just let me know." General Binney told Martin.

Martin stood up. "Thank you Sir," he said, addressing Sir Adrian.

Then turning to the generals he said, "General Binney," then he sharply snapped his heals and left Sir Adrian's office.

That night in mild air and under a misty sky, lit by a half-moon, a chill gripped around him as Martin walked the streets of central London. His with thoughts meandered through the many facets of the war, as he slowly and aimlessly made his way in the darkness. Going back into battle also consumed his innermost feelings. As he neared Nelson's column, its moonlit shadow fell just below his feet - as if it was meant to guide the direction of Martin's path. Germany, supported by its allies, was gaining control over large areas of the continent, Martin thought. They were winning against the Russians, and the Japanese were becoming aggressive in the Far East. Axis forces were ahead of us at every turn. We have had two failed attempts in Northern Africa and all looked lost. But Roosevelt and Churchill had just signed a document that set out the Allies' goals for the war, which in some small measure raised his spirits, and gave him hope for the future. There must be a way to get ahead of Germany and their allies, he was thinking. Then, with a snap, Martin's thoughts turned to his conversation with Sir Adrian and General Binney. He had a decision to make. He was a loyalist that wanted to fight for his country, and a better world, but something was nagging at him about this mission.

As he thought, a man in a black overcoat, black ascot tie, and top hat, arrived on the square. The man walked slowly towards Nelson's column in the centre of the square - as if lost in his thoughts as he plotted along. The man was Robert Lambert - a code-breaker.

Martin's path crossed Robert's as they both arrived at the Column.

"Good evening," Robert said as he neared Martin. "Fine evening we are having." "Fine evening, in deed Sir," Martin replied in a startled voice. There was only Robert and Martin in the square that evening, but still Robert's initial presence in the square was not noticed by Martin, who was lost in his thoughts.

"What brings you out tonight?" Martin asked. "I am rarely in London, and, well, when I am, I find the quiet of an evening walk helpful."

"I do as well," replied Martin. "Tonight more so than others, as I ship out for the front soon."

"I understand our code-breakers are helping the war effort tremendously, maybe they will be of help your efforts at the front as soon," Robert replied.

"Thank you," said Martin.

"Good luck to you Sir," Robert replied. They then continued on their paths, both in thought.

Robert wanted to give Martin more hope, but he couldn't. The truth was that earlier in the year, the HMS Aubrietia captured one of the new German enigma coding machines. Before this latest capture, they had made big improvements to the decryption work done by the Polish on the enigma cipher before the start of the war. But with the new enigma machine, and cipher codes captured this year, they were able to read important parts of German navy radio traffic. Things had changed, and they were winning the Battle of the Atlantic. Robert worked as a code-breaker in a top-secret research facility. He had come to London with his boss, Francis, Martin's friend, to talk with the Prime Minister about getting more resources for code breaking.

Martin continued his to walk, heading towards the north-east corner of the Square. Unaware that his good friend Francis was in London. As Martin neared St Martin-in-the-Fields church, he again shook his head at the damage from the Blitz started a year ago. Since medieval times, there had been a church in the north-east corner of Trafalgar Square. St Martin-in-the-Fields church was currently there, and had been for over two hundred years. Now it stood damaged but resolute. On seeing the damage, Martin's thoughts were that since the start of the Blitz, Britain had been losing ground to the Axis forces. Martin was instantly angered. His anxiety also grew. Why, exactly, was he eager to go to the front? He wondered. The longer he pondered this question, the angrier he became. He wanted to lash out, but at what, and why? Confused, angry, and anxious, he decided he needed to talk this over with his father - a Boer War veteran that was sure to have also faced these thoughts.

The Boers were descendants of Dutch settlers in Southern Africa. Britain had fought the Boers for control of South Africa as they sought to expand their empire in that region. Following a build-up of British troops, the Boers decided to strike before the Brits became stronger. So the very well-armed Boers and struck first. Their initial attacks against the over-confident British were extremely successful. Some years later, though, the British reinforcements and harsh counter-measures brought the Boers to terms.

Martin's father fought in both of the Boer encounters, and Martin, somewhere deep inside him, hoped that there was wisdom that his father could share with him as he opened the door to his barracks.

That night, it started again as Martin aimlessly wandered the streets. First the distant roar of the German twin engine Heinkel He 177, Greif bomber planes. Germany had named these planes after the Grief or Griffin because they were able to fly long distances and deliver powerful bombs, torpedoes, and guided weapons. Griefs or Griffins are mythical creatures with the body, tail, and back legs of a lion; and the head and wings of an eagle. An aptly named plane for the damage they were doing to Britain. This night Germany's Griffins' target was London.

The dreaded air raid sirens sounded as soon as the humming of the Griffins could be heard. The noise of the sirens wafted through the air, screeching out a deafening high and low wailing warning sound. Bringing fear and trepidation. Those in the air-raid shelters were utterly exhausted from continually being confined to a communal shelter at night - but they were safe. Others hurriedly made their way to the nearest shelter.

Then the sky became lit by the glare of the fires, some of which were caused by incendiary bombs. Air raid wardens, equipped with stirrup pumps and whistles, scampered about as searchlights illuminated the sky. The wail of the air raid sirens, the drone of enemy air crafts, the bang bang of the anti-aircraft batteries, and the shrill whistles blown by the air raid wardens were frightening. The streets were chaotic, and London was not to be spared this night. Even Martin's sanctuary in Trafalgar Square would be damaged.

That night, shortly before 9pm, a five hundred pound high explosive bomb fell on the roadway at the southern end of the Square - a direct hit. The bomb drove downwards, penetrated the road's surface, and detonated just above the Underground Station ticket hall, forty feet below. Tons of earth fell there that night - burying many who had taken shelter in the underground tunnels.

3

Through a single window the shadowy light of the evening sky, and distant fires, illuminated Martin's room at the Wellington barracks when he arrived back that evening. The raid was over; the griffins had gone; he was still alive and safely back in his barracks.

The lads at Wellington barrack had many duties - Buckingham Palace Guard, St James Palace Guard, Tower guards, and Ministry security duties. Some were members of the Holding Battalion waiting to be put into service. Martin was in the Holding Battalion and had been posted to the allied command centre while he waited to be put into service. Either in action against the axis forces or in defence of Britain's shores.

He swung the door open, stepped inside, threw his overcoat at a chair, and fell onto a couch. Night-time bombings over London had been scarce for some time. Many had felt that the blitz had ended - yet here they were again. Martin thought. He could hear the commotion in the aftermath and see the distant flames. Martin's emotions felt as if they were riding a roller coaster - up, down, around. The air raid that evening had done very little to calm him. He closed his eyes, and breathed deeply, managing his emotions - fear, anger, vulnerability.

The fear came from not being able to do justice to his station in life.

In the rigid class structure of British society, the educated middle and upper classes believed in their own moral and cultural superiority over the working classes. Even more so, they were loyalist that in every fibre of their being believed in the greatness of Britain on the world stage. Proper models of behaviour, as well as their perceived power and authority, came from here. There was no transcending the social hierarchy. The Frost family was through and through British upper class. Martin's father, Martin Frost Sr., was an Oxford law scholar and a General in a war where Britain was triumphant. After the war Martin Sr. began a successful legal career, and later went into practice with his good friend George Overy, who also studied the law at Oxford. Frost and Overy LLP were now a thriving commercial law practice, with Martin Sr. still at the helm. Martin Jr. feared he would not live up to his father's escapades. Each lost battle was cutting deeper and deeper into Martin Jr's psyche, bringing an ever-increasing fear of failure.

His anger came from the defeats on the water, in ground combat, with the air raids over Britain, and with each battleship sinking. Each taking its toll on Martin's feelings. Not because of the loss itself. No, his anger was at the core of his belief that everything was wrong about this war. Everything!

It wasn't long after he proposed to Emma that Martin joined the British Expeditionary Force and was a part of the first deployment of troops. In his mind's eye, he often recalled arriving alongside the grey imposing hull of the troopship. The gang planks were laden down with kit bags and small arms. Him being dispatched, with the other enlisted men, to accommodations below the officers' cabins at deck level.

Then came the long journey to Calais, France. A journey that saw them one by one succumb to the dreaded sea-sickness, making urgent dashes to the head, or the sides of the ship, to retch and groan. To curb the boredom of the long journey, the troops were given lectures on the German army, their uniforms, the silhouettes of aircraft, the latest information about their tanks, and daily bulletins about the progress of the war - both at home and overseas. Martin's eagerness to see the action grew steadily as the journey progressed.

But for ten long months, after arriving in Calais, through a horrendous winter, he would dig trenches in defence of the north-eastern Belgian-French border. Before, some years later, under the command of General Lord Parker, he would encounter the worst of his war. German forces invade France and swiftly push the allies to the French coastal town of Dunkirk. It would be here, during the fall of France, that Martin's inner core would be shattered, that he would lose hope, that he would face death head on.

Following a fierce defence, the allies were defeated. Martin and the British, together with other allied forces, are evacuated to Britain. But not before the harsh conditions of the French winter, the boredom of trench digging, and a crushing defeat by the skilled mobile operations of the Germans, had mutilated his pride and brought about deep feelings of resentment - anger.

Today Martin's life stood in stark contrast to his hopes, as well as the expectations of someone of his stature.

Britain was facing defeat at the hands of the axis forces, and he often felt that he would never practise the law which he loved so much. He would soon ship out again on a mission of which he was mysteriously uncertain. He honestly couldn't say why. Was it fear or intuition? - he just couldn't say.

His sanctuary, Trafalgar Square, where he sat not too long ago, fell victim, yet again, to a German air raid. The first hit on the Square was at the start of the blitz a year ago.

The damage, losing life that evening, German aggression, uncertainty, and being away from the law all deepened his feelings of vulnerability and humiliation that had grown with time.

Anger, fear, and humiliation were consuming him. He wanted so much to talk with his father, to hear his reassuring words of wisdom, his guidance, but he didn't want to sound weak, indecisive, or to appear defeated. After all, he was a Major-General in the British Army, and British upper class - resolute to the end.

Whilst at Oxford's Brasenose College, he was the Captain of the rugby team. The Blues rugby football club had seen success under Martin's stewardship. Winning the Inter-Collegiate competition and bringing honour back to Brasenose - who boast that this traditional English game was invented by a former student. He had breezed through law school and finished with an Honour's degree in Civil Law. After a successful pupillage at Frost and Overy LLP he was a barrister, and the pride of his family. The first twenty-four years of his life had seen overwhelming success, happiness, and little failure. In contrast, but for the camaraderie with lads from all walks of English society, his time in the army had been demoralising. So much more than the minor bump in his career that he thought it would be when he enlisted at the start of the war.

Later that day, just after noonday, Martin arrived in Mayfair. He had set his insecurities aside and gone to see his father. He was so glad that he did. Martin felt a sense of relief, opening the door to his parents' home. The knots that had been in his stomach instantly untangled as the tension in his muscles drain from him. He was home. He was truly safe again.

He had not seen his parents for months - since the Mayfair bombings, when this affluent area in the west received its heaviest hits from the air raids.

Martin was the middle child of the Frost siblings. The youngest, Thomas, was studying mathematics at Oxford, and there was Anne, the oldest yet the little sister of Martin's Oxford foursome. They had grown up in affluent Mayfair - amongst the British elite. Children of a war hero and destined for Oxford along with big things in the eyes of society. The war effort had done little to change such expectations held by many of the British elite. But rationing affected people from all walks of life. It was one effect of the war that bound the British society together as one - irrespective of social status. The Frost family, like many Brits, had converted their garden into a vegetable plot. Tending to the vegetables, taking care of the household, and following the news about the war effort kept Mrs Frost busy. Mr Frost - Martin Sr. - spent most of his time at the Old Bailey or with clients.

On his arrival home, Martin's mum was in the kitchen clearing up after lunch - cottage pie and fresh vegetables grown by Mrs Frost. He and his dad made their way into the sitting room to talk by the fire.

A couch and two armchairs were arranged in front of the large fireplace in the sitting room. The arm chairs directly faced each other with the couch separating them. The burning fire crackled and popped as the combustion gases trapped in the pores of the wood quickly expanded. The warmth from the fireplace took the chill out of the autumn air. Martin sat on the couch facing the fire as he sipped tea from a fine china cup. Martin Sr. sat on one of the armchairs.

Martin told his father of the fear, anger, and humiliation he was feeling. As well as the nagging feeling he had about the mission that Sir Adrian and General Binney had given to him. But not about his obsession, not about the fear he had of his secret desires being exposed. The blackouts and war time focus of the community made it easier to keep these desires a secret, and he was not about to let anyone find out now.

His dad was silent once Martin had finished talking. It was as thought that he was lost for words. Then, "Dad I have to decide by the morning." Martin eventually said.

"I understand son, and, well as you know, in war a change in strategy, a little luck, and the war is won." Martin Sr. replied. "When we fought the Boer war, it looked bleak at times but we had a breakthrough and voilà, we triumphed." He continued.

"And what about my career as a Barrister? The Law Practice? Becoming your Partner at the firm?" Martin asked.

"There will be time for that son, don't complicate matters." said Martin Sr.

"For soldier's much of their life centres around food, when they get it, how it is served, how much there is, where it is served and most importantly what it tastes like - a simple, yet demanding, life. But officers have to think moves ahead of their opponent." Martin replied.

Martin's father then said. "If you need time to think the Kings Regulations for the army allows you leave up to three months. You will need the approval of the Minister, but I can help with that - Churchill is a friend."

"Yes Sir, I could use the time. Although the war may be lost by the time I return." Martin solemnly replied.

After lunch, Martin walked away from Mayfair and headed south towards Westminster. His leave request came as a surprise to General Binney, but he and Sir Adrian received it with respect.

Susan from Churchill's office, and Martin Sr., proved to be remarkably efficient. At 5:00pm Martin received confirmation, by messenger, that his leave had been granted. He stared at his leave papers for a long time and contemplated the reality of not shipping out, and being free to leave the city.

From his sparsely furnish room at the barracks, Martin watched as the lights of London went out. The entire city was lit up like a dazzling fairyland that touched the evening sky. Then, one by one, at the pull of a switch, each area went dark. The dazzle became a patchwork of lights, here and there, until a last light was snuffed out. The darkness heightened Martin's sense of freedom. He could smell the burning tar - another defensive measure employed on the home front to create a smokescreen that impaired the pilots' vision. Guided by his senses, white paint on the streets, and nerves of steel, he again wandered the streets of London in solitude. Newspaper in hand to make himself more visible.

The Red Lion was a popular pub amongst British officers, and just a short walk from the barracks to its location on Parliament street. This was his destination. The windows and doors of the pub all had blackout curtains or blinds, and the gaps around the edges were sealed with brown paper. There was not only no leakage of light but also little air could get in or out, making the smells of the pub to linger intensely. Martin, occasionally, would stop off here for a pint. He enjoyed the atmosphere and the pre-wartime nostalgia that he would feel. The smell of hops and malt, mixed with spirits. The pleasant-ness of the warmth and smell. The laughter and banter of the men enjoying the moments amidst the uncertainty that came with war.

This evening, by chance, he met Francis in the Red Lion. It had been years since they had last seen each other. In that moment they were happy again. It was as if a beam of light had been shone into his soul? Martin sat back and let the happiness soak right into his bones. He closed his eyes and savoured the moment. For the first time in forever, his body and mind were totally relaxed. In that moment, he forgot his fears, anger, and worries.

Exuberantly, he walked over to Francis.

"Hey, I had hoped I would run into you. I passed a friend of yours in the Square last evening and he said you were in London." Martin said as he approached Francis. "Yes, Robert told me he saw you. But I thought you were heading off for the front?" Francis replied. "That's right, but not right away. My plans have changed." Martin said. The two men smiled at each other as they shook hands. Holding each other's hands tightly and lightly gripping forearms.

As the waitress passed, Martin ordered a pint of Chiswick Bitter for himself, and another for Francis. Although not as strong as before the war owing to war-time restrictions, the Chiswick Bitter was Martin's favourite beer. It was brewed right there in London's west district of Chiswick and was a favourite with too many Londoners.

"So, you are in the midlands now on some secret mission. Is that right?" Martin asked. "Yes," replied Francis, as Martin was beginning to pick up on the slight nuances of Francis' change in dialect.

Britain is very rich in its dialect, with countless accents shaped by thousands of years of history. Francis' distinct midlands accent had developed quickly since he had last seen him, but it also stood out in as it was not common in London, making it easier to for Martin to notice his friend's unfamiliar accent.

"Yes. I'm living in Bletchley now." Francis said. "What brings you to London?" asked Martin. Francis took a gulp of his beer, savoured the flavour, and hesitantly replied. "I am taking a quick break from my job as an Air Raid Precautions warden at a Government facility in Bletchley. Nothing too exciting, or secret." Replied Francis. He dared not tell Martin the truth of his highly secretive job.

"What about you, Martin? When do you ship out for the front?" Asked Francis. "Well, as I mentioned there has been a change in my plans. I had leave coming to me, and took it now." Martin answered. Martin was not ready to share his fears, nor his hesitations about the mission, with Francis. Tonight, he wanted to leave those thoughts behind and just enjoy being with his old friend again.

"So, we can both be carefree tonight." Said Francis. "Yes, if only for a while." Replied Martin. They both took a pull from their lager and looked at each other. As the evening wore on, that awkward feeling that Martin had in his flat two years ago happened again. More than once this evening, though.

4

That night Martin slept for twelve hours and woke with an overwhelming sense of loneliness. It was nearly 10 AM. Outside, gloom covered the sky, and smoke filled the air. Another air raid, more bombs, more destruction reined over the city in the wee hours of the morning.

Lying in bed, staring at what little space there was in his cramped barracks, Martin replayed the last few years or so in his mind. His gleeful proposal to Emma. Seeing Francis had reminded him of how much he loved her. His initial enlistment into the armed forces. As death surrounded him in battle. The command centre. His disillusion with the war, and now detached, confused, and ready for a break.

He could hear his heartbeat, louder, more slowly, louder, more slowly, as he had done many times before. For years, he had been surrounded by the noise of war and the constant activities of those around him, yet he had been alone in his heart, his soul, and his mind. Today, his loneliness struck harder as he recalled just how good life was before the war began. He ached in unimaginable ways. He felt like a beautiful swan that had lost his soul mate.

As Martin meandered through his thoughts, the Sergeant-Major double timed it along the Birdcage walk. He entered the barracks through an entrance next to the Chapel, glancing at the wreckage as he passed. The Chapel was bombed when the blitz had just started - now it stood in ruin as a daily reminder to the residents of Wellington barracks of how close they had come to death.

The shock of a spy that close to the heart of the allied operations had also not subsided. It had only been a few months since the German spy, Joseph Jakobs, was captured shortly after parachuting into the country. He was later hustled into the back entrance of Wellington barracks for his summary of evidence hearing. One after the other witnesses gave their statements. But for a single question, Jakobs remained quiet. His earlier interrogation by MI5 – British Secret Service - also ended without a single clue. He had a postcard from a Clara Baeurle, thought to be his girlfriend, but said nothing about his mission throughout the entire ordeal. He was court-marshalled, then executed in the summer. Leaving unanswered questions. The source of the Jakobs' threat was assumed to be German, but the truth was that no one knew for sure. The top brass was still nervous. They wanted immediate action on this new threat to their most secret facility in England.

Now Sgt. Major Wilson was on an urgent mission. The order had come from the top, Churchill, and non-delivery of this message was not an option.

Martin laid there, still in thought, when a sudden quick, and rushed sound of multiple knocks on his door interrupted his thoughts. Francis awoke abruptly. The two men were panicked. With everyone focused on the war, their guard was uncharacteristically down. There was no safe place for them to hide in the small room. Francis scampered behind the door as Martin bravely swung it open. It was Sgt. Major Wilson.

"Yes, what is it you want?" Martin said.

"Sir, I have been dispatched by General Shaw to get this message to you before you left on leave. It is urgent, Sir." replied the Sgt. Major.

The message was written on the richest white cotton paper. Then folded very carefully along the long edge towards the middle, and then again. A wax seal secured the message where the ends of the paper met. Martin recognised the seal to be the seal of Sir Winston Churchill - the Prime Minister of Britain.

With steady hands, but his heart racing inside, Martin opened the message.

His heart was racing because Martin knew that for the Prime Minister to write to him directly, it had to be important. Maybe the purpose he was seeking, maybe something worst. He didn't know, but stoically he opened the message.

"Major-General,

On a matter of urgency, and the utmost secrecy, I asked that you meet with me at Whitehall forthwith. We shall await your arrival.

Sincerely,

Sir Winston Churchill"

Dazed, Martin slowly refolded the message. He looked at Sgt. Major Wilson as if he were looking through him. As if the Sgt. Major was transparent and he could see the blank, musty wall behind him - in its entirety. He stood frozen, a deer in the headlights, for a few seconds. That seemed like an eternity to the Sgt Major. In awe of the moment, the Sgt. Major stood in silence wondering what had just happened. What does the message say? He thought.

Eventually Martin spoke. Deliberately and firmly he said, "Thank you, Sgt Major. Please tell the General that I will comply with the contents of the message forthwith." "Yes, Major-General." Replied the Sgt Major. Who then swiftly turned and began to double time his way back to Whitehall.

The day before, Churchill had received a letter brought to him personally by one of the code-breakers at a secret facility in the small town of Bletchley - sixty miles northwest of London. A seemingly unimportant place to most. But Churchill was thinking that this country manor in Bletchley, is where the war could be won. A German spy in London had only made code breaking of messages that much more important to the war effort. Britain had to get better information, and it was Bletchley that could make this happen.

The code breaker's letter began:

"Dear Prime Minister,

"Some weeks ago, you paid us the honour of a visit, and we believe that you regard our work as important. You will have seen that, thanks largely to the energy and foresight of Commander Travis, we have been well supplied with the 'bombs' for the breaking of the German Enigma codes. We think, however, that you ought to know that this work is being held up, and in some cases is not being done at all, principally because we cannot get sufficient staff to deal with it."

The letter went on to specify a list of requirements needed at the facility. There was also information about a robbery at the home of one of the code-breakers. The code breaker was arrested following the incident. Sensitive questions are now being asked by the authorities. The letter expressed grave concern for the secrecy of the facility and concluded by stating:

"No doubt in the long run these particular requirements will be met, but meanwhile still more precious months will have been wasted, and as our needs are continually expanding, we see little hope of ever being adequately staffed."

In response, Churchill immediately fired off two messages. The first to his chief of staff: "Make sure they have all they want with extreme haste and report to me that this has been done." It said.

Churchill's second message was to Martin.

Moments later, Martin, dressed in his parade uniform, took his leave through the front entrance of the barracks. His mind was racing, wondering what Churchill could possibly want with him. He took two deep breaths to calm himself and entered the door of Whitehall.

A guard stepped forward and confronted Martin. "Major-General Martin Frost, here for a meeting with the Prime Minister." Martin told him. "Down the hallway, third door on the left." The guard replied.

Martin timidly knocked on the door. Three slow knocks.

"Come in." He heard. Martin sharply swung the door and stepped forward. Churchill and General Shaw were seated at a large wooden desk. Sir Stuart Menzies, the Head of Secret Intelligence Service, was standing just to the left and behind the Prime Minister who was seated with a cigar in his mouth.

Stacks of paper were carefully piled in the corners of the desk. A portrait of the Prime Minister's wife hung proudly on the wall directly facing the desk.

Martin recognised Menzies as the new head of the SIS. He had never met the former head Hugh Sinclair before he died in November, just after the war had started, but knew Menzies as his deputy who had now taken over the service. The SIS was responsible for the covert war and used tactics and methods that were uncharacteristic of the rest of the war effort. If Menzies is here, then this must be very important, Martin thought.

Sir Adrian stood up and said. "Please have a seat Major-General." Martin sharply stepped forward and sat in the chair to the right of Sir Adrian. Martin was a little squeamish at the sight of the General's partial left limb. As such, he was happy to see the chair was on Sir Adrian's good side.

"Martin, we are glad that we caught you before you started your leave. There is a situation at one of our facilities, and we need your help. Your background as a soldier and a lawyer is needed." Sir Adrian said as he continued to speak.

Martin's interest was piqued at hearing a lawyer was needed.

"As you know there is a facility in England that decodes intercepted messages. Yesterday the Prime Minister received a letter from the code-breakers at this facility. The letter described a situation with one of the code-breakers," said Sir Adrian.

Churchill interrupted. "Martin, this facility is where I think the war could be won. But, well, we can't have the authorities nosing around. There are just too many spies. Heck, we just executed one and did not learn a thing from him. There are others out there, and the authorities cannot be trusted."

"We need a lawyer to go over there to represent our code breaker. To keep things quiet so she can get on with her job. To be secretive about their reason for being there. This is not an order Major-General, but we need your answer on this mission by 17:00." Sir Adrian said.

"The army cannot interfere with proceedings and bring attention to the place. Your father and I have been friends for several years. When we spoke about your leave, he assured me you were someone that could be trusted to get a job done. He does not know about this request I am making of you, but I trust his judgement and therefore I can also place my trust in you. But that is all we can tell you for now." Said Churchill.

"Yes, Prime Minister. Sir Stuart, General Shaw," said Martin before he stood, snapped to attention, saluted, and left the room.

Sir Stuart did not speak during the meeting. His steely eyes observed every move, as he could be seen to analyse Martin's responses, from the words to his body language.

Martin remained unaware that Francis was the code-breaker that delivered the letter to Churchill. But he was looking forward to a trip to Bletchley and seeing his old friend again.

Twenty minutes later, Martin arrived at the law offices of Frost and Overy LLP on Derby Gate. He needed to talk with his father again.

Since the start of the blitz, crime in the city had flourished. With the air raids came looting, even murder. Hiding the bodies murdered amongst the wreckage of a bomb was becoming commonplace. As were the requisitions of property and disputes under the Compensation (Defence) Act.

Despite the rise in crime, Martin Sr.'s practice made most of its money these days from property disputes. There was some, but not much, money made in the Old Bailey courthouse attending to criminal law matters.

On seeing his son, Martin Sr. smiled broadly, stopped what he was doing, and welcomed Martin into his office. He was calm and relaxed, as if he had all the time in the world.

"Were you working on another compensation dispute?" Martin asked.

"Oh no," Martin Sr. said.

"I leave those matters to the other lawyers in the firm. Most of my time is spent over there, he said, pointing in the general direction of the Old Bailey with the look of pride on his face. Martin thoughts became inquisitive. He was wondering what exactly it was that his father did. But he put off asking that question.

"Enough of that," Martin Sr. continued. "How are you doing son?" He asked in a tone of sincere concern for his son's wellbeing.

"I'm okay Sir," Martin said and immediately felt his heart begin to race. Take control of yourself, he thought. He swallowed hard and said. "It's been a difficult twenty-four hours. After our talk yesterday I thought I needed some time away from the army. I requested and received leave. Thank you for your help. I was allowed to put off going to the front. But today, the Prime Minister himself has asked me to take a special mission. I do not know much about the mission, just that it is secretive and I will get to be a lawyer."

"You can be a lawyer right here, son. We can use the help over at the Old Bailey." His father replied. "There are a lot of looting and murder cases these days." Said Martin Sr.

"I'm sorry, Dad, but I can't see myself in London handling looting and murder cases at a time when the war is being lost. These looters and murderers that you speak of need defending, but it's not for me." Martin replied. "I need something more meaningful." He continued.

Martin Sr's shoulders sagged a bit. The smile went away. "It's not all bad, son. I had one case were the defendant was charged with looting because he and his men shared a bottle of whiskey they found in the rubble when searching for survival. Looters can be executed, and he certainly didn't deserve to be executed." Replied Martin Sr.

"What do you think, Martin?" His father asked.

Martin listened, sipped his tea, and reminded himself of the Prime Minister's words - he would help to protect a facility where the war could be won. He wanted, no, needed, this exciting change of direction in his life.

"Sounds like meaningful work," Martin managed to say. "We need to defend people's rights in law, even in times of war." But it didn't take much longer for the father and son to decide what would be next for Martin.

At 16:30, Martin arrived at Sir Adrian's office. He was immediately allowed to enter.

Without hesitation, Martin said. "General I am honoured to be chosen for this mission and accept the offer. Please tell me the details of the mission."

Sir Adrian replied, "Martin, we are happy that you are accepting the mission. You are the best choice. You will be going to Bletchley, where we have our secure code breaking facility. For this mission, you will be going as a civilian lawyer. You will report to the law offices of Dunham & Associates LLP. Matthew Dunham, the managing partner, is unaware of the purpose of the facility. Most living in the area think that Bletchley Park is a mental asylum."

"You have to ensure the secrecy of the facility is maintained throughout the proceedings involving this code-breaker. The code-breaker's name is Sharon Howes. Matthew is a friend and needs the help so he has agreed to seeing you. He will give you the details of the case. He has been told that you are on leave from the army and, as a lawyer, that you wanted to help out."

"Thank you, Sir. When do I start?" Asked Martin. "Right away," replied Sir Adrian. "Yes Sir," replied Martin before standing, saluting, and heading towards the door. As Martin made his way to the door, Sir Adrian shouted.

"Good luck Major-General, the fate of this war might be in your hands."

5

Matthew Dunham ran his low-budget legal practice from an abandoned green grocery store on Park Road, Bletchley. The population had been growing steadily about ten-thousand now. Up from six-thousand before the evacuations of London at the start of the war. Mainly due to the Bletchley being designated for billeting of at least two-thousand. With the rise in population, so was Matthew's practice. He needed help and the likes of Martin would be welcomed.

In Bletchley, for the most part, the locals went about their business without too much thought about what went on behind the scenes. However, sixty miles from London in distance, and decades away in time, this quiet town had become ripe, with secrecy and petty crime, since the start of the war.

Dunham and Associates LLP, Matthew's practice, was small. He had been the managing partner from the day he founded the practice twenty-years earlier.

Ruth and Jonah Cook were long-time residents of Bletchley. They ran Cook's music and radio shop adjacent to Matthew's law office. Inside the Cook's shop, there was a telephone that Matthew would use when his own phone was not working and he had important business to speak about urgently. So he bee lined to the Cook's to jump on a call to his General friend as soon as he received the message to call. Learning that Martin might be coming to help him as a favour for a General in the army was certainly worth the trek across the road to the Cook's shop. Even though he often wondered what the Cook's did with the information, they would glean from his calls and important business.

After their father, old man Cook, as he was known to the kids, died in a tragic accident. Herbert - 'Bert' - Cook, the brother, was rumoured to have become involved in the local radio activities of the secret service. A rumour that intrigued Matthew, but he was always too busy to be bothered to investigate a rumour. Best he kept to himself and his work, he thought.

With his office phone working again, Matthew awaited the call from Martin that the General said to expect. It was days later when the phone rang, and thankfully, it was still working. Matthew picked up the handset. The heavy black cord had become entangled, as it often did. But this time, the tangled cord caused Matthew's heart to race. He wanted the call with an Oxford educated lawyer to be perfect. Giving his usual greeting, he said. "Hello Matthew Dunham, here."

A very assertive voice from the other end said, "Hello Mr. Dunham, this is Martin Frost. I am ringing you as arranged by General Shaw."

"Thank you, Mr. Frost. I was surprised to receive Sir Adrian's suggestion that you came out and helped me while you were on leave. He told me you were due to lead a division at the front, is that correct?"

Evasively, and sure not to give any confidential information over the phone, Martin reply, "You could say that, yes."

"Well, we've never had a lawyer from Oxford work with us. To bc frank I am excited to have the opportunity to work with you. We certainly can use the help. The war has brought this country together in a lot of ways, but crime is on the rise. There is no shortage of people with problems here in Bletchley. Have you ever been to Bletchley?"

Martin had not. He had been raised in London's upper-class establishments. Only leaving the city to attend law school in Oxford. He had never ventured elsewhere in the country. "I'm afraid not," replied Martin in a respectful tone. Matthew's voice was cheerful, but reserved, and Martin felt he needed to be respectful. His midlands accent also brought back memories of Francis and slightly panicked Martin. Francis was a secret that cannot be known to anyone. Especially not a fellow lawyer.

"Well, it's not London." Matthew said. "Okay Mr. Frost, look, the job does not pay and it's not guaranteed. Even though we are happy for the extra hands there is a process. You will have to be properly interviewed. Can you come here for a look around?"

"Sure, certainly, I could take the train up." Matthew said. What else could he say? Any hint of reluctance would get back to Sir Adrian and he would rightly be scolded. He wasn't ordered to take on this mission, but a court-martial wasn't out of the question either. "When did you have in mind?"

"Today, Tomorrow, the next day, whenever. We have lots of work coming in, there will be no shortage of it whenever you arrive. But I guess the sooner the better if you want to get involved in the Sharon Howes case."

"I can be there tomorrow afternoon, I suppose."

"Okay David Smith, one of the lawyers at the firm, and I will be available tomorrow afternoon. We won't have much time for an interview, but I don't think it will take long. We will probably end up just just welcoming you to the team."

"That is, if we like you." Continued Matthew jokingly.

Martin closed his eyes for a few seconds to put the call, and the pass few days, into perspective. Three days ago, he was relaying messages in the command centre, a seemingly important job at the heart of the allied operations. Now, he was hours away from a mission given to him by the Prime Minister himself. He would be a lawyer as well. His passion had been stoked, and he was excited.

Returning to the moment, and mustering as much humour that he could in his words, Martin replied, "There is a train to Bletchley leaving at noon. It takes about ninety minutes to get here. Do you want to say we meet at three tomorrow afternoon?"

"Yes, okay, I'll see you then."

"Thank you, Mr. Dunham."

"No, thank you, and call me Matthew."

A year earlier Bletchley station was a probable target for German bombing. A train was gunned, and four high explosive bombs were dropped in the vicinity of Bletchley Park. Two nights earlier, London was also bombed. But, as did most in Britain, Martin did not usually live in fear of imminent death. Today, though, Martin was uncharacteristically feeling on edge. There is so little shelter in Bletchley that he could meet his end. So that night he decided to have dinner with his parents before he left the London.

Martin arrived at his parents' Mayfair home just after seven in the evening. Thomas, who on break from his studies, smiled from ear to ear as he firmly gripped and shook the hand of his brother. An officer in the British army, the proud younger brother was thinking. Thomas was so proud of Martin and his accomplishments that he often even bragged about him to his teammates. Thomas, now a member of the Blues like his big brother, was hoping to be a captain like him, too. Anne, although living with her parents in London, hadn't seen

Martin in months. He had passed through the office in such haste earlier that week that he did not even look for his sister. It wouldn't have mattered, though. In addition to working with her father, Anne was part of the Women's Volunteer Service, an organisation that helped the war effort in many ways. When Martin stopped by for lunch, she had been visiting households in Chelsea, helping people to understand more about the air attacks, what they can do to protect themselves, and to protect the community. Martin and Anne hugged at the sight of each other. Anne's eyes watered from joy. She was so happy to embrace her brother, after so long.

"Anne, I am sorry I didn't come by to see you when I visited dad earlier." Martin said.

"It's okay, I understand. Anne Replied.

"I saw Francis for the first time in years the other evening. He was in London meeting with someone. He was all secretive about why though. Intelligence stuff."

"Have you been in contact with Emma," asked Anne.

"No, I haven't been able to make contact. Do you know if she married?"

"I am afraid so Martin." Anne said in the most solemn of voice that she could muster.

"I heard from Ruby. You know the girl that had the buck teeth and sat in the front row in you and Emma's Tort class at Oxford?

"We have been keeping in contact, and she told me that she had finally heard from Emma.

"Emma thought that you had died in Dunkirk, and her mother talked her into marrying some bloke from their home town.

"I don't think she is happy though." Continued Anne.

Martin breathed a deep, heavy sigh. He had always feared this new one day, but on hearing it, he couldn't contain his sadness. As his shoulders slumped and his spirits sank, he was visibly shaken. A moment worse than the death that he had seen was passing. Loneliness struck him in the strangest of ways.

With a deadly silence in the air as he grieved, if but for a few moments, Anne interjected and cheerfully changed the subject.

"So, what do you think about dad taking on criminal case?" She asked.

Martin didn't think too highly of his father representing looters in a time of war. He felt there was something morally wrong about what they were doing. Instead he replied, "everyone needs a defence, and dad seems happy. It must be a pleasant change for him."

"I think he grew bored and wanted to try new things." Anne said.

"Over the summer he wanted to represent Joseph Goebbels - the German spy. Being an ex-soldier and a lawyer he was excited to be in a military court. But in the end it didn't work out. Something to do with a highly classified intelligence operation that needed an enlisted man."

"However, I think he likes criminal law now." Continued Anne.

Out of habit, Thomas sized up his brother from head to toe and made his assessment. He could see the smartly attired military man, that was usually confident and composed, was on edge.

"Martin, is everything okay in your life?" He asked.

"Thomas, a lot has happened in the past few days. But we can talk about that later. How are things with you? How are the blues making out this year?" Martin replied.

"The blues could win the Inter-Collegiate competition. As for me, Oxford is going well. Last week a group of us were selected to go to America. Both Oxford and Cambridge have been invited to send some of us over to Harvard as a safe haven and for academic exchange. Dad, said I should go. What do you think?"

Martin's mind began to fill with questions. It must be the lawyer in me, he thought.

"How many students? When would you go? What does the Dean think of the offer?" Martin asked.

"I don't know how many, maybe one hundred, I guess. The Dean was hesitant at first, but the message was delivered by the hand of a Dean from Yale. So, our Dean thought it was authentic, and an excellent offer." Thomas replied.

Before agreeing to send students, if their parents agreed, our Dean even visited Yale to see the programme." Continued Thomas.

"And when would you go?"

"That has not been decided, arrangements are being made."

Martin was hesitant, but replied, "I think that is excellent. It seems to be legitimate, for now anyway."

"Now, what about you Martin?" Asked Thomas.

Martin told Thomas about the past few days. The front, leave, offer to go work with their dad, the visit with the Prime Minister, and his plans to go to Bletchley the next day. Thomas, always the younger brother who revered his sibling, was in awe. He couldn't help but stare, with his eyes wide open, and mouth slightly ajar, as Martin spoke. It wasn't until Martin Sr. came down the stairway and greeted Martin Jr. before the awe-struck Thomas snapped to his senses again. Within moments of their father's arrival, a somewhat less awestruck and slightly embarrassed, Thomas was off to help in the kitchen.

As quickly as he could, Martin told his father about his decision to go to Bletchley. He was careful not to tell Thomas or Martin Sr. about the secrecy of the mission, just that it was arranged by Churchill himself. Both knew it was important by knowing the Prime Minister was involved. There was an awkward moment of silence when Martin finished speaking.

But in that silence, Mrs Frost thankfully announced that supper was ready.

They were all starving.

6

It took an hour in Harrods to buy the civilian clothing he needed for his Bletchley mission. Martin bought two suits - basic grey, and a dull faded blue - a few shirts, ties, and a hat. He hadn't purchased clothing in years and was surprised by the quality. The rationing of materials for civilian clothing was not even noticeable. The store clerk marked off twenty-four coupons in his clothing book. Martin paid, then made his way back to the barracks.

Not long after arriving back at the barracks, there was a knock on his door. Three quick taps, a pause, then two more taps. Martin knew that familiar knock. It had to be his dad. He opened the door and sure enough, Martin Sr. was standing there - apparently out of breath. Martin Sr. took a deep breath to steady himself. "Good morning son, I am glad I was able to catch you before you left for Bletchley."

"Why, what is the matter dad?" "Oh, nothing son. I just wanted to tell you one more time that you can come work with me at the law firm during your leave."

He continued to tell Martin how he was making a mistake. That missions like this from the Prime Minister sound sinister, and that he was rushing into a dubious situation. He pressed

Martin Jr. nonstop, as his son did his best to be respectful. He remained silent. Until his dad finally got him to speak.

"Dad, no, no thank you, I don't want to come and work with you. Plus, I have already taken the mission to go to Bletchley. There is no guarantee, I have to interview, but I am sure I will get the job."

"You're making a mistake, son, but I will respect your decision."

"Thank you, Dad."

"I love you son. Take care of yourself."

Martin disembarked at the Warren Street bus stop, turned right onto Euston Road, and fell in with the stampede of commuters leaving the city for a weekend break. Near Euston Station, amongst the crowd of people, and the many uniforms, Martin saw a familiar face. It was Sergeant-Major Wilson - a short, heavyset, stocky, redheaded man. His girth and distinctive red hair made him stand out in the crowd. The Sgt. Major spoke first, "Good morning Major-General, it's me Sergeant-Major Peter Wilson, we met two days ago at your barracks."

"Yes, I recall Peter, how have you been?"

"Very well Sir, just taking a bit of R&R this weekend. And yourself? What brings you this way? Why the civvies?"

"I am on leave for a few months, heading north to Bletchley to interview for a temporary job. It's as a Barrister so I thought the civvies would be best. How are things at the front? Any news on the eighth?"

"The boys should be steaming up the Mediterranean right now. The eighth will form in Algiers, like you know, and then over to Tobruk. We are still taking heavy losses on the ground, but handing out quite a bit from the air. But the news is that the Germans are advancing in Russia and have Moscow in sight. It is not looking good. Britain may be invaded."

"Well we will be ready for them Sgt. Major. Enjoy your leave."

"You as well, Sir."

At Euston Station, Martin stepped inside and took a table in a quiet section of the coffee shop towards the window overlooking the platforms.

Martin was a staunch believer in having a good breakfast. The waitress came over. He ordered black coffee and the English breakfast. As he began to enjoy the solitude of a quiet breakfast, away from the day-to-day army routine, Francis stopped by his table.

"Hi Martin, funny seeing you here. Where are you off to?"

"Hi Francis. A lot has happened since the other night when I saw you. Most of all I am on leave from the army now."

"How? Why?" A surprised Francis asked.

Being careful not to say anything about a secret mission. Martin told Francis about what had transpired over the past few days. That he was on his way to Bletchley for a job interview and hoped to spend his leave working as a lawyer in Bletchley. Then asked, "Are you leaving London?"

"Yes, I am on my way back to Bletchley. My secret mission is in Bletchley is over. Between the two of us, I tell people I am in the Home Guard, stationed at Bletchley Park. But I do more than that. One day, when I can, I may tell you?"

"Okay I will keep your secret," replied Martin.

In the pause of their conversation, the friends' eyes met. Another awkward moment.

"Well we must get together whenever we can in Bletchley." Stumbled out of Francis' mouth as he broke the awkwardness.

"Yes." replied Martin.

The train for Bletchley is boarding from platform one came over the loudspeaker. The two men made their way to the platform in silence. Seated in different cars on the train, the men, as they approached the platform, said their goodbyes and went their separate ways.

Martin inched his way along the platform and into one of the compartments towards the front of the train. Army, navy and air force personnel packed the train and there was standing room only. Martin's officer's reserved seat was taken, but he decided to not to ask the soldier to get up. Probably best, he thought, as he was not in uniform. Too many questions that would make him too visible when he wanted to travel in secrecy. Instead, he found a spot between the first and second compartments where he could use the outer side of the train to brace himself. Here he settled in for an uncomfortable journey.

Just as the doors to the train were closing, four men, also dressed in civvies, jumped haphazardly through the closing door. They crammed into the compartment with Martin and a few army personnel. Although it was not yet noon, the men appeared to be inebriated and were talking loudly. Drawing both Martin's anger and curiosity as he listened to the men.

Anger at how loud they were amongst the other passengers. Curious about what these four men, with American accents, were saying.

Jim, the loudest of the four, was doing most of the talking.

"Our work at Bletchley Park will be finish next week. We have all we need to get started now."

His travelling companion, who had a strong southern American accent, spoke next, "Yes, we do, we are ready to start, Donovan will be happy with what we have discovered. But it is a shame Goebbels' man got caught coming into the country."

A third companion, who seemed less inebriated, signalled Jim and the other man to be quiet. "Hey, shush, shush," he said as he scanned the compartment to see who could be listening. Martin, who had seemed to be looking towards the floor, and not directly at the men, used his periphery vision to notice this behaviour. The man's mannerism peaked Martin's curiosity even further. He spoke and acted as if there was a secret being told that should be kept quiet.

Donovan was not a common name in these parts, and Goebbels was certainly German, thought Martin. He knew from his time working in the command centre that William Donovan was the Head of the Office of Strategic Services. He was responsible for all the American spies. There was also Joseph Goebbels, the Minister of Propaganda in Germany. But these would be odd names to be associated together, Martin thought.

Suddenly, a commotion began in the second compartment. A Sergeant in the army and a Petty Officer in the navy were arguing. It was just a loud rumble that Martin could hear, but it captured the attention of those in his compartment. The rumble grew into a fight, and the commotion into a fracas. Martin decided to move further down the train away from the events. Somewhere a bit more civilised was on his mind.

Towards the rear of the train, he was motioned over to a vacant seat by a woman. "Come, you can sit here," she said.

"Will he not be returning," Martin asked.

"No, he was called to the front of the train because of some commotion, and said he would be getting off at the next stop."

"Okay thank you." Martin said as he took a seat next to her.

They exchanged pleasantries. She spoke with a perfect Liver-pool accent and introduced herself as Clara Baeurle, a singer and actress. Getting into the character of his secret mission, Martin told her he was a lawyer.

Martin had maintained the muscular physique developed during his days playing rugby at Oxford. This physique, his smile, debonair demeanour, and strong chin captured Clara's eye. In his presence, she felt both safe and admired. She was also curious and deliberate in her contact.

In that moment, Martin noticed a depth to Clara's beauty. The innocence of her face, soft and smooth as it was, could not hide any of her emotions. She was like an open emotional book to him. Her pain was noticeable in the crease of her brow and the down-curve of her lips. But her eyes, her eyes, revealed her soul. They were a deep pool of restlessness, and oceans of hopeless grief. As Martin looked into her eyes, he could not escape his thoughts. Not since Emma had he been so swiftly captured by a woman in this manner. Although all the beauty of the world could not surpass one thing he saw in her eyes - mystery.

Mystery turned her eyes of beauty into orbs of the brightest fire, and in those orbs, he read she would not let the world break her. She would fight to the bitter end for her life. Mys-terious as she was, she immediately appeared as someone that would cling to their principles with passion. A mysterious facade, signs of principled passion, laid her ever so beautifully in front of him.

"Every young man in Britain is either, in the Army, Navy, or Air Force - why aren't you?" she asked.

"I was in a tough battle in France. We lost a lot of men to the axis forces, and were forced to withdraw. The battle left me, well, ah, in an unfit state for duty." he replied.

"How terrible this war is on all of us," she said.

"When do you have to return for duty? Do you have to return?"

"In a few months. I am hoping to spend the time in Bletchley practicing law, and healing. What about yourself, are you on your way to Liverpool?" Martin asked.

Clara had never been to Liverpool. With her eyes in a hazed, awkward steer past Martin, and into the compartment behind him, she searched for a reply. She thought about her past and how she came to be at this point in her life.

Her early life in Austria, as the child of fruit handlers. Losing two of her siblings at a very young age - which still saddened her to this day. As well as meeting her childhood friend, Joseph Jakobs, who had always brought joy into her life. It was Joseph that brought her to England and how she came to be sitting here beside Martin.

Not too long after the Great War - World War I - Joseph told her that he had been recruited by the district leader of the National Socialist German Workers' political party - the Nazi Party - to be a part of a secret operation. This is where it all began for Clara. The event that set in motion her becoming a spy, but for whom she was now uncertain.

Until the summer of 1939, Joseph and Clara lived a simple but happy life together. Clara singing and acting, and Joseph travelling on missions for Goebbels - the man that recruited him into the Nazi Party. His duties for Mr Goebbels were always simple. Tell the stories he gave to them to people they encountered or were told to meet. Stories that supported the Nazi Party and got people to support Germany's aggression - revenge for what was done to Germany during the Great War is what they were told. Clara was told to develop her English speaking.

By the summer of 1939, when Joseph and Clara had to separate, Clara had developed a strong Liverpool accent. That summer, she was told to move to England and get settled into a life there as a Brit. While Joseph was to join the Wehrmacht - the German armed forces.

While in England, she provided accommodations and help to the spies that would come from Germany. Many of whom were sent on reconnaissance missions to understand the British resistance capabilities. Which targets were best for the German air raids? Where to spread the propaganda given to them by Mr Goebbels.

But occasionally she would be told to help spies she knew were not Germans, even though they spoke German with her. They spoke English in public and it was their English that gave them away. Their attempt at a British accent was flawed with American or Canadian. She was unclear - but gradually grew more and more suspicious.

When Jacob did not arrive in England on schedule in the summer, she knew something had gone drastically wrong. The fake German spies had also not arrived as planned. Now she suspected the worst and was determined to find the truth.

Returning to the moment, she looked at Martin and replied, "No, no, Liverpool was a long time ago. The past year or so I have been living in Bletchley." Martin was pleasantly surprised at the prospect of seeing more of Clara while he was in Bletchley. He smiled, an endearing smile that caught Clara's eye as well.

However, their moment was interrupted by the sudden jerking of the train as it came to a stop at Leighton Buzzard - rattling, Clara and Martin forward, and then side to side, causing their bodies to gently bounce off each other. Martin could smell the sweet scent of her shampoo. It was rare for him to be this close to a woman. He became aroused, but remained outwardly calm.

Until the final jerking of the train before it stopped resulted in their bodies colliding and Clara's handbag falling from her lap. On the floor, the contents of her handbag were revealed. At first, nothing too suspicious. The normal things women carry. Lipstick, scarf, hairbrush. Then there was the unusual a pistol.

Martin's eyes were drawn to the pistol, a Browning Hi Power 9mm semi-automatic handgun. He carried the same gun when he went into battle, but was surprised that Clara had one in her handbag. Not many, and especially not a woman, carried handguns in Britain even during these times, he thought.

As Clara scrambled to repack her handbag, Martin calmly asked, "Why the handgun?" Clara, in a state of paralysing surprise, replied, "It is for protection."

"Ah, you fear that the country will be overrun by the Germans? Well not if our boys have anything to say about it." Said Martin.

Clara stopped for a second. She glanced out the window, took a look around the compartment, and then said, "This war is not as it appears. There is so much more that I need protection from than the country being overrun by the Germans."

Silence ensued for quite a while after that comment as Martin tried to understand what he had heard. He was reluctant to ask questions out of fear of being drawn off his mission to help a 'damsel' in distress. Fortunately, the train stopped in Bletchley and the awkward silence was broken. In a cloud of smoke and dust, they disembarked. Martin looked at his watch: 2pm. He had time. He asked Clara if she would join him for a coffee. Despite the awkwardness, he was still attracted to her. He also didn't want his time with her to end just yet, especially not on that awkward note of silence.

The two walked the full length of the high street and took in the sights for the full ten minutes that it took to get the layout of the town. Near the end of the high street was the Bull Commercial Hotel. Martin checked into the hotel and left his luggage at the front desk. Clara and Martin then went to the hotel cafe. The cafe was empty, so they had a choice of seats. "Where would you like to sit?" Martin asked. "Over there by the window," Clara replied. They ordered tea. Martin preferred his with sugar and lemon, but Clara preferred hers strong and without sugar. She also insisted on having digestives with her tea. A habit she had picked up from practicing to be a Brit from Liverpool. She had to have a digestive for her dunking biscuit. Martin wasn't a dunker, though. The years in combat had taken away any urge to dunk. It was just the basics for him these days.

As their tea arrived, two men entered the cafe and sat at a table in the corner. The men, dressed in civvies, had a clear view of the entire cafe. They strategically place the backs of their chairs were against the inside wall.

After taking a brief look at Martin and Clara, the men seemed otherwise uninterested.

Clara became unnerved. She looked out the window, around the cafe, and attempted to look nonchalantly at the two men in the cafe. Martin noticed Clara's actions and asked, "Is everything okay?"

"No, it isn't. Those men have been in Bletchley since the summer and keep showing up where ever I am. I think they are following me." She replied. "Is that why you have the pistol?" Martin finally asked.

"Yes, I have been looking into the movements of the Americans in Britain, and I don't think they like me. I fear for my life."

"Do you really fear for your life?" Asked Martin suspiciously, as it seemed so strange for a woman in Bletchley to be looking into Americans. "What is really going on?" He asked.

She paused and looked away for a second. "We have had three women from the Bletchley Park Government facility go missing. Their bodies are later found among the rubble in London after an air raid. You have to be careful around here. Especially the women it seems, as neither of those women should have been in London."

At that moment, a tall man also entered the cafe. He was at least six feet, thin, dressed in a dark grey suit, with greying temples in a well groom head of dark hair. This older man walked with purpose towards Martin and Clara, drawing their attention as he approached their table. "Good afternoon Martin, I am David Smith, how was your journey? Matthew is out of court a bit earlier than expected and wants to see you now. If that is okay with you?"

"My journey was okay, and yes I can see Matthew now. But how did you know where to find me?"

David replied, "It's a small-town Martin."

7

With a girlish smile of admiration Clara thanked Martin for the coffee, and the conversation, as they left the Bull Commercial Hotel. They shook hands and promised to have lunch someday. David, with Martin at his side, continued along the footpath on their way to the law offices.

It wasn't much shy of 3:00 p.m. when they hustled past Cook's Radio Store. Two men in the radio store, dressed in American armed forces uniforms, caught Martin's attention. He squinted and scratched his head in puzzlement, but did not comment on them to David. Maybe another time he will ask what happens in that store. He thought.

As they made the turn onto Park Road, a brisk wind hit him in the face, and a chill consumed him. He shuddered, drew his overcoat tighter, as he looked towards the wind swiftly descending from the distant hillside that surrounded the town. In the hills, dark grey clouds were gently flowing into a lighter grey mist. A sure sign that the town would soon be engulfed in the darkness of another chilly winter night.

A bell clinked on the door when they entered the front room of the offices. Martin paused, looked around, and took in the surroundings. An empty reception area with a cluttered, paper filled desk stood boldly in front of him as a certain indicator of a busy law office. Someone was usually there to answer the phone and greet the clients, he surmised.

The offices were in an early nineteenth century building, as were many of the brick-built offices in this Victorian railway town. A hallway to the right of the reception desk disappeared to what could be a kitchen or break room, he thought. Stairs directly ahead of him went up a few flights to what he imagined was a rabbit warren of small rooms with offices and files, perhaps. In the room, to his left, was a table and several chairs. Martin guessed this to be where they saw clients. The offices had a feeling of old and well used about everything that he saw.

A faint smell of wall plaster filled the air. The oak flooring was dusty and well worn, creaking as he walked through the reception area. The walls were a cream colour from the floor to the trim of the vaulted ceiling. Giving the offices a feeling of being functional and professional - where serious business was conducted.

On the wall, behind the reception desk, hung a large oil painting of a woman elegantly posed against the backdrop of a sprawling oak in an English countryside. She was dressed in an early Victorian period, powder blue, lace and silk dress. She had the ideal shape of the Victorian woman. A long slim torso emphasised by wide hips giving her a low and slim waist. Corsets were tightly laced and extended over the abdomen and down towards her hips. A beautiful, seductive woman. Martin thought. A change from the other smaller black and white photographs arranged haphazardly on the surrounding walls, but an odd painting to be found in this office, he thought. Still, it really brightened up the reception area, and that may have been its sole purpose.

"That is a lovely picture," Martin said. "Yes, it is. Matthew thought it would liven up the offices."

"I think he is right. It certainly brightens up things." Martin replied.

"It has been in Matthew's family for some years," said David.

"Is it of someone special?" Matthew asked.

"It is of Matthew's great grandmother. Painted sometime around the turn of the century by a local artist." replied David.

Martin could hear the footsteps of someone coming down the stairs quickly. The stomp, stomp, stomp on the wooden stairs echoed loudly in the sparely furnished office. Then, there in front of him, stood a balding elderly man with glasses perched on the bridge of his nose. "I take it you're Martin," he said, walking towards him with his arm stretched out. As they shook hands, in a strong and rugged voice, the man said, "I'm Matthew Dunham. I am very pleased that you were able to come up to Bletchley for a chat."

"I am pleased to meet you," Martin said as he surveyed Matthew. The hair that remained on the sides of his head was salt and pepper, his eyes were blood-flecked, and his smile, his smile, was captivating. Martin guessed his age to be early fifties, and with that smile, plus a strong voice, he came across as one hell of a lawyer.

"In here," Matthew said, as he moved towards the meeting room just off to the left of the reception area. David and Martin followed. Once inside, Matthew closed the door and said, "I see you have met Clara. She is a mysterious person. Been here in Bletchley a year or so now. She is friendly with David and Margaret, they seem to understand her. Have a seat."

"So, what's her story, Martin asked."

"I don't know much about her. She arrived here just before the war. Has been here ever since. She is a real looker, isn't she?" Replied Matthew.

"She is stunning. Do you know why she would have a need for pistol?"

"No why do you asked?"

"On the train ride over I noticed she had a gun, said something about needing protection."

David stepped forward and leaned towards Martin. In a soft voice, almost a whisper, as if he was worried about who might hear, said, "There was a commotion over by her home a few weeks back. Gun shots, but she said she knew nothing about them. There is certainly more to her story."

Matthew spoke again and said, "Anyway, here's where we are. The General thinks you will be helpful with the Sharon Howes case. I don't have a lot of time to spend interviewing, you now. So let me tell you about the case, and if you think you can help our board will meet and decide."

"Okay, who is on the Board?"

"It basically just David and me. Janette is another lawyer here and she would be invited to the interview but she's in London. We will make a quick decision. If we decide to go with you, when can you start?"

"I am not that busy these days, so can start right away - if that is okay with you."

"Okay that's fine. About the Howes case. I don't know why the General is interested in the case, nor how he knows Sharon. But, it's a domestic matter."

"Since coming to Bletchley she has taken up with a man, Richard. He was wounded in the war and cannot serve anymore. Now he is back home, in the pub all the time, and quite frankly mean to Sharon. He ill-treats her all the time.

"The bobbies have been called several times, but Sharon never lets it go anywhere. However, this time Richard has taken a shine to Sharon's work. He thinks there is something more to what she is doing than she is letting on. He has got the bobbies asking questions, and, well, Sharon is really upset about it. The bobbies have been at it for days, questioning her. They have not charged her with anything, and she has again not asked for Richard to be charged either. She just wants it to stop, so she can get back to her routine. Is that something you can help with?"

"Yes I think so. What else will I be doing?"

"Everything from opening the mail to answering the phone to filing pleadings. You may even get the odd looting case. Did you ever get to see the inside of a courtroom before joining the army?"

"No."

Matthew hesitated for a second, as if this might be a deal breaker. "That's okay, I guess, you're lucky in one sense. But I am sure being at the front has more than prepared you for the stress of the courtroom. Why aren't you at the front now, if you don't mind me asking?"

Martin took a deep breath and thought of ways to avoid answering the question. Invention failed him and he said, "I was supposed to take over the command of a division in Northern Africa, but took leave to be here instead. Being at the front lost its meaning for me. I felt there was something more I could be doing for the country."

"Being here you think is that something more?"

"Well, no, but it is a distraction while I figure things out."

"Fair enough. Are you relieved to be away from the war?"

"I don't know how I feel, Matthew, to be honest. A month ago, I was scrambling about in the allied command centre in London, thinking that I was doing my part, and there was hope. There were dark clouds out there but I was too busy to notice. Then an air raid over London, the loss of a few merchant vessels, and suddenly the loss at Dunkirk came back to me and honestly, I became afraid of my own shadow. So, in a way Matthew, yes, I am glad to be away from the war. But in other ways I want so much to make a difference and to serve my country. I am torn."

Matthew had a solemn look on his face as he seemed to contemplate what he had just heard. War is soul destroying, he thought. "Would you go back?"

"I don't know right now. I am on leave and have to go back, but I am no longer committed to what I was doing."

"Well, Martin here at Dunham and Associates you can make a difference in someone's life every day."

David glanced at his pocket watch, a well-worn Swiss Helvetia, and said, "Martin, what are your plans for the evening?"

Martin shrugged and shook his head. "I haven't the foggiest. Didn't actually think that far ahead."

"Well, let's start with getting you settled in at your hotel, then dinner, and we can go from there." Said David.

"Okay." Replied Martin.

At the reception desk of the Bull Commercial Hotel, Martin checked in and made his way to his hotel room. David waited for him in the lobby. The cold and sparsely furnished room reminded him of his quarters at the Wellington barracks. The room's heavy curtains concealed the light from the dimly lit room. It was dark out, so the blackout continued.

Martin quickly freshened up and changed clothing, ready for whatever was in store for him in Bletchley that night. Before leaving to meet David in the lobby, he paused, sat at the foot of the bed, and reflected. He thought the events had moved quickly in the past few days. He has gone from the boring busy activity of the allied command centre to the remoteness of Bletchley, and the journey has been eventful.

His thoughts then went to Clara, the Americans on the train, the radio shop next to the law office, and his mission in Bletchley assigned by none other than Churchill himself. His curiosity about hearing Donovan and Goebbels also crossed his mind. What could all of these people have in common? He thought. His mind explored the possibilities and concluded that below the surface, there was more going on in Bletchley. Maybe this was where he was meant to be, he thought - divine intervention and all went through his mind.

With so much on his mind, he suddenly took a deep breath. Cleared his thoughts. Then snapped to his feet, took one last look at himself and left for the lobby to meet David for dinner.

"Where are we going for dinner, David?"

"My house, its just around the corner and my wife is an excellent cook. We can have a drink in the garden and talk. I can tell you about Bletchley." David said with a smile.

David pointed in the direction of travel as he and Martin left the hotel. "It's a short walk to my house."

The shops and offices were closed. They trekked along the roads that David had travelled often in the darkness of a blacked-out Bletchley. He seemed to know every step of the ten-minute journey from the hotel to York Street, a leafy row of nineteenth century, redbrick buildings lined with oak trees.

Martin took in the surroundings as they walked in silence. The solitude awoke feelings within him as he wondered where

Francis lived in Bletchley. Could he possibly be in one of these homes? Or perhaps he lived in Bletchley Park itself.

When they arrived at the Smith's home, Margaret Smith was in a rocking chair in the living area. "I told Martin that you are an excellent cook," David said as he swung open the door and greeted his wife loudly so that she knew Martin was with him.

"I guess that means that there will be one more for dinner tonight," she said with a smile. "Welcome."

"What are you cooking for dinner, sweetheart?" David asked.

Margaret said, "Baked chicken with potatoes and vegetables."

"Just what I was hoping you would say. Margaret's baked chicken is one of her specialty dishes. I think you will enjoy it." David said. "A glass of wine or a lager first?"

"A lager for me. I am not much of a wine drinker." Martin replied.

With a crescent moon for light, they drank lager in the garden for an hour. Martin drank slowly and choose his words carefully. From fear of his secrets becoming expose by accident, Martin had become accustomed to being careful in the company of others when he drank alcohol. As they talked, he politely probed David and learnt that the Smith's had two adult children who were both serving in the air force. There were two grandchildren, one from each son, that they rarely saw. Clara, mysterious Clara, had befriended them some months back. Margaret, who David affectionately called Peggy, was a Women's Volunteer Service worker. David's father was a lawyer and had been killed in the Boer Wars. Martin thought of the many similarities that he and David shared. The conversation eventually turned to Matthew.

"What is Matthew like?" Martin asked.

"Matthew is a very interesting person. He is calm, kind, while at the same time a cheerful person, and a brilliant lawyer. He knows how to find a common language with everyone. I have never known him to raise his voice or have a harsh word for anyone. He is dedicated to his work as a lawyer and enjoys the good that he does helping others. We have worked together for ten years and he has been an inspiration for me. You should enjoy working with Matthew."

Not much longer than an hour or so of Martin and David talking, the Smith's had an unexpected visitor. Clara had come by to say hello and chat with Peggy. She lived a few streets over and often stopped by for a chat, and sometimes dinner.

Surprised, but not terribly, by Clara's visit, Peggy said. "We have a guest for dinner this evening Clara. Martin Frost. He is one of David's associates, over from London, and may be here for a while working with David and Matthew. Do you want to join us for dinner?"

"Yes I would be happy to join you for dinner. I met Martin on the train ride up from London. We had a coffee after but he did not share much. It would be nice to talk with him some more." Replied Clara with a smile.

"What's that about," asked Peggy.

"I will tell you more later," Clara answers.

Peggy announced Clara to the men.

"Clara tells me that the two of you know each other Martin."

"We met earlier today." Martin replied.

"I have asked her to join us for dinner. Is that okay?" Almost in unison, Martin and David replied. "Yes, that is okay."

Peggy poured Clara a glass of wine as they both chatted while moving back and forth from the kitchen to the dining room, checking on dinner and preparing the table.

"He is so handsome. What is his story?" asked Clara.

"Ah, so the truth of the smile be told," Peggy said as she niggled a quietly snickering Clara in the side.

"He has not said much. I know he is not married. But there is a sense of restlessness in his words." Margaret thoughtfully replied, with lines forming between her eyebrows and her head tilting to the slightly to the side, showing her confusion about Martin.

The word "restlessness" hung in the air for a moment as the women moved about in silence, then Margaret announced that dinner was ready.

The men came into the dining room, where a table was set for the two couples. At least, that was what went through Clara's mind. Two couples and the start of something new for her.

Margaret served the chicken, steaming hot from the oven, with tenderly baked potatoes, seasoned vegetable, and freshly baked rolls. Clara placed a salad bowl in the middle of the table and poured water.

"Smells delicious," Martin said as he approached the table. The four sat and began eating. The conversation seemed to come to a halt for the time being as the food was devoured. Martin eventually broke the lull in the conversations and spoke first as he wanted to keep the conversation away from him. Plus, this would be a good time to interrogate Clara, he thought.

He had so many questions.

Where did she live before moving to Bletchley?

What are her thoughts of Bletchley?

What were gun shots over by her home all about?

Why did she really have a gun in her purse?

But he thought that this was not the time and place to ask all of these questions at once. He would find a time when it was just the two of them. For now, the conversation needed to remain casual and none intrusive. So, he asked about her family.

"Do you have any siblings, Clara?" He asked.

"I have a large family Martin. I have six siblings, but two of them died very young, another died in the Great War, and one is in America. The other one I do not see often."

Martin replied, "I am very sorry to hear that, are your parents still alive?"

"No, it's just me. My parents passed away several years ago. What about you Martin? Do you have any siblings?"

"I have a brother who is studying at Oxford, and a sister who clerks for my father's legal practice."

Clara lowered her head and appeared to become saddened, as if what Martin was saying had some effect on her feelings. She could tell from his replies that he had a well-to-do upbringing, and this brought back memories of her difficult childhood.

In the silence that followed, David, sensing that the conversation had become awkward, interrupted and said, "Tea or coffee for anyone?"

"I would love some coffee." Replied Martin.

Clara and Margaret decided to tidy up. The men went into the living area to talk some more about Matthew, the job, and Bletchley. A few minutes later, Clara arrived with a pot of coffee and left to continue helping Margaret with the dishes.

After his second cup of coffee, Martin grew sleepy. "I need to be leaving now, David. Thank you for dinner and the hospitality."

David Replied. "It was our pleasure. Do you mind walking Clara home? She lives along the way to the hotel."

After helping Margaret to finish tidying up, Clara said her goodbyes and joined Martin for the walk home.

The two slowly disappeared into the darkness.

8

The next morning, in the midst of the servicemen, Martin sat nursing a coffee as he waited for Francis, who must be running late, he thought. To his left were two air force men were chugging beer and discussing their last air raid over Berlin. Three navy men to his right were discussing their exploits in the Atlantic with the Kriegsmarine - the German navy. They were also knocking back whiskeys. It was not yet noon day and the armed forces of Britain were at full steam in the pub of the Bull Commercial Hotel.

Behind Martin were the three American servicemen from the train. Speaking in hushed words and, unlike on the train, when they were loud and obnoxious, they were calm and pleasant. Martin, curious about the Americans, trained his hearing on their conversation. In their whispers, Martin could only hear the odd word. He heard words like the F.B.I. will handle the situation, that Roosevelt was unaware, plausible deniability. If only Donovan had not been so reckless, one of them said.

He could not make sense of the conversation that the American servicemen were having, but could sense the secrecy. He strained to listen more intently to their conversation, but was interrupted.

Distracted by his efforts to hear what the Americans were saying, Martin did not see Matthew approaching, Good morning,
how was your evening?" he asked.

A startled Martin replied, "Fine, Matthew. I had super with
David and Margaret, and a pleasant evening."

"Good. Well the Board just met and decided to bring you
on board with Dunham and Associates. The vote was unani-
mous," Matthew said with a smile.

"We also discussed the Sharon Howes case and we are certain
that you would be able to help out there. When can you start?"
Asked Matthew.

"I'll be there tomorrow morning."

"Brilliant. We will see you tomorrow then."

"Thanks Matthew. I'm looking forward to getting started."
Martin replied with a bit of urgency and angst in his voice so
are to hurry Matthew away.

"Okay Martin, enjoy the rest of your day," replied Matthew
before moving away moments before Francis arrived.

Martin had seen Francis across the cafe, and all of his fears
came flooding in, as if the chemistry in his body had sent a
blanket invitation. Matthew left at the right time and did not
see Francis approaching. While Martin sat with his feelings.

He felt a panic that grew with each step that Francis took.
It will fade, come back again, but then do it all over again.
I can let these feelings swirl into a vortex of stupidity, or I
can breathe really slowly and let the thoughts leak into the
ether. He thought. Either way, he knew he needed to get rid
of Matthew before Francis arrived. He took a deep breath and
said, "If that is all for now Matthew I will get back to my coffee,
before it is cold, and will see you in the morning."

As Francis sat down across the table from Martin, his mind raced as he gave Martin a once over. Had Martin discussed his secret work in Bletchley with that person who just mysteriously disappeared as he approached? Or did Martin have a secret work of his own? thought Francis.

"Who was that," Francis asked.

"My new boss, I guess. I just got the job at the law firm and will be in Bletchley for a while."

"That great news. But you didn't tell him anything about my work did you?"

Martin smiles. Then quickly contained himself. He wanted to laugh loudly at Francis' fearful looking demeanour. But he held back his roar. The lunch crowd for this popular spot in Bletchley was notorious, and the cafe was quickly filling with a mixture of servicemen and civilians.

"No, not at all," replied Martin.

"You can trust me not to share your secret with anyone."

At that moment Martin's and Francis' attention was drawn to a procession of armoured cars that came to a stop on the High Street outside of the restaurant. Everyone in the cafe was watching as a contingent of heavily armed military men exited the vehicles and began to surveil the Hotel.

Shows of such military might were common in London, Liverpool, Manchester, but seldom in Bletchley.

A few minutes later, a hostess in the cafe came over to Martin and Francis and said, "Gentlemen I am very sorry, but we need this table." A similar announcement was given to several of the surrounding tables. The servicemen, being used to orders from higher ups, appeared to take the announcement in stride. Many vacated the cafe.

A thin framed, balding elderly gentleman dressed in civvies stood up and rudely replied, "I am sorry chap but we will not be moving." When standing, he stood greater than six feet tall. The hostess stood only a mere five feet and was unnerved by the man.

"Please sir, we are preparing another table for you. But we need these tables," she said in a firm, but pleasant voice, as her hands trembled in both the fear and anxiety of the moment.

Martin and Francis eased away from the table, observing, along with everyone else, what was taking place outside of the restaurant. There were murmured whispers about who it could be that commanded such special attention. Could it be Churchill?

Eventually, the big shot emerged and was escorted inside. The crowd, frozen in their activities, stared with open mouths. Men armed with M3 sub-machine guns formed a perimeter to create a private table in a section of the cafe. The three American men from the train sat at the private table. Everyone watched as they were joined by the big shot.

Martin and Francis were escorted to a table in a corner of the cafe. The table was secluded. An out of the way table where service from the hostess wouldn't be too good, but it was in line of sight of the private table with the big shot and the other Americans. Such a perfect location, thought Martin, as they took their seats. In the line of sight to satisfy his curiosity, while secluded so that he, and Francis, can speak freely. They could also share their emotions without the fear of their feelings being discovered.

As they took their seats, Martin glanced over at the big shot. It was William Donovan, the head of the Office of Strategic Services – the American intelligence agency that handled all the American spies. Martin knew him from his time in the allied command centre in London. Donovan sometimes met with Stuart Menzies, who was in Churchill's office when Martin was assigned this mission to Bletchley. He is not well known in Britain, so a public meeting might have gone unnoticed, had Martin not been there to see it for himself.

He had heard Donovan's name on the train as well. The three American servicemen who were now meeting with Donovan had mentioned his name in their inebriated state. Could they be spies, Martin thought. He could hear nothing of what they were saying, and Francis was here in front of him. So he focused his attention on Francis instead.

In his head Martin had planned this time with Francis carefully. He felt his inquisitive nature rising to the surface. This desire of mind to get all the details is perhaps what made me pursue law, or it may have been instilled in me by my father, Martin thought. Nonetheless, it was in his nature now and Francis was in his sights. This new phase of his relationship with his long-time friend was stirring feelings deep inside. Feelings that he was not understanding but enjoying. Still, he hoped that today, in the Bull Commercial Hotel, he had planned to get some answers. He had so many questions, but needed to take care of how he asked them. He did not want to scare Francis away. He started slowly.

"It is good to see you. How have you been keeping?" Martin asked.

"I have been well. It is really good to see you in Bletchley. What do you think of the town?" Francis replied.

"Is that normal for the army? You know, being granted such a long leave in the midst of war?" Continued Francis.

"I haven't seen much of Bletchley but it seems okay. The billeting seems to have taken a bit of a toll on the town. Crime is on the rise with all of the extra people, I hear. So plenty of work for me." Replied Martin.

"No, it's not normal for service men to get long leaves at this time, I don't think. But, my father knows the Prime Minister personally, and, well it was kind of a favour to my father that I was granted the long leave. But it is all within the King Regulations for the army, so nothing special just for me. I wouldn't have it any other way." Continued Martin.

In a somewhat rhetorical response Francis asked, "Your father knows the Prime Minister personally?"

Martin smiles and asked, "So about the other night. It was a first for me. Where you surprised the next day? Any regrets?"

"Your first time?" Francis said with a smile.

"Well you know my story somewhat. Just who I am attracted to, and who I am not."

"But no regrets at all," continued Francis.

"Martin, you see that man sitting over there? The big shot?

Strangely enough, I saw that man, the one sitting right over there, at Princeton, when I was asked to stay on. He came by and met with my e professor. He was interested in my work on a "universal computing machine. I had built a machine that could multiply. I had completed three of the four stages of the machine when he showed up asking questions." Replied Francis.

"Which man, William Donovan?" Martin asked. "Yes," replied Francis. "And now he is here," Martin mumbles under his breath.

"And now you are on a secret assignment, here in Bletchley?" Martin asked.

Francis did not answer Martin at first. He was a little wary of the lies being a part of the code breaking team. He also sensed that Martin was not telling him the whole truth about himself.

With Martin, he felt the urge to tell the truth, but contained his emotions for now. Instead, he found out Martin's truth first.

"So, Martin, what was the real reason for your leave from the army? If your father had to speak with Churchill there must be more to your story. And how did you get to spend your leave in Bletchley as a lawyer?"

Martin was startled by the question. He paused, his eyes widened and his mouth shut tight, as he thought for a moment.

"Francis what I am about to tell you is extremely confidential, and I have to have your word that you will not repeat it to anyone. Do I have your word?" Martin eventually asked.

"Yes Martin, certainly." Francis replied.

"Martin trusted in Francis' reply and said, "I did not want to go back to the front as I had lost my belief in that being where I needed to be. We were losing the war, I thought. The Germans were gaining ground everywhere. To be honest, I was scared and confused. I needed time to think."

"How did that lead to you ending up in Bletchley?" Francis asked.

"I was ready to take leave, and stay in London or just head north. Bletchley was not on my mind. But I got summoned by the Prime Minister, to a meeting with him, a general that was responsible for intelligence, and the head of the SIS. They asked me to come to Bletchley to help keep quiet a secret they have here." Martin replied.

"In Bletchley there is a secret code breaking facility that the Prime Minister thinks is important to the war effort. So here I am, in Bletchley on a secret mission." Martin continued before saying, with tongue in cheek, that he felt like a spy.

"I am so pleased to hear that," Francis said.

"Why is that," Martin asked as the brow of his forehead creased in curiosity.

"Martin, I am going to be completely truthful with you too. I am going to tell you about what I really do here in Bletchley." Francis said.

"Oh, then what is it that you do here?"

"When I returned to Britain from America, I was asked to join the Government Codes and Cypher School. The GCHQ was moved to Bletchley Park when war was declared. So, you are here to help to protect what I am doing in Bletchley. That is why I am so pleased."

"You were in America?" Asked Martin.

"Yes, but we can talk about that another time, okay?"

"Oh, okay let's talk later about that." replied Martin.

"But it's good to share our secrets. I feel like a weight has been lifted off me. Keeping that secret from you would have been hard for me. Continued Martin.

In the awkward silence that followed, the two men observed their surroundings. Then, to break the silence, Francis spoke.

"Don't be so distraught about the war Martin. Just a few months ago we cracked the German enigma code. Gordon and I have developed a machine that we call Bombe and it can decode the secret messages sent by the Germans. We started with a machine given to us by the Polish, who cracked the early codes after the Great War. Now we can tell the allied forces where German navy ships are and tell the allied command."

"So, the messages that I was passing along in the command centre were coming from you?" Martin asked.

"Well not me but my team in Hut 8."

"Your decrypted messages helped us to win the Battle in the Atlantic." Martin said.

"Yes, and we can decrypt all of their messages now. We are also sharing our decryption methods with the Americans. There is hope for the war Martin, so don't be despaired."

Francis and Martin had been close friends in uni. They had shared so many things about themselves and their lives in the years since. But nothing they had shared compared to the duty and the loyalty of that duty. Each had declared their loyalty to the war effort, and the secrecy of their assignments was paramount to that loyalty. But today they broke that secrecy and now felt a deeper connection to each other. Their unbreakable bond was even stronger.

As they sat taking in the moment, they were disturbed by a loud commotion inside and outside of the cafe. The servicemen were clearing a path and securing the way for Donovan to leave. Armoured vehicles were starting their engines, and the crowd was gathering for a last peek at the big shot. Donovan rose to his feet and took his leave from the cafe. The Americans from the train left as well. Though both left in armoured vehicles, they went in different directions.

As the commotion began to subside, the closeness of the moment Martin and Francis were sharing before submerged. Their feelings were stronger now than before. The two men looked at each other with smiles. Martin left the table first. He slid away quietly, paid the bill, and sauntered in the direction of his hotel room. A few minutes later, Francis got up from the table and walked in the same direction as Martin.

When they finally reached the hotel room, Martin fumbled with his key as he desperately tried to open the door, slamming it with the heel of his foot once it was open.

Francis nuzzled Martin onto the bed before crawling slowly on top of him. Trailing kisses up and down Martin's neck as he moans, "finally, all mine again." Francis said.

Francis found a sweet spot on Martin's neck and started sucking. Martin moaned. In a spontaneous and intimate action, his hips thrusted upwards. Francis moaned in unison with him and smiled as his lips moved to Martin's mouth. He kissed him deeply, drawing Francis into an immobilised state of pleasure.

"Francis..." Martin moans, a pleasurable moan, as their lips disconnected. Almost as if to say don't stop. The two then began to peel the shirts off of each other. Slowly, deliberately, they exposed the tenderness of their bare chests.

Once they were both completely shirtless, horny, and wet at the tips of their shafts, Martin took a deep breath and pulled forward to Francis. Sticking his tongue out, he tenderly licked the skin behind Francis' ear in a teasing motion. Francis' emotions deepened. Butterflies began to swirl in his stomach. Francis let out a groan as Martin pulled away, leaving salvia to drip down Francis' face and onto his neck. Francis closed his eyes, smirked at Martin's pleasure, and rubbed Martin's inner thigh.

"I like having you like this," Francis mumbles as he caressed Martin close to the sensitive skin around his hard erection, but not quite there. "My big strong army man. So sweet. So, so, sexy."

"Damn Francis!" Martin cries out as his hips desperately bucked forward. But Francis pulled back, took Martin's zipper between his two fingers and said, "You are going to have to wait."

Martin's mouth hung. He breathed heavily as Francis pulled down Martin's trousers, while trailing his face down Martin's naked chest as he did so. He eventually had Martin's erect manhood in front of him. With his trousers off, Martin looked even bigger.

Martin took Francis' zipper between his fingers. Then, with a quick jerk, Francis was unzipped. Francis crawled further up the bed, pulling down his trousers as he did so. Giving Martin complete access to his manhood in the middle of the bed. As Martin approached Francis' manhood, Francis pulled backwards. Martin smiled. Gripping Francis by his hips, Martin lean in and gently licked the tip of Francis' manhood. Wrapping his tongue around the tip, slurping, sucking, and then taking Francis deep in mouth for a second before falling backwards on the bed. Martin groaned loudly. Francis shook with pleasure.

Laying side by side on the bed, Francis caressed Martin's thin with the tip of his index finger. In Francis' gaze was Martin's manhood. With more than a hint of desire in his sultry tone Francis said, "You are so hard for me." Martin mumbles, as they rubbed their naked bodies together in a motion that had them both leaking pre cum like a fountain.

Suddenly Martin flipped Francis over, and raised him in the air above his erection, then pulled him down hard. His penis slipped between Francis' butt cheeks and quickly inside him. Francis let out a pleasurable cry as he was penetrated. Martin filled him completely.

Martin's hands reached around and clutched Francis' erection. Francis let out a moan of ecstatic pleasure – but then he didn't move. Martin pushed Francis' hips forward until the tip of his manhood was all that was left inside Francis, then thrusted his hips forward, penetrating deeply inside Francis. Slowly at first, and then faster. His shaft thrusting in and out of Francis. His arms were wrapped around Francis' thin muscular body. In his hands he held Francis manhood. While penetrating Francis from behind, his hands slid up and down Francis' erection. Martin could sense that Francis was nearing orgasm, and sped up. His shaft sloshed around Francis' slippery inside as pre cum leaked out and down the back of Francis' thighs. His hands tightened and suddenly Francis released a tidal wave of pleasure. As Francis moaned, Martin grabbed him by the hips and moved him up and down on his shaft. The movement caused Martin to let out a fountain of cum inside Francis. Martin kept going, pushing Francis on and off his shaft through his orgasm before finally allowing the two of them to drop onto the bed. Francis' naked butt was resting against Martin's manhood, causing him to orgasm for a second time, as did Francis.

Francis moaned loudly. Cum flowed out of him and over his chest, arousing Martin, who pulled Francis up and down once more before the two finally dropped. As they both drifted off to sleep, Martin thought about how incredible Francis was, and how he would always long to make sweet, sweet love to him, exactly like they had just experienced.

9

Refreshed, Martin awoke.

Francis laid peacefully by his side.

With a gentle swipe of his hand, Martin brushed the hair from Francis' face and gazed at him. A content, loving, and curious gaze. The innocence of his soft and smooth face revealed a new depth to Francis. There was a lingering of pain in the crease of his brow, and the down-curve of his lips. But it was his eyes that said everything they revealed to his soul, thought Martin. He wondered about this pain before his thoughts were interrupted by Francis' gentle awakening.

As their eyes met. They both smiled. A satisfied and content smile. Content, not only from their desires having been extinguished, but also because of the trusting comfort of the moment. A dealing that Martin had not experienced before with another soul. There was a calm inside of him. A focusing calm that reduced the entire world, a troubled and war-torn world, down to this moment in time. He could see, hear, feel, not think about nothing more than where he was, and who he was with, at this time.

Looking deep into Francis' eyes, with the broadest of smiles brightening his face, Martin could not back escape this calm. A calm that inspired unsettling, yet beautiful, thoughts. In Francis' eyes, Martin could see a deep pool of restlessness, oceans of hopelessness, and grief. In those eyes Martin could also see that Francis, odd as he was, clung to his principles. He could also see that all the beauty in the world could not surpass one thing he saw in those eyes. Passion, passion that turned Francis' beautiful eyes into orbs of the brightest fire. He also saw a loving man that would fight to the bitter end for those that touched his soul. Francis' love and passion made him beautiful, Martin thought.

Although he had experienced urges with men, Martin had never been with any other man. This, what he is experiencing now, was mesmerising. Even with the women he had been with, there had been nothing as beautiful, and pleasant, as these moments. For a fleeting moment, he thought, 'it's just a phase' and 'it's half way to being only with men'. But I don't feel that way now, and I didn't after the first time either, ran through his mind.

Francis was fluttering in and out of a gentle sleep as Martin's mind wandered. He was now in a gentle sleep, which gave Martin time to think.

He was wondering if there were other men like him? Men that enjoyed being with other men, as well as women. He also wondered if he went to those places where you pick up men. Would he know what other men, attracted to men, thought. Could he even have a conversation with them? But that wasn't him. The thought of going looking for sex with men was repulsive to him. It was more of a chance attraction to whomever caught his fancy, captured his feeling. Be that a man or a woman. Right now it was Francis, his friend from Uni and a man.

Martin's thoughts then drifted to when he was much younger. His young adult life and childhood were such confusing times for him. He had spent years trying to reject his attraction to boys. This didn't work, though. Feeling that he liked both boys and girls really messed him up good back then. He went through a spell of felling like he was 'turning into a homosexual' when he first realised he was attracted to boys. That was when his obsession with fondly looking at naked pictures of men started. It was hard on him at first, before he gave into his attraction to boys. However, giving into his feelings came at a price.

As a child, he was suicidal, and had spells of depression, anxiety, as well as other mental disorders. His parents just didn't understand, and he dared not tell them the whole truth. Then, as a young adult, he hated himself, because he just wanted to be what was thought to be 'normal'. He wouldn't just accept that he was a homosexual, because he wasn't. He was still attracted to girls. But then it was sometimes boys and sometimes girls. Though Martin just wanted to like boys, or girls, so he could categorise himself. So that he could understand.

This went on until he met his first serious girlfriend. It was in his first year of Oxford, and her name was Shirley. She was gorgeous. Martin was instantly attracted to her. But after almost a year together, Martin walked into their flat in Oxford to find Shirley upset and crying. Martin and Shirley shared the 4 bedroom flat with two other girls, and another boy. Shirley was upset and told Martin that she had been sexually involved with one of the other girls living in the flat. That it was her first time, and now she was confused and upset about having betrayed Martin.

Martin tried comforted he by telling her that didn't care and if anything, he was even more attracted to her. He then told her of his confused past and attractions to boys. That's when Shirley changed. She became angry. She started to pace around the room. Shouting at Martin at the same time.

"I knew it!" She said.

"You're a homosexual!

"I tricked you, I have not been with a girl, but now I know you're a homosexual!"

Martin was devastated. Shirley was the first person he had talked to about his attraction to boys, and she acted like that. In that moment, now thinking his attraction to men wasn't just a passing fade, he vowed, to himself, to never tell a soul ever again. He then swore to Shirley that he had never been with a man. That he had not been attracted to anyone, male or female, since they were together. Also that his attraction to boys was a long time ago.

Shirley accepted Martin's words. The two moved on with their relationship and repaired the damage of that day. However, in time, Martin did experience attraction and rages towards other men, but would feel guilty afterwards for some reason. Like he was doing something wrong, but after a little while, those feelings of guilt went away. He came to accept who he was but never, until now, had he acted on any urges towards men.

Eventually Shirley and Martin did breakup though. It was when Martin met Emma. Although he wasn't in a serious relationship with Emma, he could think of no one else, and Shirley gradually became a thing of the past. Since which had also not been attracted to a man. That is - until that day in his flat. The day that He proposed to Emma, his now fiancée, who may be married to someone else now. That was also the day that he had felt that something about Francis come over him. It was an attraction, an urge, and now here he was. Lying beside Francis, a man, and feeling no remorse, no guilt, no confusion, but his mind was a washed in other thoughts and questions.

As Francis' eyes slowly opened again, Martin decided it was time. The time was right to get some of his other thoughts settled.

"Hey Francis we have been friends since Uni, and now we are here, but we really don't know much about each other before Uni. Plus we have the few years when the war started. Tell me about you. Okay?" Martin asked him.

"We have been friends for a long time. You know me already." Replied Francis.

"Yes, but not everything. Some things I have never asked you about."

"Like what, Martin?"

"Who was your first?"

Francis blushed and after silence, he started to talk. "As you know I moved around a bit. My family was living in London when I was born, but we moved to the coast, Hastings then Dorset, when I was young."

"It was in secondary school in Dorset when I met Christopher. My first." He said as he looked away, in thought of that time with Christopher.

Martin could see that Francis was fighting back tears, his face was flush, and his eyes were wet.

"Christopher was important to you, wasn't he?" Martin asked.

"Yes, Christopher was more than just my first. I loved him. He was my first love too. He shared my interest in many things - mathematics, chess, logic, and problem solving.

Francis smiles broadly and then continued, "I wasn't well liked by my teachers though."

"Oh, why was that?" Martin asked with a smile, knowing the truth all too well, as he had heard this story before.

"They would get annoyed with me often because I received high marks in exams despite not paying attention during lessons," Francis replied with a chuckle. "I always had good grades at maths, and my secondary school maths teacher thought I was a genius back then." He Continued.

Martin gave a half smiles, a light-hearted laugh, and said," Well you did do well in maths in Uni too. So you just might be a mathematical genius?"

"What happened with you and Christopher? Are you no longer together?" asked Martin.

"He died some years ago - tuberculosis," replied Francis with his eyes now swimming with tears.

"I am sorry," Martin replied.

"It's okay Martin." Francis said as he whiffed his head from side to side for a moment. Almost as if he was shaking away the feelings he held for Christopher. Removing them from the surface. Burying them deep inside again.

"Since Christopher's death I have devoted all of my energy to the study of science. I desperately wanted to fulfil all of his potential. He meant so much to me. He is the inspiration that has led me to where I am today. That's how I honour him. That's how I keep him close to me." Francis continued.

"Christopher and I both believed that a mere machine can be built, and taught to add, subtract, multiply and divide, and if it can do that then it can do almost anything." There was a hint of excitement, on top of the sadness, in Francis' tone when he spoke of making a machine that can play chess.

"What did you do after Oxford? I kind of lost track of you for a while. Until your father passed I think."

"After Oxford I went to America, Princeton, to continue my studies in mathematics and cryptology."

"They wanted me to stay on in America, but I decided to come back to Britain." Continued Francis.

"Did you come back to Britain to work at Bletchley Park?"

"I came back when my father died. That's when I saw the advertisement that took me to Bletchley Park."

"I thought so," said Martin.

"What about you Martin? What is your story being here with me? Throughout Uni, and even after, I never thought of us like this. Now here we are."

"As a child, I was interested in girls all the time. Then when I was around the age of maybe fourteen, or so, I saw a naked man in a magazine. That got me thinking about boys. I then went through a horrible time of confusion. That ended when I met Shirley in Uni. You remember her don't you?"

"Yes, I remember Shirley, that ended a bit abruptly. All of a sudden there was Emma." Said Francis.

"Yes, but that is a much longer story." Martin replied before continuing to tell Francis about how he came to be here with him.

"I never knew I could like both men and women. So I convinced myself that I like women. Until that day in my flat when I proposed to Emma. That was the first time I had a powerful urge to have sex with a man come over me. That man was you."

"I am flattered," replied a blushing Francis.

"What about you? Has it always been boys for you?" Martin asked.

"Yes, I guess. I have never really taken a fancy to a girl. Not that I am not attracted to them aesthetically. But I am just more attracted to boys sexually. I have been with a girls though." Replied Francis.

"Why do you think it is that certain men are attracted more to men than they are towards women? Take you for example. You are probably attracted more towards men. But me on the other hand I would say that I'm more romantically and emotionally attracted to women. Although I do have feelings for you?"

"I don't know. But I think that we are multi-faceted in that we live in a continuum of potential attractions. It's just the way I am, we are." Replied Francis.

Continuing, Francis asked, "Now that you have been with a man do you have any different thoughts or feelings?"

"It seems they like the sex aspect of being with a man might be more intense. Or it could be just being with you. I don't know for sure. But if it is more intense with men, then I see nothing wrong with having a sexual preference that leans towards men whilst my aesthetic, physical, romantic and emotional attraction are skewed towards women."

"Well, that's enough of that." Francis said as he reached over to kiss Martin, who was now at full mast. After a brief kiss, he slowly rolled Francis over and was deep inside him.

Wore out, the two men eventually left the Bull Commercial Hotel separately.

Returning to their lives of secrecy.

10

The next morning, Martin entered the offices of Dunham and Associates at 7:45 a.m. wide eyed and ready to get started. Orientation and then on to the Sharon Howes case, he was thinking.

Matthew had different plans for Martin. As an early riser, he had been there since 7:00a. His usual start to the day consisted of coffee and the newspaper. The news that day was very similar to the day before, and the day before that as well. Hitler's Luftwaffe did this, and the R.A.F. did that. So his attention was always drawn to the crime reports. Crime had increased two-fold since the war had begun. The looting that had risen during the Blitz had been subsiding as the air-raids decreased. But what has commanded Matthew's attention was the rise in juvenile delinquency.

With the London evacuations, there was a rise in the number of children in Bletchley. Many of them had formed in gangs which just added to the peer pressure. The children eventually took to the streets, creating problems. Despite birching being regularly handed out as punishment, the delinquency continued to rise. The Bletchley Police blamed a combination of boredom, restrictions, and a lack of parental control for the sharp rise in juvenile delinquency. Matthew paid close attention as his business grew. Now Martin was here to help.

Martin's orientation consistent of an 8:00 a.m. meeting with a new client. The meeting was controlled by Matthew, who was well prepared. Martin whispers to Matthew, "What do you want me to do?"

"Just take notes, frown a lot, and look intelligent," Matthew replied with a half-grin on face. "No problem" – that was exactly how I had survived in the allied command centre, he thought.

The client was James Moss, a sixty ish father of three whose wife had died, and his sons were off in France fighting the Axis forces. James was a soldier in the Great War, Warrant Officer Class 2, in the Royal Artillery. When the war was over, he left the army and became a postman until the Hitler's war. Since the start of the Hitler's war, in 1939, James had the task of caring for his two grandchildren, boys, while their mothers were at work. Alan, 16, the oldest of the two, was in the police jail over on Simpson Road. The building was notorious for plagues of flies during the summer due to its proximity to the sewage works. Fortunately for Alan, it was autumn, and the flies had subsided.

Martin, frowning and taking notes, surmised that the Smith's had to live a hard life. James' rustic appearance and coarse language added to his thinking. From the first sentence, there was nothing but hard luck and misery flowing from James. The family of six, nine before the boys went off to war, lived together in a four-bed house in Stony Stratford.

Alan, who had become harder and harder to manage since his father had left, had taken up with one of the gangs of street kids that usually wandered the about creating mischief. Mostly during the blackout hours. Everything from picking pockets to sexual assaults by some of the older kids. They had started off by just bumping into women, using the excuse of the blackout, before moving on to grab them or taking their belongings.

Alan's crime: Theft. He had been caught buying food for the family with ration books that were not theirs. During the war, nothing encapsulated the ideal of "all in it together" than rationing, which required everyone to sacrifice to ensure there was enough to go around. Martin knew too well the importance of this ideal as he knew of the many merchant ships filled with tons of food from America that were destroyed by German U-Boats in the Atlantic.

Alan was facing a birching of six lashes, and the family a fine of one hundred and forty pounds. There would be further lashings and repercussions if the fine was not paid.

Martin was angered, and saddened, on hearing of Alan's crime. Angered by the lack of respect and sensitivity to others, that Alan and his friends had shown in stealing ration books. Saddened by the thought of food being sought after by someone as young as Alan. But ultimately, how will those that had their ration books stolen survive? Do the Smiths have enough food to survive, where the thoughts in Martin's head?

"He is a wonderful child, that just fell in with the wrong lads," James said. "There is no need for the lashes, and we cannot afford the fine. I don't know what to do. His mum is depending on me to sort this out, but I need help. Is there any way you can help me?"

Martin's eyes narrowed, watered, and his face became flush. The war was taking people, and lives, in many ways. Martin had seen the loss of life on the battlefield. He had heard of the family turmoil and shattered lives on home soil. But the plight of the Smiths had unnerved him more so than any battle he had been through. Now, as he fought back tears, he was seeing first-hand the many ways that the war taking lives.

"Of course," Matthew said with enough optimism to bring a smile to James' face.

"I've had some success negotiating with the Police and the Courts.

They are used to lawyers getting involved. They know the kids need things to do and can get into mischief. They are pretty understanding. They only want a just outcome, especially in these times. We can get him out, but he may have to go into a remand home for a period of time, and you will probably have to make restitution to the family who had their ration book taken."

"Give us a couple of days and we'll put together a plan. Feel free to contact Martin here if you have questions. He'll know everything about your case."

"So, we will have two lawyers?" James asked.

"Yes, you certainly will."

"We cannot afford to pay for one lawyer, let alone two lawyers."

"It is okay, James. We know that the war has been hard on all of us. Especially the kids. We will not charge you for our services. Let's just work on getting Alan back on track."

James was elated. He covered his face with both hands, and silently wept.

Martin had not yet recovered from the meeting with James when he was summoned by Janette, who thought it was time for him to meet Sharon Howes.

Janette had lived in Bletchley all of her life. Despite having dreams of leaving Bletchley one day and moving to the city, she still lived in her parent's house. The same home she had had since birth. London, and her own law practice, had called many times, but she never answered the call. It was always some reason not to. Now, though, that dream seemed even farther away. Since her husband was killed in Dunkirk, Janette the widower lost all interest in venturing out. She refused to take time to grieve. Buried herself in her work, and looked the part as well. Dishevelled, and rushed as always, she hurried Martin into a cluttered room next to the meeting room. Here Martin met Sharon Howes. His whole reason for being in Bletchley. His secret mission.

Sharon was a twenty-one-year-old graduate from mathematics at Cambridge. Five feet six inches tall, blonde, stunning, and very smart. No one knew what she saw in Richard, but there she was. A lot of tears and emotions as she told her story of Richard, the bobbies, and just wanting it to end.

Just a little more than a year ago, she received a telegraph that meant everything to her. She had longed to be able to do something meaningful after college, and the war effort seemed like the perfect opportunity.

The telegraph read:

"You are to report to Bletchley Park, Buckingham, in four days' time. Your postal address while at Bletchley Park is Box 117, c/o The Foreign Office. Show this telegraph on your arrival. This is all you need to know."

Sharon knew that this was the one chance she would get. But now she has ruined it by taking up with Richard, she thought. She took nothing from Bletchley Park home with her, but this day, of all days, she had accidentally taken home codes she was working on that day.

"Richard came into my flat and robbed it. He is really violent when he drinks. He sometimes takes money from my flat when he is like this. But this time was different." Sharon told Martin and Janette.

"He has taken some of my papers from my work. The bobbies now think that I am a spy, but I am not." Sharon continued to say as she started to cry even more profusely.

With a calm voice that soothes even Martin, Janette, said, "Sharon, this is Martin, he is a lawyer from London that has come up to help with your case." Sharon's eyes widened, she snapped her head towards Martin, wiped her cheeks with the back of her hand, and suck in to dry up her tears. Martin said to Janette, "Would you get Sharon some water please?"

Once Janette had left the room, Martin continued to speak. "I know about your special assignment in Bletchley Park. You have signed and agreed to the terms in the Official Secrets Act. If you abide by those terms, then everything will be okay. Leave everything else to me, okay?" Sharon smiles and said, "Okay."

On returning with the water, Janette returned announced that she had another client in fifteen minutes. With that announcement, in her usually dishevelled and rushed manner, she left Martin to continue with Sharon.

"We will go to the court today and get a restraining order to keep Richard away from you. If he violates the Order, they will throw him in jail.

"What about the bobbies?"

"I will go to them and let them know that I am your lawyer, and they can speak to me if they have any questions."

"What do they have that they are questioning you about?"

"They have codes from transmissions that were on paper in my flat. Will I get in trouble? It was a mistake." Replied Sharon.

"There shouldn't be any trouble. But we will have to give the bobbies a story about the codes. Is there anything that you think we can say."

"We can say that Richard is mistaken. That he was too drunk to remember where he got the coded papers. Maybe he took them from someplace else."

"We can say that then. With Richard always drunk, it will be easier for the bobbies to believe that he was mistaken. They might still go on about the spy nonsense, but at least you won't be involved. Let's do that and see what happens next." Replied Martin.

"For now, you go back to your normal routine, and let me know if there is any more trouble." He continued.

At 9:00 a.m. David Smith arrived and escorted Martin to his new office. Talking the entire time as they made their way up the winding staircase to the second floor. After a few quick words about dinner the other night, he moved to Martin's journey home with Clara. He wanted all the details. Martin, feeling uneasy about the conversation because of his own secret, slowly became unnerved. But David, oblivious to Martin's changes in mood, pressed the conversation and asked, "When will you be seeing her again? I know you must have taken the opportunity to get more time with her." Feeling the pressure of the conversation, Martin replied, "We are having dinner tonight." Something that he will now make a reality.

On arrival, Martin's at the new office. David apologising for the dustiness of the room said, "We take care of ourselves around here, I hope that is okay with you," as he pointed towards a small room with cleaning supplies.

"Oh, before I leave you. Janette has agreed to let you live at her parents house while you are in Bletchley. Her parents house is an old Victorian era building with a detached garage. Nothing special. But above the garage is a two-room annex. Janette lives in the main house, but the annex is yours while your in Bletchley." David said, before scurrying out of Martin's dusty new office.

Alone in his office, among the maze of the rooms on the second floor of Dunham and Associates, Martin closed his eyes and breathed deeply. The office was tiny and cramped. The heavy dust gave an appearance of the office not having been used in years. A small office desk, an empty filing cabinet, and two visitor chairs filled the room. His office had a small window. If Martin looked carefully out the window, through the adjacent buildings, he could see far across the English countryside. Martin looked, smiled, and was thankful for the view and the minuscule light the window offered. It was a far cry from what he had in the command centre of the allies.

Just as Martin began to settle into his office, Janette popped her head inside of Martin's office and said, "There is a new client that just came into the office. He said that he needs a lawyer. David and Mathew have left for court, and I am busy with another client. Do you think you can take care of the new client?"

"Yes, that will be okay for me to handle," Martin replied as he wondered what he had got himself into.

Elizabeth ran the reception on a part-time basis and had greeted Martin earlier that morning. She directed Martin towards a small room off the reception area. The room that Martin had recently met with Sharon Howes.

The new client's name was Hugh Tucker, a local farmer. On entering the room, Mr Tucker greeted Martin. The two men spoke for a few minutes about Martin. Oxford law, growing up with a father who was a lawyer, and coming to Bletchley. Mr Tucker was a careful man who wanted to get to know Martin before putting hi. trust in him. Martin assured him he was indeed a lawyer that could be trusted, and soon after, the two men were off and running.

Hugh was going through a rough spell; he was grateful for being able to talk with someone about his troubles. In those times, farmers were required to grow at least two acres of potatoes. This growth was ordered by the Ministry of Agriculture so that there could be food for everyone. But Hugh was now being charged with failing to grow two acres of potatoes. He could be fined as much as one thousand pounds. A fine that he could not afford. For all manner of reasons, growing that many potatoes was also not possible. Martin could see Hugh's frustration and need to vent. So, despite his day having turned into a busier day than he planned, Martin let him ramble. Just before lunch Hugh left the office's content. Martin was able to convince him that everything will be alright. That he would review his case with his associates and get back to him.

Wednesday lunch at Dunham and Associates consisted of brown-bags in the meeting room where they greeted clients. They would eat while they discussed clients, and cases, and other matters pertaining to the practice.

As the new boy in the practice, Martin was encouraged to speak. He started by saying, "I need some help with a new client. Mr. Tucker a farmer that is being fined for not growing the requisite amount of potatoes."

The name Tucker drew laughter before Matthew, back from court, finally spoke. "Hugh Tucker is a regular to our offices. He has not been a farmer since before the war started. He comes in for the company and to talk." By this time, David and Janette were red in the face with laughter.

"But he was so sincere," Martin replied.

"He always is," replied Janette.

"We take turns talking with him. It's the least that we can do in these times. We are a community practice, after all." said David, while the others nibbled on their sandwiches.

Eventually, as the laughter began to dwindle, Mathew said, "Consider yourself welcomed to the practice. We are really glad to have you, and hope that you enjoy being with us."

The rest of the meeting was extremely zestful. They moved quickly from topic to topic, and in forty-five minutes they not only covered the pressing business of the practice but also talked about the war, the rise in crime, and, of course, David's favourite topic, Clara. Martin was convinced that had David not been a married man, he would take up with Clara.

Mathew broke up the meeting with a terse, and abrupt, "Okay everyone, back to work."

11

Later that evening, Clara quickly pulled the door shut as he disappeared into the darkness. Another one off on some clandestine operation, she thought. She was becoming weary of her role as a German spy in Britain. It weighed heavily on her most days, and nights, now. But not tonight. She had other things on her mind. Tonight she was glad to be alone with her other guest.

The red silk dress was handmade for her seductive figure. It was a good choice for what Clara had in mind. In perfect unison with her body. Her dress of seduction draped over her hips, accentuated her thin waistline, and full bosom. The neckline was cut just low enough to reveal a bit of cleavage, but not too low to dissuade thoughts of her gracefulness. Lace accessorised the dress and was gently touched by her flowing straw-coloured blonde hair. Her blue eyes glowed as bright as Sirius - the brightest star in the night sky. She was ripe with anticipation as she prepared for her evening with Martin.

While she was not in a committed relationship with Jakob anymore, she had known him for so long that she was feeling guilty. However, her attraction to Martin could now not be contained. It was an instantaneous attraction that she thought may have waned. But this has not been the case. It was an attraction that had grown consistently since they first met. He was all she could think about. Goosebumps graced her skin whenever she thought of him.

Martin arrived at Clara's house promptly at 7:00 p.m. Dressed smartly in a blue suit, and carrying flowers as a show of respect, not affection - he thought. But this gesture did not help, as in Clara's mind, he had now shown that he shared the same desire for her that she felt for him.

Her voice rang deep and sultry as she opened the door. "Good evening Martin." The casual, but inviting, smile on her face let Martin know she was truly happy to see him again. Standing five feet nine inches, with a flush skin tone, she was stunning.

But such beauty in a woman was lost on Martin this evening. He had other plans. In his mind, he had rehearsed his inquisition over and over until he knew the questions by heart. He had even prepared "what if scenarios." These questions occupied his thinking as he calmly and coldly presented her with the bushel of flowers that he held clumsily in his hands.

Taking his overcoat, she asked, "Would you like a glass of wine?" He wanted a lager but felt compelled to drink wine with her, and politely replied, "Yes, thank you."

"Dinner will be a few minutes more, she said." Everything had to be just perfect for this evening. She had spent hours preparing the food. But that wasn't all she had prepared. She also had an inquisition of her own to conduct. She did not hesitate and quickly started in on her questions. The most important things first – does Martin have a wife – is what she wanted to know. But she could not be so bold as to ask directly. Being subtle, she casually asked, "Are you from London?"

Martin spoke freely and told her more than she had asked. "Yes, I am from London. I have never lived elsewhere actually.

My family is from the West End, *Mayfair. My brother Thomas, sister Anne, and me all grew up there. Thomas is off at Oxford now, and Anne is working with my father in his legal practice. But we are a close family, and I miss them all the time"* He said.

Clara, though, wanted to know more. She did not find out what she really wanted. She wanted to be a bit more direct and ask, What about you, Martin? Do you have a family of your own? Wife? Children? But instead, not wanting to rush things along, she asked, "What do you think of Bletchley?"

"Quaint, and interesting," he replied.

"It's the children though that have caught my attention. With so many of them in Bletchley it must be hard on the entire community." He continued.

"I have never really thought about the children." Replied Clara. "But it is good that they are not in London I guess. The raids over London saw a lot of lives lost. Having children there would have made things so much harder." She continued before moving on to the next question. All of which was leading up to her plan for the evening.

She had thought about this time with Martin ever since they first met, but now her inquisition was not moving along fast enough. She had planned to find out if he was married before seducing him. Starting to feel awkward about the direction of the conversation, but being patient, she asked, "Will you be staying long?"

"The crime up here seems to be about the same as in London. So, there will be lots to do for a lawyer. I like the lads at Dunham and Associates and will enjoy working with them, I think. But I am afraid, I will not be staying longer than a few months." Martin replied.

"Oh, why is that she asked? I thought you liked it in Bletchley."

"I do. But I will have to go back for duty at some point in time. I am sure they will summon me."

Wanting to break up the direction the conversation was heading, then start fresh, Clara said, "I am sorry Martin, let me check on the dinner. I will be right back."

A few minutes later Martin heard the words dinner is ready, coming from the dining room. The two ate dinner as Clara shared stories about David, Margaret, and her time in Bletchley. She didn't seem to have many friends in Bletchley, which Marin found odd. He didn't comment on it, though. Martin was content to listen and enjoy the dinner. Shortly after arriving in Bletchley, she met Margaret at the Co-Op. She had been friends with the Smith's ever since. He also learnt that there wasn't much to do in Bletchley. That Clara often travelled to London, and to the countryside, which she found to be beautiful. As she spoke non-stop, while Martin listened patiently, Clara's feeling for Martin were aroused even more. Handsome, strong, and such a gentleman, she thought. Her emotions were stoking her inner desire. She began to tingle as she gazed across the table at Martin. She felt like a teenager all over again.

After dinner, Clara was ready to make her move. The night was getting late, and it was time, she thought. Hoping to arouse Martin's loins, she slowly ran her fingers through her hair, while twisting and curling the ends. Looking directly at Martin, holding a steady come hither gaze into his eyes, Clara began to speak. In a sexy girl like tone she asked, "Do you have a wife in London?"

Her tone made Martin uneasy, as he could tell she had become interested in him. Although stunning, Martin simply was not looking at her like she was him. Tonight, he had other things on his mind for her. How do I handle this without giving away my secret? He thought.

Eventually he replied, "No, no attachments, just me. I have been too busy to find myself a wife." The words just settled in Clara's mind. They were the words she wanted to hear. Rising to her feet, gently swinging her hips, she seductively approached him. The fullness of her red lips were striking, alluring even. But her eyes, her eyes, said it all. She wanted him.

Martin watched her every move with a quiver inside him. His palms became moist. Fear, maybe, anxiety, possibly, but a certain movement in his loins were the cause of his rise in body temperature.

Clara placed her arms on his shoulders and began running her fingers through his hair. As she slowly brought her lips towards his, she said with a smile, "There would be no one that would get upset with me for doing this then."

The kiss began softly. Her lips gently touched his, and Martin felt his manhood come alive. First a tingle, and then, then as Clara's kiss lingered, and her tongue slipped slowly inside of his mouth, his tingle started to turn into an erection. Martin wasn't expecting this from her, or to happen to him so soon after his experience with Francis. Martin was confused. He stepped clumsily backwards. On his face, in his posture, and in Clara's eyes, Martin looked like a deer caught in the head-lights.

Clara, was startled by Martin's reaction and asked, "What is the matter? Did I do something wrong?"

Not since Emma had Martin looked at a woman in the way that he knew Clara was thinking of him. Then, having recently been with a man, Francis, for the first time, Clara's advances unsettled him. Could he be with a girl so soon? He was think-ing.

He could not tell Clara the truth, but he had to speak. "No, No, you did nothing wrong," he said. "It is perhaps a little too quick for us. We hardly know each other, and, well, don't you think it would be better to get to know one another a little more first?" Was about all that he could muster to say.

Clara, confused, and hurt, by Martin's rebuff, stepped away then meekly said, "Yes perhaps you are right. I am so sorry." She then shrugged off her disappointment and began to move past this awkward moment.

"What did you mean earlier when you said you had to get back on duty?" She asked.

Realising that he had never told Clara that he was in the army, Martin nervously collected his thoughts. What secret will he be revealing by letting her know he was in the army? Could this lead to why he is really in Bletchley being found out by Clara? He asked himself before replying with, "I am a Major-General in the army. I decided to take leave for a short while. Now I am here in Bletchley as a lawyer. It is good to be pursuing the law for a change. But my leave will end, and I will have to go back to the army."

Martin's eyes narrowed. He hung his head and continued to ramble on in a mono-toned voice. "I am not looking forward to my leave finishing. I am not afraid of battle, but the war seems so hopeless now. The Germans and their allies have been winning in many battles. It is as if they know what we are going to do next, and we know nothing about their movements. A little intelligence here and there but nothing."

"There must be so many of German spies in Britain, they must be the reason why Germany is winning so many battles. We even caught a German spy named Joseph Jakobs over the summer, and he told us nothing before he was executed." He continued.

On hearing the name Joseph Jakobs Clara's breathing became rapid and shallow. Her pulse pounded in her temples, and her stomach knotted up. She needed to remain calm on the outside so as not to alert Martin to who she really was - but inside; she was hurting. Nervousness and heartbreak were beginning to consume her when she said, "I will take these dishes into the kitchen and put on the coffee," as she skirred the room.

Minutes passed, then Martin followed Clara into the kitchen to refill his glass of wine. Speaking as he approached the kitchen, he said, "I do not want to be a spy, but I just think there is something more for me to be doing for Britain in this war. I am hoping to figure that out as well while I am on leave."

On entering the kitchen, he saw Clara with her hands over her face, and her back to Martin. She was startled by his arrival. There was redness in her eyes and moisture on her face. She had been crying.

As Martin approached her, she stood, turned towards him, and embraced him. Her hands clutched at his jacket as she sobbed unceasingly into his chest. Martin gently rocked her as her tears soaked into his chest. The pain she felt must have come in waves. As there would be breaks in her sobbing when there was silence, then she would start again.

She eventually spoke, saying, "I am sorry Martin, forgive me, as you did not come over to see me sob."

"It's okay, Clara. Was it something that I said? Are you okay?"

"Martin, I have not been completely honest with you, and I am very sorry. You seem like a good person and I do not want to deceive you."

"Deceive me?" Martin asked.

"Yes, you said that you think there is something more for you to be doing in this war. I think there is more to the war than we know."

"Why do you think that?" Martin asked.

"You said you don't want to be a spy. Well I am a German spy, and Joseph Jakobs was my friend. We met as children in Austria. Over the years we grew close. That is why I am sad and was crying."

Martin stiffened from the inside out. He drew backwards, then away from Clara. Her words not only puzzled him, but also invoked his inner senses of defence. Instinctively, his hand was sent to where his holstered pistol would normally be. But no pistol, nothing was there. He was nakedly unarmed in the home of a German spy. His heart raced as he said, "Clara, why are you telling me this now?"

"Because, well, I am scared, I have no one to turn to, and I trust you, you seem like a good person. So, before you turn me in to the army, let me explain myself, okay?" Martin nodded slowly. Hesitantly giving his approval to hear her out.

She then told him of her past. From her modest beginnings in Austria. Losing her siblings, and her childhood friend Joseph Jakobs. How he had been recruited by Joseph Goebbels not too long after the Great War. How he later recruited her to be a spy. She also told him that she operated a safe house in Bletchley for German spies. That the gun shots that people heard the other night was one of the spies coming to her safe house being chased by the National Guard. When she told Martin about expecting Joseph Jakobs in England over the summer, her tears began to gush like a broken dam. She could hardly get out the words, 'he did not arrive'.

"I suspected the worst with Joseph, and when you confirmed it tonight, I became emotional." She said. But it was what came next that not only peeked Martin's interest but also gained his trust.

"On occasion there are spies that come to stay with me that I am sure are Americans. They try to portray themselves as Germans to me, but I can tell when they speak English that they are not German." She said.

"Americans?" Martin replied with his eyes wide open.

"Yes, and the last time that they stayed at my house was just before I was expecting Joseph. They had an accent that I remembered hearing before the war." She said.

"Before the war there was a man meeting with Joseph Goebbels one evening. I heard them speaking. They spoke in English, but the man was dressed in a German army uniform. I remember talk of mathematicians and scientist in Germany. They spoke of nuclear fusion and the German scientists Otto Hahn, Lise Meitner, and Fritz Strassman."

"The Americans that stayed with me over the summer had the same accent." She said as Martin's interest grew with each word that she spoke.

"I saw that man, the one that met with Goebbels, again in Bletchley just this week. He was dressed in an American army uniform this time. He arrived in an armoured caravan and went into the cafe of the Bull Commercial Hotel before leaving again. That is why I am sure there were American spies in my safe house, because that man is an American officer of some kind."

This was the second time Martin had heard Goebbels and Donovan together in the same circumstances. His suspicions of something more sinister to the war were growing.

As Clara continued to speak, she told Martin that, "Adolf Hitler has been listening to Goebbels from before the war. That Goebbels helped Hitler to get control over Germany before the war, and influences everything now."

"What do the Americans have to do with all of this?" Martin asked.

"I have suspicions that the Americans' involvement in the war isn't as they portray. But I cannot prove anything. I have been making notes, and investigating things, but I can't put all of the pieces together yet." Clara replied.

"Why Bletchley?" Martin asked.

"Bletchley Park is where the British code-breakers work," she replied.

Martin was shocked to learn that she knew this information. Immediately he thought of what do the Germans know of Bletchley Park. If she is a German spy, then they must know this as well. But there have been very little air raids over Bletchley, and none that directly targeted Bletchley Park. Why? He thought.

Clara continued by saying, "We've known about Bletchley Park since the start of the war. There was a Dutch Army Intelligence Officer, and two British agents, captured on the border between Netherlands and Germany, near Venlo. Major Stevens and Captain Best were the British agents I think. They thought they were going to meet a German general who was plotting a coup against Hitler. But the SS found out captured and interrogated them. They told us a lot about British intelligence service including that most of the code-breakers have moved to Bletchley."

"So is that why you came to Bletchley?"

"Well, yes, and Bletchley is close to London. Makes it the ideal transit point for our spies when they come to Britain on their way to London."

"What do you know about Bletchley Park now that you have been here for some time?" Martin asked, trying to extract everything out of her while thinking that this may be his calling to help the war effort. That one thing, one place, where he could make a difference. But he needed to be careful not to become a source of information for Clara. After all, she is a spy for Germany, he was thinking.

"I broke into the Bletchley Park facility one night and discovered that they were working on breaking German codes," replied Clara.

"I don't know everything but that is an important facility," she continued.

"I also followed one of the code-breakers from Bletchley Park to London. He met with Churchill. I was coming back from following that code-breaker - Francis Lambert – when I met you on the train. So, I know that Bletchley is important to the British. Then when I saw the American that met with Goebbels here in Bletchley it confirmed my thinking - there is something important going on in Bletchley."

"His name - the American you mentioned - is William Donovan. He is the Head of the Office of Strategic Services in America." Martin said, being grateful that Clara didn't say she saw him and Francis together in London. She was being open with him, so he was confident that she first saw him on the train.

With a quick nod to acknowledge what Martin said about Donovan, Clara continued, "There is another code-breaker at Bletchley Park – Sharon Howes. I convinced her boyfriend, Richard, to gather information for me. It was easy, Richard is always drinking and a few quid was all it took. He was able to get me some of the papers Sharon worked on at Bletchley Park. I think they have a machine that can break codes use by the Germans, but I have not confirmed that as yet. But I have no one to share this with now that Joseph is dead. He was my only link to Germany."

"Do the bobbies know about the code breaking papers from the Sharon Howes case?" Martin asked.

"No, they were questioning her to try and find out things. I hear that they think she is a spy." Martin was relieved to hear that the bobbies knew nothing. He also did not share

his involvement with Sharon. He couldn't, even if he wanted to. Sharon has a legal right to confidentiality, he reminded himself. Martin then asked to see her notes. She
did not hesitate. She showed him her notes – dates, times,
even messages relayed to Germany.

Some of the messages sent to Germany were about allied troop movements, and then the allies lost badly. She
was partly the cause of the allied battle losses that had
frustrated Martin. But other information sent to Germany
appeared to be given to the allied forces and not the
Germans. Which he found odd.

From his days in the command centre, he recalled some
of the allied actions around those times. Germany was
told that the allies knew about their troop movements, but
continued to do exactly as they had planned – almost as if
they had never been told anything - this puzzled Martin
and Clara. "There must be a back channel between the
Germans and the allies where this information from spies
is being acted on." They both concluded.

"What about Germany, do they know about Bletchley Park
now? Do they know who is in charge of the ode breaking?"
Martin asked.

Clara was not sure how much to tell Martin, but she decided
to be open with him. She needed a friend and someone she
could trust. Martin was going to be that friend, she decided.
She looked Martin in the eyes. She hesitated, then spoke. Her
voice was low, and Martin could sense the sincerity in her
words when she said, "Joseph Jakobs was coming over to help
her find out everything about Bletchley Park. What they knew
and how they were doing things, before telling Germany. We
feared that giving bad information to Germany would be met
with harsh consequences for us, because it would delay the
war while Germany changed their cipher machines. Then if it

was later found that we were wrong, it would be bad for us - especially me!" Clara replied.

"He never made it and Germany does not know anything new since before the war." She continued.

Speaking with a hint of excitement, and some fear, in her voice Clara asked, "Please don't turn me into the British army. It is the Americans that concern me most now that Jakob is dead. We must work together to figure all this out. Can we do that? Can we trust each other?"

On hearing those words, Martin's brain seemed to stutter for a moment. It was as if a ferocious jolt of electricity had just struck him. His jaw dropped. His eyes opened in disbelief. His whole body paused to allow his thoughts to catch up. Clara stood frozen, too. Fearful of what might come next. Fearful that this would be it for her. But to her surprise Martin replied by saying, "This is not what I was expecting from you. But what you say about the Americans worries me too. If there is something sinister to this war and they are involved then they should be discovered."

Thinking she was home free, Clara let out a gasp of air and said, "Yes, they should. We can do it together. We can expose them."

Martin paused, thought, and asked. "Why don't we go to the British with what you know. They would welcome you and help us?"

"We can't Martin! The British will think I am lying. They will torture me, then kill me! Also we don't know who is involved. Germany yes. America maybe. Bit Britain maybe too. There is no one we can trust other than each other. That is if you trust me." Replied Clara.

"Right now I do not trust you! But I also will not go to the British Army for now. I need to think about everything. This is all a bit much and can become even more for me. I need to think! I need to think about you, what you have said, what we know, and what I want to do about." Martin said as his voice trailed off from a stern beginning to a rather benign soft rambling.

12

T ime stood still for Clara as she awaited Martin's answer. Time that she haphazardly used to make plans to run if needed. Every day, every waking hour, she looked over her shoulder. Checking, asking herself: is that them? Have they come for me? Did Martin turn me in to the British?

Martin, on the other hand, was in a time warp, travelling at the speed of light it seemed. He did not have time to think about Clara. He needed to focus on his mission in Bletchley. He needed to be a lawyer? He needed to prepare to be in a courtroom.

Generally speaking, Martin's experience with court rooms had been non-existent. Yes, he had been to court to observe. Once when he was an associate with his father's law firm. But also when he was at Oxford. It was mandatory for law students to spend time in courtrooms. While at Oxford there was a case that involved innovative that Martin found very interesting. So he travelled to Lancaster, where the case was being trialled, and spent days in court following the trial of Doctor Buck Ruxton.

Dr Ruxton had been accused of murdering his wife and house maid. The prosecution of Ruxton's murders was highly publicised. Because of his occupation, and the extensive mutilation he inflicted upon his victims' bodies, Ruxton became known as the Savage Surgeon. Martin was fascinated by the whole case which went by the names Bodies Under the Bridge due to the location where the bodies were found. The case was also known by the Jigsaw Murders because of the painstaking efforts to re-assemble, identify the victims, and then determine the place of their murder. The lawyers pored over the details. Battling daily, on the centre stage of the courtroom, as Martin looked on. It was the case that had shaped Martin's view of the ferociousness of courtroom battles. Now today, centre stage belonged to him, and his nerves reminded him of the ferociousness of the courtroom. But he was ready for the battle.

Weather-beaten terracotta tiles covered the roof of a Lincolnshire Limestone building. Inside the building, the dusty foyer displayed fading portraits of the town's legal heroes scattered amongst the neatly stapled legal notices. It would be here, in this building, where Martin would start his courtroom experience. The building has been a feature in Bletchley for over a century. Now the building housed the courts, the police station with its jail, and had in recent times become the centre for applicants wishing to join the Local Defence Volunteers. Also, with the rise in crime, following billeting at the start of the war, the officers' clubroom in the building had been made into a juvenile court.

Silence lingered in the air. A small sigh of anxiety leapt into his mouth as he arrived at the courthouse. His eyes flickered at the thought of a building that just a few days ago hummed with of exhilarating excitement, but now seemed so intimidating. When he saw her, a muscle twitched involuntarily at the corner of his right eye, and his mouth formed a rigid grimace. Somewhere deep inside him, he had hoped she would not show. That he would escape what he feared. But this was not to be the case. Sharon confidently strode up to Martin and Matthew. Now this uncharacteristically sunny morning in

Bletchley would either see the dawn of his life as a solicitor, or a sharp end to his dreams.

Sharon was dressed like many other young women that he would see in London. She smartly wore a pink dress, a waist-length jacket, and a colourful neck scarf. Her face was made up, but not overdone, and her long black hair was pulled back into a ponytail. But what Martin noticed most was that there was something in the way she held herself. Her limbs extended naturally from her body, and gently swung as she walked. Whereas the average person just walked along, barely aware of their surroundings, her eyes moved quickly over everything in front, to the sides, and every few moments also behind. In those brief moments, as she briskly stroked her way towards him, she portrayed a sense of confidence that settled even within him.

The trio made their way to the Bletchley main courtroom on the second floor, where they were greeted by the bailiff – an elderly man with a cheerful smile - that ushered them into the courtroom. As they eased through the double doors of the main courtroom, Martin's eyes widened. Several spectators, watching and waiting for justice to be dispensed, filled the room. Martin looked around the courtroom like a child on the first day of school, taking in the sights with both excitement and fear. The limestone walls were bare. Three tall widows were interspersed with on either side of the room. A judge was working at his bench as lawyers, at the tables to the front of the court, shuffled papers as they argued back and forth. A few clerks chatted with the lawyers as they went about their business. The jury box to the left of the room was empty. It must have been a bench trial in progress.

Matthew cornered a prosecutor, a man he quickly introduced to Martin and Sharon as Frank, the lawyer assigned to Sharon Howes' case. Martin told Frank that he represented Sharon, and that he will be filing for a restraining order of Richard

Brown, an acquaintance of hers. "How much do you know about Sharon's case?" Martin then asked the Frank.

The four of them moved to a quiet location near the jury box so they could speak in private. Frank said, "The bobbies say that Ms. Howes is a spy that was caught by her boyfriend, Richard". Sharon replied, "I am not a spy, Richard spends his time in the pub drinking and when he is drunk, he thinks all manner of things about me." Matthew interjected and said, "Ms. Howes is a clerk over at Bletchley Park. She types, makes tea, and things like that. Nothing sinister about what she does."

"Then why would Richard think otherwise," Frank asked. "You know Richard, he had it rough in the war and isn't himself. That is why Sharon fears for her safety. We need to get the restraining order and this nonsense against Sharon dropped." Replied Martin, who knew that he needed to make sure that Sharon was left along. It was the reason he was in Bletchley and what Churchill expected of him.

"Ms. Howes has been dealing with Richard for some time. She does not want to press any charges, the war thing with him and all, but she wants her piece of mind," Martin demands. "Who is this again, Matthew?" Frank asked.

"He is a lawyer from London sent over to help us out for a bit," replied Matthew. Frank looked at Martin, casting his eyes from head to toe, then glanced quickly at Sharon before replying, "Okay, I will get the charges against Sharon dropped, but you will need to get the restraining order sorted with the bobbies and filed with the Judge before you leave today." Matthew nodded, agrees, and said, "Thank you, Frank."

"Thank God there will be no trial," Martin mumbles as they turned away from Frank.

Juvenile Court day was every other Thursday, but gradually it became every Thursday, and now every day. Today was

Thursday and Martin had to rush over to the Juvenile Court for his next case.

Alan Smith, and two other kids, were marched into the courtroom and seated in the front row. Their handcuffs were removed, and one of the bailiffs stood close. The three boys were members of one of the gangs that were terrorising the streets after dark. They wore faded blue overalls and were a mess. It was also evident, from the smell, that they had not bathed for some time. James was there to support his grandson through the ordeal.

The juvenile court was a miniature version of the main courtroom that Martin had just left. But his familiarity with the layout and proceedings did nothing to ease his nerves. His palms were sweaty, and his hands were shaking as he waited to speak on Alan's behalf.

William 'Bill' Denning, the Prosecutor, was a friend of Frank's whom Martin had passed earlier. He was a fixture in the courts, prosecuting everything from juvenile delinquency to murder. Bill, who was smartly dressed in a black suit, placed his white wig on the table in front of him. He must have a need for the wig later that day, as formal court attire, with wigs, was not a requirement for juvenile court. Something that Martin appreciated, as he was not prepared for that degree of formality today.

A pair of well worn, fading, suspenders strained under the load of Bill's mid-section. The suspenders looked ready to pop, which caused Matthew to smile broadly as he contemplated that eventually. Matthew, commenting on the size of Bill's stomach, whispers to Martin, "that thing seems to be growing by the day." Bringing an uncomfortable half smile to Martin's face as he held the intensity of his first court appearance representing a client in his mind's eye.

Bill leaned over to Martin, extended his hand and said, "Bill Denning, pleased to meet you." Martin lightly shook Bill's hand, almost as if fear was preventing him from touching Bill. He introduced himself, then turned his head awkwardly towards the Judge. But Bill was not finished talking and again leaned into Martin whispering in his ear, "these lads need discipline, such a curse this war is on the kids." Martin smiles and nodded, as if in agreement.

When the judge called Alan Smith's name, Bill and Martin snapped into focus. Alan stood before the judge, with Martin to his right. Bill stood to Martin's right as James looked on from the gallery. They introduced themselves to the judge, stating their business in the court on this occasion. Bill then started in on a rambling narrative of Alan's involvement with gangs, the seriousness of rationing in war times, and the affront of such behaviour as stealing ration books has on not only the victim, but the entire British solidarity. Alan's hands were trembling, and his eyes were moist as Bill spoke. This was a first for Alan. He was tough and strong with the gang, but still only a young boy. He was scared.

The judge, a graceful old gentleman with a slick head of white hair, calmly scanned the audience and asked, "Is the alleged victim in the courtroom." Bill looked over his shoulder into the room, and found Mrs Moss, a widower, seated at the rear. "Yes, My Lord," he said as Mrs Moss stood to be acknowledged by the judge.

"Are you here alone," the Judge asked.

Posturing for a sympathetic ear from the judge, Bill interrupted, saying, "My Lord, I am afraid that Ms. Moss' husband recently died from cholera." The sympathy of the judge could be seen in his face. His face dipped downwards and his cheeks soften to give way to a lifelessness that showed deep sorrow. The judge replied, "I am very sorry for your loss. There are so many servicemen being sent to serve in countries, where there is all manner of diseases at epidemic levels. Then they return infecting an increasing number of Brits. Especially children and infants, who had weaker immune systems, in alarming numbers."

Turning to Martin, the Judge asked, "Mr. Frost, do you have anything to add?"

Martin turned his head to squarely face the judge. "My Lord," he began with as he explains to the judge that he represented Alan at the behest of his grandfather James, who is here with his grandson today. He went on to tell of the plight the family has faced since the start of the war. James' service to his country in the Great War, and to request leniency for Alan. The Judge replied that he was inclined to agree with Martin and asked Bill for his commentary on the matter. Bill, in the grandest of flash, spoken language, and far too many words, agreed with Martin and the Judge. That Alan, for the sake of his grandfather, would be given a chance this time.

"What do you have in mind, Mr. Frost?" the Judge asked.

"My Lord, I would suggest that Mr. Smith be confined to a remand home where he will have less freedom of movement, and be able to grow into a productive young man without the drama of repercussions from this incident. His grandfather has confirmed that Alan is a good lad in need of closer supervision which he cannot give at this time." James, a rough but distinguished man, asked to speak, and the judge granted his request. "My Lord, I am appalled by the actions of my grandson. Having served my country, I understand the importance of unity. Rationing is the greatest unity we as Brits can demonstrate and I would like to make any restitution to Mrs. Moss that, My Lord, thinks appropriate. But please be lenient with young Alan."

"Mr. Frost, do you have a period of remand in mind?"

"My Lord, young Mr. Smith is 16, he will be able to join the service in two years, I would suggest remand until he is required to begin his service."

"Mrs. Moss, as to restitution, what is it that you seek?" The Judge asked.

"I do not want anything My Lord. It is difficult for all of us during these times. Having the lad get good guidance in a place where he will not harm others is good enough for me."

"Mr. Denning?" the judge then asked.

"My Lord, I am in agreement with Mr. Frost and Mrs. Moss."

"Then it is so ordered."

Turning his attention to Alan Smith, the Judge then said, "Mr. Smith you are to spend the next two years at a remand home. I wish you well."

Martin was feeling a bit rattled, but exhilarated as well. He had not only survived his first encounter in the courtroom, but enjoyed it and was ready for more. James was remorseful as his grandson was led from the courtroom. But he thanked Martin and Matthew for their help. After a quick stop at the court clerk to file the restraining order, Martin returned to Dunham and Associates. The rest of the day was client-free, thankfully. His nerves had had enough for one day and he needed to reflect.

His journey to Bletchley had been rich in new experiences and information. Though it was the information that weighed on Martin's mind as he sat and looked out the window and across the countryside. Closing his eyes, and gently massaging them with his fingers, his mind wondered through the pieces of information he had gleaned from Francis and Clara. What stood out, and nagged at him most, was the American connection. He could reconcile the Germans - their spies, Clara, and even the secret facility at Bletchley Park. He had also reconciled to work with an admitted German spy, Clara, to uncover what was taking place with this war. But William Donovan and the Americans still puzzled him.

At five o'clock, he finally called it a day. He was tired, his head was hurting, and his mind was full of possibility. He stopped by Matthew's office on his way out. They recapped his work with the firm. So far so good, though he was still rattled from committing young Mr Smith to confinement followed by service in what was sure to be a war, maybe even death. "it was for the better, and an eventuality something that Alan wouldn't have escaped," Matthew assured him. "I've been doing this for twenty-five years and I have seen it all. Young people are resilient and the war is not your doing," he said.

Martin felt fine leaving the office and walking to his flat.

A slow drizzle was falling, and the town was growing dark as he climbed the stairs behind Janette's garage. He had not seen Jannette in the office through the day and felt compelled to be polite. He would stop over and say hello a bit later. He thought. Right now, he just needed to rest.

Janette was a lovely middle-aged widower, who had main-tained her physique over the years, and was very easy on the eyes. She had not taken an interest in anyone since her husband and had grown accustomed to eating alone. But was pleased to see Martin at her door.

He gently knocked on the blue door at the front of her house. The door opened in an instance, as if she was waiting for him. A combination of lilac from her perfume and a musty smell from a lack of ventilation greeted him. "Hello Janette, I do not want to intrude. I just wanted to thank you again for letting me have the flat," he said as she appeared in the doorway of a dimly lit entranceway.

"You are not intruding. I had just arrived home and saw you come in right after. I had hoped that you would stop by."

"Why is that?"

"There is not much to do in Bletchley. In fact, there is nothing to do if you are not one of those that tend to church business three nights a week, or go to the pub every night."

"And you don't tend to much church business?" Martin asked, trying to continue the pleasantries. So far, in his brief time in Bletchley, he had come to understand that religion was significant. There were Methodist, Anglican Catholics, all hunkering together to give hope and help to a community that was buckling under its expanded population.

"I attend sometimes on Sunday, but don't get involved in the business of church," Janette said.

"Oh, forgive me, come in, come in, its wet outside" she said.

The weather in Britain is so unpredictable. Bright and sunny in the morning and now cold and wet, as the day drew to a close. Something to do with the cold polar air from the north and warmer air from the Tropics push against each other to create the changeable weather and unpredictable winters. Because of these changes Brits had grown custom to making snarly remarks about the weather, at the start of each conversation. Janette was a typical Brit. "Some weather we are having today," she said.

Sensing that she was getting uncomfortable with the company, Martin tried to lighten the moment by replying, "Well you know our King prefers Reign over sun."

Following a hardy chuckle, far more than the moment deserved, Janette said, "I was just about to start dinner, would you care to join me?" With her schedule she had very little time to cook. Evidently, cleaning was not a priority either. After supper the two cleared the table and stacked the dishes in the sink. Grateful for the company, and wanting it to last longer, Janette then said, "Let's have some tea, and talk." With nothing else to do, Martin said yes. "Make yourself comfortable in the living room, I will bring the tea in shortly." Replied Janette.

She brought two cups of steaming tea, handed one to Martin, and said, "Let's sit on the couch and talk." As they settled in, Janette began to talk. She spoke non-stop for what seemed like hours to Martin, who politely listened and occasionally nodded. She spoke mainly about her childhood, growing up in Bletchley, and how she had enjoyed it so much. She was saddened when she lost her parents, and then later when her husband died. She went from very happy times to sombre and sad times. Martin could tell that she was lonely and unhappy.

Once there was a break in Janette's rambling monologue about herself. Martin used this time to get a few words into the conversation. "It's hard to believe that you are not pursued by all of the men in Bletchley," he said.

"There is not much going on here. I made the choice to stay; now I live it, but its okay."

"Your choice?"

"Yes, there have been a couple of nice men since my husband, but no one I wanted to be together with. One fella was twenty-years older. I am forty-six and I just couldn't image myself loosing another husband as he grew older. "I understand," Martin said.

As the evening was drawing to a close Martin's mind started to fade away from the here and now. With a relaxed mind, and a clear head, he started to think about Clara. She is really a spy, he thought. His time in the army was more direct. He had heard of what spies did, but never had he actually encountered a spy. This was a big deal for him. Instinctively he thought that he must turn her in to his superiors. It was his oath as a soldier, as a lawyer, as a loyal British subject. Still if he turns her in, and she is right in her thinking that there is more to the war then the world may never know. Is the pursuit of the truth, the pursuit of justice, not also his oath he contemplated. He thoughts went back and forth as Janette rambled. Then suddenly it struck him. Some sort of cosmic energy came over him and he knew what he had to do. At the next lull in the after dinner talk he quickly interjected, "It is getting late, I had better be getting off to bed. Thank you for a lovely evening Janette."

Despite Martin's wandering mind it was truly a good break from the world to spend time talking with Janette. The two said their goodbyes in the threshold of Janette's doorway. Now it was time to return to reality.

As the door to Janette's house slowly closed behind him, Martin bee lined towards Clara's house. He didn't even look at his flat above her garage. He had something to say to Clara that he had to get done now. It was late in the evening but he knew Clara would see him. She must be waiting, expecting to hear from me, he was thinking.

Seeing Clara, telling her of his decision, did not take long at all. Martin went directly to the point as soon as she opened her door. "I have no choice Clara. I will not work with a German spy against the interest of my country." He said.

Stunned, and visibly shaking, Clara stood in silence while Martin continued to speak, "In the morning I shall be going to London to be with my family over Christmas. In London I will be debriefed on my time in Bletchley. They will know of you soon." Tears rolled down Clara's cheeks as he spoke. Martin remained stoic as he tried to not give in to any feelings that may be developing. Before abruptly turning and briskly walking away Martin spoke his last words to Clara. Martin then disappeared into the darkness of the night. Clara watched his every move until she could no longer see him.

His last words to her echoed in her head. "Leave Bletchley, leave Briton and never return. Go now before I arrive in London. Go now!" He said.

13

After leaving Clara's, the night before, Martin didn't sleep a wink. It was a long night for Martin. He just counted the minutes, and the seconds, as his mind raced from thought to thought. He worried about who could be trusted. He worried if there is more to the war as Clara has said. He feared for his own life if he talks about what he knows about Clara, but is not believed.

Tired and weary he arrived at the train station bright and early the next morning. Way before its scheduled departure time. It was one of those days when dawn was slowly proceeding, as if it were not ready to come, but must as schedule demands its entrance. The joy on these days, when it feels as though dawn is dragging its feet, is the beautiful morning sounds of the birds.

Wood pigeons, wrens and warblers, were just beginning to join the serenading of the pre-dawn sounds of robins, black-birds and thrushes. Sparrows, great tits, blue tits, and finches will chime in later in the light of the new day.

The station was busy with passengers and people seeing them off. Many of the passengers were saying, "The train's late!" Which only adds to Martin's feeling of weariness. However, to his delight, the train to London arrived just before its scheduled departure time.

On arrival the train was as crowded as usual. Everyone at the Bletchley stop raced to grab a place to rest their bodies. So did a tire and weary Martin.

Martin's ride on the train to London marked the end of a roller coaster of a visit to Bletchley. As soon as it began, he felt a mixture of relief and anxiety — relief that he was travelling on a train away from Clara the spy, and anxiety about what she had told him about the war. He worried about Clara's fate. Yet it was the feeling of relief that over powered the moment. He was getting away from it all, and it felt good.

The train crawled along patiently and faithfully pulling its load. Stop after stop the crowded train grew fuller and fuller with passengers impatient to see their families at Christmas.

The next morning Martin awoke rested. The solitude and safety of his barracks proved to be just what he needed to settle his anxiety. Or maybe it was sheer exhaustion that allowed him to rest. Still dishevelled from his time away from active duty he dressed in his parade uniform to up-date Churchill on his time in Bletchley. Sir Stuart Menzies, the Head of Secret Intelligence Service, will also be there and this would be his chance to tell him about Clara. The Head of Secret Intelligence Service, and the Prime Minister, would be the safest people to tell. They would be able to be trusted, and would do the right thing, he thought.

On arrival at Downing Street, a huge ex-Guardsman that everyone called 'Panzer', the German word for tank, greeted Martin. Panzer looked disapprovingly at Martin's hair, which had grown unsightly outside of the army standard during his leave. Panzer then presented himself in the most pleasant and soft-spoken manner. Panzer was a gentle giant.

Panzer knocked, then entered Churchill's office with Martin in tow. Inside Menzies and Churchill were waiting on Martin's arrival. "Come in. Please have a seat Major-General." Churchill said. As Martin took his seat Menzies looked sinisterly at Churchill. A look that gave Martin an eerie feeling. He was certain what to make of the look. Maybe his mind was working overtime. Clara's words that 'there was more to the war' played on his mind more than he had known. He was now thinking that everyone may involve. Still, he had a duty to share what he knew about a German spy during war time.

Once seated Churchill was the first to speak. "How are you making out in Bletchley," he asked.

Before Martin could speak Menzies also chimed in and asked, "Do we have anything to worry about in Bletchley?"

To Martin it felt like an onslaught. He had much to tell about Clara, but not so much about Sharon Howes. The case that they had sent him to Bletchley to handle.

Grasping for what he might say Martin started with a preamble. He thanked the Prime Minister and Menzies for their opportunity and their confidence in him. Pausing often, and talking slowly, as in the back of his mind he pondered the Clara situation, Martin continued to speak, but say very little. "Sharon Howes is a lovely lady. It as a pleasure to meet her. Matthew and David also took great care of me while I was there." He said.

Churchill could be seen to becoming impatient so Martin moved on to what he wanted to hear. "There is a bit more to do with the Sharon Howes case, but it should not be a problem for us. Martin said with both Churchill and Menzies smiling in relief as they heard that the matter may end well. Once hearing that the situation was in hand, both Churchill and Menzies raced Martin off.

"Thanks, you for the update," Churchill said standing to usher Martin out. "Enjoy your Christmas. Update us when you are back from Bletchley again." Menzies said as he too stood to usher Martin out.

Under his breath Martin said, "There is one more thing I need to tell you." But neither man heard him speak. They seemed to be in a hurry to have him leave. Martin also got that eerie feeling again and decided to take leave. "Thank you, sir," he said then exited Churchill's to find Panzer standing outside, ready to ensure Martin left the building.

Martin left the meeting with Churchill and Menzies and decided to get a few Christmas gifts for his family. With rations and ration books the pickings for gifts were very slim. However, Martin braved the crowds shopping for the popular gifts of gardening tools and fertiliser to replenish his parents' supply. For his siblings he got reading books. As the day slowly passed, he handmade cards for each family member. He also couldn't shake that nagging eerie feeling that came over him in Churchill's office.

Throughout the rest of the day, he could hear Clara's voice, even see her in his mind eye, as she told him that there was something more to the war. As she asked for his help to uncover the truth. He remembered the Americans on the train. Hearing Goebbels name mentioned along with Donovan's. Yet he still found the thought of Clara asking for his help annoying. For her to think that he would betray his country hurt him. The look of innocence as she spoke disturbed him to his core. She was trying to pull the wool over his eyes. He kept repeating to himself that north good could come of helping a German spy. Chaos and noise filled his head until he could take it no longer. He was troubled beyond the point that he could recover. As always though, in times of trouble, he would turn to his father do his wisdom and guidance. This was one of those times of trouble and he was looking forward to getting his father's advice over the holiday.

Seeking wisdom Martin arrived in Mayfair knowing how fortunate he was to be with his family. As for many it wouldn't be easy to celebrate Christmas this year with many of their families, and loved ones, separated by war. As he made his way towards the front door it opened slowly. A wizened face peered out from the open wedge of the door. On seeing his father Martin rushed into his arms. Young and frisky for his age Martin senior, with his mottled scalp save a sparse fringe of white, embraced his son with vigour. His heavily lidded eyes, weighed down with wrinkled folds that it was almost like talking to someone asleep, watered from joy as he held his son. "Welcome home son." His father finally uttered. Thomas, Anne, and Mrs Frost also rushed to greet Martin.

That Christmas thousands of incendiaries, and nearly 500 tons of high explosives, were dropped in the Greater Manchester area. London also got its fair share of bombings on the nights just before Christmas Day. The royal family were whisked away to a secret location where the King gave his Christmas broadcast. Traditional carol singing was also cancelled due to the bombing and blackout. One concession was a doubling of rationed tea and sugar allowance.

Also, that Christmas, amid the bombing the Frost family enjoyed camaraderie, good food, and a modest gift exchange. It was a needed break for all. Especially Martin who not only desperately needed the break but also needed the wisdom of his father. His mentor and confidant. In the days following their Christmas meal Martin and his father spoke many times about the one challenge that haunted Martin the most — Clara.

He told his father everything. That he was sent to Bletchley by Churchill to help keep the code breaking facility at Bletchley Park a secret. How the Americans were making a raucous on his train to Bletchley. That he overheard the Americans on the train speak of Goebbels and Donovan. How he met Clara on the train when he moved away from the raucous. That he has developed feelings for Clara, but she has told him that she is a German spy. Also, that she thinks there is more to the war as she has seen Donovan and Goebbels talking. As well as that she has also asked him to help her.

Martin Sr., seeing the angst in his son as he spoke, would often interrupt him. He wanted to calm him. To focus him. "Son," he would say. "Calm is always best. With calm comes clarity, and what we need is clarity." Those word would always get Martin to focus. There was also a small respite from the bombing on Christmas and Boxing Day which helped Martin to focus.

As the two men spoke off and on over the Christmas holiday Martin Sr. Asked many questions to help Martin come to his own conclusions. "Why would a German spy tell you she is a spy? What does she want from you? Are you sure she is German?" Where some of the questions that sent Martin off to think, to become lost in mind as he pondered the possibilities. Each time he returned to talk with his father his thoughts were clearer, but he didn't have any answers. Martin would simply say, "I don't know or I am unsure."

By the 29th December, many families in London were again rushing for the safety of air-raid shelters once more. The outlook for the war still looked bleak. As the Londoners scrambled for safety, and others were fleeing the City, Martin senior decided to give Martin his parting words. He said o Martin, as they sat in front of the living room fireplace, "Son, she is either genuinely in need of your help, or she may not be German but British Military police testing you out ahead of a bigger role." Hesitation proceeding Martin's next words. With the crackling and popping of fresh fire in front of him Martin slowly asked, "How would I know the difference, Dad? What shall I do now?" The fire seemed to reach a roar as Martin senior put another log in the fire before slowly, very slowly, answering his son.

"Remember that nagging feeling that prevented him from telling Menzies about Clara? That is your inner compass. Trust that compass and you will know what to do." Martin senior said then gracefully, as a senior statesman would, he turned and slowly walked away. Leaving Martin to digest, understand, and decide for himself.

Then, just as Martin thought his father was finished speaking with him, in a distance he heard the words, "But have a backup plan. A backup plan son." Shorty after, Martin made his way back to Bletchley.

The anxiety and relief that Martin felt when leaving Bletchley was now replaced with feelings of enlightenment and nervousness on his returning. Enlightenment squished upon him like a whirlwind. One minute he was casually riding the train back Bletchley. Moving the thoughts he had developed with his father about in his head — from one side to the next, up and down, like one of those slide puzzles, as he tried to complete the picture that was forming. Then it happened. Looking out at the trees, veiled in the lightest of mists, with sombre brown trunks, and frost cracks that gnarl the bark, Martin achieved enlightenment. He knew, he knew what he needed to do about Clara. Nerves then overtook him. He was so nervous he thought he was going to throw up. He could feel sweat beading on his forehead as the train chugged along, moving closer and closer to Bletchley. His heart pounded. His hands became clammy as they rested on his bouncing knee. It would be long now, and he will know. Did Clara run? Is she still in Bletchley? What does she think of me now? If I didn't trust her will she ever trust me again?

The town was covered in fog as the train pulled into the station. Martin's eyes travelled to the edge of the buildings as they became ghostly silhouettes against a blanket of white. The town, a happy hug of shops and houses, had expanded bit by bit over the years. Now it was about to be a place of reckoning for Martin. Either he will find Clara or not.

Martin leapt from the train before it had come to a stop at the station. He scurried his way over to Clara's house. His footsteps echoed like stones off a cave wall. Around him he could smell the damp trees not yet in bloom. On arrival he knocks. No answer. He tries the door handle. The door opens. Which is usual for these parts. Even with the crime rise after the billeting few folks locked their doors. He enters calling her name. "Clara, Clara, are you home Clara?" But there is no answer. Her home looks the same. Nothing disturbed. She must have run. He thought. Leaving quickly and taking nothing with her?

His heart was in his mouth as he turned to make his way over to David and Margaret's house. Here he would find out if they have seen Clara over the holiday. He knocks. Paces back and forth as he waits for David or Margaret to open the door for the inquisition. As he paced with his back to the door, the door opened. On turning, to his surprise, there she was standing in front of him. She hadn't run. Clara was still in Bletchley.

Moving swiftly to her, taking her by her hands and twirling her around, Martin says with the greatest smile of happiness, "It's really you!"

"But why?" He asked.

"I had faith in you. I knew our journey wouldn't end the way you left it."

"Was I wrong?"

"No, you were right. You were so right."

"I want t work with you. I believe there is more to the war. I believe that we can find out more about the Americans that visited town at Bletchley Park. We should start there."

"Okay," replied Clara before the two, now in an embrace, we're drawn into each other. Clara eyes trained on Martin lips, and his on hers. Then just as they could bear it no more, Martin's lips met Clara's. The warmth of her month sent a current running through his body. He was nervous no more. Clara threw her arms around Martin's neck as she lost herself in his soft lips and manly touch. His hands held up her butt as she pressed her body closer and closer. She had long for this moment and now it was here.

14

B letchley Park was chosen as a location for the gov-ernment cipher operations because of the privacy of being its own estate. It also had its own power, and a secure source of drinking water, which helped with secrecy. Clara had once considered breaking in and contaminating their water supply to put an end to the code breaking. But they would only move the facility and she would have to start over, she thought. The other reason that this location was chosen was because the train station was located next to the estate, making it easy for graduates from Oxford and Cambridge to slip in as code-breakers. She would often watch the trains coming into Bletchley and take note of new people going into the estate. They would be wide eyed, young, and with an air of enthusiasm mixed in as they wandered confusedly towards the estate. She could pick the new code-breakers out from a mile away, she always said to herself.

Tonight, without the wide eyes, she would be making her own way into the estate. Martin would be by her side. It had been days since they agreed to go inside Bletchley Park for a look around. They were both ready to explore.

The ride over was made at dusk with just enough light to find the path. They pedalled along the cliff's edge the entire way. Martin was certain that they were going to fall over, but with nerves, and skill, they travelled deeper and deeper into the forest. They were surrounded by oak, walnut, and gum trees, when she said, "This is it, we start here."

"How far away are we?" Martin asked.

"I have been using this trail to gather intelligence on the code-breakers for a long time. More and more code-breakers arrive from the universities, and they keep expanding their operations. Visitors live in the cottage where they are closely monitored. We will have to get in there while they are at the mansion for supper. The estate is almost six-hundred acres, but twenty minutes hiking along this trail before we are at the cottage," she said.

"There are buildings that they call huts on the eastern side, but we will not have to pass them. Before the war started, they had only one hut with a machine that was built by the Brits. Over the past two years, since I have been here, they have added another seven huts. I have been in all of them, and I think I have figured out what they do in each.

"That many? I didn't think their operation was that big. Why so many, huts?"

"They work on police and military codes from Italy, Portugal, Spain, Japan, and maybe other countries. Some huts are for capturing and decrypting messages. Others for passing on the content to the allied command centre. It's all in the books I showed you."

The hike began at the end of an abandoned foot trail to the west of the estate. Dressed in neutral colours, and wearing boots they started off on foot. Martin was thinking that the artillery fire, noise, and machinery at the front had done nothing to prepare him for the stealth that this required, but he was up for the new experience. Clara though, had explored these parts since arriving in Bletchley and knew every trail. If blindfolded she could travel them without being seen.

Earlier that day Martin had gone to the co-op and purchased new boots and tan clothing for the mission, at least that was what he was calling it, a mission. In silence they made their way towards the cottage. The incline was gradual, the undergrowth thick with the remnants of the spring growth of bluebells, wild garlic and wood anemones, natural foliage for these parts. She moved at an easy pace for his benefit, but there had been other nights when she had all but sprinted along the trail.

It was mandatory for all army personnel to keep up with their physical training. Martin, who jogged daily when he was in London, sensed that she was being careful because of him and said, "We could move a bit faster and hopefully get more time in the cottage."

"Okay," she replied before picking up the pace.

The new boots grew heavier with each turn as they zigzagged upward. Soon he was panting and sweating, but he was determined to stay on her heels.

They stopped at the edge of the woods and looked through. It was dark. Lit only by a semi-crescent moon. "Just barely sufficient enough light to manoeuvre around the campus," she said.

"The big building directly in front of us is the Mansion. The three buildings to the left are the cottages. Cottage one, is closest to us. This is where one of the caretakers live. Cottage two the next one over, is a feed store with hay loft, and Cottage three, the one furthest away, is where the Americans would be staying." They paused as Martin took in the scenery. Then, like a tour guide who needed no prompting, she went on. Nearby there was a lake and lots of trees that they manoeuvred in to stay hidden. They passed the new buildings where all the code-breakers work, the mansion, and the first two cottages. As they passed Hut 8 Cara said, "Over to the left of the where they are staying is where the chap that went to London works. But that is for another day."

"What does he work on?" Martin asked, knowing the answer of course.

"That is Francis Lambert's work area; he works on German military intelligence. But he has another private work area. I don't know what he does in there."

Near the third cottage she sat her backpack on the ground and pulled out binoculars. Through them she scanned the grounds and found what she was wanted. She handed the binoculars over and said, "Over there, at one o'clock, you can barely see them in the blue and grey uniforms." He looked through the binoculars, focused them and said, "Okay got them."

"Those are the guards on patrol. They should be passing the mansion soon. When they disappear behind that building, we can make a run for it."

"We will head to the northern corner of their cottage and wait." Continued Clara.

As the guards vanished from sight the two hustled to their next vantage point. Clara stood slightly ahead of Martin, gazing in a distance as they caught their breath.

Martin was panting profusely. But it was the pain from the new boots pinching at the arches of his feet that bother him most. The panting was not as much from the physical exertion but the adrenaline rushing through them that brought on his exhaustion. Martin was not use to covert work. In battle he had always attacked his enemies head on with them fully aware that he was coming.

But Clara was in her element, and brimming with confidence. Her right hand instinctively reached back over her shoulder and pulled a gun from her backpack. There was hardly a breath coming out of her as she stood in silence, casting her eyes around like a hawk eyeing its prey. Martin recognised the gun to be the same, browning semi-automatic handgun, that she had on the train. Again, he asked, "What is that for?" Don't worry we're safe," she said before for the second time replying, with a smile on her face this time, "protection." This time, though, Martin finally understood the need for the gun. Clara pointed to her right and said, "There, there is a guard just there - lagging behind the others. Let's sit here for a moment."

There was a rotten log, and a pile of firewood, behind the cottage. Behind the firewood and log was their next stop. It made a pleasant resting place as they shared a bottle of water. Clara didn't ask how Martin was doing, and he didn't inquire about the guard. He was content to wait on her next move. She had obviously done this before. Martin took another sip of water and wriggled his toes to get some circulation in his feet. Clara reached into her backpack, removed two bread rolls and handed one to him. "Thanks, I could use that about now." Martin said.

Then very nonchalantly, as if they were out for a casual stroll, and chat, Clara asked, "Does David and Peggy know that we had dinner together?"

"I work on the assumption that David, Peggy, and probably Matthew know just about every move I make. It's a small town after all."

"I've asked, they know nothing, and best we keep it that way." replied Clara. Martin smiled, took a large bite of the bread, but said nothing.

Minutes, which felt like an hour to him, passed in silence. She scanned the area continuously, keeping her eye on the straggling guard who was relieving himself in a bush. As the guard was finishing his business she spoke. "It's time, she said as she began to ease her way into the open space. With Martin snapping quickly into action behind her.

In the fading light they managed to find the entrance to the cottage and slipped inside. "They never lock any of the doors around here." Clara said.

"I guess they think it is a secure area so there is no need." Replied Martin.

Cottage three! their destination, was once a tack room old estate. Today though it has been converted into accommodations. An open plan one and half story room. A Victorian teak staircase ascended to the loft that overlooked the ground floor. The entire accommodation was of the highest quality of workmanship. Remnants from when the estate was privately owned by Sir Herbert Samuel Leon. He was a meticulous man that not only made a number of upgrades but also insisted on the finest quality of workmanship. On the lower level bunk beds lined the northern wall. Storage cupboards adorned the southern wall. While on the upper level there was a double bed, dressers, as well as a sitting area with a couch and chairs. The upper level was obviously the officers' quarters. As the two of them stood in the doorway of the dimly lit room Clara said to Martin, "Donovan and his entourage would sleep in here were its secure. The bunks on the lower level would be for his entourage. He would be on the upper level. But I am guessing the boys from the train are staying outside of the estate. That's way they would get the best sense of what is going in the town, and be able to give Donovan an early alert.

"If there is going to be anything of value in here it will likely be on the upper level seemed," Martin said in the softest of voices so as not to be heard by a passing guard outside.

"Possibly. I we will start on with those cupboards to the left. Why don't you with the bunks," replied Clara.

Clara started to search the cupboards methodically, looking for any new intelligence that she could find. In the past she found hand written orders from superior British officers. Even notes from operations conducted by the Germans. Gathered by American spies, she had assumed. She was always careful not to take anything, in order to not reveal that she had been there. This time, with the head of the American intelligence agency visiting, she was hoping for much more. Martin began riffling through the belongings of those sleeping in the bunks. The two moved quickly and in silence. Five-minutes, ten-minutes, fifteen-minutes passed, and they had nothing.

Meanwhile, in the mansion nearby, Donovan and the boys were finishing a fine English spread. Rationing was spared for visiting dignitaries. Their host, Brendan Bracken, Churchill's Minister of Information was an unruly member of Britain's upper class. Known to be a close associate of Churchill's he commanded the attention of Donovan during supper. He was also well travelled, and in an unruly manner as he could muster never hesitated to speak of his travels. As Bracken boisterously shared stories of his time in Australia with the men they ate, they talked, and friendships with the British grew stronger.

With nothing to be had on the lower level Clara and Martin knew they were running out of time. Empty-handed they quickly hustled up the stairs and started in on Donovan' belongings. "Here, I have something," Martin whispers. Clara swung her attention to Martin who was holding a book of some sort in his hands. It was a rust coloured, leather bound, book with handwritten notes inside of it. The two, stood side-by-side, their shoulders touched, and the soft sensual smell of her hair filled the air. Martin could not help but be distracted, if only briefly. They held the document inches away from their faces. In the moonlight that peered through a double window overlooking what they now knew to be Donovan's bed they scoured the first few pages of writing. Parts of the document was written in plain English; others parts were in a code of some sort. They flipped through the pages quickly stopping only to read the highlights. "It's his memoirs I think," Clara said. "Yes, it looks like it. He seems to have been involved in some kind of plan that was drawn up after the plan the Great War," said Martin. "Yes, but I can't tell who else is involved, it's all coded. Just seems to talk about how Donovan and others devised a plan to obtain world supremacy." Clara said. "This is big," Martin replied?

Eager to get a better look at the notes they decided to take a risk. They knew they could be discovered by a guard if they pulled back the blackout curtains to get a better look. But they pulled them back, anyway. Sure enough the light from a window in the cottage caught the attention of one of the guards. Having seen several battle plans Martin said, "this isn't a battle plan. It's a plan to politically destabilise the world somehow."

"We might have been seen. Plus Donovan will be back soon. We need to get out of here, but What should we do about these notes?" Clara said.

"If we take them they will know we were here." She continued.

"We can't leave them. This is big. Just what we were hoping to find. I say let's take the, and get out of here! Unlikely they will know it was us, but I f we get caught here, we will be executed." Replied Martin.

Clara placed the notes, and her gun, in her backpack. The two headed for the door. To their surprise, as they scampered around the side of the cottage, a guard yells out to them, "Stop, Stop." Knowing the consequences the two sprinted for the tree line at break neck speeds.

They were just beyond the tree line when they heard gun shots. There was a loud pop, followed by two more pops. A bullet whistled past them. Nearly missing Martin who was trailing behind Clara. Stopping for nothing they zigged and zagged through the trail. After some minutes of running, they took refuge behind a cluster of trees. "We can wait them out here. It's dark but they will still follow so we must keep quiet." Clara said.

They laid there in silence as three guards passed by them in a distance. Shortly after the passing of the guards they began a hurried descent down the trails they had come up. "It unlikely they will pick up our path in the dark. But at first light they will be back looking for signs of where we went." Clara whispered.

After a few hundred yards of careful jogging they slowed down to catch their breath. "Are we okay?" Martin managed to ask in between breaths. "We're fine," replied Clara calmly. "They don't know the trails like I do. Plus they do not have the dogs to pick up our scent."

Not long after they resumed their retreat there was the welcomed sight of their cycles came a hundred yards away. Clara paused for a second to see if there was anyone else around. "They haven't found us," she said as they pedalled off into the dark.

Clara stayed on high alert as they raced through the country side of Bletchley. Clara had made this journey several times before. She was in her element moving swiftly along with Martin close behind. Martin's heart was beating a mile a minute. But the two said nothing as they made their escape. Nearing the end of the trail with the town buildings coming into sight Martin asks, "Do you think they will be waiting for us at the end of the trail?"

"Oh no, they will be careful not to draw attention to themselves. Even if they are waiting, we will deny everything. They won't search us, but just in case let's hide the notes. I have just the place." Replied Clara.. As they neared David and Margaret's house Clara nodded in its direction and said, "We had better split up here. David will be sure to hear us and ask questions."

"Meet back at my house in one hour, okay?"

"Okay."

Martin was grateful for the blackout curtains. They kept out the light, and the eyes, from inside Janette's house. He jumped off his cycle. His heart was beating rapidly, sweat dripped from his brow, his feet were aching, and his mind was racing. Looking, with his eyes wide open, at the doorway, and all the windows, he eased past her entry in silence. Carefully he ensured that he was not seen. When he finally sat down on the couch, in his one-room flat above the garage, trepidation and exuberance consumed his emotions.

Trepidation from having broken into a secret government facility. His actions were treasonous. This weighed on his mind. He didn't think they were recognised, but couldn't be sure. Could I explain my actions if I am found out, he asked himself?

Exuberance because he finally felt like he was making a difference in the war. There was something happening here that he needed to expose. Something big. He liked the thought of being the person to expose it.

The time went by quickly as his mind raced from thought to thought. Arriving back at Clara's she greeted him at the door saying, "Quickly, come in, shut the door." Martin could tell there was a lot going through her mind. She was not the same calm and collected person who had not too long ago faced down gun shots. Then calmly made her way through the wilderness. Now she was talking quickly, mumbling incoherently, and as she spoke, she trembled. Having just steadied his own feelings of trepidation Martin felt he knew what she was feeling when he said, "Clara, what is the matter with you?" To his surprise, in an unsteady and trembling voice, she said, "I am just so angry right now."

"Angry? How so?" he asked.

"Jakob lost his life believing he was serving his country, but he wasn't. They've trick us!"

As she spoke her voice trembled more and more. Clara eventually broke down completely. She buried her head into Martin's chest. With her arms around him she held tightly. With a soft whimper she sobbed. Gently rocking her Martin, with his arms around her, offered comfort. As the two stood in their soft embrace for minutes, their feelings consumed them. Feelings of fear but anger, mostly. Martin's earlier feelings of exuberance were now deep within. They both wanted revenge.

Their embrace was broken when Martin, in a soft and gentle, almost serene, voice said, "We need to get them. All of them. Tell me about the notes. What have you discovered?"

She stepped backwards, calmed herself and said, "I've looked at the notes closely. It is definitely Donovan's memoirs. I don't know why he has written this stuff down. A lot of it is in code but what isn't in code doesn't just tell of a plan to destabilise the world politically, it also talks about how. But I can't tell if it was who is behind it. Donovan is just a puppet it seems. I am pretty sure they are not German though.

"How do you know he's not working for the Germans?"

Clara with a straight face hastily turned, looked at him, and said, "Martin, the Germans are not behind this one. I would know. Plus it starts when Germany was reeling from the Great War. They were too weak to plan this stuff!"

He could tell that she was angered by a suggestion that Germany may still be at fault for her situation, Jakob's death in service to them, or even the entire war. Her visible angered piqued his interest. His eyes narrowed. The lines off his brow became visible. His anger had caused his face to tighten. He knew he had to tread carefully with her and said, "Okay Clara, calm down, get the notes and let's go through them together."

The two sat at her kitchen table, drank tea, and looked at the notes line by line for hours. In the notes Donovan described a pact formed between three people who met in Versailles at the end of the Great War. The names of the three people were in code. It was obvious though that they were each from different as were the countries. "Who do you think the three men are?" Clara asked.

"Donovan is one of them, for sure. It possible that Goebbels is another. The third man I can't say. We will have to break the code to know."

"I know someone that can help." Martin continued.

"Who?"

"I can't say. You are going to have to trust me."

"Well Martin, we are in this together so okay. I will trust you."

More details of the plan came to light as they made their way through the notes. They assumed that the pact was made during a secret meeting in Paris at some point during the Great Depression. One man, who went by the code name Chowder, had brought the men together.

There was a second man, an inside man in Germany. At the height of the Depression he was charged with finding a leader in Germany. Someone boisterous and gullible. Once found he would help this person rise to power in Germany. The next step, once Germany had a leader they could control, it was time to push this new leader towards war. Another Great War. But this time things will be different in the end. The second man had a code name of Doctor. He was often referred to as Doc in the notes.

Razor was the name given to the third man. His mission was the same as the Doctor's. A new war was to be started from two different countries in different parts of the world.

Martin and Clara read the notes carefully. There were a lot of details about the plan in Donovan's memoirs. The primary aim, though, was to manoeuvre key aspects of how the world was run covertly with a new war started, so that they would have central control of the world once the war was over.

After quite some time reading Martin and Clara paused as the plan settled in their minds. They paced the floor in different directions before Martin said, "So if Donovan is the leader is the plan to make America the most dominant country in the world? Some kind of stealth war on the other nations of the world?"

Clara did not respond to his thoughts. She knew instinctively that he was thinking out loud. She just let him continue to think. To find answers where there were perhaps none - at this time at least.

Instead she said, "And if Goebbels is the inside man in Germany then Jakob and I have been tricked. He gave his life for an unjust cause. Now do you see why I was so angry?"

"Yes, I do." Martin Replied.

Returning to the notes, burying their heads in, they flipped backwards and forwards. They were getting angrier. They were also becoming amazed by what they were reading.

"Such a clever plan," Martin said as they took another break from reading, sat, and reflected. His admiration quickly turned to deep thought about how the pieces of the puzzle where coming together. The plan had a section titled people, another titled science, and a third titled process.

In the people section were the words, *'capture, entice, trick, or by any means necessary get the smartest people in the world.'* It went on to include that these people will help us achieve our plan. Then when we are successful, they will become the seed population for our greatness. The names of people they wanted in their program were also in code. It was hard for Martin and Clara to understand what they had in mind in this section of the plan. But they knew it was not good, some kind of human breeding program that they would start after they had gained global dominance.

The science section was a little easier for them to understand. They would steal the best ideas, and inventions, from the countries around the world. It would be hard for these countries to create new ideas because they had taken the smartest people. One part of this section, code breaking, struck a chord with Martin and Clara. "This explains why the Americans are in Bletchley," she said.

"Yes, but look at this part here. The code breaking can be developed into some type of machine that can be programmed to do other things. Machines can be made to do what people can do," replied Martin.

Clara had spent enough time with spies, Jakob, and Goebbels, to think of the possibilities. "With the smart people, and this science, they can create better weapons, machines that can fight for them, think for them, they can do almost anything," she said.

The process section is where it all came together. Martin and Clara had initially thought that this was going to be about the way they would achieve their plan. But no this was about how they planned to keep control of, and run, the world forever. No one country can run the world they thought. However, when they read this it, all started to make sense to Martin.

"Roosevelt and Churchill recently laid out their vision of the world after the war. It's called the Atlantic Charter. There are some admirable goals set out. But one thing the Charter says all makes sense now. Disarmament of aggressor nations this is how they plan to keep control, I bet," he said.

"So they do not have to control the world by themselves, they just have to get agreements like this one in place to be able to keep control. As long as they are the only country with arms they are in control," Clara replied.

"Yes, I think this is what the process part of their plan is saying. We need to try and decode the other sections to see who is involved. Then we can justice for the people their plan has hurt. Including me." Clara said.

"But how do we even stop them? How do we obtain justice." Martin asked.

"Let's worry about that after we find out who is behind things. For now, let me take these notes to my friend and see if he can help with the decoding. Don't worry we can trust him."

15

L ittle did Martin and Clara know that what they had stumbled upon, in Bletchley Park, began years ago when the count finally came in.

After two and a half years of standing neutral. Staying silent when merchant ships were sunk by German U-boats. Maintaining patience in the light of outcries from British sympathisers. As allies of aggression formed against us. After a lifetime of thumb twiddling while the politicians went about their deliberations, with Europe watching like hawks, Congress had voted. The House voted almost unanimously, leaving the final vote in the hands of the Senate. One by one, eighty-two Senators had proudly stood behind the President's call to arms. Only six of them stood in dissension. The year was 1917, the count was in, and America was finally entering the Great War.

It wasn't normal for President Wilson to be asleep when the sun shone, but the sleepless nights that he and Junior spent poring over the thousands of pages of material, produced by the Inquiry Committee, had taken its toll on him. The following late nights preparing his war request speech to congress had also added to his need for sleep. With a fourteen-point plan for world peace, and the Senate in deliberation, nearly twelve hours passed as he slept.

"Wake him, wake him up", was the command Junior barked at the President's secretary.

"Sir, he has asked not to be disturbed unless the vote was in, is it?"

"Yes, damn it, yes, just wake him, I will be right there," shouted John D. Rockefeller Jr into the telephone before slamming it down and rushing for the door.

The wealthy Rockefeller family originated in Rhineland in Germany, was powerful, and had always had the ear of the American President. Junior, as he was commonly known in close circles, was the last of five children. He was given his father's namesake - John D. Rockefeller Jr.

Life for the Rockefellers, in America, began with Junior's grandfather William Rockefeller or "Devil Bill" - a scoundrel, a con-man, and bigamist, who disappeared amidst controversy. His disappearance left the Rockefeller family name tarnished on many levels. But one thing Devil Bill did before he left was to instil a sense for business into Junior's father. With Devil Bill's teachings, and a strangely profound, genuine belief that being successful in business was his God given gift, Junior's father - John D. Rockefeller Sr - amassed the family fortune. Along the way became John D Sr. became one of the most hated men in America – monstrous, evil, ruthless, and cruel, were the words used to describe him.

Seemingly blind to his own misgivings John D. Rockefeller Sr, or Senior as he was sometimes called, set out with drive and determination to devolve himself from the evils of his father. As for his own misgivings, well, he remained resolute in his belief that his business dealings, no matter how they may appear, was his gift from God. There was no need to change that gift.

With time, and success, Senior grew closer and closer with the church. It was through the church that he met, and married, his deeply religious wife Laura. Convinced that riches led to sin Senior raised Junior, and his siblings, in seclusion on the family estate. Ruthlessly teaching them wealth, power, and most importantly, thrift. But it was Junior's mother that had the most profound effect on him. From his mother Junior learnt that his purpose in life was goodness. He was to serve others.

Such variation in his upbringing led Junior to grow into a strange, confused, and aloof, individual. A Yale man at heart but, at the insistence of family and friends, he attended Brown University, a Christian school. It was at Brown where Junior became radicalised by his studies of politics, economics, and the social sciences. The free-flowing spirit of reform that prevailed on campus also contributed to his radicalisation, leading Junior to break away from his confined upbringing.

Brown, like all the Ivy League Schools, was also rich in tradition. One such tradition was the existence of, what became known as, secret societies. Junior had always expected that he would be tapped into the Skull and Bones secret society had he attended Yale. So it did not surprise him when, at Brown, he was tapped into the Franklin Society. Through his involvement with the Franklin Society he became intimately familiar with the workings of secret societies. An experience that began his journey into the world of what he was now seeing as the societal norms outside the family estate.

Ultimately though it was Marxism, and the role of the social class structure in society, that shaped, the young and impressionable, Rockefeller's world view.

After Brown, Junior's foray into the family's oil business had proven his dislike for business and confirmed his mother's teachings. Junior had become convinced that his purpose in life was goodness. With this understanding he took to philanthropy. He took the reins of the family's philanthropic operation - The Rockefeller Foundation - where he set about dispersing the family's multi-generational wealth to "good causes" - so he said.

Nonetheless it was through philanthropy that the doors of the world had opened for Junior. Philanthropy brought the ear of the President ever so close to him. An ear that today he will use to give a fine young man a boost in his military career. That man, William Donovan, was a Columbia Law graduate, a Captain in the New York National Guard, and a Fellow member of the Yale Club.

The Yale Club was a private members' club for Yale Alumni and a few others. Junior was one of the others that, with his philanthropic activities, he was graciously accepted. William Donovan was also another with a stellar public profile. Junior had a good sense of who would work well with him. He instantly took to Donovan when they met at the Yale Club.

He saw Donovan as a maverick who had carved out a reputation for himself as being aggressively anti status quo. Just the type of person who Junior thought he might need to bring about change one day. Junior also saw having a military ally could be strategic to his philanthropy. For these reasons Junior was going to help Donovan rise the military ranks.

***

Arriving at the White House Junior made his way to the door of the Oval and belted in the most pleasant of voices he could summon, "Is he free, Janice?"

Janice was the President's secretary, a twenty-one-year-old fracked red head. She had a perfect figure, and a radiating charm that added to her beauty. She not only caught the eye of every man in the White House, but was highly effective at her job. Nothing, and no one, got past her. She had her suspicions about Junior, and didn't like him much. She struggled, on each occasion, not to let Junior see her distrust of him.

"Yes, Mr. Rockefeller, he has been waiting on your arrival. I will let him know you are here." Janice politely replied in a monotone voice. Not showing her dislike for Junior, but also not inviting and friendly.

"Mr. Rockefeller is here to see you Mr. President."

"Send him in Janice." replied the President in a flirty, but respectfully, tone. He too could not help but to, in soft tones, be drawn to Janice's beauty.

"Mr. President, very good to see you again. You delivered that speech to Congress spectacularly," blurted an eager Junior as he entered the Oval with an outstretched hand.

"I am pleased that the Progressives, and Republicans, heard the message in it." Replied the President.

"Well I was certain Roosevelt would whip his Progressives into supporting the request. Since he formed that third party, after losing the Republican nomination to Taft. He has mostly voted in line with the Democrats anyway. But Jeannette Rankin was a surprise. Wasn't she?!"

"Well not so much. She is the only woman in Congress so a bit of pressure, but she held firm to her pacifist beliefs. She didn't cave in a bit to pressure from the Republican whip." Replied the President.

"Good on her I say," He continued.

"Well we have the war we hoped for, Mr. President. The Generals can handle the military action from here. They shouldn't need much of your time. But I was hoping that we could get going again on international affairs post the war Sir." Junior said.

"You mean the League, Mr. Rockefeller?"

"Yes, Mr. President. Are you ready to continue our discussion?"

"I still believe that a League of Nations, as we discussed, is the best way forward. You have also convinced me that it would be best if America pushed this forward with the other countries. But why the rush to talk about it now?" Junior said.

"Mr. President of the fourteen points that we discussed the League is the most important. It will take the most time to get started. Plus, it will galvanise the nation's resolve during this Great War, and into the future. We must make that our immediate priority!" He continued.

"I understand Mr Rockefeller, but why is it so important right now, I would say that there are other points that need my attention first."

For Junior the League meant so much more than he was letting on. The League would be a platform for him to disperse his goodness internationally, amongst other things. It was for this reason that he gave the financial support of the Rockefeller Foundation to the Inquiry Committee that was looking into solutions for world peace.

"Mr. President, last year our Foundation sent William Donovan, the man we spoke about, over to Belgium to negotiate with Britain and Germany for a shipment of food and clothing into Belgium, Serbia, and Poland. Mr. Donovan's report has convincing needs in it for the immediate establishment of an organisation like the League. It is the right humanitarian thing to do, and this is why it is imperative that's we get started right away." Replied Junior.

"Mr. Rockefeller, I admire your zest for the League of Nations however there are other more pressing matters to address at this point. I will, when the time is right, enlist your further support in making the League a Reality. We all know it is desperately needed."

A demoralised Junior could only but mumble, "Thank you, Mr. President," as his obvious hopes for more were dashed. But he was happy for small victories. Getting the President to agree to involve him, even at a later date, was one of those small victories. As would be his next request of the President.

"One more thing Mr. President, thank you for putting in a word with General Pershing about William Donovan?"

"I mentioned him to General Pershing Mr. Rockefeller but it was the General's decision to take on Mr. Donovan. I emphasised that to the General as well. I told him the this had to be his decision, not mine!So you can thank the General."

"I will, Mr. President," said Junior as he took his leave from the Oval Office.

With the possibility of the League being set in motion again Junior moved on to the next item on his agenda - William Donovan. On the President's word following his meeting with Junior the State Department had Donovan, or "Wild Bill" as he was often called, return from Belgium.

Once in America Donovan took his New York National Guard cavalry troop to the Texas border to join Pershing's army. Before Donovan's arrival in Texas months had passed with Pershing in the hunt for the Mexican General Pancho Villa. Wild Bill's arrival brought enthusiasm as well as a disregard for the rules. However there was no success in cornering Pancho before Wild Bill received his field promotion to major. He was on his way to just the type of power Junior had hoped he would attain.

Texas with General Pershing was a great opportunity for Wild Bill, he proved himself to be just what Junior needed to get things done. With the rank of Major it was time for "Wild Bill" to take his next step in Junior's plan. He was returned from Texas to join the "Fighting Irish Regiment" in Buffalo - a raunchy bunch that suited him perfectly. On his return to the New York Donovan swore to repay the good deed that Junior had done for him. He was now indebted to Junior. A debt that Junior recorded in his mental ledger.

Donovan on the other hand sensing that his star was rising began to capture his journey in written notes. His memoirs will one day not only cement his place in history but also tell the story of his rise for his young children to know. He cherished his family and missed them dearly each time his was away from them. It, his memoirs, were his legacy should he be killed in battle or otherwise meet his demise. Now his legacy was in the hands of Martin and Clara.

***

In December 1917 America finally joined the war, but Russia had left so Germany held a powerful position until the start of 1918 when the tide of the war changed. Britain and France counterattacked strongly in March, the German Navy went on strike, and Germany and her allies eventually realised they couldn't win the war. Once the leaders of the German army had told the government to stop, Kaiser Wilhelm, Germany's ruler, stepped down and the Great War ended. The League of Nations was established and the fourteen-point plan - Junior's Plan - for peace agreed.

In years following the Great War the work done by the League was a disappointment for Junior. President Wilson remained true to his word and called upon Junior to lend for his help with setting up the League. However, the President had otherwise withdrawn his own support. America did not join the League. Other countries also began to invest in researching better transport, technology, and communication, to get an advantage over their enemies. This was not what Junior had in mind. Peace and goodness in the world was being threatened. The League was powerless. Yet Junior had hoped the League would be a force in the world that would control everything. Then he, Junior, would control the League. The balance of power in the world was also shifting away from Junior's control.

Then came the Great Depression. Misery and despair spread as havoc was wreaked on the social norms of the world. As, with the Depression, even the wealthy found themselves in breadlines, and having to mingle outside of their class. Amidst the misery and despair crime rose, and religion faded. Roosevelt's plan for relief, reform, and recovery from the in its infancy even the very nature of humanity grew darker by the day against the difficult odds of the Great Depression. The darkness of human nature had seen the popularity of human breeding also rise. With human breeding came a particular interest in the inheritance of "undesirable" traits, such as mental disability, promiscuity, and criminality. Junior observed this human breeding phenomenon with his own particular interest but otherwise had turned his attention building the Rockefeller Centre. His vision for the Centre was a City within City. But little did Junior know it would be on one of his visits to Manhattan that would garnish an even greater vision.

****

In Manhattan the sun only aligns perfectly with the street grid twice a year. First as the sun moves toward the summer solstice, and second as it returns southward. On these days the most beautiful spectrum of colours form over the City. The yellows flow into the oranges, reds, magentas, and violets, giving the City the most pleasant and peaceful glow imaginable. These days are amongst the finest the City enjoys.

It was on one of these perfect days in Manhattan, when the sun was moving towards the summer solstice, that Junior reached another plateau of his enlightenment. Almost as if the darkness of the depressions years had suddenly given way to a new light. A light greater than the meagre construction of the Rockefeller Centre. This enlightenment, this new vision, came to Junior as he strolled along Vanderbilt Avenue. The first building of the Centre had just opened. His wife, Abigail was at his side. The setting sun was high in the sky colouring clouds a majestic array of orange through brown. It was tranquil on the surface but Junior's mind was a bee hive of activity, processing the events of his life that had brought him to this moment. Then it happened.

Junior's past, present, and future came into brilliant focus. With each step towards the Yale Club he meticulously aligned each event in his past, and from his present. As well as each sign post of his future. Just as an architect might craft a master blueprint.

Maybe it was the tranquillity, or maybe the success of opening the first building of the Rockefeller Centre, or the presence of his beloved Abigail that released the most intense endorphin rush that Junior had experienced. With each step, with each of Abigail's lovely smiles, his thoughts grew clearer as he sifted and sorted his life's experiences. The teachings of his mother about his life's purpose, doing good. The designing of the Rockefeller Centre. His success and failure in business. The faltering League of Nations. The growing tensions in Europe. As well as his life in the secret Franklin Society. On this day, as the sun moved toward the summer solstice, in his mind's eye, Junior saw a clear path. A path that was set in motion on that fateful day when the Senate voted in favour of America joining the Great War.

***

For most the Depression brought misery and despair, but for Junior it brought enlightenment. He had a plan, he had an epiphany, he had a new name. It was May 29th 1933. A day Junior recalls vividly. It was the day Junior was forever changed. On this day, in May 1933, with the setting sun beautifully aligned on the streets of Manhattan, Junior ceased to exist, and Chowder was born.

Chowder, the code name that Junior would take on, realised that he could not achieve his purpose in life without more economic control over the affairs of the world. That he could not achieve his purpose in life alone. That it was a responsibility of society's upper class to protect the future of humanity. That had it not been for depressed economies, the harsh conditions of the Treaty of Versailles causing dissent in Europe, and a tranquil Manhattan day, all would have been lost.

16

The Great Depression also left the Japanese economy in dire straits. Their exports were halved, leading the Prime Minister to decide that exporting weapons, and armaments, was a good decision. He later fatally reversed this decision. Fatally as it wasn't long after Prime Minister Tsuyoshi changed his mind, about producing weapons and armaments, that he was assassinated. Though no one ever knew for sure, it was rumoured that his assassination was the work of the Black Dragon, also known as the "Kokuryūkai."

The Black Dragon was known for its secrecy. No one knew for sure who were members of this clan. However, it was known in Japanese circles that the Kokuryūkai wielded considerable political influence over Japanese foreign relations, particularly on Japan's relations with China, and other Asian nations. It was also known that the Kokuryūkai supported the sale of Japanese-made weapons internationally. Mainly to Germany at the time.

***

By 1933 many of these secret societies, like the Black Dragon, existed throughout the world: each with their individual goals, each growing increasingly discontent with the League of Nations; and each wielding power and influence that rivalled governments.

In Europe the Illuminati was leading the charge. In America Societies, such as Junior's Franklin Society, and the Yale Skull and Bones, were in full swing. Little was known about the membership of these Societies. Each secret society also operated independently. That is until Junior's Manhattan epiphany led to the creation of The Commission, a coming together of the world's most powerful secret societies. Despite their secrecy Junior's prominence was able to attract their attention. Four societies were represented in The Commission: The Black Dragon, the Illuminati, the Skull and Bones Society, and the Franklin Society. Each represented by the Master of that Society. Each with their own code name. All now with a common vision. Junior's Manhattan epiphany vision.

Master Hideki Tōjō "Razor", was the Black Dragon representative. The Illuminati were represented by Master Joseph Goebbels "Doctor". The Skull and Bones was represented by Wild Bill Donavon "Architect". Junior "Chowder" represented the Franklin Society.

Other than Junior they were all military man with talents that worked in unison.

Goebbels was the charmer. He had a quick tongue, and they could win anyone over. He was the mastermind behind the recruitment of Clara. Goebbels saw a bit of himself in Clara. She too had an uncanny charm that, with her beauty, could move mountains. Goebbels's charm was an immense asset to The Commission.

Tōjō was the realist. In perfect balance to Goebbels optimism and charm Tōjō brought routine, discipline, and the sound execution of any plan set in motion by The Commission.

Donovan was an egotistical planner. However, his propensity towards being an aggressive rule breaker was only overshadowed by his strategic thinking. He was a Master strategists. Once he saw Junior's vision he carefully, like a master building, architected the means to accomplish this vision. A blueprint which his ego led him to capture in his memoirs.

Junior was the visionary. He made himself the Grand Master of The Commission and oversaw every detail as the other members plan, congealed, and convinced the world to follow their lead.

On December 23, 1933 all four men arrived in Paris for the inaugural meeting of The Commission. That night a heavy fog blanketed the City, and the surrounding area, when the crash occurred. Twelve miles east of Paris the Strasbourg express smashed into the rear of a train bound for Nancy. On impact the last five cars of the Nancy train splintered, the Strasbourg train derailed, and over two hundred people going home for Christmas were killed, many others were injured. In the City, people rushed in every direction. Worried about their love ones they raced to hospitals, or anywhere they could find out information. A horrific and unfortunate event was unfolding, but as tragic as it was the crash was an opportunity, not a tragedy, for The Commission. An opportunity to move about the City undetected amidst the panic.

As the streets of Paris swarmed with people Junior and company made their way to the centre of the city, to the Ile de la Cité - "Island of Paris". Their destination, the Notre Dame Cathedral, one of many Cathedrals built during the French gothic architectural period.

The Gothic architecture was distinctive with its very intricate designs. The Last Super, The Gateway to Heaven, and other distinctive designs graced the exterior of these buildings, giving hope to all who entered. On entering anyone would be captivated by the beauty, wide expanse, and serenity that unfolded. These gothic Cathedrals brought together hope and faith. Not unlike the hope and faith held by the city's occupants during the late Roman period, when Paris was called Lutetia, when the Ile de la Cité was a much different place than that night. A time when the highly religious Romans, who attributed their success as a world power to good relations with the Gods, built temples of worship to many Gods. When Church and State were analogous, and priesthoods were reserved for the elite classes. With the Church and State as one, the elite also ruled over the vast Roman empire.

With time though Lutetia, the Ile de la Cité, and the world, transformed. Rulers, Gods, and temples, all changed. Rulers became many Governments, the central control from Rome faded, Gods grew fewer, Church and State separated, and all that could be seen changed.

What did not change was what lied below the Cathedral. Far below the Notre Dame Cathedral was, the completely intact, Temple of Minerva a shrine to the goddess of wisdom and strategy.

In Junior's mind the Notre Dame Cathedral perfectly symbolised the vision of The Commission. However, it was what was not seen that made the Cathedral the fitting location for The Commission to meet. Not seen was The Temple of Minerva as to this day it lays hundreds of feet beneath the gothic church of Notre Dame, A Temple that existed in Rome, the City that was once the epicentre of the world, A Temple that existed in a time when the world was as it ought. A time when hope, faith, wisdom, and strategy existed as one in the steadfast hands of the Rulers. This ancient world was, but for the pagan Gods, was as Junior visioned the future of the world. Something that he understood clearly, and believed in fully. Except, in Junior's vision, The Commission members were the Priests that would wielded the power. Yes, this Temple, that symbolised all that Junior desired, was the most fitting place for The Commission to hold its inaugural meeting.

One by one the men arrived at the Cathedral. Each entering the wide expanse of the worship hall, giving their respects at the altar, and lighting a candle of hope, before entering a confession booth. Inside the booth a three-foot cross adorned the rear wall. At the centre of the immaculately kept polish brass cross sat a covered key hole. Each man quickly slide the cover on key hole, inserted an ancient brass key, pulled the key downwards, and then turned it to the left. With their key they each unlocked the secret passageway to Minerva. As they slide the rear wall of the confession booth a dusty pathway, lit by a single glowing torch revealed itself. Grabbing and unlit torch before setting it alight the men one by one made journeyed down a narrow, winding, staircase. Creakily step after creakily steps they made their way. At the bottom of the staircase six three story columns and a grand, marble covered, courtyard greeted them at the entrance to the perfectly intact Temple of Minerva.

Junior was excited for this night. He had worked tirelessly to find, contact, and not only create a shared vision amongst the world's most powerful secret societies; but to also to unite the economic and political control over the affairs of the world in his hands. This pew, this control, would, in Junior's mind, allow him to achieve what his mother told him was his life purpose. To do good in this world by making it a better place.

With all of the men present Junior began the meeting.

"We are all here!" he exclaimed.

"In the words of the philosopher Lao-Tzu, a leader is best when people barely know he exist. When his work is done, his aim fulfilled, they will all say: We did it ourselves. This is what we are here to achieve. We are here to be good leaders. To lead this world to greatness in the fulfilment of our vision. A vision where the strong lead, the weak are neutralised so that they can cause no further harm, and the world is unaware that it is us who has saved them." Junior continued, before going on to set out the two objectives of The Commission.

The Commission's first aim was to bring back a single centre of power and control. In stating this objective Junior explained that, in the days when the world lived in peace and prosperity it was by the unitary rule of Rome. That to achieve such peace and prosperity again the world must have but one ruling power. That, with the League of Nations having failed to create such central control, it fell to The Commission to fulfil this daunting responsibility. The Commission's second aim was, for the good of the world, to ensure that there never again seizes to be a single centre of control in this world.

Once having laid out the objectives of The Commission Junior then asked Master Chowday - Wild Bill - to tell everyone of the plan. "Master Chowday is a brilliant strategist. He has devised our plan to achieve these objectives. He will now tell us of his plan." Junior said.

Wild Bill, ever flamboyant, ever convincing, flashed into his explanation of the plan he devised. In a slow, almost whisper of a voice, he began to speak. Wild Bill began by saying, "Before there was peace and prosperity under centralised Roman rule there was war and upheaval. Yet the conquered people grew to appreciate the rule of Rome. For The Commission to bring about peace and prosperity, as did the Romans, we too must go to war."

His words were just loud enough to be heard, and low enough that the men focused and paid attention to be certain of what he was saying. This was Wild Bill's way of drawing people into him as he spoke. Still, before Wild Bill could get into the explanation of his plan, Hideki Tōjō "Chow", the Japanese military man, interrupted him and said, "We have no army how do we go to war?"

"Germany is in upheaval, they are angry, and they have withdrawn from the League. They will lead the war that we need." Replied Wild Bill.

"Wouldn't it just end the same way?" Master Chow asked.

"Perhaps, but it is not a victory for Germany that we seek. Through war we seek peace and prosperity for all. Germany will lead, Italy will follow, and I am sure that Japan could be convinced of the need to go to war to save their economy, their people." Replied Wild Bill with a smirk on his face.

"Then with the world in chaos there will be a need for control. The Commission will provide that control by controlling a new League of Nations." He continued, as Goebbels sat in awe nodding in agreement. While Junior said nothing, shared no emotion. But in his silence was approval. After all, he and Wild Bill had crafted the plan.

"But how do we control the League?" Asked Master Chow.

It was at this point that Junior choose to speak again.

The years since the Great War had taught him much. Junior had grown from a young man believing that his world view best, to a mature adult with a worldly understanding. The Depression years had brought about a realisation of the importance of political power, economic power, as well as the need for smart people to achieve the control he sought. Over the years Junior had developed a new world view.

He answered Master Chow's question with the poise and confidence that the years had afforded him.

"The Commission will not seek to control the League." He said.

Junior explained that, "As the Roman Empire expanded their centralised model struggled to keep control. Eventually they needed to rely on local governments more and more. They created Consuls loyal to Rome that governed locally. They intermarried within the populations, especially the local elite. They brought Roman ingenuity to the locals. The people were even made citizens of Rome, they were treated good, and not treated as conquered people. Everyone flourished. Central control the the empire was maintained. This is what we will do as well. We will systematically control the people, the science, and the ingenuity. The League will be our throne."

The men all nodded in agreement.

Wild Bill then said, "Each of us will operate autonomously. We will only communicate at these meetings. In this location. It has to be an absolute emergency otherwise."

"One more thing protect your key to the Temple with your life. It should not fall into the hands of anyone for fear of us being uncovered. Anonymity is our way to keep control that key may draw attention. Also outside of this room we shall be spoken of only by our code names." Junior chimed before beckoning the men that the meeting had concluded.

Unlike the complex and lengthy meetings that took place in the Palace of Versailles at the end of the Great War - this clandestine meeting was short, simple, and to the point. The plan was presented and agreement reached in breath-taking speed. Each man arriving separately, alone, and under the cover of darkness. The outcome? A pact formed, a stealth war against the nations of the world declared, and The Commission in top gear.

Long in patience, but resolute in their desires, The Commission members - Goebbels, Donovan, Tōjō, and Junior - Left the confines of the Temple of Minerva. On leaving their clandestine meeting the men made their way swiftly through the streets of Paris.

The chaos from the train crash that evening had subsided. Yet the devastation of a city, whose streets and buildings, that not too long ago was massacred by German bombs was still visible against the night skyline. Having vowed never to be seen together they disappeared into the blackness of the night after their business was done. Unaware that one day, through the meticulous memoir notes of Wild Bill, that their blueprint to change the world would be found.

***

Not much time passed after their Paris meeting before the initial shots in their war were fired, three shots into the heart of the people prong of their three-pronged plan.

The first shot: Charles Davenport was placed deep inside the inner workings of two of Germany's most influential racial hygiene journals. Davenport, an American biologist, believed strongly in improving the genetic quality of the human population by excluding inferior groups and advancing other groups thought to be superior. Once he was in Germany, riling Hitler up proved to be a straightforward assignment for Davenport. In no time at all Hitler was promoting encouraging healthy, smart individuals, to reproduce and discouraging the poor, who were considered unintelligent and unfit for reproducing. Money from American corporations - IBM, Rockefeller Foundation, Kelloggs, and others - poured into Germany as the eugenics ideals of America took root in the country. Germany was moving quickly towards a war footing. Shot one fired, and a resounding success.

The second shot: Broaden public support. With sterilisation as the primary method to discourage reproduction the critics of forced sterilisation laws believed that these laws violated the Constitutional rights of Americans. To broaden public support the architects of the plan in Donovan's memoirs decided to prove that the laws were constitutional. To do so, they needed someone who could challenge the law in the courts. They chose Carrie Buck of Virginia. Seventeen years old, pregnant, unmarried, and with her mother at the Lynchburg Colony for Epileptics and Feebleminded, Carrie was classified as "feebleminded". After her child was born, she too was committed to the Lynchburg Colony. Eased into it, officials at the Lynchburg Colony pushed to sterilise Carrie. But first, an appeal of their the decision in the Virginia courts was arranged by these same officials.

Although the appeal was in her name, Carrie Buck had no voice in the process, and the evidence in her trial came from the Eugenics Record Office established by Davenport. Ultimately, in the American Supreme Court, Carrie Buck lost her appeal and was sterilised. Citing the best interests of the state, Supreme Court Justice Holmes affirmed the value of a law like Virginia's in order to prevent the nation from being "swamped with incompetence." Justice Holmes' words, "Three generations of imbeciles are enough," sparked an outburst of public support from as high in America as the President. Also, other states enacted sterilisation laws. In his propaganda book, Mein Kampf, Hitler, unaware of the plan in Donovan's memoirs and his scape goat role in it, even proudly refers to the American laws supporting a master race. Shot two fired, also a resounding success.

The third and penultimate shot: improve the gene pool was in the making.

The initial signs of The Commission's success came on the first day of September 1939. The day that Germany invaded Poland marking the first battle of the second Great War. The United Kingdom responded with an ultimatum to Germany to cease military operations. An ultimatum that was ignored by Germany bringing France, Britain, their empires, allies, and Martin into a new war.

A war that has now brought together an odd combination of a lawyer, a spy, a code breaker, and the mysterious memoirs of the "Architect", in the English country town of Bletchley.

17

First the door opened. Then there was the loud deliberate slam as the door was shut. Panicked, Frederick jerked upright, but his wrists refused to move. Something sharp and cold dug into his skin. He looked down and saw there were handcuffs holding his arms to the metal frame of the bed. Groggily he looked around the room. Empty, just the bed, a table beside the bed with a tray of uneaten grub.

"I am Sergeant Davis one of the training officers here at Kedleston Hall. I am here to tell you that you will face a court martial. If you are found guilty you will be sent to a military camp. Do you understand?"

Still groggy Frederick nodded slowly, shaking his head as if to say no.

"Who do you think you are?" The Sergeant said angrily stumping his way to the bedside. Frederick stayed silent. "TELL ME." The Sergeant repeated sternly. Goosebumps appeared on Frederick's forearms as the cold air wiped across the room. He was scared and trembling when Sergeant Davis wrapped his chilly hands around Frederick's throat and squeezed. Frederick's feet rose off the bed as he kicked and squirmed, but it was of no use.

Just as his vision started to blur, another uniformed man came in, "STOP, STOP THAT," he shouted. "His lawyers are on their way here." The Sergeant whipped around, dropping his hands, and was led out while Frederick laid there panting for breath.

***

David drove and talked while Martin took in the scenery. The highway to Kedleston meandered through the rolling hills and valleys of Derbyshire, rising and falling, giving breath-taking views of luscious greenery, then dipping into valleys filled with neatly organised farming patches. Barley, wheat, potatoes, all being grown and under the strict production guidelines of the Ministry of Food. It ran for miles on end in perfectly architected straight lines, giving way to right-angled turns that would take you to yet another village nestled in the midlands. The architecture of the region - its buildings, churches, and roads - were all that remained of the Roman occupation of Britain.

More than a century had passed since the Romans had organised their conquest over the Catuvellauni into the Province of Britain, but the stamp of the Romans remained so visible in these parts. The contrast of the open roads with the towns and cities was startling. The uniformity and grandness of Roman highways on one hand. Contrasted against the meandering twists and turns off the narrow roads that had organically developed through the Middle Ages. Still the beauty in the intricacies of the churches was consistent in a country steep in architectural history.

As they rolled over one of the many hills that surrounded the farm lands, a long lorry approached from the other direction. It was dirty, covered in dust, and loaded with service men. To the front and rear were tillys, small utility vehicles, loaded with supplies. After the convoy passed, flying down the descent, Martin said, "I assume those were new recruits heading off to their deployments."

David checked a mirror for another look at the convoy, as though he would be able to tell if they were new recruits from a rear look. "Oh, yes. They are coming from Kedleston Hall it's an army training camp. You will see more of them when we get there."

"I did my training in London but knew there were other camps in these parts." Replied Martin.

"Convoys like those are everywhere. A lot of the country manors have been requisitioned now. They are being used as mustering points and training camps."

"Clara talked about them yesterday. She said that she sees convoys heading the other way as well. Full of troops injured in the war, heading to medical facilities in the country." said Martin.

He assumed David knew everything about his excursion with Clara last evening. He waited a moment to see if there would be a mention of it. There was not.

"Yes, the medical facilities in the manors are a regular occurrence around here as well. I'll bet we send almost as many out as we get back injured," was David's reply.

"The army just patches them up and sends them back out. I have seen many of them, young impressionable, scared mostly. They come back from being patched up, some and are gun shy in battle afterwards." Martin said.

They topped another hill and began a descent onto one of the long straightaways. Then David said, "Let me show you something. It won't take long." He hit the brakes, made a sharp right-angled turn onto yet another straightaway. A sign said Quarndon, Borough of Amber Valley. Before long they arrived at a small village with buildings centred around a beautifully designed church. The Roman influence on the church was clear. They stopped by the church. St. Paul's the sign to entrance read. "There look," David said. The steeple to the church was missing. Debris laid on the ground and the surrounding buildings had been destroyed.

"This happened when the Blitz started. A German plane had mistaken cars travelling together without blackout mask on their lights for troops near an important facility, they think. First the machine gun fire, that killed two - one by splintered glass, and one by a bullet - and wounded 5 others. Then the aircraft dropped four high explosive bombs."

"How bad was the loss of life?" Martin asked.

"There were five more killed. Another twenty-five wounded. All taken to the same medical facilities that we carry soldiers from the front. Just like the lorries we saw earlier."

"Such a horrid state of affairs. They have destroyed so much of the British way of life, it makes me sick," replied Martin.

With frayed emotions they continued driving in silence for some miles. Until Martin asked, "What is the story with our guy, the guy we are going to see?"

"Our guy is a 20-year-old coloured man named Frederick O'Cora. He is one of the conscientious objectors being held at Kedleston Hall. His CO hearing before the tribunal left him serving in the military. He is okay with serving now but wasn't at first. However, he fears for his safety. That's why we are going there."

"One of the conscientious objectors?" Martin asked.

"There are about a half dozen or so of them there."

"What was his argument with the tribunal, do you know?"

"He argued that he had had a hard struggle to get the job he had owing to the colour bar. He was a riveter before conscription. That he didn't want to take part in military service in war time, when he was not allowed to join in times of peace."

"Sounds reasonable to me, but is that an objection based on conscience?"

"Well, let me finish. The tribunal asked him: if he felt, as the result of the war, that he would be treated as an equal would it change his opinion. When he said it would, they turned down his application. That's why he is here now."

"You said he fears for his safety, how so?"

"Unless you are or you're likely to have to serve. Those opposed to the war for philosophical or political reasons are forcibly inducted, court-marshalled, and sent to prison. So are those that are refused non-combatant duty, or didn't want to do compulsory military training and service. Some may be assigned to service jobs in military camps. But the men placed in military camps are ridiculed, physical abused, and subjected to cruel punishment. Frederick is about to be moved from Kedleston Hall to a military camp and fears for his safety."

***

Kedleston Hall was a magnificent Palladian structure. A three-floored house with three blocks linked by two curved corridors. It showcased one of the many architectural periods of Britain. An architectural period when the designs of Andrea Palladio were in vogue. At the outbreak of the war the owners offered it for use by the War Department. Now it served two main purposes: young men came here to be readied for battle, and as a collection point for messages before they were sent to

Bletchley Park for decryption. Of course, it has its detention barracks which are common to all of the military facilities.

Servicemen going through their paces filled the courtyard as they drove into the sprawling estate. They parked in front of the central block next to a lorry and walked inside the marble hall. Hand carved stone columns lined the middle of the circular hall, creating a beautifully represented corridor from front to back. The hall rose three stories to expose the dome shaped skylights that added to the grandness of this room.

David and Martin paused to take in the expanse of the grand hall. They surveyed the layout of the building. "Such a lovely house isn't it?" Martin said. "Yes, it is. I am guessing our guy is in the east wing with the other conscientious objectors. They had him out back in the detention barracks but with us coming over they said they would move him." Replied David.

***

Frederick O'Cora was a tall muscular young man. He sat waiting for them in what was once a state room servants. The small room had been furnished with a wooden table and four chairs. The room was pristine but Frederick was not. His smooth, chiselled face may have hid the worry that he was carrying, but his brown sorrowful eyes told the true story of how he was feeling. With just the furniture and Fredrick in the room when they entered, their attention was immediately draw to him. Dressed in army fatigues he quickly rose to his feet, snapped off a salute, and gave them his full attention.

David spoke first, "Good morning Frederick, my name is David Smith and this is my associate Martin Frost. We are from Dunham and Associates and have been assigned to help you. Mr. Frost is a lawyer and a Major-General in the army.

He has spent time at the front and is now on loan to us. I thought he would be able to help with your case." The men exchanged brief pleasantries before Martin suggested they sit and get started.

"Frederick, David has filled me in on your case. How you ended up here. That you no longer are objecting to service. That you are to be transferred to a military camp, and you fear for your safety. Is that about, right?"

"Yes Sir."

"Why do you fear for your safety? This is not Hitler's Nazis shouldn't you be perfectly safe in the service of the British armed forces?"

"I was born in Kingston, Jamaica, and moved to Britain with my family as a young child. My father struggled with the colour barrier when he arrived, and I struggle today. But if fighting in this war will help to change that for people of colour, I am all for it. But I hear stories from the men. I hear that with the yanks coloured servicemen are confined to non-combatant units, and treated really badly by the servicemen. Different with us Brits, but for me if I get to serve like they said it won't be in a non-combatant unit and a promotion was unlikely even if I am qualified to do the job. Because they don't want coloured personnel in charge of white servicemen. Oh, they have excuses for non-promotion but they only apply to the men of colour.

But, you see, I don't care about that I just don't want to be in a military camp like they have said. They say because I was originally a conscientious objector that they don't want me in their army. One of the other COs was in a camp over in Scotland and he said it was horrid, worst for people of colour."

"Horrid, how so?"

"He said that the men are tied three out of four nights to gun carriages. They are placed in solitude and made to live off only bread and water. They don't pick deliberately on the men of colour but seems that they get the worst of it. But I still don't think I will make it out of a camp alive. While in the detention barracks I was choked near to death by a Sergeant. Said I am going to be court marshalled."

"Why are you being court marshalled?"

"They say I violently refused an order. But I don't remember any of that. I was in the yard working. Just cleaning up. One of the other COs was being picked on by a Sergeant, and I spoke up. It was not right! The next thing I remember is waking up in the infirmary. Is there something you can do to help me? I just want to serve. It's what they said I would be doing."

David looked at Martin as if to say help me too. He was stomped for what could be done, but managed to say, "Martin with your background in the army do you have any thoughts?"

He had heard of many situations in the army, and as a divisional leader had had to deal with some of them personally. But never anything like Frederick's case. It all seemed to be within the norms for servicemen as far as he knew. After a momentary pause where Martin massaged his eyes, something he did when under pressure to think, Martin replied, "This type of situation would be new for the army to handle. What we would have to address are the individual rights of a person. We fight the Nazis to stamp out evil and ill treatment but in some ways we have it here in Britain too. The Magna Carta and the Bill of Rights are good documents for us to use in our argument. They both assert individual rights but from what I have seen in practice there are exclusions - women, people of colour, and members of selected social, religious, and political groups."

"You just want to serve in a combat unit, right?" David said.

"Yes, that is all I want."

"Well I think we can help with that, tell me about the other COs that are here."

"What do you mean Sir?"

David said, in a calm voice, not wanting to rile Frederick who he suspected could get riled easily, "Well are they coloured or white men? Are they still objecting or like you wanting to serve in a combat unit? Are they being transferred to a military camp like yourself?"

"Oh, okay. There are six of us. I am the only coloured CO, and it's only me that is being transferred to a camp. Also, I said I was okay serving, but the other COs are still objecting for different reasons. Why do they get to go to a combat unit and me to a camp?"

"What do we need to do, Martin?"

"We would have to argue this matter in front of a military court. Try for equality of treatment." said Martin.

The ride back was less adventurously than the journey over. The men travelled in silence for most of it. David was concentrating on his driving and the need to get back to Bletchley before dark. He was driving as quickly as his 1935 Talbot-Ten would carry the two men.

A battered sign announced their approach to Bletchley. They topped another hill and could faintly see the rolling meadows covered in the evening mist. David breathed a sigh of relief and spoke, "What is your take on the fear that Frederick has about the camps? I have seen some of the coloured GIs in town and the folks treat them really well. I can't believe our servicemen are not doing the same." David said as he finally spoke.

David breaking the silence offered some respite from Martin's turmoil.

"I have had coloured men in my command. The lads treat them well, nothing special either way but I hear stories too. Maybe his fear is warranted. But as I understand it, he just wants to serve as an equal. It's all fresh territory for me." Replied Martin as they continued to speak.

"That is what he wants. But if our lads are not treating folks equally then we are no different than the damn Nazis." Replied David.

"The Bill of Rights is so vague that it does not help when it comes to the specific rules these men must follow. But there may be some policy around to help. I'll do some research. Then we will have to get in front of a military court."

"There is will be a military court session here in Bletchley sometime soon. I will try to get you on the docket."

"Okay, Replied Martin."

As they neared David's house just before dark, David said, "Margaret will have supper waiting, you're welcome to join us."

"Thank you for the offer but I will pass. I have some things I want to catch up on. I am also meeting a friend for a quick bite to eat." Martin was not but wanted to be alone with his thoughts and a quiet meal. He thought a quick white lie to get away wouldn't be harmful.

Assuming his friend to be Clara, David smiled, an eerie, devilish smile, and said, "Okay, we will talk later."

As he swung the door open and stepped into his flat, he felt a hand in the middle of his back. He was pushed inside and quickly joined by another person. Not expecting company Martin was startled, but pleasantly surprised when he turned to see Francis standing in front of him. A deep embrace was followed by a long passionate kiss, as the two men held each other closely. All the tension just drained from his body as he stood there with Francis in his arms.

"What are you doing here," he asked.

"I wanted to see you. I was longing for you and have been waiting some time, so I am afraid I don't have much time now. They will miss me at the estate."

"I am sorry I had to see a client in Kedleston. If I had known I would have been back sooner."

"It's okay I understand. It's just that there was an intrusion on the estate the other night and they are watching everyone. Otherwise I would stay. But I am glad I at least got to see you."

Martin eyes watered as he melted into Francis' arms. He could feel the genuineness of Francis' longing and he felt likewise. Their relationship had become incredibly intense. It was passionate, and it was becoming a love relationship. But as in any relationship, one never knows, really, what the other person is feeling. You can't know, you can believe you know.

He was deeply touched to see that Francis was less interested in the sexual side — although he believed there is a sexual side that deepens this relationship — but the intensity of the emotions they felt for each other, was ultimately the most gratifying thing about him and Francis.

"Francis, I must tell you something. Don't be upset and hear me out. As I will need your help."

"Okay, anything Martin."

"It was me that was the intruder on the estate."

"What?! Why, Martin?!"

"I met a woman on the train to Bletchley. She turned out to be a friend of David at the office. So we have been talking at different times. It also turns out she is a German spy."

"A German spy, what the hell? Did you turn her in to the army?"

"No but let me finish, okay?"

"We believe there is something more sinister going on with this war. She is working with me now to get to the bottom of it. It's not a trick, she is genuine. She has lost a lot and wants to find the truth. We found what we think is Donovan's memoirs. In his memoirs he discusses how following the Great War some men got together and conspired to start another war. But the men we think are from different countries. Some are in it for money for themselves. But there is at least one that is in it for world dominance. It's a stealth war and we think Germany is a pawn in this war that we are all fighting now."

"That's ridiculous Martin!"

"We have the memoirs and other evidence. But parts of the notes are coded. We do not know who is involved or which country is leading the operation. We need your help to decode the plan. Will you help us?"

"Anything for you Martin. Even if it is only to prove you wrong."

"Okay here are the memoirs we found at the estate. But be careful, they may search you on your return."

18

M ore than a week had passed since finding the memoirs when Clara scanned the crowd on the high street. She couldn't see any sign of him. She moved amongst the servicemen, her eyes darting more wildly. One second, he was making his way towards her and then no sign of him. Heads turned in every direction as the soldiers scrambled about. In the grip of the confusion, silent panic set in. Her heart raced and her brain was a mental soup of conflicting instructions. Something was up and she was worried for Martin, for her too. An elderly gentleman, moving slowly towards her, caught her eye. Tapping him on the shoulder she asked, "Do you know what is going on?"

"Their looking for a spy. There was some sort of intrusion and the yanks are up in arms. They have the guards out door to door. To tell you the truth it scares the heck out of me."

Suddenly there was a sound coming from inside the cafe. Tap, tap, tap she heard. It was Martin signally her to come inside.

"I didn't think they would come looking for us?" She said.

"Calm down, if they knew it was us, they would have picked us up by now. They're just acting on orders but can't know anything about the memoirs. I am sure of it. Donovan isn't going to tell anyone about them. They are probably just rounding up strangers for interrogation."

Clara who was normally calm and collected took a deep breath and steadied herself. "Why do you think it took them more than a week to come looking?" She asked.

"I don't know. More than likely Donovan had to report back to someone before he could take any action. That could have been the delay, Or maybe they have been searching in secret. Now they want to rattle the intruders out of hiding. Either way we just stay calm and it will be okay." Replied Martin.

"I guess you're right. Is your friend going to help us with decoding the Notes? We need to know who is involved. I am also getting very nervous about the use of my safe house. I am not certain who I am helping anymore."

"Yes, he has agreed to help us. It will take time and we have to be careful though. He has an important role and we can't jeopardise him. Right now He has the notes and I will meet him later to hear his thoughts. But with all the confusion out there, I hope we can still meet."

There was a long silence as the two watched the soldiers move about. Stopping and checking anyone they did not recognise. In the silence, as they steered through the window onto the high street, they each had other things racing through their minds.

Martin's work in Bletchley was coming to an end. The Sharon Howes case was finished. He has even helped Matthew and David with other cases. Even though Frederick's case was just starting, it won't be long before he would have to return to the front. With these thoughts Martin was contemplating how and when to tell Clara. She had become vulnerable and dependent, which bothered him. Perhaps he would just jump in and say he was returning to London. Or just slip away on the train leaving her a letter. Maybe he would invite her to move to London, that way she could feel secure in the crowds. But going missing from Bletchley may raise alarm bells.

Clara, whose stomach still fluttered in the presence of Martin, was thinking about a life together with him. The two had become friends, and she was thinking of the possibilities. Solving this mystery together, settling down somewhere after the war, having a family. She spoke first, "Do you ever think about life after the war? What will you do when it is over?"

"No, not so much. Being a soldier, you learn to take the war one day at a time. Any day could be your last in battle. Plus, who knows what will happen, after the war, if Germany invades England."

In a soft, almost solemn, and distant voice as if she was talking to herself but also just thinking out loud Carla said, "I often think of times together after the war. A family like mines with lots of children. Maybe even in another country far away from Europe. Maybe America?"

"There are so many from Europe that have found a new life and happiness in America. Maybe you will one day too." Replied Martin while being careful not to lead Clara to think that he shared the same thoughts.

"Maybe, if I had a husband and a new name it would be possible. But a surname like Bauerle tells of my Austrian heritage and, well, it would be hard to be free of hatred towards me in America."

Not convinced of the possibility of happiness in America she continued to speak, her voice tapering off into silence as she said, "yes, maybe," in a tone that reeked with uncertainty and sorrow. Martin's heart sank, he could feel the pain, loneliness, and sadness in her voice.

He pondered her words. She was right. Inequality, bigotry, and hatred spewed about because of religion, colour, or nationality. Why should she be persecuted? Anything done by Hitler's Nazis was not her doing. It may not even be the doing of Hitler who could be a pawn in someone else's stealth war. This was the same as with Frederick O'Cora he thought.

***

Some days later, without Martin having received word to return to London, he was back at Kedleston Hall.

The military court martial convened promptly at 11:00 AM with the Sergeant in Arms saying, "All rise!"

In an otherwise empty room, nine enlisted army servicemen sat in their booth, ready to cast judgement. At the table to their right sat the prosecution team - Captain Mark Phillips, a small framed man with steel-rimmed glasses and ginger hair, and his second chair. Martin and David nervously awaited the start of the proceedings. David tapping his fingers on the table. Worried about his first court room trail Martin fidgeting aimlessly with a pen.

"All those having business with this general court-martial, stand forward and you shall be heard. The Honourable Wayne Alexander is presiding." the Sergeant in Arms shouted and the lawyers suddenly became razor focused.

The Judge Advocate, Alexander, began the proceeding by asking if the government was ready to give its opening statement.

"Yes Sir," replied Captain Philips as he rose and walked to the Panel box. "This is a case of a disobedient soldier. On the day in question Private Frederick O'Cora, when ordered to board a transport vehicle, refused to follow the order. Now, as you all know when a soldier refuses to follow an order life can be lost. Disciple and obedience are fundamental to the working of the army. Without which our country may just be overrun by the Nazis. It is that simple."

He paused as if thinking, but really to let those words sink in with the Panel. The fear of a Nazi invasion of Britain would certainly focus the Panel's thinking about the seriousness of the matter.

The captain continued, "Now, Major-General Frost is goanna try to pull off a little magic act, he's goanna try a little misdirection. He's going to shock you with stories of Nazi beliefs. Tell you that this case is more complex. He might even go after a few officers. It might even sound plausible and righteous. But when you get to the end the facts will be the facts. Private O'Cora disobeyed an order."

"Major-General Frost."

Martin, for dramatic effect, remained seated as he began to speak. He was now running on adrenaline when his first words were uttered. "We tell our soldiers to fight for those that can't fight for themselves, to stand up for right and wrong, then persecute them when they do." He said.

He then rose and walked to the Panel box, before continuing to speak, "Let me say those words again, to stand up for right and wrong". Following a short pause to allow those words to cement into the panels' mind he continued. "This is not a simple case of disobedience as my learned friend would like you to believe. Mr. O'Cora is here today because he wants to do the right thing, and any attempt to prove otherwise would be futile." That was it. With his heart was racing Martin went back to his seat. He didn't believe in long opening speeches. Make one, maybe two points, and move on. That way he thought his points would be remembered in deliberations.

"Is the Government ready to call its first witness?"

"If it pleases the Court, the Government calls Corporal Johnathan McGuire."

Corporal McGuire enters through the double doors of the court room. A tall, heavy set man, greying around his temples suggested he was in his mid-forties. The wooden floors creaked under his weight as he marched his way to the witness box.

"Corporal McGuire, would you state your full name and occupation for the record, please?" The Corporal gave his name and rank in the army before the proceedings continued. The Corporal is sworn in and he told the court of the incident he witnessed.

Corporal McGuire told the court that: Frederick was in the yard. There was a CO, an Indian fella, being picked on, slapped around a bit, by a Sergeant Davis. Fredrick became angry, approached Sergeant Davis and told him to stop. It wasn't right to treat our men in that way. It was not right, Frederick repeated a few times. Sergeant Davis told Frederick to go back to what he was doing. He didn't. The Sergeant then hit him with the butt of a rifle knocking him unconscious.

Martin's cross examination consisted of one question. "Did Sergeant Davis order Fredrick to cease his interference and board a transport vehicle for a military camp?"

"No," replied the Corporal.

Captain Phillips then called a handful of other witnesses who all told a similar story. Martin asked each of them the same question until he came to cross-examine Sergeant Davis.

"It wasn't an order, was it, Sergeant? After all Private O'Cora wasn't is a combat unit, was he? Surely as a non-combatant orders aren't really orders are they?" Martin asked.

"This is the army. Every order is an order, without question."

After a few more probing questions, aimed at getting the Sergeant off balance, Martin then asked. "Would you read the following for the court please?"

"I do swear that I will well and truly serve our Sovereign King George in the service of the British army, and I will do right to all manner of people after the laws and usages of this realm, without fear or favour, affection or ill will. So help me God."

"Do you know what that is?"

"It's the Oath of Allegiance."

"Would you be obeying your oath to do right if you give an order that is to do wrong?"

Captain Phillips immediately rose to his feet, "Objection," he shouted.

The Judge advocate replied, "Sustained."

"Thank you, Sergeant," Martin said knowing that the seed of right and wrong had been planted.

Frederick O'Cora was the only witness called by Martin. Frederick told the court how he was originally a conscientious objector. About his hearing before the tribunal as well as his expectation to be in a combat unit. He went on tell the court about what he has been doing since he began his service. How he had stepped in to speak up for a fellow serviceman being ill-treated. During his account of being choked, his eyes watered, and he eventually broke down as he spoke. His emotions from the years of struggle as a coloured man, to his struggles today, had got the most of him. Martin thanked him for his testimony.

"This would be a good time for a recess," the Judge Advocate said.

David and Martin both made their way to the toilet. David took a quick look around the toilet before saying, "You did good Martin, are you ready to close?"

"I am nervous as hell. Not too sure how this will go. Phillips is right, an order is an order. How do you think the Panel is leaning?"

"It's hard to read them, but I did get a glimpse of sorrow or shame on their faces when Frederick was in the box. Let's see how the close goes. Just hang in there. Remember during the close make eye contact with each of them. Make them feel his pain."

When court resume the Judge Advocate said, "We will hear closing arguments now. Captain Phillips are you ready?"

"Yes, Sir."

The captain stood, turned and faced Frederick. He caught Frederick's gaze and held it for a few seconds, which felt like minutes to the court room. He was able to succeed in drawing the courts attention to the defendant. He then slowly walked to the Panel box, scanned the jury, catching the eyes of each before he began to speak, "Right and Wrong, that is what Major-General Frost would have you believe this case is about, and he is right." He spoke in a monotone, without emotion, a very calming presentation. When he said that the defence was right, the Panel's attention seemed to shift to him. His intention all along. Now they were listening to try to understand where I am going, he thought. Martin and David showed no emotion. While limited on courtroom experience Martin knew better than to show the Panel when he was amazed, confused, or impressed by the prosecution.

After a short pause the captain continued, "Etymology, is an interesting word founded on the Greek word for truth - 'etumos'. We talk of etymology when we look at the meaning of words. The etymology for soldier tells us about determination in defence, just as a we see ants come together in large numbers to accomplish a task in defence of their own existence. We are at war, we are defending our very existence, and the existence of our comrades. That is the right thing to do! Soldiers' humans or insects must work together to be successful. Working together to accomplish the right thing means following orders. This case is about right and wrong. Private O'Cora is a solider doing the right thing for his country. He was wrong to disobey an order from an officer and you must find that way. Less we fail to do the right thing by condoning wrong."

The words "Major-General Frost," we're spoken as Captain Phillips walked slowly back to his seat with the eyes of the Panel fixed on his every move.

Martin, anxious to draw the attention away from Captain Phillips rose quickly from his seat and March directly over to the Panel box. Phillips had not made sat down when he began to speak,

"Over seven hundred years ago our forefathers had the foresight and fortitude to create a charter that protected the individual freedoms of our country man and women. They believed so much in its doctrine that they called it the Magna Carta, to distinguish it from smaller Charters. That's right Magna, the greatest and most important charter protected individual rights. It took almost four hundred years for those rights to become the English Bill of rights and the law of the land that we know today.

Earlier the Court heard that every soldier takes an oath to defend the laws of our law. As the Magna Carta states, and our law for over three hundred years have upheld, individual rights are the most important right.

This case is about right and wrong. But what you must decide is which right is most right. Private O'Cora stood up for another human whose individual right to be treated fairly was being trampled. He did not obey and order that was intended to stop him doing so. He did the rightest thing and you must honour this Country's tried and proven history of individual rights by finding him not guilty. Let Private O'Cora continue to fight for those rights."

"The Panel will now take its leave for deliberations," the Judge Advocate said as Martin walked back to his seat. The Sergeant in Arms again shouted, "All rise!"

As Frederick O'Cora was led off by the guards in handcuffs he glanced at Martin, smiled, nodded his head in appreciation, then stood upright and walked. His pride was brimming.

Once the court was cleared David spoke first, "That was a good summation, Martin. I could tell you left the Panel with something to think about."

"I was so nervous. I did not want to fail Frederick. Human rights and freedom from tyranny is what this war is all about. It felt good fighting for that in a place where I could possibly make a difference."

"You have done all that you can. We just have to wait now." Replied David.

After three hours of deliberation the Panel returned to court. Prosecution and Defence both sat nervously waiting for justice, their justice, to be dispensed.

Again, the Sergeant in Arms shouted, "All rise!" Again, Martin's nerves turned to mush as he stood, with David to his right, and a proud Frederick to his left.

A court clerks handed a piece of paper to the Judge, who quickly read it then asked, "Has the Panel reached verdict?"

"We have Sir," the Head of the Panel responded.

"Please read the verdict for the court."

"On the charge of disobeying an order this Panel finds the defendant guilty," he said. Frederick's, David's, and Martin's heart sank. The blood rush into Martin face as his blood began to boil. In Oxford he was taught not to show emotion when a verdict is read. Neither of the three men showed any emotion.

The Judge Advocate then asked, "Does the Panel have a recommendation on punishment?"

"We have Sir," the Head of the Panel responded.

"What is the Panel's recommendation?"

"This Panel finds that in disobeying an order that Private O'Cora did act in the interest of the greater good. It is our recommendation that he be deployed to a combat unit at the first available opportunity. That he be confined to a detection barracks unit until his deployment. It is the Private's desire to fight for right and equality. This is the war that this country finds itself in now. We need soldiers like him at the front."

"The Panel is dismissed. Private O'Cora is ordered released and is to be deployed at the earliest opportunity."

Martin turned to Fredrick and said, "Do us proud son." Frederick snapped Martin a salute, then a big smile, before exiting the courtroom.

19

The following day in Bletchley was a typical early December day. The wintry sun was just beginning to peak its head over the eastern horizon. Ready to take centre stage as the morning unfolded. For now, though, the skies were grey, and the morning was gloomy. At Dunham and Associates Matthew and Martin looked out through the tiny window in the meeting room. They could see the occasional farmer's lorry heading into or out of the market. The streets were otherwise bare, not a single soul braved the early morning brisk. Then, in true English weather fashion, the skies opened. Rain gushed from the heavens, hard rain, that rain that stung as it contacted your skin. Large rocks of hail pelted the ground before slowly melting away. Despite the wintry sun it was looking to be a cold and wet day in Bletchley. Martin knew the court house was not far away. He had walked it many times before, but it will seem like forever in this weather. Better to wait this out, he thought.

Across the road, at Cook's Radio Store, old man Cook stood in the door way, eyes wandering. Up at the skies, down at the rocks of ice, and at the occasional lorry as it passed. Letting the time go by on a slow wet morning looked like something he had done on many occasions. It was not too long ago that

Martin had seen the two Americans oddly standing inside the radio shop. With what he knows now his thoughts raced from one question to the next. What were they doing in there? Is the old man Cook one of them - a spy? His thoughts were interrupted when Matthew said, "It's really coming down out there. We will have to wait this out, I will make tea."

Standing, alone with his just thoughts now, Martin's gaze caught an elderly woman preparing to cross the road to the Co-Op with her parcels. The on again, off again, showers looked set to settle into a misty drizzle as she opened the door to her lorry. This could go badly he thought, as he too prepared for the weather outside with a hero's dash to help on his mind. Old man Cook also had his eyes trained on this woman.

As the rain slowed surely enough, the woman jumped from her lorry and began a quick two step towards the Co-Op. After a few steps a loud shriek was followed by the woman on her backside. Coming to her rescue in a flash, Cook was the faster of the two men. With Matthew still off making tea Martin made his own dash for the door. Not to help, he had something else on his mind, an opportunity. A quick breeze at the doorway hit Martin flush in the face. A chill rippled down Martin's spin as he stepped across the threshold onto the curb.

At the doorway to the radio shop, he quickly looked over his shoulder. No Matthew peering out the window. All the other windows also looked clear. There were no eyes on him. He could also see no one on the streets. This was his chance to get a look inside the radio shop. But he didn't have not have much time. He also didn't know what to look. Whatever he would find it wouldn't be in main store. There was no heating of any kind in the main store. A trail of condensation followed him as the warmth of his breath hit the cold air. Various radios, encased in wood, aligned the shelves of the shop. For the enthusiast there were headsets and a section for parts as well.

With his adrenaline pumping Martin bee lined for a door behind the glass sales counter. On the door were the words 'Private Keep Out' painted haphazardly. Martin opened the door. The office was colder and damper than the main store, which explained why the old man always donned a winter coat. Leaving the door ajar, so he could hear in case old man Cook returned, he Stepped inside. His private office behind the counter was small, messy, and dusty. Probably because old man Cook preferred to spend his time idly in the shop's doorway rather than working in his office. Nether the less his private office was horrendous. Two desks to either end, a work bench along the wall, storage cabinets on the other wall, and equipment everywhere.

Martin's eyes darted from object to object, nothing out of the ordinary caught his attention. He stepped further inside and started to open cabinet doors. He had only minutes, so he moved quickly, being careful not to disturb anything, or leave a trace. The first cabinet: more radios in different states of repair. The second cabinet: tools of the trade; and then the third cabinet: radios again. But something on top of that forth cabinet caught his eye. A bulky black machine covered with a black cloth. It wasn't a radio. The black machine had a key pad, and rotors. It was the Converter M-134. An American message encryption machine. Martin recognised it from his field training. All officers were shown pictures of encryption devices with instructions to seize and protect these, if ever they found one in battle. Martin was stunned. His hands trembled, but he knew he had no time left and there could be no hesitation now. Fearing the old man's return he made a quick exit from the radio store, looking in every direction to be sure he was not spotted. The old man was still in the Co-Op so he was safe.

Wet, and out of breath, Martin arrived back in the meeting room. Matthew was sitting drinking tea and reading from a file. It looked to be the case file of Hannah Gruber.

***

At the outbreak of war potential enemy aliens in Britain who, it was feared, could be spies or willing to assist Britain's enemies in the event of an invasion were called before a tribunal. They were classified into high-risk cases, doubtful cases, and no risk cases. High-risk cases were immediately interned, low-risk cases were left at liberty, and doubtful cases were supervised. Hannah was a doubtful case, but with the outbreak of spy fever last year she had become a high-risk. She was to be interned. However, Matthew intervened and kept her free, but supervised, until now. A short hearing on this matter, later that morning, was on Matthew's agenda for the day.

Hannah was a war bride. She had married Captain Christopher Davies, an R.A.F. pilot, shortly after the outbreak of the war. With Christopher off fighting, she has been a target of Churchill's "Collar the lot!" round up of German's and Austrians in Britain. If unable to prove her marriage to Captain Davies, she would be sent to an internment camp.

"Where did you go?!" Matthew asked.

Stammering, Martin managed to get out a few words that seemed to settle Matthew's curiosity. "I went out to help an old woman who had fallen in the wet weather, but old man Cook beat me to her rescue. There he is now returning from his hero's mission." A little white lie to cover up his venture wouldn't hurt, he thought.

Matthew looked out the tiny window to see the old man hasting his way along. "He is smiling. She must have caught his fancy," he said with a half grin on his face.

Eager to move the conversation along Martin asked, "Is that the Hanna Gruber file? How do you think that will work out?"

"Well, it depends, we are in a bit of a crisis right now. I am hoping that the priest that married her to Captain Davies makes it down here from Birmingham in time for the hearing. Those internment camps are nothing more than the British version of concentration camps. I am worried for her."

"My father told me about our camps. We used them during the Boer Wars. They were horrid, but useful, he told me. But they got out of hand during the Great War when we used them to simply control civilians from other countries." Replied Martin.

"Churchill is doing the same thing now," Matthew Replied. "Last year in one of the Polish camps, we have let them setup in Scotland, a Jewish prisoner was shot dead. We turned a blind eye to the killing. The courts even ruled that the guard, who killed him, used his weapon in the execution of his duties."

"How do you reconcile these actions with what we say the Nazis are doing wrong?" Martin asked rhetorically before the two men sat in silence while the intensity of the moment settled on them.

Breaking the silence Matthew eventually said, "It looks like we can get going."

***

The weather-beaten terracotta tiles of the court house now glistened in the sun which had overtaken the skies. Inside a line of applicants, young men, too young to serve at the front, and a few elderly men, former soldiers most of them, formed the queue. "That is an unusually long queue," Matthew commented.

"Must be the weather. It is something about a rainy day that brings the soul searching and patriotism out of people." Replied Martin.

They hastily made their way to the main court room, being careful not to fall on the slippery tiles. The usual array of characters filled the courtroom. Bill Denning was there for the prosecution. Hannah sat at the defendants table awaiting Matthew's just-in-time arrival. She was thin, blonde, and with nearly twice the usual amount of neck. With her long extended neck she crane over at Bill looking for some sign of what might come. They had just enough time for greetings before the Judge entered and the proceedings were called to order. There was no jury, just a hearing before the Judge, who would decide her fate.

In their haste Martin had not noticed Clara sitting in the public gallery. She sat at the rear of the gallery taking everything in and making notes. It was not her first time either. With a name that was clearly Austrian she regularly attended any proceeding that involved war brides. She knew her Liverpool accent won't keep the authorities away forever. She needed to be ready for her upcoming hearing. Being interned would even be better than being killed as a spy.

Bill presented his case to the judge, as Matthew nervously tapped his fingers on the table, snapping his neck around each time the door opened. He didn't have a case without the priest that married Hannah. The judge called on Matthew to present his defence. Matthew slowly rose to his feet and began to speak, "My Lord, I am afraid my witness is delayed. May I beg the Court's indulgence for an adjournment so that I may ascertain his whereabouts?" Bill interjected and said, "My Lord, this is a matter of national security. Ms Gruber is a risk to the war effort and I would beg the court to rule at this time.

There has been plenty of notice for the defence to be able to ensure the presence of their witness." The Judge denied Matthew's request for an adjournment. Matthew's head fell and his heart sank. Tears came to Hannah's eyes.

Suddenly the double doors to the courtroom swung open. A giant of a man was standing in the doorway. His face was almost completely hidden by a long, shaggy mane of white hair and a wild, but neatly groomed beard, but you could make out his eyes, glinting like black beetles under all the hair. He was a big, beefy man with hardly any neck. He wore a dark suit and a clerical collar. Matthew eyes widened, and a broad smile came to his face, before he asked the judge for a moment to confer with his witness. Vicar Reverend John Donaldson in a soft scraggly voice said he was ready to confirm Hannah's marriage to Captain Davies, in Birmingham, before the war, and before the anti-fraternisation rule for men in Britain's service.

After hearing the testimony from the Priest, and seeing the marriage license, Bill had no objections. The Judge ordered Hannah be left to her own liberties. Everyone then rose to their feet as the judge left the room. It was in these moments that Martin caught a glimpse of Clara as she was leaving. Taking his leave from Matthew and Hanna he rushed to catch her. "Clara, Clara," he shouted as he approached her. She turned, obviously caught off guard, her flush red face showed her discomfort.

"What are you doing here Clara? Is everything okay?" Martin asked in quick succession.

"I am embarrassed to say," she replied. "What is it Clara, you can tell me."

Clara so strong in the face of other dangers feared more than anything the being killed as a spy in Britain. Her interest in Martin was because of this fear and she was embarrassed. Her only choices to avoid them were: to return to Austria, but she did not know what the Germans would do to her; or what sadistic assignment they would send her on; or, as she was hoping, she could marry in Britain, change her name, and blend into the population. Through the many hours he had spent in court she had learnt that she would need a civilian husband because the anti-fraternisation rule did not apply to civilians in Britain.

"Martin, I am looking for a British husband. I come to the court to learn about the law and rules for war brides. Also, to maybe find a lawyer, judge, or policeman as a husband. It is more import now that they have summoned me to a hearing. I know on that day my fate would not end like Ms. Gruber's. I will be killed and you know why."

"That explains it," Martin said.

"Explains what?"

"Your interest in me and why you would be embarrassed for me to find out.

It's okay though Clara, I understand. I am sure it will all work out for you.

Clara's heart slowed as she became more comfortable with her fear.

"Thank you, Martin," she said.

"I have another matter to deal with here at the courts. Can we meet tonight?" Martin asked.

"Come to my house later," replied Clara.

***

The officer in charge of the Sharon Howes case was Detective Samuel Rueben, a second-generation Jewish lad, that had attended Cambridge and was as smart as a whip. He quickly sized Martin up as he approached the two of them. Martin in his blue suit with Sharon at his side dressed modestly in a dark suit. They were there to have Sharon's work papers returned to her and this matter finally put to rest. Detective Rueben offered no resistance to their request. Sharon was no longer of interest to them. He also told them that Richard Brown had been in the police jail for the past month serving time for an unruly pub fight. He could not afford the bail, and the Judge ordered that he be jailed for three months. "Richard would be carefully supervised by the bobbies on his release," the Detective said. After a few additional minutes of exchanging pleasantries, and assuring Sharon that Richard would not be bothering her, the Detectives strode off as proud as a peacock in his position of power over the small community.

Mart mission to Bletchley. His commitment to the Prime Minister, and his orders from the General were finally accomplished. Sharon was relieved, as was Martin, when they both said their goodbyes.

***

In what had become a day of crises yet another erupted moments after Martin arrived at Clara's house later that evening. She was waiting for him. "Martin, they have finally summoned me." She blurted out. "They will find me out. I will be killed! I will be killed!" She continued without even a pause to breathe. Martin hadn't even made his way inside. Her voice was unexpectedly calm, though tears rolled down her cheeks. In her panic she repeated her words yet again, "I have been summoned, what am I going to? I don't want to be killed!"

Martin stood helplessly by, lost for words to console her, his discomfort was overcome by his desire for her safety and, from time to time, he would muster up the words, "Francis may be able to help."

"Francis may be able to help." Martin softly said again as he eased his way into Clara's house. In doing so the two inadvertently moved closer to each. They were now standing side by side, almost in an embrace. They moved so close he could feel her breath on his face. Her soft blonde hair hung ever so slightly over her sparkling blue eyes. In their closeness her hand gently touched his wrist awakening something inside of him. His manhood slowly began to respond to the heart breaking, yet sensual moment. Embarrassed that he should be consoling her, not desiring her, Martin tried to resist his natural urges. Still his eyes slid over her body, adding up her pluses and minuses. She was a 10. In their almost embrace stoically Martin continued to repeat the words "Francis may be able to help," until the softness of his voice and the warmth of his body next to him settled her anxiety.

***

In the weeks that followed Martin spent much of his time in Bletchley trying to circumnavigate his emotional quagmire of: love and attachment; depression; and anger.

Love and attachment were spurred on by his growing fondness of both Clara and Francis separately. Something had sparked in Francis, feelings perhaps, that he had not experienced with other men. He was growing ever more attached to Martin. Which was unnerving Martin as he did care for Francis but it was not love that he felt he was experiencing. Clara, Martin could also tell was fancying him more and more. With Clara he could see the potential of a spark that may ignite something truly special. Or maybe it was just that he found women more affectionately attractive. Either way he was definitely growing in his attachment to both.

Martin also experienced a deeper sense of depression. Before his leave, his time in Bletchley, it was depression brought on by his sense that Britain was losing the war. Now his dark moments of depression were the darkest he had ever experienced. He could just not reconcile the injustices that had unfolded around him. His intimate encounters with Francis could see him thrown in jail. It was against the law. Why he asked himself? Is not love, just love, no matter who? Frederick's case may have ignited the fuse on his depression again. He wasn't sure, but it grew deeper after that case. The mistreatment of people of colour just did not settle with him. Yet he was unable to speak of it, or of it, or do much about it, in the world as it was today. Then there was the loss of life in Dunkirk. The blood, the screams of young boys as they met their end, the death it was all around him. Yet now, with Donovan's memoirs, it all seems to be so contrived. So senseless. Depressing.

Yet today the silver lining to his depression was that it always brought about his anger. Anger was a silver lining because it renewed his resolve to uncover who was the mastermind in the plot Donovan speaks about in his memoirs. He grew angrier each time his heart would sink with depression. He was angry that this whole war may have been someone's plan to appease themselves. Or in some twisted way to improve the world through death and destruction.

Amidst his quagmire, unfolding and circling around him, it was still left to Martin to keep both Francis and Clara focused on the memoirs. Though, even with the anger that would sometimes rage inside of him, it would be hard to keep his own focus amidst emotions.

Focus had become a struggle for all three of them before the world erupted into an evolved state of chaos that captured their attention. Immediately refocusing all three, Martin, Clara, and Francis.

20

The eruption began at 7:53 AM with the signal to attack *"To, To, To" – in Morse Code.*

At the insistence of General Hideki Tōjō, the sleeping base in Honolulu had been hit by over three hundred Japanese air crafts, in what they called the Hawaiian Operation. Within minutes, much of America's Pacific fleet had been destroyed, thousands had been killed, and a massive psychological blow dealt. The attack continued for two hours. Fighters, level and dive bombers, and torpedo bombers struck in two waves, launched from six aircraft carriers. Indiscriminately levelling their targets in Pearl Harbour, before disappearing as quickly as they arrived.

A couple of hours before the Pearl Harbour attack Japanese forces also landed in the British colony of northern Malaya. This landing was the real mission, the Southern Operation, directed against Malaya, the Philippines, and the Dutch East Indies. Their target, Tōjō explained, was the oil and rubber in the Dutch East Indies and British Malaya. The attack on America was only a diversion to weaken the American's ability to help the Dutch and British - General Tōjō had told the Emperor.

In a brilliant sleight-of-hand Tōjō gained the approval of the Emperor to go to war against America. After years of patiently biding his time. Rising through the ranks of the Imperial Japanese army. General Tōjō had become a trusted advisor to the Emperor. He had now used this trust to fulfil The Commission's mission to bring America into this new war. Within hours America had declared war on Japan, Britain was readying its forces to defend its Asian colonies, and Martin had been summoned back to London. He was ordered to London on matters of national importance. Depression, Love, and attraction had to all be set aside. Active duty awaited.

***

Yesterday had seen Martin's world upended. Today he skipped his usual five-mile morning run. There would be no time for running today. Plans had to be put in place. The work on the memoirs had to continue. He needed to see Francis and Clara before leaving Bletchley..

At Clara's he told her that the war had intensified with Japanese attacks in the Pacific. That everyone including himself was being called back into action at the front. Clara's shoulders slumped and her body went limp on hearing the news of Martin's return to action. She did not show any signs of anxiety. On the contrary she was calm, very calm. Her face was no different from if she had just learnt that her childhood friend Joseph Jakobs was alive. When she finally spoke her voice remained as the Pacific Ocean in summer. She simply said this was expected one day. Martin, surprised by her reaction leant into her calm, and told her that the time had come for them to make a plan for the work on the memoirs to continue. They then made a plan and agreed that she would meet Francis for the first time in the morning.

Later, near Bletchley Park, he met Francis. They discussed Martin's return to the front. The need for Francis to work with Clara. Together they devised a secret code using of cryptography and steganography, so that the three may communicate while Martin was at the front. They also discussed Clara's predicament with the war. She may need to marry soon Martin told Francis, who quickly agreed that he would take care of it if needed.

The crowds had already begun to gather at the train station when the trio was completed by the arrival of Francis. A more jubilant Clara, meeting Francis for the first time, wore a black dress that accentuated her confidence. A quality that she felt Francis might appreciate. An immensely blue sky, with white silvery clouds gliding almost imperceptibly against it, was slowly beginning to give way to a golden ray. After introductions the plan was shared. Martin, Francis, and Clara then watched, in silence, as the rays grew into a big ball of fire changing from dark orange to dark yellow as it moved gracefully across the sky. Their mission was clear and their plan was set.

Clara was the first to leave after Martin's departure on a standing room only train to London. Her golden blonde hair flowed down her back as she made her graceful exit. Glancing over her shoulder to see if Francis was watching her. He wasn't. Francis was in a trance, thinking, wondering what would become of him and Martin, and worrying about Martin's safety as he headed off to war. For Martin the train ride to London took the rest of the day. Stopping at every station, and waiting for repairs on the track following a late-night Luftwaffe strike near London, severely delayed his journey. Giving Martin plenty of time to contemplate the magnitude of his experiences in Bletchley. Something sinister was taking place with a war that was taking millions of lives. It was reprehensible.

At midnight he pushed open his door at the Wellington Barracks. Where, in the lonely solitude, the emotional weight of the past months hit him like a ton of bricks, crushing every fibre of his emotions. The uncertainty of surviving battle, and the certain deepening loneliness he faced, had taken all the strength that Martin had mustered. Now though, the life drained from his body as he fell into his bed, with thoughts of exposing the covert actions of Operation Checkmate, and obtaining justice, weighed on him. He was lonely and growing increasingly afraid. In Bletchley he had Francis and Clara to be with and share his inner most thoughts - his fears, his love, his hopes for the future. But tomorrow he returns to the army and will be sent into battle. In battle he would be surrounded by soldiers that looked to him for their strength. He would not only need to be strong for all of them, but he must also find a way to bury his emotions deep inside of him and cast himself into the darkness loneliness of his life. Deep inside will be his love for Francis, his concern for Clara, and the knowledge that the war he was about to fight in again was a sinister plot. That night, in solitude, Martin cried

Himself to sleep. In the morning he was to report to the war office.

***

The war office was inside Whitehall, which is a flat, ugly building, crowned with four turrets that seemed out of place for the structure. Next to Whitehall was a concrete bombproof structure, which, like an iceberg, concealed its bulk below the surface. This iceberg structure was called the Fortress. Both Whitehall and the Fortress where almost opposite Downing Street, and together the three buildings made a secure underground complex for the Prime Minister. As such Martin half expected to see the Prime Minister. He hoped to update him personally on the Sharon Howes case. But such an update was not going to happen.

Once arriving in London Martin was to report to General Binney in the War Office. Here he would be briefed on the campaigns of the South-East Asian Theatre - the name given to the allied military operations in the Pacific.

Martin entered the vast hall of the War Office. Halted at the Security desk where his papers were examined. After a telephone check, made with the General, he was issued a temporary pass-card. The briefing room was in the basement, next to Churchill's lavish bedroom - which he hardly used. Martin had been told to report to the Sergeant-Major, whom Martin recognised as Panzer the gentle giant.

Martin followed Panzer to the briefing room. There were six of them in the cramp and dimly lit room when Martin entered. General Binney was leading the briefing and introduced Martin to the others: British Navy, Airforce, Army, and Intelligence gathered together to discuss the Allied response to the Japanese attacks in the Pacific.

The outbreak of war in the Pacific couldn't have come at a worst time, the General explained. British forces in the area were critically overstretched and weak in almost all arms. The General had called Martin into action to lead a division of Allied soldiers that included the Scottish Gordon Highlanders, and the Suffolk Regiment.

Martin had seen action with the Suffolk Regiment in Dunkirk and had heard of the heroics of the Highlanders. He was pleased to be leading both. They were to be called the 18th Division. Unlike the last time he was called into action, Martin was ready now. He was looking forward to deploying for Singapore in the morning. The war effort, and the lives of his fellow countrymen, needed him. No matter what the real reason behind the war he was ready to answer their call to arms.

Up next on Martin's agenda was lunch with Thomas who was back in London for Christmas, and a break from his studies at

Oxford. They met at the entrance of the Piccadilly Circus tube station then crossed the carriage way to the Lyons Corner house on Oxford Street. The Lyons Corner house, a gigantic place with food being served on four floors, was a popular spot, in the mornings when very hungry people came rushing out of the shelters. Martin and Thomas had arrived after the morning rush and had the run of the place. They chose a third-floor restaurant. It was famous for its hamburgers - the "Whimpy" burger it was called.

The restaurant filled quickly as the two ate lunch at a table near the entrance. Away from the noise and the crowds that formed near the window tables. It was a brightly lit day. Sun this time of year in London was very unusual, but then again there it was - sun in December and the crowds scampered for the light as they entered the restaurant.

Only a few pleasantries were exchanged as they ate. Talk about their dad, his boredom in his practice, his yearning for something more, the war, Martin's shipping out for the front, and their sister Anne, occupied most of the conversation. It wasn't until after they had eaten, and the conversation was dying off, that Martin's thoughts wandered towards what was really on his mind. Words in Donovan's memoirs that he and Clara had discovered in Bletchley Park ran through his mind. The words, *capture, entice, trick, or by any means necessary get the smartest people in the world*, echoed in his head. Could bringing Britain's elite from its top universities be a part of this plan, he was thinking.

As he pictured in his mind's eye the three men secretly meeting in Paris, his eyes moved around the restaurant with no particular focus. He was dazed. Lost in thought. What could have brought these men to this place of such devastation? The loss of life, a world in chaos, must have greater meaning. How could anyone think in such a manner? Is my dear brother now a pawn in this scheme? He wondered. He could not fathom the good that could come from such a plan. Lost, bewildered, and in a complete daze his mind continued to wander. Interrupted only by the clumsiness of a woman, clad in the red and black skimpy uniform of the severs, as she collided with a co-worker while moving swiftly in the crowded restaurant. The loud splatter of dishes and silverware crashing to the floor, with china breaking into tiny pieces, caught the attention of everyone. Martin was startled to life, and instinctively blurted out, "Thomas, how are the plans for Yale coming long?"

"Are you okay?" Thomas replied, with the widest of grins. His pale skin turning pink and flush as he enjoyed a rare moment. His brother, usually not rattled by anything, had become startled and was laid bare before him. This amused Thomas.

"Yes, Yes, the noise startled me. I guess my nerves are on high alert, having to go into action full time soon," Martin said.

"So, how are things going with Yale? When do you go to America?" he asked again.

Thomas' grin dropped and his normal ruddy complexion returned. Then he spoke in a soft monotone voice of seriousness, or maybe fear. "The Chancellor has requested that everyone that is going to America be vetted before they are allowed to be included."

"Does the Chancellor's request worry you," Martin asked.

"No, it doesn't worry me. It's right to be certain that the people going to America really want to go. There is only room for a certain number and you can't change your mind easily once the ship sets sail."

"Then what is it then Thomas? You have a look of concern on your face."

"Well, to be frank, it's the questions, they don't feel right to me. There are questions that really probe into our family history."

"How so," asked Martin.

"There are questions about the family history with things such as pauperism, mental disability, dwarfism, promiscuity, and criminality. The criminality I understand but not the others. What do they have to do with going to America to study?"

"That is a bit strange," Martin replied.

"One more thing, Martin, there have been whispers among the students about experiments and some sort of pool of people being gathered together. The mothers of the children that went to Yale for refuge last year are writing letters that mention eugenics. Have you heard about eugenics? What do you think that is all about?"

Martin knew nothing about eugenics, but his thoughts went back to that night, not too long ago, when he and Clara poured over the Donovan's memoirs. He wondered if there could be a connection. There was that section of the plan that he recalled. The words, *"capture, entice, trick, or by any means necessary get the smartest people in the world" and "seed population for our greatness"* echoed in his head yet again. Could this eugenics thing, and the students from Oxford, actually be a part of this plan he thought. He knew now that Francis being able to decode the names in that plan was crucial to understanding what was going on with this war and who was behind it all. In reply to Thomas, Martin simply said, "I don't know, but let's be careful about you going to America, okay?"

Martin knew more about eugenics than he let Thomas believe. The topic was widely debated during his time at Oxford. But he had not kept up with it since leaving his college. Out of fear for his safety, or maybe just the cautionary lawyer in him speaking, Martin felt that the least Thomas knew at this stage the better it would be for him.

Thomas, somewhat hesitantly replied, "Okay. "A one-word reply uttered slowly, in a low distracted voice, almost a whisper that trailed off and ended abruptly with him asking Martin to gently look over his right shoulder."

"What am I looking for," asked Martin.

"The two men at the table near the window."

Martin, stretched his arms high above his head then slowly turned to get a glimpse at the men. The glare from the unusual sunlight in December obscured his vision. He saw enough of them though. The two men were both dressed in dark suits and, aside from being young men that for some reason where not in armed forces uniform, they looked normal to him.

"What about them," Martin asked.

"I am not sure, but I think they have been watching us. They arrived just after we sat down, and appear to be taking turns looking over at us and talking."

"Probably just a coincidence. They could be just looking over at the entrance and we are in their line of sight." said Martin.

Following lunch with Thomas Martin wanted to find out more about the current state of eugenics. A visit to the London Library directed him to the Eccleston Square, near the historic Brockwell Park in south London. Here he would find the Eugenics Society Offices. Debris laid everywhere as he bobbed and weaved his way to the Society's offices. Eccleston Square had been heavily bombarded by the Luftwaffe air raids. The offices of the Society were vast, but cramped, a 19th Century, Victorian style home now purposed for offices.

At 3:00 PM that afternoon Martin arrived the Society's office, where he was immediately greeted by an elderly lady. A pleasant lady, immaculately clad, well spoken, and alert. Martin could tell she was stunning in her youth, and from British upper class. Not wanting to draw attention to his motives Martin expressed an interest in joining the Society and asked where he could get more information. The elderly lady asked Martin to wait in a small room next to the reception area while she fetched someone to help him. Minutes later a wiry young man entered the room and introduced himself as Julian Huxley, the Society's Vice President.

At Martin's request Huxley explained the work of Sir Francis Galton who, after a study of upper-class Britain, believed that through selective breeding humans could direct its future. Huxley liked to hear himself talk. He rambled on non-stop. Explaining that Galton believed that an elite position in society was due to a good genetic makeup. That Galton was the first to use the word eugenics. That the Society was established to continue his work. Huxley, proud in every word he uttered, told Martin how the eugenics movement in America had grown to surpass that in Britain where it began. In America, Huxley said, they focus on the removal of negative traits in society through sterilisation, but in Britain the Society promoted the breeding of positive traits. "Even Churchill and President Roosevelt where supporters of eugenics," he told Martin.

After what seemed like hours at the Eugenics Society, but in reality, was only thirty minutes, Martin was dismayed by his findings. Maybe his thoughts were not too far off track. This eugenics thing could be a part of the plan he and Clara uncovered in Donovan's memoirs, he concluded.

***

Dinner that evening with his family was a sedate affair. Thomas and Anne where remarkably quiet throughout the evening. Maybe it was their fear for Martin's safety, as much of the conversation was about his return to action. Martin senior, however, incessantly gave his advice. Martin's mother, visibly nervous and concerned for her son, flapped about in the kitchen. Perhaps it was the lack of sincerity with which he spoke, but Martin's assurances and promise to write often did nothing to calm her, nor his siblings. As, after difficult farewells, Martin arrived back at the Wellington Barracks. Echoing in his head were the sombre thoughts that this might be his last time in this building, in Britain, or for that matter tonight might have been the last time his family would see him.

In the solitude of his barracks Martin wrote the first of his coded letters to Francis and Clara.

To Francis he began his letter with the words, "My Dearest Frances, Tomorrow I will leave Britain to lead our troops into battle. You will be in my heart and my thoughts." He finished the letter with the words, "take care of what we have started. Remain resolute." Being careful of his secret life with Francis, knowing his letter may be read, he changed the spelling of Francis name to the feminine version. The letter also encoded the word eugenics knowing that Francis would understand. What they had started would also be clear to Francis that it was the decoding of the memoirs.

To Clara his letter encoded the words, "help Francis." He also told her that tomorrow, at 6:00am, he will join the men of the 18th Army Division for the journey to Liverpool. Then onto a troopship that would carry them to action in South-East Asia.

In the months that followed both would write back to Martin. But to no avail.

21

The small farming village of Braemar, in the Scottish Highlands, was notorious for its harsh winters. Yet the village had enjoyed many years of prosperity. In the summer and spring, the lush greenery, and fertile soil, were ideal conditions for farming. Crops would flourish and the produce - milk, cheese - would be plentiful. Surrounded by the Grampian Mountains and woodlands, with the River Cluine running smack through the middle, and the River Dee nearby, the village was rich in fish and meats all year. The markets of the nearby Aberdeen, despite the heavy bombing, overflowed with the Braemar villagers selling their goods.

The Mackenzie's had been a part of Braemar since the days when the Romans occupied Great Britain. Archibald Mackenzie and his wife Jane, who lived there today with their six children, were also rumoured to be descendants of Scottish royalty. They were god fearing Catholics that enjoyed the village prestige that went with their rumoured royalty. A rumour perhaps started as a result of the Mackenzie family's dominance in the annual Highland Games held in the village.

The Highland Games were contests of strength – jumping, running, throwing, and riding. They were held all across Scotland every year. It is said the games originated from Ireland in 2000 BC and crossed the water to Scotland with the fourth and fifth century migrations of the Scots. They were introduced in Scotland as a means of selecting the most able men for soldiers and couriers. In Braemar royalty had always attended the games giving rise to the rumour of the Mackenzie royalty.

With the heavily wooded area nearby, links to royalty, its closeness to Aberdeen, and the home of the Highland games, Braemar had also become the ideal troop training ground. At the outbreak of the war the Gordon Highlanders had been stationed in Braemar for their training. They were a Scottish Regiment of two battalions. Archie, and his eldest child William, immediately joined the Highlanders. William was assigned to the 1st Battalion and Archie to the 2nd Battalion. They were both dispatched to Italy.

The Gordon Highlanders were among the first to set their feet on the soil of Europe. They landed on the beach in Tripoli and fought the Axis forces there before marching day and night to meet the Germans in Sicily. After scaling the walls of the castle Vizzini they eventually drove the Nazis from that part of town. In Sferro the Highlanders met the desperation of the Germans head on. Having withstood an onslaught of intense bombardment from the neighbouring hills, and lived against the tank and infantry counter-attacks, they took up the chase to Messina and drove the Nazis from the island.

These days at the front were particularly brutal on William who had long suffered episodes of depression. As a young lad, not more than ten years old, in an episode of his depression, he had strung a rope around his neck and leaped forth off the chair he was standing. His hopes of bringing an end to his suffering did not deliver results this day. The loneliness, the depression, often continued to give way to mornings when William woke to thoughts and wishes that he had not lived to see this day.

Inside the family they were forbidden to talk of the troubled child, so little was known of William's inner struggle, but it raged on. For a while it wasn't much that would push him to the edge, but with time he had learned to live with the depression deep inside, and place a smile on the outside. Day by day he had moved on and suffered in silence - depressed on the inside, and the Mackenzie cheer on the outside.

In the summer of 1938 William, then a young man of twenty-one years met and married Catherine, a young lady that had caught his fancy in the local pub. After a short honeymoon and a period of bliss, when the depression seemed to have subsided within him, the two settled into an uncharacteristically mundane life together. When his leave from the Highlanders ended William returned to the front leaving a then pregnant Catherine in Braemar.

In late autumn 1940 William, after a spell of intense fighting in Europe, returned to Braemar. On returning he noticed Catherine was quieter at home than before. He spent his days in the pub catching up with village gossip, and in the evenings he and Catherine sat in front of the wireless in silence, or he would be rambling on while Catherine knitted. Amongst this mundane routine were the scatters arguments, brought on partially by William's inner feelings of depression, and partially by the frigid nature of Catherine's reception of him. From time to time the two would argue over the most trivial of things - heated arguments in vain - as they would repeat over and over.

The truth about Catherine came to light when her secret past was exposed during an argument between the pair. The only child of the marriage was a product of a seedy relationship that Catherine had while off in Aberdeen before their marriage. The arguments went on for days before William found the will to reconcile. On the surface he moved on, but inside his depression was raging out of control. He would find ways - dark ways - to distract his attention, and reduce the flames of his inner depression, but it would not be long before it surged back. This cycle of depression was draining his will to live, reigniting his thoughts of not wanting to wake to another day.

December 2nd 1940, however, would not be one of those days. On the eve of this day William inhaled a trembling breath, sweat accumulated on his icy cold skin. Outside the cramped garage the fog, which had settled on the village, engulfed the midnight air. Inside the smoke swirled, wrapping around his body, and down his throat as he drifted further and further away. Death was on him, and it wasn't as beautiful or peaceful as he had previously imagined. His stomach turned in on itself and the gases were eating away at his insides, tearing away at the tissue there, leaving him but a rendered slab of dying cells. The drool and snot had turned to liquid much like his mind. He tried to move, tried to reach the door handle, to escape, as the pulsating engine of the Hillman Minx roared. Froth gathered forth near his lips in pungent yellow as he sat frozen - as time stood still. Death was nowhere near as merciful as he had dreamt of it being.

The villagers talked about his death being a way of William avoiding the fight. "What a smear on the Mackenzie name," were the whispered words that echoed throughout the small village. But little did they know that he had long been in turmoil - a troubled soul since his youth. The seemingly frigid union with Catherine, the betrayal, his desperation for a closeness, love, affection from her, was but the straw that broke the camel's back.

Archie, generally happy-go-lucky, was devastated on hearing of his son's death. Resolute in upholding traditions he set about with determination to ensure that William did not become the forgotten son. After a Mackenzie family send off, with almost every occupant of Braemar taking part, he summoned the family together. Ashamed, the family wanted to never speak of William again. They certainly did not want to relive his death in perpetually. After much discussion it was agreed that they would honour his birth, not his death, and with this agreement the Mackenzie family traditions were forever altered.

***

At noon on the 15th of January, 1941 a stunning 22-year-old blonde scanned Liverpool's Capaldi Catê and spotted him. He matched the brief description given to her - 26 years old, moustache, freckled, and piercing bright green eyes. A small scar on the left side of the forehead confirmed he was Donald Schiffer, a British naval Officer. She approached him and asked, "Are you by any chance Mr. Schiffer?" Donald was expecting an elderly man - tall, wrinkled, with a rustic Seafarers' complexion. This was to be an information gathering meeting about the seaways around the Liverpool port and across the Atlantic.

Surprised and speechless he managed to mutter something in the affirmative. Dressed in an elegant white dress, with a smooth rosy complexion, and red covered silky lips the woman took a seat next to him. Explaining, as she sat, that she was a freelance journalist writing a story about wartime transport, and had been instructed to meet him and be as helpful as possible. The pair spent the day together—sipping coffee in cafes, watching a film at a local cinema and enjoying a late dinner. Like every Officer Donald had been sworn to secrecy, and he always took his orders seriously. However, by the evening she - Clara Bauerle - had learnt practically all there was to know about him, and the allied operations in and out of Liverpool. It wasn't long after this day that the port at Merseyside in Liverpool had become the focus of the German blitz.

As a strategic port in the Battle of the Atlantic, and easily found from the lights of the nearby neutral Dublin, the bombing became relentless. The allies quickly began rounding up, and interning, any foreign national in Liverpool. Huyton's internment camp quickly became home for many innocent German, Austrian and Italian civilians - mostly low to medium risk, and waiting to be shipped to the Isle of Mann or Canada. It was during this time that Clara fled Liverpool for her new assignment in Bletchley.

Since Clara's departure from Liverpool the Luftwaffe air raids had been consistent but had done nothing to slow the use of the port, which remained a buzz with activity when Martin arrived in Merseyside, over a year later. By this time America had officially entered the war and there were thousands of allied servicemen - Americans, Canadians, Irish, Scottish, English, and Welch, scampering about the port - some heading for troopships others rounding off the numbers on ships forming convoys. Amongst the service men were a splattering of civilians - women seeing their husbands, boyfriends, and children off.

Martin's attention was drawn to two men, standing in a distance, seemingly watching his movements. Their dark suits were first to capture his eyes, but then he recognised them as the men from the restaurant. This is not a coincidence, he thought to himself, as he, and his men, headed straight for the USS Mount Vernon - an American troopship.

Once he had found his quarters Martin beelined for the officer's mess. Twisting and turning his way through the halls of the Mount Vernon he hustled to the mess hall - shushing people out of his way as he moved along. In his haste he recalled his father's words that, "a soldier's life centres around food," and an instant smile came to his face.

Men from the combined allied forces had filled the mess hall - laughing, talking, drinking, and eating as they emotionally readied themselves for battle. Martin was awestruck by the sights. One table in particular caught his attention, as he stood at the entrance way of the mess hall - mesmerised. Gathered around the table were men of the Scottish Regiment, mostly Highlanders, but some Black Watch as well. At the centre of the table sat a stocky fella, with a dark beard, freckled skin, and auburn hair, he was not only cheerful, but captivating as he gallantly told a story of an ancient battle.

In Scotland the culture and the tales traditionally told in stories were a part of their Irish ancestry - dating back to around 500AD with the Irish invasion. In these Celtic countries it was an art form that never failed to capture the imagination - especially when told by a seasoned story teller. Archie, who was at the centre of the table, was a seasoned story teller.

Martin listened in while he ate and drank.

Hours later, inspired, and upbeat about seeing battle, Martin returned to his cabin - a shared cabin for officers. Shortly after he was joined by his cabin mate who he instantly recognised as the story teller. The now very inebriated story teller. The two managed to introduce themselves before Archie was comma tossed in his bunk. The next morning when they awoke the convoy was on its way to Mombasa, Kenya.

The port in Mombasa was not only a mail stop for the convoy; it was also a transfer point for troops. From here the Mount Vernon, now ladened with Archie, Martin, and men of the newly formed 18th Infantry Division of the allied forces set out in a convoy for Bombay, where they would pick up their last transport to Singapore - the HMT Rhona.

Once on board the HMT Rhona Martin set about making final preparations for his Division's arrival in Singapore. The Japanese had now fully entrenched themselves in the Pacific Islands. Australia's 8th Division and a few British units were putting up a strong fight in Malaya, but Japan's superiority in air power, tanks and infantry tactics were slowly winning. Things looked bleak for the allies.

At dawn the next day the HM Rhona streamed into the British Naval Base in Singapore. Between the wars a major building project, designed to ensure security of the empire east of Suez, took place to fortify Singapore. The island now had batteries of guns guarding the sea, an airbase, and tens of thousands of men. Singapore was widely assumed to be impregnable, to be able to hold out any attack until a fleet sent from Britain arrived. In the region Australia and New Zealand looked to Singapore to aid their security against the Japanese threat. It gave them peace of mind having a base where a fleet despatched from Britain could be based. The island was a deterrent to any enemy.

Martin had been awake for hours. With the comfort of a secure base in Singapore in mind, he was expecting to engage the enemy in Malaya and push them back to Japan. To aid the battles ahead, he needed to find words of inspiration for his troops before they went ashore. In his head he had gone over the words of his speech many times. But now the time had come for him to address the troops. With nerves of steel, and a confidence that beamed with every step, he made his way to the bridge. Far out to sea streams of pulsing light saturated the surface of a slothful sea. Ebbing ever so gently there was a peaceful Neptune-blue glow, with a golden haze, as far as the eye could see. The horizon seemed to be stitched with a line of silver. There was a strange irony in such beauty amidst the turmoil that existed only a few miles away.

On the bridge he snapped a salute to the ship's captain, stepped up to the microphone, took a deep breath, and began to speak. His words echoed throughout the ship. The rising sun laminated the bridge with warmth as he spoke and a silent, chilling feeling, of peace and hope filled the air. The men listened intently as he said,

"Gentleman, when Jesus choose his disciples, he knew that one was the devil and one was Judas. Yet he believed in the good of

men kind and choose them. I believe and we must all believe in the good of men.

Over this horizon guns are blazing and men are fighting. Soon we will be among them face-to-face in battle. When we do let us stand resolved in our belief. Let our courage not fail us, for while a time may come when the courage of men fails, when we forsake our hearts and break all bonds of good and just, but this is not that time. A time may come when evil triumphs over good and all belief is lost, when the age of good comes crashing down! But this is not that time! Now we fight! We fight together for all that is good and just! We fight with honour, belief, and courage! We fight for our future, our families' future, our friend's futures, and the future of our country! We fight! We fight! and We fight!"

22

The morning after Martin's arrival in Singapore he called together his senior officers to assess the threat of a Japanese invasion of the island. He needed to plot the defence, and counterattack on Japanese soil, that the Commonwealth forces will conduct.

Gathered in the briefing room with him were Archibald Mackenzie of the Scottish Gordon Highlanders; Jasjit Singh Commander of the Indian forces, the Australian John Wilks, and Andrew Hamilton who led the Canadian forces.

Martin, now a General following a quick promotion ceremony after the death of General Percival, began the briefing with his officers by saying that Britain placed a high value on Singapore as a staging point for attacks into Far East. That the island must be held at all cost. Our intelligence tells us that the Japanese have many troops in Malaya, but as a base Singapore was designed as a formidable fortress and is impregnable, he told his officers.

"However an attack on the island is inevitable, so we ought to focus our attention on how best to defend the island." Martin said.

"We all know that on the same day that Japan attacked Pearl Harbour, half a world away, they simultaneously bombed our Air Force bases in the north. Our Navy responded by sending the battleship 'Prince of Wales' and the battle cruiser 'Repulse' with a fleet of ships, but both were torpedoed." He continued.

Everyone knew of the Japanese attacks, Martin only mentioned them as a formality, and to focus the men on what was about to come. Still, even though the men knew the Japanese decimated the British naval and air forces in the Asian Theatre, Martin's officers remained lethargic about an inevitable Japanese attack of Singapore. The air of lethargy and arrogance was rampant, not only amongst the officers but also among all the colonial forces stationed on Singapore.

The only exception to this arrogance and lethargy was fury. In a rare revealing of emotion for a Scot, while not under the influence of alcohol that is, Archie, the only Scot in the room, began to boil inside. When Archie finally spoke his fury could be seen and heard in every word.

"As Scottish I feel a heavy burden to live up to the legendary heroics of our ancestors, but I am also cautious and calculating." He said.

"As you all know by now I am not one to show my emotions, but this situation with the Japs he got me riled up. They are not fighting fair, I hear that they are not taking prisoners, killing everyone, it's just immoral and unethical." Continued Archie.

"We have to stand up to these bastards!" He shouted.

Then, in a much calmer, almost fearful voice, Archie said: "But ... But, Britain's naval and aerial capabilities had been completely destroyed, leaving the island defenceless to assaults from both air and sea. If the Japs decided to invade this island then we are the only hope of retaining control of the island."

"Those attacks on us were shrewd and well thought out. The Japs must have something else planned, and we have to be ready for them. Does anyone else see this as I do, or are we all so sweet on ourselves to think that the Japs can't hurt?" He then asked.

Jasjit then interjected with the air of arrogance, that he had been known to project in all situations.

"Eliminating the Air Force's ability to both retaliate and to protect the ground troops was a shrewd and incredibly well thought out attack. But we are impregnable here, plus the best they can do is get thirty, or forty, thousand troops here. We are ninety thousand plus between the British, Indian, Canadian, and Australian forces. It doesn't matter what the Japs have planned - they will fail." He said.

"With enemy troops in Malaya numbering so large, we have fallen back over the causeway and will be able to defend against a Japanese sea attack safely." Hamilton, the Canadian forces leader, said.

The causeway he spoke of was the long bridge joining Singapore and mainland Malaya.

"Yes," replied Martin. "But Archie is right, let's play this all the way out in any case."

He then asked the room of officers, "What do we know of the Japanese troop movements since the attacks in America and our bases, and that humiliation in Jitra?"

The Australians always seemed to have the best intelligence on the Japs, and it was John Wilks stepped up and replied to Martin about what was known of the Japanese troop movements.

"Over the past month or so, since regrouping here on Singapore, the waters have been quiet around the island. The

Japanese appear to be contained in Malaya and not likely to risk attacking the island." He said.

Over the next hour the officers planned the defence of the island. Relying on their strength in numbers they agreed on the deployment of their soldiers.

As it was a much simpler way for the Japanese forces to attack by sea Martin and his officers expected the Japanese to attack from the sea. It was just not likely they would send their troops through the treacherous jungle of mangroves and swamp. However, there were large guns facing out to the sea, so it was a possibility that an attack would come over land. With a sea attack in mind Martin ordered his troops to be deployed to the coast line all around the island.

However, the Japanese were unexpectedly swarming south, through the jungle from Kota Bahru and, across the cause-way towards Singapore some 600 miles south. Following a diversionary attack the Japanese launch their primary assault over land. An assault, that when it finally happened demon-strated not only their military prowess but also the ruthless-ness, brutality, and fearlessness of their soldiers. The attacked happened with such speed and savagery that Martin's men were caught completely by surprise. The Japanese soldiers did not take prisoners. They simply executed all those in their path and swept through Singapore with the force of the most ferocious tidal wave, leaving utter destruction in their wake.

Having a mandate of not taking prisoners also allowed a speed of attack for which the British-led forces were not prepared. They did not need to stop, restrain, and corral enemy troops. They moved quickly across the ground during the day and at night.

Over estimating the defensive nature of the jungle was a grave mistake that left Martin's troops completely outmanoeuvred. By the time Martin became aware of the Japanese attack through the jungles it all seemed hopeless. He ordered his troops to spread over 70 miles of land in order to face the oncoming onslaught. With far superior numbers of men he thought that his troops would be able to repel the attack, but the Japanese seemed unstoppable. Just seven days after the attacks began, on 15th February Singapore fell to the savagery and tenacity of the Japanese army.

Across all of Singapore the battlefields saw fathers, brothers, and husbands fighting to their last breath as the young army of Japanese conquerors savagely, and mercilessly, slaughtered all that they saw. All now laid quiet on the field of battle as it had become a graveyard of the unburied. Corpses laid among the sand and foliage, and in the jungle crevices. The battle had been lost. The enemy had won.

The final day of battle was a typical wet and humid day in Singapore, nothing to speak of, but somewhere far away mothers and fathers, brothers and sisters, wives and children waited in vain. For Martin and his offices it was all unbelievable, shocking really. They had been sent reeling, unable to comprehend or process the what had transpired right in front of their eyes. As they sat, trying to come to grips with surrendering, Martin couldn't help but notice how time is so much like water. Time can pass slowly, a drop at a time. Time can stand still, or freeze like water, and time can rush by in a blink like a raging river. The clock says it is measured and constant, tick-tock, part of an orderly world; but the clock lies. The past six hours had passed like thousands of camera frames per second shown one at a time. In Martin's slow time-bubble every sound was louder, hotness was hotter, and colours were brighter. All the while his insides felt as if there was nothing there, nothing to need feeding, and nothing to have need of anything at all. Then the time to surrender was upon them. The officers would surrender themselves to the Japanese for internment, and then their men would be rounded up too.

They assumed Changai prison in the south of the island, if they were lucky, otherwise they might find themselves performing hard labour on the railways in Thailand or Japan, was where they might end up. However, their fate lied in the hands of one man, General Yashamito, who had established his headquarters in the Ford Motor Company factory, which made cars before the war, planes during the war, and will now become the site of humiliation for Martin. It was here, that Yashamito, and much of the Japanese army he led, awaited the surrender of the British-led forces.

The Ford Motor Company factory building was a modern, and glamorous, building, that was the eastern hub of a great Company, and once full of life. However, when war broke out again in Europe, it wasn't long before the factory's state-of-the-art assembly equipment was taken over by the British Royal Air Force to assemble fighter air crafts. The building continued to be full of life, a new life, but life, as it churned away assembling air crafts, not cars. Life, this time around, was eventually sucked from the building when the potential loss of Singapore to the Japanese became an eminent possibility and all the aircraft parts were flown out. The building then laid abandoned.

In recent days, though, there had been many battles fought against the Japanese around this building. There had been the buzz of new life again for this great structure. Life... Yes, but on this turn around, today, death could be felt all around the building.

Death, though, won't be what defines this building today. For today this building will not be the poster child of positivity, as it was before the war. Nor will this building be the backdrop of death that it had recently been. No ... today this building will bear witness to the end of the worst British military defeat of the war so far. A defeat that is said to have left Churchill stupefied. A defeat that will give rise to yet another new chapter in the many lives of this structure.

Normally sunsets on the island came in the kind of oranges that brought warmth to the eyes and soul. Today though, for Martin's crew, the beautiful island, which boomed with tourist a few years earlier, had now become a dusty dirt brown tomb of humiliation. Still, Archie, John Wilks, Jasjit, Andrew, and Martin were resolute in their belief that they had the bargaining strength to negotiate favourable terms for their surrender.

Their nerves were frayed, and their bodies, dripping with sweat brought on by the heat and humidity of the island, rocked from deep within their cores. Internal tremors that would measure a seven on the Richter scale. There was no doubt that, inwardly, fear and trepidation was upon them, but they men shown none of their fear outwardly as they walked briskly toward the Ford Motor Company factory building. As they marched along every thump of their boots hitting the dirt echoed sharply on the deserted pathway. The thumping sound was loud, overly loud in their own ears, like the booming heartbeat of a condemned prisoner.

At 5pm, through the dusty graveyard, and against a setting sun, Martin and his officers approached the factory. The once abandoned building glowed golden in the sun light. It was as if the building had a soul, one that was stoic and sobering.

On arrival at the building they heard the echoing of footsteps in the concrete walls and corridors of the building. It was at this point that they questioned themselves yet again. How could we have come here so boldly? Did we really have the strength to negotiate? How did it all come down to this? Were but a few of the questions that played over and over in their heads.

From around the corner walked an unarmed, battle worn, Japanese soldier whom Martin assumed was General Tomoyuki Yamashita's second in command. The soldier, a young man, did not walk with the same confidence as Martin and his men. His steps were tentative, and measured. His feet seems to flail about as he walked, as if he was being carried along by a force not of his own. Tired? Perhaps? Nonetheless, certainly not the air of confidence that Martin's men expected.

No words were exchanged between the men, just a gesture, made with their weapons, told Martin to comply and follow these men. Led through battle torn concrete corridors, the men followed, they followed until they arrived at what e must have once been the office of the General Manager of the factory. An expansive office with a huge metal desk at the fore, accompanied by chairs of steel and leather. Sat at the centre of the table was an older man whom Martin assumed to be General Tomoyuki Yamashita, the leader of the assault of Singapore. Gestured again, but this time to be seated, Martin and his men sat.

Confident yet uncertain, and fearful yet strong willed, the men were reticently ready to negotiate their surrender. They knew that the Japanese had recently showed that they would follow the Geneva rules Relative to the Treatment of Prisoners of War, and would observe the Hague Convention of 1907 outlining the laws and customs of war. So they felt confident in their starting negotiating position despite the fact that Japan signed, but never ratified the most recent Geneva Conventions Relative to the Treatment of Prisoners of War. Therefore, with an expectation of being treated in accordance with the Geneva conventions, Martin began the negotiations with General Yamashita.

The two Generals immediately jumped into trying to assess the true strengths, and plans, of each other's forces. Yamashito was particularly worried that the British might discover the truth about the actual situation of his troops, especially their numerical inferiority compared to the British, and their shortage of supplies and ammunition. Martin, aware of the brutal savagery attacks of the Japanese as they made their way across Singapore, was worried about what may happen to the civilians once the Japs had control of the island.

Martin started the negotiation by requesting to keep 1,000 men armed to guard against any Japanese retaliation against the local population. He also wanted a delay the ceasefire to allow all of his men to receive their orders on time.

Over the next hour the tug-of-war of words went back and forth, no one wanting to give into the other. Yamashita pushed to close the negotiations quickly as he also worried about the possibility of British reinforcements arriving. He repeatedly threatened to carry on with the attacks planned for that night if Martin did not acquiesce to his demands of an unconditional surrender.

Eventually, faced with no other choice, Martin signed the surrender documents at 6.10pm. Once signed the world was completely still. Eyes darted around the room, but no one moved, within the silence there was a ghostly calm, a calm that kind of just lingered in the air. It was over.

The true question though was who were the victors and who were defeated. There was no celebration that evening amongst the Japanese. There was a solemn silence and a feeling of sorrow in the ranks of the Japanese army. Each man was loyal to the Japanese empire, mired in tradition, and ready to die for their country. However, surviving the battle that they had just experienced required more than loyalty. These soldiers needed to give up a part of themselves that will never return to them. They needed to go into their primitive brain, and stay there as some semi-drunk, for they had been called upon to commit the most heinous acts.

23

That night sleep had not come easy for Martin. It was a humiliating defeat, the worst ever for Britain, and he had arrogantly presided over the whole battle. Then now this ... His troops being ruthlessly and dishonourably rounded up from every corner of the island, marched into captivity, and sorted into groups like cattle on their way to slaughter. A group for those suited for hard labour, another group for those who might have vital information, and a final batch of those suited for dying.

Armed soldiers controlled the procession of the troops, and controlling the armed soldiers were the Kempeitai.

Officially the Kempeitai were the Japanese military police, but unofficially they were a ruthless secret police. The commanding officer of the Kempeitai was Lieutenant-Colonel Masayuki Oishi, a young and ambitious man of only twenty-four years. Oishi commanded over two hundred Kempeitai officers and one thousand army auxiliary recruits. He made his way to the head of the Kempeitai with a cold, calculating demeanour, and a willingness to do whatever it took.

***

There were three barracks being controlled by the Kempeitai that evening. Kitchener Barracks, that used to house the British Army's Royal Engineers. Roberts Barracks, where the Royal Artillery were assigned, and the Selarang barracks that held Gordon Highlanders, and had now become Martin's prison. Today though there were no barracks assignments just men being cattled into confinement, and into buildings that were once their refuge but had now become their prison.

The barracks, and the surrounding base buildings, were built as a part of a massive defence construction project which created "Fortress Singapore" and were located in the Changi area of the island. The Changi area derived its name from the massive Changai tree. A tree that grew so tall that it could be seen for miles. Trees that had To be brutally chopped at the top during the construction of the pre-war base buildings, so as not to give the enemy a range marker to the base lands.

While the base guarded the northern approach to the island, the southern approach was guarded by heavy gun batteries, and troops, permanently stationed on the islands of Blakang Mati and Pulau Brani. When completed, these batteries, in the north and south, held the greatest concentration of heavy artillery outside Great Britain.

However, no such weaponry was able to prevent Martin's troops from being overrun by speed, ingenuity, and ruthlessness.

The island had fallen to the Japanese just as the tops of the Changai trees fell to ground. Both with finality, shock, and a thudding felt by all within the grasp of these two events. Martin was one of the few men that had witnessed both events, and the thud, thud, thudding of the Changai trees falling to the ground haunted him during his brief sleep that night. Images of the trees falling, his men falling in battle, the unceremonious surrender to General Yamashita, and the thud, thud, thudding sound, echoed in his head as he slept.

***

From the Selarang Barracks Martin watched the Kempeitai in action until exhaustion got the better of him. For as long as he could bear to watch his troops were herded into Selarang, and the surrounding barracks.

The next day, as the sun crept over the horizon, Martin woke to a field of soldiers, fifty thousand of them, every one of them wet, war torn, and tired. On first sight he could feel the bile rising in his throat, before sickness and despair, turned to hope, and hope to pride, as he watched over his troops. Every one of them, in the face of such shocking horror, stood unbroken and rooted in resolve - like tomorrow was guaranteed.

Amongst the troops were pilots that he had sent into battle when working in the London command centre, combat soldiers that he had trained personally, friends, and officers in his direct command. Conor, a young 19-year-old Irish recruit, was also there in the field of tattered and torn men.

Conor lied about his age and enlisted in the British Army at only 16 years of age. As a scrawny, but scrappy, little fella he quickly rose through the ranks and became an ace pilot. Martin recognised Conor as the young pilot shot down above the Dunkirk beach. Martin watched as Conor's plane became a fiery ball of melting metal. In the sky nearby the burning metal he saw the white shoot strapped to Conor float gracefully to the ground. Dragging Conor to safety that day made Martin a friend for life. It was also one of Martin's proudest moments in the war. Now there Conor stood amongst the men certainly destined for hard labour.

As he looked at Conor his mind drifted to Thomas, his younger brother. Conor had always reminded Martin of Thomas. He thought of the times he a Thomas shared as kids, playing football in the street, running laughing together. Much simpler times than now, he thought. He also wondered what had become of Thomas since he returned to the front. Did Thomas go to America to study? Has he now enlisted? Has he too been in battle? Is he alive? We're all thought that went through Martin's head. He could barely look on at Conor and the men without welling up. His eyes watered. He wanted to protect Conor. To protect all the men. To somehow throw a force-field over them and keep them from what they were about face. It was a rare moment in which sentiment reigned. Yes sentiment, the one weakness he knew he couldn't afford.

After that day life continued in Selarang unabated, and in relative calm. Martin was in the group of men selected for information. His days were, for the most part, quietly idled away marred in routine. The men roamed freely from barrack to barrack. Labour was limited to those things necessary for survival - tending to crop, cleaning, and health maintenance.

The first, and most urgent problem, that Martin faced was the lack of toilet facilities. Each barracks building only had four to six toilets, but the Japanese cut the water off, and these toilets couldn't be used. There was only one water tap and the line, which would last all day, would start from the early hours of the morning. As the senior officer in the barracks, and a lawyer, Martin diplomatically arranged a queuing system with officers being the first in the queue on alternative days. Each man was also allowed one water bottle of water per day, just one quart for your drinking, washing, and everything else. It wasn't much for bathing but under the circumstances there wasn't much bathing being done, anyway.

The nights were hot, sticky, and a struggle to sleep for those that tried. Martin and his officers were not amongst those trying to sleep as they beavered away on their escape.

However, it was not so much the same for the group of men that were destined for hard labour on the railway. They were sent to various destinations throughout the Pacific and Southeast Asia, journeys that carried with them a taste of the horrors to come. Packed onto vessels with tens of thousands of other prisoners one in five of them didn't survive the cramped, disease-ridden journey. A passage that was so horrible that the vessels eventually became known as "Hell Ships." Another two in five died of disease, starvation, or exhaustion. Though the worst of it for these men was the disease.

From time to time the Kempeitai would select one of the officers for interrogation, torture really.

The interrogations were the worst part of the day-to-day life for Martin, and the men at Selarang, or at least that was what Martin thought at the time. Although, not selected often, each man had to undergo interrogation. With the Kempeitai interrogation meant torture using their chosen method for that day, and they had a lot of choices.

Waterboarding, rice torture, flogging, electric shock, kneeling on sharp instruments, sharp objects, nail treatments, heat, jiu-jitsu, ants, and burying were all on the list of choices.

The waterboarding was worst when the Beast was on the island. The Beast was a Japanese army interpreter, who worked for the Kempeitai, and who developed his own version of waterboarding. He would prop a ladder on a slope, tie the prisoner to it, feet higher than head, pound something into their nostrils to break the bones so they had to breathe through their mouth, pour water into his mouth till they filled up and chocked, and then it was talk or suffocate.

With rice torture the victim would be starved for several days and then have a large amount of uncooked rice forced down their throat. They would then be forced to swallow a large amount of water. The rice would expand leaving them in excruciating pain for several days. Flogging was the most common of the cruelties used by the Kempeitai and was made more painful and terrifying by the use of wet sand pressed into the skin. Jiu-jitsu was another form of beating carried out by Japanese martial arts experts.

The knee spread often lead to permanent disability as the victim was forced to kneel with a pole inserted behind both knee joints. The joints would spread and pressure was applied to the thighs. This torture caused immense pain, and separation of the knee joints.

The use of ants was aided by the earlier impaling of Chinese. The impaled head were hung in trees and the captives made to stand under the tree while thousands of kerengga or weaver ants were dislodged onto the prisoners.

Martin experienced all the choices but remained unbroken until a humid and wet evening took him beyond his breaking point.

As a senior officer and friend Martin was called to the bedside of a dying soldier. It was Conor. After months of hard labour and suffering the young man couldn't go on any longer. He had been dying slowly, stoically withering away for days, though it was the malaria that was finishing him off.

When Martin arrived at his side, he could see the end was near. Conor, one that would never quit. Tears began to roll down his cheek on seeing Martin arrive. "Help me, Help me Martin," he squeezed out between laboured gasp for air. His eyes told the whole story. Quickly closing them, reopening them, and repeating the process. Conor didn't have long to live, and there was nothing Martin could do but watch. As Conor sweat profusely Martin did his best to keep his brow dry and he body comfortable. Then it happened. Conor closed his eyes, and through his jaundice mouth he took his last, loud and laboured breath.

That was all that Martin could bear. It is one thing to lose a soldier, a friend, in battle. It happens quickly and is to be expected. But to lose a friend in captivity is another level of sadness. Having to watch young Conor wither away then die on a hot humid night like this night was too much to bear. As Conor exhaled his last breath Martin threw his head into his hands and cried out loud. He wept, and he wept at the bedside of Conor without any shame nor concern for his rank. The enlisted men left and Martin remained, crying, and crying some more. Martin had finally broken! Before long, the shrieks of even the enlisted men could be heard throughout the barracks.

Maybe it was Martin's link to Thomas that Conor kept alive. Maybe it was the sheer mental and physical fatigue getting the best of him. Or maybe something else. Whatever lead to Martin's an unusual display of sentiment didn't matter. Such a display had allowed all those standing strong in the horrors of captivity to exhale. To feel a sense of relief, even if short-lived.

24

H ideki Tōjō demonstrated no such similar sentiment as Martin when, one month before the attack on Singapore began, he summoned Lieutenant-Colonel Oishi Masayuki to his home in Yonago, a tiny Japanese village on the northwest coast of the Sea of Japan.

***

Perched on a narrow pier, Yonago felt like it could be on the edge of another world. Quiet, peaceful, and void of that buzzing sound you hear in busy war ready towns and cities like Tokyo — a city that had been on a perpetual war footings, or at war, for what felt like centuries. In Yonago there was the quiet sound of peace captured in a seashell.

Overlooking Yonago is the holy mountain Daisen that rises from sea level to dominate the terrain for miles around. Holy because of centuries of occupation by Buddhist monks. Dominant as from Daisen you can see the whole of Yonago and the surrounding villages, including Tōjō's home.

Just as Daisen dominated the terrain of the region, Tōjō's home, a castle, the terrain of Yonago. The castle, positioned on the highest hill in Yonago, had walls made of the strongest things for miles around, yet when looked at carefully the simplicity of mere stones could be seen. The walls were built of stones of varying sizes and shapes, each one unique. From a distance it is uniform grey, from up close it was a mosaic of humble rocks, each of them nobody would think anything of where they lose by the roadside. But together they are a castle, the crown of the landscape, and the home of the protector of the people.

Prime Minister Tōjō would retreat to his home in Yonago for Commission business, and to escape the pressures and prying eyes of Tokyo.

***

Oishi was nervous and shaken, not so much to be visibly shaken though, when he received the summons to attend a meeting with an undisclosed purpose. The ambitious and outwardly fearless Oishi vigorously climbed the myriad of steps to Tōjō's home in Yonago. Not one step at a time, but several in unison, almost a sprint up the winding stairs. Once at the top Of the stairs he was greeted with an entranceway to a towering six story castle, and Japanese Imperial army soldiers. Moments later Oishi and Tōjō met for the first time in what would become, for Oishi, a long journey with a modest benefit.

Tōjō, now the Prime Minister of Japan, and the Commission's eastern leader, was following the people section of the plan when Oishi was summoned.

He began the conversation with two words, "jakuniku kyoushoku" which when translated to English means survival of the fittest.

"Do you believe this?" Tōjō asked Oishi.

Oishi didn't believe this at all. He was raised in a Buddhist family with the basic teachings of kindness, humour, and compassion towards other people. He actually believed that there should be no agenda other than to help someone, not survival of the fittest, or any master race type of teachings. However, to survive and prosper, Oishi had evolved.

An ambitious, and willing to do whatever it took, Oishi knew the answer Tōjō wanted and replied; "Yes your Excellency."

"Good then you will take command of the Kempeitai when our troops arrive in Singapore." Tōjō said.

"Just one thing though, when the opportunity arrives slaughter them." Continued Tōjō in reference to the Chinese whom by the Commission's plans were an inferior race that needed to be exterminated.

With those words from Tōjō being said the meeting was over, and a young man, willing to commit atrocious acts, now had both the power and ambition that could lead to grisly outcomes. A long journey, a short meeting, modest benefits for Oishi, but far-reaching consequences for so many others.

Two months after Martin's surrender Oishi, who was now the Kempeitai commander, met with Major General Kawamura Saburo and General Yamashita. Kawamura, a lowly infantry brigade commander had been only the day before been placed in charge of Japan's Singapore Garrison.

Yamashita, who only days earlier defeated Martin's troops, had ordered the men to meet at the Army Headquarters where Yamashita placed Kawamura in charge of carrying out mopping-up operations on the island. Yamashita then listened in as Kawamura consulted with Oishi. Kawamura listened in horror as he learned of the duties facing him.

"Our Prime Minister has ordered us to purge the Chinese population. They are an inferior race and as we have seen from our allies in Germany they must be eliminated from the face of the earth. Only those not a threat to Japan and not likely to procreate can survive." Oishi said once the proceedings were turned over to him.

"Have all Chinese males between the ages of 18 and 50 report come to us. Tell them that it is just a screening to know who is on the island. Tell them that it is for their protection and that we will be giving out medicine for their families." Continued Oishi.

"Yes, sir," replied Kawamura.

Within twenty-four hours, on the evening of 17 April 1942, the slaughter began. Over the next few days Chinese men were, loaded onto lorries, taken to the coast, or to other isolated places, and machine-gunned and bayoneted to death. For good measure Oishi sent those captured soldiers that were suited for dying along as well. Tens of thousands of men were exterminated.

***

When news of the Singapore exterminations reached Junior, in America, he sent an urgent radiogram for Wild Bill to meet him in Switzerland.

Junior was in Switzerland personally attending to another shipment of gold. He preferred gold to the other artefacts that Goebbels ships over from time to time.

Junior's thoughts were that gold was a good metal that could assume a multitude of forms: bar, coins, or pieces of jewellery. Plus it could be easily exchanged for more liquid currencies. Junior generally would visit the gold refinery and have the gold re-smelted to disguise its origin before shipping. It was at the gold refinery where Junior had instructed Wild Bill to meet him.

The men met in a small dusty room adjacent to the smelting area of the gold refinery. Every movement in this room sent a vortex of dust into the previously stagnant air. Despite the dust, this meeting allowed Junior to keep an eye on his gold while he, and Wild Bill, decided the fate of their once Commission compadre - Hideki Tōjō, who was now a target for demise,

With the rotting door to the room wide open, the dusty particles reflected the sunrays taking on the appearance of glitter, gold dust, or perhaps pixie dust, rather than a dull grey sheen over the flag-stones. Within this pixie dust Junior began the meeting with an explanation of the gold smelting process. In the finest of detail Junior rambled on and on as Wild Bill grew impatient, but there was a reason to what Wild Bill thought was madness.

Speaking metaphorically, in the calmest of voices, after the most detailed explanation of the smelting process, Junior said, "New beginnings are often disguised as painful endings."

Junior was quoting Lao Tzo an ancient Chinese philosopher. He was also referring to the painfully high temperatures used in the smelting process to produce pure metals. However, what he was really telling Wild Bill was that some Commission members needed a painful ending so that The Commission could start its new beginning.

Then in an abrupt switch in the conversation, and the tone of his voice, Junior said: "As for General Tōjō, now that the Japanese have attacked on American soil, there is an inevitable end to his reign in sight. The public will rally to have America enter this war, and Japan will be squarely in the cross hairs. This is an opportunity not to be missed." His tone was not aggressive, calm, nor provoking, neither did he raise his voice one octave. But sternness was clear and the fact that he meant business obvious to Wild Bill.

"What do you think needs to be done?" Asked Wild Bill, ready to take action, and thinking that in these last words spoken by Junior was the man he knew and respected. Wild Bill was always enamoured by Junior and would follow him to the ends of the earth.

"With the Singapore eliminations I am now more sure than ever that we can create the right circumstances to stoke Tōjō's on his conscience towards restoring honour to himself and his their families. The Japanese call it Seppuku, we know it as Harakiri." Junior replied.

"You just have to ensure that the appropriate military support is given, and action is taken, when the time is right. I will get things lined up on the world stage to set this in motion." Junior continued.

With patronising words, a shift in his stance to show his respect, and an astute scholarly look on his face Wild Bill simply replied, "Our own The plan in Donovan's memoirs mop up exercise".

Proud as a peacock could not describe Junior any better as he stood there admiring what he had created. Wild Bill had become the perfect disciple. It will be such a shame when it is his time. I will make sure he is last, and it is a good death thought Junior before replying with a single word, "Yes," he said with a broad devious and misleading smile on his face.

Wild Bill took Junior's smile as a nod of approval and merrily retired from the clandestine meeting to continue on with his mission, at least that is how he saw it, a mission given to him from some higher power.

***

The worst of Martin's time at Selarang, was not the interrogations as he once thought, the worst happened on the evening of the 30 August 1942. Six months into his captivity, having endured all manner of interrogation he was, on this evening, stunned into silence. It was the kind of moment that you witness but your brain just rejects; you can't believe what you just saw. He crouched there, nestled behind a small shrub, lost in his thoughts, saying nothing.

They had made their escape in the early morning of the 30 August 1942, before the sun had broken the darkness of the southern skies. After studying the guards' movements and planning their escape down to the minute Martin and five others slipped through the guards and into the Changi woods. However, freedom would only be short-lived for some of these men. Four of the escapees; two Australians, Rodney Breavington and Victor Gale, and two English soldiers, Private Harold Waters and Private Eric Fletcher were recaptured that same evening. Martin and Archie managed to evade recaptured and were now watching the proceeding from the Changi woods.

With Martin and Archie remaining free Oishi had ordered the next in command Jof the British and Australian troops in Changi to attend the execution of the four recent escapees: Breavington, Gale, Waters and Fletcher. One of the Australians, Breavington, pleaded to no avail that he should be the only one executed as he was solely responsible for the escape. Yet Oishi ordered his Kempeitai to executed all four by rifle fire. The initial rifle volley was non-fatal, and what happened next stunned Martin. Oishi, on seeing that the four were still alive, slowly walked to Breavington and with a single swoop of his sword slice his head off clean. He repeated this action until all four men had been decapitated.

***

Witnessing the men executed sent Martin into a state of turmoil. His heart and head seemed to be racing in different directions.

In his heart there was a kaleidoscope of feelings spinning and twirling.

He was angry with himself and the world. With himself because he felt that he had failed as a soldier, as a son, and as a moral person. He couldn't even return to battle after Dunkirk. Granted he had seen more blood, body parts, and death than most, but a failure nonetheless. As a son he had let his war hero farther down. As a moral person, he was not, how could he be after having sex with a man.

His anger with the world came from knowing of so much injustice, so much death, and so much treachery. Injustice in Frederick's treatment as a coloured man having to fight for equality. Injustice in the lives lost to the unconscionable actions of those who brought eugenics to life. The same eugenics that Hitler, and Tōjō, were now following as they exterminated people by the millions. Death in war, and the treachery of those behind the plan discovered in Donovan's memoirs riled him in his very core.

He was sad as a picture of hopelessness was starting to form in front of him. Hopelessness about a world gone wrong. Hopelessness about his own inability to make things different.

He was confused about how he could develop feelings for Clara, but be with Francis. He was also confused about how the law that he loved so much could see him as a criminal for being with Francis. Was this also an injustice thrushes upon him because of who he was? Much like Frederick's injustice because what colour he was?

He was happy to have had the chance to practise law were he helped others to enjoy their lives. He was also happy to have found the memoirs. Maybe in bringing to justice those behind the memoir plan he could live again.

At the same time, in his head, he was scouring through the memoirs that he and Clara had found. As he pondered the ramifications of the plan, he continued to become stuck on how it was to be carried out. He needed to know who was involved, and then connect the lines of the various pieces of information. Using aliases for the names he didn't know, he kept analysing the words of the memoirs until he could think no more.

In his head he also replayed what was most horrific for him in those moments. That it was he who had encouraged the escape. He who had told the men that under the prisoners of war had the right to attempt to escape and they are not to be punished if they were recaptured. That even though Japan was not a signatory to the Geneva Convention, they had recently agreed to honour the conventions. The lawyer in Martin felt confident that the men would be okay even if captured. But now the man in him was left stunned, speechless, and even more horrified as he tried to process if this, this war, was orchestrated by a secret faction.

His turmoil continued until his heartstrings pulled so tightly on him that his brain turned to mush.

This was when Fletcher's decapitated head fell to the ground and Martin's turmoil turned into a trance. All of a sudden it was like his soul was outside of his body. From his onlooking soul he saw himself frozen in horror. He saw the blood spewing from decapitation heads, and body fissures from where the bullets had stuck. Archie was stunned, but calm. Silence ruled the moment. Physically his heart was beating at an enormous pace, and his blood was boiling over, as he fought to restrain himself. losing the battle of restrain Martin leap to his feet and began to March towards Oishi. A March that was quickly halted by Archie, who silently moved Martin further away from the scene of executions.

"What are you doing Martin?" Archie asked as he continued to pull Martin away as silent as he could.

Martin was still in his trance and did not immediately respond to Archie. He pushed, shoved, and tussled with his friend in an effort to reach Oshi. Archie could see that his friend was not himself. He swiftly gripped Martin from behind. He arm was around Martin's next as he applied pressure. He continued to applied pressure to the throat of his friend until he could no longer move.

Resting Martin in a safe spot Archie watched over him until he awoke. Dazed but aware Martin asked, "Why did you stop me?"

"Because you were about to get us both killed." Replied Archie.

"I am sorry my friend. I didn't think of the consequences for you. I am not urge what came over me. The only thing I knew was that I had to do something, even if it meant death for me."

"I understand Martin. It has been difficult for you, possibly more so than me. I can't imagine the horrors that you must be fighting."

"Archie, I was ready to die. There is so much treachery going on around us that I couldn't bear it anymore. I can't tell you all of it. But I believe that there has been senseless death and destruction."

"War brings death and destruction Martin. That is what it is."

"Yes, but not when it is a contrived war for other reasons. Then it is just inhumane. Much like decapitating those men."

"I am not sure what you mean by contrived. But do you think that your death will make it better?"

"No but I don't see how I can make a difference by myself. It's hopeless Archie. We are all doomed. It may as well be sooner rather than later."

"That's not the Martin that I know. The Martin that believes there is good in the world. That he can make a difference even if a small difference, day by day. The Martin that became a lawyer to help others. Where is that Martin?" Archie asked.

"That Martin is gone. It is better to die now than face life in this unjust world."

"Martin! Martin! Snap out of it," Archie said as he slapped Martin across the face. "You have to fight on. There is much left for you to do."

"Archie, do you think I can actually make a difference? Do some gone with my life?"

"If anybody can it's you Martin. I have seen you get through the worst that life can throw at you and still fight on. Don't give up now! Your needed to help! There is much more for you do."

"Okay, Archie. I will give it my all again. I promise."

"You promise Martin, because you know I will hold you to your promises. A smiling Archie said jokingly.

"Yes, I promise. I was was lost for a time I guess, but I am back now."

"Are you sure you are back with us now? Or do I have to give you another nap?" Archie said with a smile that also brought Martin to a mild laugh.

"I am sorry to have put your life in danger. But yes I am back now."

"Okay good! Let's get moving before we are found." Archie replied as the two men lipped off into the darkness of the Changi forest.

***

In the pursuing days s E. B. Holmes, and his deputy, eventually gave in to the Japanese demands that each man sign a pledge not to try to escape. Initially the prisoners remained firm however as the days ensued Oishi became furious at the mass display of insubordination and ordered all prisoners, except three who had agreed to sign, to congregate in Selarang Barracks parade square. The men remained here without food, with little water available, and coupled with latrine pits, kitchens, and hospital beds crowded into an area of about a square kilometre. Dysentery broke out quickly, and the sick began to die. Realising that more would die needlessly Holmes, under duress, ordered his men to sign the pledge. After five days the men returned to their barracks, but the loss of life was telling. By the time the Selarang incident was over the number of prisoners who had been originally taken to Changi, six months earlier, now numbered less than half. Many had died of hunger and disease, some were slaughtered like animals alongside the Chinese, and many more had been taken to other destinations to be put to work as slaves.

Also by this time Martin and Archie were well on their way back to Britain.

25

Two things happened the night that Clara disappeared. One, Clara had a visitor. Two, Clara made an impulse decision.

Clara's visitor arrived shortly after Francis left for the evening. It was the night of 12 June 1942. There was nothing special about the night. A moonlit night with the typical warm, wet, and drizzly air that had that fresh just rained smell. Clara had just hugged Francis, and promised to meet him at their usual breakfast place in the morning, when she heard a familiar knock on her back door. George Dasch, who was making his way from Germany via a network of underground safe houses, clandestinely arrived at her door. Dash was one of eight saboteurs skilled in explosives, chemistry, and secret writing. The saboteurs, all trained at a secret location in Britain, were now on their way to different spots along the English coastline where German U-Boats would pick them up and take them to their final destinations. As Clara helped to prepare Dasch for the next leg of his journey, she learned the details of his mission.

Clara's impulse decision came when she heard that the saboteurs were on their way to strike a blow in America's war efforts. Dasch for no contrived reason held the detail about America to the last minute. In doing so he left Clara with little time to think. However, on learning that there were U-Boats heading to America her mind strobed with scenes from her past. Frozen as if blinded by a bright light she stood still as the scenes flashed repeatedly on a loop in her mind's eye.

The first scene that flashed in Clara's mind's eye was a childhood memory. When you are a child everything is different: trees are higher, colours are brighter, the days get more interesting as each one passes, and most importantly sometimes things happen that stay with you forever. We all have that childhood memory that is with us for life.

In vivid colour Clara's saw one of those lasting childhood memories. The day she first met Joseph had been with her ever since. Clara was five years old and living in 1923 Austria. The Great War had recently ended, and the country was spiralling out of control. Austria, once a powerhouse in Europe, had been reduced to a small struggling nation centre around Vienna. Unemployment was high, those that were able to find work did so for meagre wages, and housing was also difficult to find. The Austrians were resilient though, amid hyperinflation and their troubles, life continued. Clara's family survived on the sale of their fruit from a small store in the heart of Vienna. This store is where she first saw Joseph. The day was no different from any other day. Clara and her siblings ran through, around, and about the store as their parents sold their produce. On one of their infrequent breaks from romping around laughing, smiling, and oblivious to the economic struggles of the country Clara stood still. As she looked out the window pane of the store, into the vast white remnants of the snow storm the night before, she saw him. There were three of them Sloshing through the trample snow, but Clara's eyes were drawn to only one of them. The smallest of the three. He was a skinny, scrawny, boy, about the same age as her and dressed like a man in an all grey outfit. He was with his parents, he was Joseph, and this was Clara's first image of him. On seeing him, for some unknown reason, her face lit up with a gremlin grin. The two of them went on to see each other every week when Joseph's parents would come to buy fruit. However, her lasting childhood memory would be that first sighting on that winters day outside her parents' store.

The second scene was one that felt so real, as if she had witnessed it herself, but no, it was imaginary. It was a scene that she has had many times before, each time with the same result, and this time would be no different.

The sky's are a pasty collection of greys and gloom as sawn breaks on the horizon. Josef stands upon one of the many bridges of the Tower of London looking down into the slow-moving waters of the moat twenty feet below. Josef's wrist are bound with a cord, his hands behind his back.

The sky is a gloomy, pasty, collection of greys as dawn breaks on the horizon. Josef is atop a hill on the north side of the Tower of London. His wrists are bound with a cord, his hands behind his back, and he is sitting in a chair, blindfolded, with a black hood placed over his head. In a distance he can hear the slow-moving waters of the river Thames. In a strange way Josef, who was Clara's brave hero, was at peace with what was about to happen. Two sentries, soldiers of the British Royal Army, stand at each end of the public access to the hill, each with their rifles in the patrol position, that is to say, the muzzle end of the rifle is pointed towards the ground as the rifle is held horizontally across the chest. These men seemed unconcerned about what was going on atop the hill; they merely blockaded the two ends of the road given public access to the hill. Seeing the sentries in her vision always opened the flow of tears down Clara's cheeks. How could these men care so little about someone who meant so much to her? She would question.

On top of the hill a line of eight soldiers stood with their rifles aimed at a white cotton target, the size of a matchbox, pinned over Josef's heart. A lieutenant stood at the right of the line, he carried a sword, the point of which rested upon the ground, his left hand rested upon his right. The captain stood to the left with folded arms, silent, observing the work of his subordinates, but making no sign. Midway between the men and the Tower were the spectators - about a single company of soldiers in line, at parade rest, with the butts of their rifles on the ground, the barrels inclining slightly backward against the right shoulder, and their hands crossed. With the exception those at the centre of the proceedings, not a man moved. The company faced the Josef, staring stonily, motionless. The sentries, facing the public could have been easily confused with statues.

As the preparations completed the lieutenant raised his sword into the air and yelled, "READY". The eight men tightened their focus upon the target on Josef's heart. At this point in Clara's vision Josef replies, "Shoot straight, Tommies". Something Josef has said to her in jest many times before. Then almost in a single motion the lieutenant swooped his sword to the ground and yelled, "AIM," followed quickly by "FIRE." In a single volley, almost in unison, the men fired. Josef falls limp, his body lifeless. By this time in her vision Clara's tears that had begun to flow earlier are now gushing. But that's not all. This vision, which she has had before, makes her fiery angry again.

The third scene was the tipping point. With tears now gushing down her cheek, and anger in her heart, her mind's eye fleetingly turns to the night that she and Martin found the plan at Bletchley Park. She remembers cowering in the woods as men with guns hunted her. Only for a moment though before the scene in her head is over taken by the anger in heart. Anger drives her to imagine what she envisaged was the start of it all. Wild Bill and a group of men in a dusty room in America plotting to start the war.

After a few loops of these scenes Clara was fuming mad and blaming America for Josef's death. In anger Clara snapped out of her stasis and, as if possessed by something, she blurted out, "I am going with you!" Dasch did not argue with Clara as deep down he was actually hoping she would want to join the mission. No Dasch didn't argue, he simply replied, "welcome to the front", as he smiled broadly.

Just before dawn the two arrived in the coastal town of Hastings. The town's residents had mostly been evacuated following Luftwaffe air raids since the start of the war. Still just to be sure the Germans had targeted Hastings a few weeks earlier. On Sunday, May 23 1942, the bombing was relentless. It was the most devastating raid on the town to date. Many shops and buildings were destroyed, people were killed or injured, but most of all, they were now afraid. Nights, from dusk until dawn, were spent hunkered down in makeshift bomb shelters clearing the way for the costal activities that were taking place on a regular basis.

On arrival Clara watched the waves swirl, mesmerised, as if the movement of the water choreographed her thoughts. From the shore Dasch flashed a light in coded form. The sea returned a similar coded flash of a light- then it appeared. A submarine. It had emerged from the sea with the speed and impossibility of a stage illusion. One moment there was nothing and then it was there in front of them, ploughing through the sea toward the beach, its engine roaring, water streaking off its grey casing and churning white behind it as it moved along. The submarine had no markings, but Clara knew it wasn't English. The shape of the diving plane slashing horizontally through the conning tower and the tail rudder at the back moved the waves around feverishly. The waves broke around the rudder in the shallows, their foam crests becoming a chaotic lace over the dark blue seas. Clara shivered. She never thought a machine could actually emanate evil, but this one did. It was as dark, and as cold, as the water that lapped around it. It looked just like the bomb it had become.

Once inside the submarine Clara learnt more of the mission. There were two subs, ready to cross the Atlantic as, with Dasch now on board, all eight of the saboteurs had been picked up. Four saboteurs dropped off the coast of Long Island, New York and the other four of the coast of north eastern Florida. The sub with Clara and Dasch was heading for Long Island. However, after arriving in America the mission went awry.

Dasch a gifted, intelligent, man with an extraordinary memory struggled to maintain sameness in his life. This sameness was wildly interrupted through by his journey across the Atlantic. By the end of the journey Dasch, while eager to be in the fight, had become undone. Pain built in his brain like some sort of electrical headache, and the sensory overload was too much. His brain was feeling the need to explode, his nerves were frazzled, and he was shaking. So much so that once Clara, and the other saboteurs, was released from the sub onto Long Island Dasch beelined to the offices of the nearest F.B.I. offices. It wasn't long after this that Clara and the other saboteurs were being hunted. From the start of the hunt things moved quickly. One by one the saboteurs were picked up by the F.B.I.. What became of them after their capture was a mystery, but certainly nothing good.

When word of the F.B.I. scooping up the saboteurs reached Clara images of Josef's death seized control of her thoughts, her anger changed to fear, and her fear to a need for flight. So much for seeking those responsible for Josef's death, thought Clara as she began her journey to the America's west coast.

Drawing on her network of spies Clara fled to Blaine, Washington, where she would meet Satoshi Nomura inside Peace Arch park. Blaine was on the border between Canada and America, and Peace Arch park was at the northern tip of Blaine. The park got its name from the Peace Arch monument erected in the centre of the park to symbolise the long history of peace between two nations. The park was known for its serenity and the town for its easy access to Canada. Satoshi, a Japanese-American, and a spy, was much like Clara, he operated a safe house for German spies who he mainly helped to escape America into Canada.

Despite the submerged fear held by everyone on the west coast, following the Pearl Harbour attack, Peace Arch Park at noon was still a place for lovers. When Clara arrived at the park, every place to sit was taken by a couple gazing into one another's eyes or else laughing at a joke. Yet by a fountain stood, statue-like, a lonesome gent. His face was clean shaven and utterly serious. His eyes were hidden behind a pair of round sunglasses that mirrored the scene in front. He stood there every lunch-time, rain or shine, in case someone arrived with the code seeking his help. He dressed in scrubby corduroys and wore a well-used coat that spoke of impoverishment, but not destitute, much like most in the park. Although alone in a sea of couples the man almost belonged, but not quite.

When Clara approached Satoshi his wizened face peered out from under a wedge of blue hat. On seeing Clara, through eyes that were so heavily lidded and weighed down with wrinkled folds that it was almost like talking to someone asleep, Satoshi said "Are you lost?"

Clara had been expecting the croak of old age but Satoshi's voice was more like a sergeant major, strong and distinctly assertive, but strangely calm and inviting at the same time. She was shocked and stuttered once she was able to muster up the courage to speak. "Yes, what is the best way to get to the bus station?" She replied to Satoshi.

"You could walk, but it's a long walk, probably about ten blocks."

"That's fine, I could use the exercise."

With the spy words exchanged Satoshi knew that Clara was a German spy and it was safe to speak with her - to help her. As Satoshi suggested walking and said nothing about taking a taxi cab Clara also knew it was safe to continue to speak. Taxi was the abort word in case Satoshi was under surveillance.

Clara then told Satoshi of her journey from Bletchley, of Dasch's betrayal, that the saboteurs were probably all in the F.B.I.'s, and that she needed to flee America. They decided that she would travel back to Bletchley by convoy from Halifax. That night the two drove across the border into Canada, and Clara, with fake identity papers, was on her way back to Bletchley.

Months passed as Clara made her way across Canada. It wasn't until the 1st February 1943 that Clara arrived in Halifax and boarded the Pacific Enterprise, a British vessel. There were 51 ships in the convoy which sailed undisturbed by German U-Boats across the Atlantic. Elated, exhausted, and eager to see Francis Clara arrived in Liverpool on the morning of the 14th February 1943.

Arriving back in Bletchley that night brought a strange feeling of emptiness over Clara. Her emotions had been running high for almost a year. She journeyed to America with anger and hope in her heart as she sought to strike a blow against the American lead covert war. However, her emotions quickly turned: anger and hope to fear, and fear to nervousness as she journeyed on the Leerdam. With so much behind her, and now back in a familiar place, but with a failed mission added to her woes, Clara felt lost. She felt as if there was nothing that could be done to stop, of even expose, the Americans to the world. Nothing come be done to obtain justice. She felt empty and powerless yet still intent on not only revealing those behind the plan she found but also in obtaining justice for Josef who lost his life under false pretences.

In the morning she went to look for Francis at their usual breakfast spot. It had been a long time since she had seen him, and finding him there was a hopeful long shot. However she had to try anyway, but Francis never arrived for breakfast. There was no sight of him at his flat either. For days Clara repeated her routine search for Francis - first the breakfast location, outside of Bletchley Park hoping to catch a glimpse of him, and at his flat in the evening. Then, on the morning of the 1st March, as Clara made her daily walk to the break-fast location things changed. It was a rainy morning where the drops fell so hard on her umbrella that they practically drowned out any other sounds that could be heard. As Clara neared the hotel, and breakfast hall, two women walked in front of her heading to the hall as well. With the rain so loud Clara could hear them speak of friends of theirs that had travelled to America. She listened intently, as she knew the women to be co-workers of Francis, but could only gleam that a group of men from Bletchley Park had left for America less than a month prior, and had not returned as yet. Clara wanted to ask if Francis was one of the men but dared not out of fear of drawing attention to her relationship with him.

For now in Clara's mind Francis would remain as missing but with hopes that he, and Martin, may return to Bletchley one day.

26

F rancis was indeed one of the men from Bletchley Park that had travelled to America. A visit that was shrouded in mystery before Francis even set out to sea. Mystery that began nearly a year earlier in Rockefeller Junior's smoke filled room beneath the earth of his Cleveland mansion.

Not long after Junior, Hoover, and Wild Bill concluded their meeting there was another meeting held that night. Only Junior and Wild Bill were in this second meeting though.

As soon as Hoover had made his departure through one of the underground passageways of the mansion, Junior, began the second meeting.

"Now that Hoover has left let's talk about those British code breakers again." Junior said.

"Why all the mystery around the British code breakers?

"Is there some reason why Hoover couldn't be present?" Wild Bill asked as he looked over his shoulder to the doorway through which Hoover had just vanished?

"Quite frankly Hoover can be dangerous. He is a little too loyal and too ambitious. I worry that he might use the knowledge of what we need to do with the code breakers to his own gain. If he does anything out of step with us it would hurt our efforts. We could all be exposed."

"What is it that you think we need to do with the British code breakers?

"I thought we wanted them neutralised?"

"No, not just the three that discovered the plan you carelessly left lying around. We need the knowledge the gleaned in their code breaking centre in Bletchley. There is so much potential there beyond the war we started. The Brits are so caught up with the war that I don't think they have yet realised the potential of what they have. The science part of our plan needs that knowledge."

"So what are we going to do?" Asked Wild Bill.

"Roosevelt is a classmate of yours from Columbia Law; isn't he?" Asked Junior.

A somewhat confused and quizzical Wild Bill hesitantly replied "Yes."

"Ernest King has just been appointed Chief of Naval Operations, when Admiral Harold Stark stepped aside. Only a few months earlier, with that attack on Pearl Harbour, he was moved up to Commander in Chief of the United States Fleet. His star is rising and he is likely both influential and still very much ambitions.

"Roosevelt has also been pushing the Navy, he seems to have a soft spot for that outfit especially the ONI - Office of Naval Intelligence."

"Where are you going with this Junior?"

"Use your friendship with Roosevelt to plant in his head that the Brits are not sharing details about decoding the Enigma machine which could help with Naval operations. Once Roosevelt learns of this he will surely pass it on to King, and with King's ambition he will push the Brits to know more."

In a quick and decisive meeting Junior and Wild Bill set in motion plans to advance the science part of their plan. By November of that year, 1942, Francis and others were on their way to America to share details of how he cracked the Enigma machine. It would be Francis' second visit to America a country that he detested. A hatred that began several years earlier when he lived in New Jersey, where he was a graduate student in the Department of Mathematics at Princeton. A hatred that grew even more so when he decoded the plan and learnt that Americans were covertly behind the start of the war.

However, after a call from Roosevelt to Churchill, and an insistence from the American Navy that the Brits share details of their cryptography programme, Francis was summoned to a meeting in London. He had been to 10 Downing Street only once before when he had requested additional support for code breaking from Churchill. During his first visit to Number 10 he was welcomed as a future saviour of Britain. This time his visit was different though, this time Sir Stuart Menzies, the Head of Secret Intelligence Service, led the meeting and Francis felt more like a spy than a saviour when the meeting had concluded.

Sir Menzies was clearly a bitter man when it came to the subject of American code breaking. On seeing Francis Menzies quickly went into a rambling tirade about the Americans.

"The yanks have never been good at this stuff. When they entered the Great War back in seventeen they didn't have any experience at all. Over here though we were years ahead of them.

"They raced around trying to catch up then, and their doing the same thing now. They only began recruiting code breakers a few months before their Pearl Harbour and if you asked me it wasn't because they were concerned about the war going on over here. They were gearing up to steal our secrets is what I would say." Barked Sir Menzies.

Francis' senses went into overdrive on hearing Menzies mention stealing secrets. He knew that he had a few from his code breaking work, but more so he wondered if Menzies knew about the plan in Donovan's memoirs. Could Menzies be an ally that could help Martin, myself, and Clara he thought? Menzies actions and tone looked and sounded genuine, he was angry about this topic and it showed. What's coming next also ran through Francis' mind.

"The damn yanks can't even get it right amongst themselves. The Navy has their little team of code breakers and the army has another team. Wouldn't you think having one team sharing ideas and techniques like we have over hear would make more sense. How daft can they be over there in America?" Rhetorically exclaimed Menzies.

"Now their President has somehow convinced our Prime Minister to send you and a few folks from your code breaking team to America to help them out." Menzies told Francis.

That was when the penny dropped for Francis and he knew why he had been summoned to this meeting. "So what do I tell them he asked?" "Do you want me to tell them everything?"

"Everything?" asked Menzies.

"Yes, I have developed a code breaking technique that can decipher strategic messages; well almost any enciphered message. The technique works on messages encoded by the Lorenz cipher machine. It's a complex technique that has already helped to decipher important German strategic message."

When Menzies said not to share his latest work with the American Francis began to think that maybe he too was involved in the covert plan that Martin and Clara had found. Why else would he not want the Americans to be able to decipher messages or words that were of strategic importance? Did he know that the technique could be used to decipher the coded words in the plan, Francis queried to himself. He wanted to know why not, but was fearful of asking such a man to explain himself.

However, in a burst of courage or stupidity, he rushed in and blurted out, "Why?"

To his dismay the question didn't faze Menzies at all. He was forthright and even calmer in his reply than he had been when he first began to speak.

"I don't trust the yanks. They have some sort of competition going on between their army and their navy with all this stuff. They just don't seem to be coordinated and in control. Strong chance that there might be leaks so let's keep the latest stuff to ourselves, okay?"

America was detestable to Francis. He had lived in New Jersey some years earlier when he attended Princeton, and did not develop a pleasurable taste for the country. His second visit wasn't to be much different.

Francis arrived in Washington D.C. on a cold winter day in mid-November 1942. It was the sort of cold winter that felt as if your blood could freeze. There was no fanfare for Francis when he arrived, but there was Claude who over the next four months was there with Francis as his emotions ran the rapids. There were times of calm waters, times when things looked so dire that death felt certain, and times when Francis almost burst with excitement.

At first the waters that he found himself in were calm, and Francis endured. Limiting what he said helped little, and his days were painfully routine. Much like the ship that he sailed on to America he talked of his exploits in code breaking to those that they propped up in front of him. Calm on the surface with so many deep undercurrents of thoughts, all of them with their own purpose. All of them setting the stage for the rapids that were to come. His nights were very much the same as his days - painfully calm. He spent his nights pondering the threads that bond the covert American plan to start, and benefit from, a war with the thousands he saw daily unwittingly fevering away with patriotic pride. Often thinking to himself about the origins of goodness and what "humanity" really meant in these times. All the while, willing to give up an eternity of code breaking progress, to simply solve the great mystery behind Donovan's memoirs.

For Francis his stay in America took a turn of events when he felt that he was facing certain death. It was at a Christmas function for the code breakers when Francis' amygdala kicked his body into high gear. There is a region of the brain dedicated to detecting how much something stands out to us. A threat stimulus, such as the sight of a predator, triggers a fear response in the amygdala, which prepares our motor functions for fight or flight. It also triggers the release of stress hormones.

During the Christmas function Francis' stress level spiked, and his fight-or-flight reaction oscillated on seeing one of the guest at the function.

The function started as the typical Christmas shindig. Claude, who seemed to know everyone, promenaded Francis around the room, introducing, and showing him off, to dignitaries and academics. What triggered Francis' was the way that they looked him when he was introduced. Watson, Kellogg, Donovan "Wild Bill", and Rockefeller Junior looked at Francis as if he was a Christmas turkey that they will be consuming later that evening. Junior wanted him silenced out of his own fears of what Francis might know, while Kellogg and Watson saw him as a "cash cow" full of ideas from which they will grow their business wealth?

On hearing the name Rockefeller Francis became trans like. Rockefeller was one of the names that he had encoded from the memoirs. Now he is here with Donovan, covered in secrecy, and full of code breakers caused his amygdala to trigger a flight response. These men were predators to him. Inside him his brain began to move at what seemed like a hundred times it normal speed, but outside his head the world and everything in it was frozen. He could hear his brain tick. His eyes were darting around the room, over and over, until they came to rest on a door. The world was suddenly alive again, and Francis took flight.

The door led to the bathroom and the bathroom to a small window through which Francis climbed. In the snow covered garden he stood, without an over coat, but his adrenaline filled body wasn't cold. No, he was in full flight mode, death felt certain, and he was on high alert. There were people mingling about, mostly women, code-breakers. However, in the sea of women two men hurried to the fore. He wasn't certain but could swear he had seen these men in Bletchley.

Francis began to run, and the men began to chase. He'd been chased before by those seeking to expose his secret desires, but this was different. He ran fast to escape the eyes of these two men. In these moments running, his brain was on speed-mode - ultra focused on the escape. The two men ran fast to try to catch up with Francis. Their intentions unknown, but they pursued, and he fled. Once clear of their eyesight Francis hid, a doorway off an alley to the rear of building made for good refuge. The two men searched about for him at the end of the alley. Francis could hear them moving about and knew they will be in the alley way next. So as soon as they had passed Francis move quickly. First to the rear of the building, and then lodge in a group of men leaving the function, he made his way back to his room where he remained frighten, and on high alert, until the next day.

Inside the hall the Christmas function continued, as did the search for Francis. This time it was Claude that searched for him though. As for the two men that chased Francis, they returned to the function and beelined to Wild Bill. In the huddle the three men Davis and Delaney - the two F.B.I. agents - plus Wild Bill whispered before Wild Bill called Junior over. As Junior approached Davis and Delaney, with heads held low like kids scalded and sent to their rooms, walked away briskly.

"What was that about?" asked Junior.

"Davis and Delaney thought now would be the opportune time to take the British code breakers out. They saw his reaction to meeting you and wanted to get ahead of things. They didn't want him saying anything. Fortunately they didn't hurt him. He managed to evade them, and I assume return to him."

"I have given them a right scalding."

"Good, as we can't have anything happen to him that leads to more questions. Especially not on American soil."

"I have sent them back to Bletchley to keep an eye on things. The right opportunity will present itself and I want them there and ready."

"Okay, keep me informed."

Francis, in his room, in total darkness, was pacing. The usefulness of his thoughts had long evaporated but his mind was still churning out of control like a runaway train. He was sure that this had to be the same Rockefeller from the plan in Donovan's memoirs. But were they? Then there were the two men that chased him. Had he seen them in Bletchley? Were they chasing him? Or was it his mind playing tricks on him?

His amygdala was still engaged and his adrenaline infused body could not be motionless. Then there was the not on the door that sent everything into hyper speed. Only to be slowed when he heard a familiar voice.

"Francis, it's Claude, are you in there?" sounded the familiar voice.

"I have your overcoat open up." Claude continued.

Francis slowly opened the door and ushered Claude into his room. He then paused at the doorway, leant over the threshold. His eyes scanned the hallway in all directions before he closed the door and turned his attention to Claude.

"What happened? Why did you leave so abruptly?" Claude immediately asked.

Francis, sworn to secrecy by British intelligence, and vigilant about almost everything else wanted to diffuse things with Claude. However, he was feeling alone, confused, and overwhelmed by the immensity of the burdens he was carrying. Yet, still, he managed to restrain he urge to unload all that he knew.

Instead he simply replied, "it was nothing I got confused about a few things and needed to leave, to clear my head. Thank you for returning my overcoat."

Claude, an astute mathematician, knew there was more to the story but did not push the issue. He appealed to Francis' intellect instead and replied:

"Confusion a conflict between your conscious and subconscious understanding of events.

"Confusion comes when your conscious brain isn't able to process the narrative that you have, but subconsciously you are able to process the narrative.

"My suggestion is to take it slowly. Give it time. Step away from what is confusing you. Clarity will come with patience and time. Wisdom is often slow to develop, like a photograph. It will all be clear in the fullness of time."

In those few words Francis found both the security he needed to move on from the events of that evening, as well as a friend. He knew Claude suspected much more but respected Francis enough not to pry. This gesture of support without compromise was endearing to Francis.

That gesture began a conversation that evening which lasted for hours. The men began talking about confusion and how the brain worked, but ended, hours later, talking about building an electronic brain. This conversation was one of many that excited Francis over the following months of his time in America. He continued to look over his shoulder for danger, but mostly from that night onwards he remained excited about the possibility of using his code breaking techniques to build an electronic brain. His excitement was so much so that at times he felt as though he would burst. His visit to America was indeed a good visit in Francis' eyes.

It was also a good visit in the eyes of Watson, Kellogg, Donovan "Wild Bill", and Rockefeller Junior who extracted every bit of information they could out of Claude, their covert operative assigned to befriend Francis. To learn all for these American business giants.

Francis arrived back in Bletchley on 14 March 1943, two weeks after Clara's return. He quickly fell back into his old routines. To his amazement, and joy, he also fell back in the company of his old friend. Clara had remain vigilant and dedicated to knowing Francis' whereabouts. She visited their breakfast spot daily and circled about Bletchley Park often. Then one week to the day after his return to Bletchley she found him, there he was just sitting in their usual spot. Francis had returned, and the two had so much to catch up on.

They embraced and began their journey to unveiling a sinister American plot. Still missing one of their travelling partners the pair was ready to get back to work.

27

The mountains of the Swiss Alps is where Junior had chosen to bring all of them together for the first time in over a decade. The Black Dragon, the Illuminati, the Skull and Bones Society, and the Franklin Society all under the same roof again. The shared vision created by the secret societies, when they met in Paris for their inaugural meeting, was falling apart and all the parties needed to meet, even those that were not members of The Commission.

Gathered together were the who's who of secrecy and power: the money brokers were W.K. Kellogg, Thomas Watson, and Junior. The other Commission members: Tōjō, Wild Bill, and Goebbels, were also there along with Charles Davenport.

The eugenics activities had grown out of control, especially in Germany where it had become an obsession for Hitler. It was made worst by Davenport prodding and poking around the edges of every global conversation about it. Most of the other scientists in the fold had stopped supporting eugenics due to the rise of Nazism in Germany, but Davenport remained a fervent supporter. Junior had even seen to his funding at the Carnegie Institute being pulled, but this did not slow Davenport down. No not one little bit of a hesitation created in Davenport. As such Junior now feared that it won't be long before somehow this was all linked to him and his supporters.

On August 15, 1942, the men gathered together in the sleepy village of Zermatt, in the Western Alps' Canton of Valais. A beautiful village and a far cry from the hot and humid Changi forest where Martin was being held captive.

Late summer was beautiful in the Alps. For as far as the eye could see peaks in all shades of brown, some capped with white, rose majestically from the green pastures. Although Switzerland was neutral, and Zermatt was high in the mountains, most who would normally be resident there had vacated the area in fear. German was largely spoken Valais, and those that fled were scared that German troops may visit the area for refuge.

Mont Cervin was the only hotel that remained open so this is where Junior decided to meet.

The stated intention of the meeting was to discuss the eugenics activities.

However, for Junior, it was just another step in the dismantling of The Commission. To the others, like Kellogg and Watson, it was another step towards repatriation of the world's best scientists to America. It was also, for these money brokers, another move towards their economic and political control over the affairs of the world.

Following an elegant dining experience, and a lull in the chatter, the men looked to Junior to take the next step. With an initial cough to attract attention Junior said: "So, to business?" He made sure to catch the eye of each man at the table to secure their agreement before speaking again.

Junior explained that Hitler's Nazis had taken eugenics too far into the public eye. That under Hitler's instructions eugenics had become the scorn of the world's leaders. That it was now not good for business, not good for the world, and definitely not good for those in the room. Tōjō even spoke up and said that he feared that Oishi may be going too far and is becoming unstoppable in his mass executions in Singapore. Word was spreading and others in the Japanese Imperial Army were beginning to follow Oishi. The suggestion was to end everything to do with eugenics and allow Hitler to be its only champion. However Davenport, now seventy-seven years of age, and obviously sickly, had made eugenics his life's endeavour and was not willing to stop advocating it at this point in time. All the men became infuriated with Davenport. He could ruin it for all of them.

Kellogg was the one that couldn't contain himself, after all he had the most to lose if this, this Davenport debacle, could not be fixed. He had swallowed his anger months ago, starting when it was a fire-seed, and forgot to drink something cool. Now it had grown in his belly and was racing to come out as hot as any dragon has ever flamed. On whom the men did not know, but it was clear that he had activated his emotional indifference. There was anger in his eyes, anger that said he could kill and not care one bit. So back off.

When we see something that frightens us, a primitive part of the brain is activated to produce aggression. It is fear that brings anger and turns it into rage, a biological button better left alone. It was too late though, Kellogg's rage button had been pressed, that hot burning anger inside of him had led him to seek to harm, to take decisive action.

"Davenport, my dear man, would you care for another brandy?" Kellogg asked.

Kellogg fearing Davenport's rejection of abandoning eugenics from the moment they were all summoned to Valais had taken steps to end this once and for all. His plan was to drive Davenport's heart over a cliff. For months he had cured digitoxin from his foxglove plants for just this eventuality.

Davenport who was known to be arrogant, noticed Kellogg's rage, but could not fathom that such a man would attack him himself. No Kellogg was the kind of man that would have someone do this type of deed for him, thought Davenport. On accepting Kellogg's offer of another brandy he had sealed his fate. The drink was spiked, and within minutes after a few sips Davenport, to no surprise of the others, fell to the floor in pain. As he laid there holding his chest the men began to contemplate and plan their next moves. Davenport would be dead soon but he could not simply disappear. Uncomfortable questions would be asked and they would be found out. Davenport's death needed to be confirmed as natural causes by a medical professional, and they were ready to make this happen. Then ... Then to their horror they noticed a couple at the window of the dining room. The couple had seen it all.

Wild Bill quickly rushed out of the room to retrieve the couple. At gun point a young man and his wife were brought into the room with the men. Farmers returning from a day of milking their cows it seemed. The men acted quickly from this point. Junior called the local ambulance service for Davenport, while Kellogg and Watson piled the couple, and their milk, into a nearby truck before driving away into the night.

The doctor tending to Davenport pronounced him dead shortly after arriving at the scene. In the days to come his death would be recorded as complications resulting from pneumonia. Heart failure was not an unexpected consequence of pneumonia.

That evening high in the mountains of the Western Alps, were snow still covered the ground, Kellogg and Watson disposed of the bodies of the two farmers. Wild Bill carried out his duties as instructed. His duties? Capture the burial in photographs just in case. The two men buried the bodies in a pool of water at the bottom of a ravine, that was sure to freeze overcome winter, concealing the bodies in what might later be thought to be a mountain accident. The couple simply disappeared that day. The whole burial captured in film.

After Davenport's death, Junior used the activities of that evening to formally disband The Commission. The world was in disarray and the foundation was laid for the dominance that he sought. In a secret meeting, with only those who had attended the inaugural meeting, he announced that given the state of things we had better disband. The other men were in agreement. However, Goebbels did say that the Bletchley trio needed to disappear like Davenport and the farmers.

Junior agreed that he would handle the disappearance of the Bletchley three. After all, he had already decided this with Hoover and Wild Bill. Goebbels and Tōjō would also be silenced in Junior's plan.

At this point all the men, that met on that fateful day, only some weeks before the Selarang exterminations, went their separate ways never to meet again. They had a secret that would bind them beyond the days of The Commission. For Junior the added protection of photographs of Kellogg and Watson disposing of the bodies would be useful leverage one day.

On his return to America Junior was pleased to see that the military draft was in full swing. America's once meagre military forces were now in the millions, and continuing to grow. Factories were also in full production mode. This definitely pleased Junior. Not only had his personal wealth grown through his intricate financing of war bonds, but also, as America's military might grew stronger, the world was starting to revere the country. America a country that was decimated by their participation in the Great War, and an economic depression, was quickly becoming the epicentre of world power.

Junior now only needed to ensure that this power continued, and that his wealth grew even more. Not surprisingly he had a plan to ensure that these things were accomplished.

In Bletchley news of the fall of Singapore had long reached Francis and Clara. They feared for Martin's life. Had he been captured or killed? So many men returning to Britain spoke of dysentery and illness has this befallen Martin? It was a difficult time for Martin's Bletchley accomplices but life had to go on. A difficult time made even worse when Clara mysteriously disappeared in the night.

Francis first became concerned about Clara when she didn't show up to have breakfast with him as they had done almost every day since Martin left. As he waited in the breakfast hall of the Bull Commercial Hotel, his concern grew ever intensely. His concern changed to fear when he went to her house to check on her. Having spent the previous evening with Clara reviewing the memoirs for clues about the coded parts or the authors he was fiercely disturbed to find her home abandoned. Everything was composed in a way that he did not expect. Tidied from the night before. Not rumpled and in a disarray. Francis thought for sure that her home would show signs of her being taken, if she had been taken. So he concluded that she had not been taken by someone. No she appeared to pack neatly and leave, as if she planned a long journey. Why she didn't tell him about leaving Francis didn't know. But as disturbed, and fearful, as he was, he was also hopeful that she was well. However now he was alone in Bletchley.

With his Bletchley associates gone Francis continued to work on decrypting German naval communications. Many at the cryptanalysis unit that he headed had been stomped by the complex communications used by the Germans - but not Francis. His success in decrypting the naval enigma messages was helping to direct allied convoys away from the U-boat 'wolf-packs'. However, decrypting the coded sections of the Donovan's memoirs had continued to elude Francis. It wasn't until one month later, July 1942, that he inadvertently had a breakthrough.

In July 1942, with Martin missing in action, and Clara's where-abouts unknown, Francis completed his development of a code breaking technique that was able to decipher messages encrypted with the 'Lorenz' cipher machine. A machine used to encrypt German strategic messages of high importance. Breaking this code not only allowed his code breaking team to decipher strategic German communications but also by a stroke of chance he was able to decipher the coded sections of Donovan's memoirs with this same technique. He now knew all, but did not know who to trust nor what to do with this information. If only Martin and Clara were here to help he often thought as he continued his daily life trying to contain this new found knowledge within him.

***

In Singapore Martin and Archie were recaptured fifteen miles from Selarang and taken to Seletar, a base in the north that was once occupied by the British navy but was now under the control of the Japanese. When captured, to their surprise they were not alone, they were loaded onto a truck with other soldiers. Stragglers that evaded capture when the Japanese took over Malay.

At Seletar the soldiers were unloaded from trucks and lined up. Then, from a stage, a Japanese officer in very good Eng-lish told them that they were to be under the control of the Japanese Navy. That if they did not obey them they would be punished, and if they tried to escape, they would be executed! Fortunately for them the Japanese did not have good records of prisoners and they were thought to be captured for the first time.

Over the next several months Martin and Archie remained prisoners of the Japanese Navy. During this time they were put to work on a multitude of jobs, but generally they were still better off than those prisoners working on the railway. Forty plus prisoners were always supervised by a dozen or so Japanese navy soldiers. As prisoners Martin and Archie first repaired a river boat captured from the Chinese. They also completed several other jobs, including the building of an airstrip. However it was the river boat, the HMS Siang Wo, that held the most significance as, once repaired, it became their new prison.

For months their daily routine consistent of Tenko, or roll-call, where they had to line up and number off or by counted by the Japanese. Immediately following Tenko they took turns rowing ashore. At night they were given a small bag of weevil ridden rice and a bag of peas. They could also fish but there are not many fish in the Johor Straits. After some months malnutrition started to affect the men. Most had an illness of some sort; beri- beri, dengue fever, malaria, dysentery plus a lot of skin ailments. It was these illnesses that allowed Martin and Archie to escape the Japanese for a second time. One of the Japs that held them captive was older than the others, kinder as well. His name was Hinata, and he befriended Martin and Archie. It began with him given them cigarettes for English-speaking lessons and grew to the point where Hinata helped them to escape. One evening Martin, Archie, and other prisoners, were being transferred to another prison with better hygiene. The new prison was Loyang, another former Royal Naval Base, with shower facilities and a chance for better food. Hinata knowing that this would be the only time for the men to escape, and not be noticed, allowed Martin and Archie to disappear into the woods as the others were loaded on trucks. There were no records kept of prisoners and Hinata would just tell the new captures a different number for Tenko.

That night Martin and Archie headed east to the coast and were rescued by a merchant ship, the SS Bedford. They were immediately set to work cleaning the ship before it took on 2,500 women and children in Java. The Japanese bombed many of the ships in the wharf at Java, but lucky for them they did not get hit. They received a few shocks though.

After a day or so in Java they set off for Colombo. They arrived in Colombo and had a few days there, before setting sail for Durban, South Africa. After Durban they called into Cape Town and then left for Britain.

Not all the women and children had cabins; some had to sleep in the troop sections. The crew generally felt sorry for those that had to sleep amongst them. It was boiling and sticky, and there was very little privacy, so the crew tried to make things as easy as possible for them. They took them drinks and sweets, and mingled with them on deck whenever it was possible. They played games and found other ways to help because it was no fun for the children. The situation became better after Durban as some families stayed behind which made the rest of the journey easier for the rest.

Other than the bombing at Java it was as safe a journey as could have been under the circumstances. However, the dangerous part of the journey, out into the Atlantic where there was a heavy U-Boat presence, was yet to come. So on leaving Cape Town they increased speed and had lookouts everywhere. They did this and still kept their passengers entertained. There wasn't a submarine attack, but the weather did become welcomely cooler, and the seas got a little bit rougher, as they sailed north, near the coast of Britain.

Throughout his journey Martin's resolve grew stronger and stronger. With a renewed vigour, and his promise to Archie to fight on, he was ready, anxious, to return to Bletchley. Here he would make them pay. Whoever they were behind the plan in Donovan's memoirs. He had seen enough. Been through enough. It was time to find them, expose them, kill them if necessary.

Both men were anxious to get home. Martin to seek justice. Also they had learnt as in Durban that they had been posted by the military as 'dead'. Martin feared what his parents must be going with the thought of his death. Archie knew that his village must be beyond itself. They had lost others to war before, it was expected, and they were brave people, but Archie was a folk hero. Revered by his fellow villagers.

As they sailed up the river Mersey and saw the 'Liver Birds', tears came to their eyes. There were crowds of people, flags flying, and bands playing. The Red Cross people took both men home, each arriving to streets lined with a banner saying "Welcome Home". On Martin's street there was not a soul in sight. However, as he got out of the car, out of nowhere came a mob of people, his father came out first, then his mother, his sister and his brother, neighbours even joined in, and everyone was crying. That was it, he would be home for good now!

28

Waking up is a transition from the world of dreams into the day. It is good to take a little time to allow the transition to be made gracefully, as such moments of transition allow us to ponder the messages of our dreams, to weave them into the realities of our lives, and feel ready to take on the day ahead. Martin, though, awoke suddenly as if his one button had been pushed. Sailing up the river Mersey, 'Liver Birds', the crowds, and banners had invoked emotions held deep inside him. However, as his brain adjusted to the day's reality, the fanfare of his return from captivity quickly vanished into a memory. The noises of the day were in full swing. His eyes took in every ray of light. Every thought was in high definition.

He knew the war raged on and, that national service was still enforced. He also knew that he had no desire to return to battle. In his mind he was home for good, but he must now make his desires a reality. He raised his heavy eyelids half way only for them to fall shut. He raised them again and swung his bare feet to the cold carpet. They room was damp; rain fell to the roof, the ground outside, and splattered against the window. From a carousel of what was once random ideas came some order, a strong awareness of who he was under a flow of thoughts loosely connected to his waking life. The tasks that lay ahead formed and demanded that Martin think about them, find solutions, and get results under seemingly impossible conditions. He was now awake and there was no retreat. Dressed and fed, in a fraction of the time it usually takes to get into his full dress uniform, he left without a thought of taking a warm hat or gloves.

The time to get from Martin's parents' home in Mayfair to Whitehall seemed instantaneous. Martin's mind was awash in thoughts, adrenaline was pumping through his body, making the rain soaked ground less than a minor inconvenience. He was focused and ready. He was also stressed. He was on a collision course. He was never getting out of the army without first getting past his briefing, and his interrogators were not going to make things easy for him. It would all play out, in the hollows beneath Whitehall, in the days, maybe weeks, to come.

The General poured over the mission report for the hundredth time and found nothing that could have been done differently, at least not by Martin and his officers. They were in a heavily fortified location, they were without full intelligence reports on the Japanese forces in the area, and they were carefully measured in their defence of the island. Yet they suffered the greatest military loss in British history. Commonwealth troops were captured and remained in captivity. Their commanding officer was here though, free. What did he do? Did he share any vital information with the Japanese about the Allied forces in the area? He didn't know but was determined to get answers. Martin's head as well, if that resulted from his debriefing.

The Admiral, and the Air Marshall, watched Martin pacing back and forth in the hallway adjacent to the briefing room. There's a manned desk at one end of the hallway, a steel door with a wire-meshed glass window at the other end. They had studied him closely. Beads of sweat adorned his forehead as he paced. They counted the twelve strides he takes before he turns and retraces his steps. Martin's lips were moving as he paced, probably rehearsing his response to questions. However, he was clueless about how hard they're going to go at him.

Over their shoulders they glanced back into the interrogation room. A bright beam of light bathes the wooden chair where Martin will sit, where he will soon be squirming. The poor bastard doesn't stand a chance, they thought. They decided to give him a few more minutes to stress out before they ushered him in.

Eventually, dry and stoic in the face of what was to come Martin entered the briefing room inside Whitehall, snapped to attention, and announced himself.

"At ease Lieutenant-Colonel Frost. Take a seat." Came a voice from the room.

"My name is General Watlington. I'm am leading the review of the fall of Singapore.

"I will be the individual that will mess with your mind, paint you into a corner, and get to the truth of what really happened on that island.

"To my left is Admiral Jameson. He will be looking at what happened from the Navy's perspective. To my right is Air Marshall Smith, his fly guys had a small role to plan in the Singapore fight and he wants to understand why.

"As you know we are getting ready to launch another offensive in the Pacific Theatre and what we learn from you could be very helpful to our efforts.

"Also I know that a prisoner of war has a duty to try and escape, but you are here and your men are still in captivity. I don't like that, and you're going to find that I can be a really bad guy when I don't like something."

General Watlington then pressed a buzzer on the wall behind him. Two privates in service dress led Archie into the briefing room. The men in the room watched as Archie looked around at the surroundings. Martin sat in silence as Archie is left standing and thinking for several minutes as the white noise blasted into the room, and took its toll on Archie. They watched him rub the palms of his hands against his pants and then reach up and tug at his shirt collar. He was nervous and ready to be taken down. General Watlington led the briefing again.

"You know Martin here don't you Archie?" He said.

"Our paths have crossed, Hi Martin." he said jovially.

Martin's eyes widened. "Archie?. What're you doing here? I thought you went home and would be in Braemar with your family."

"I did, and now I am here. Only two of us made it out and they wanted to look into the whites of our eyes at the same time I guess."

"General Watlington," says Archie. "Why am I in this room? Surely you know we followed everything to the book." Still jovial he tries to laugh but a sinister cackle comes out instead. He was so nervous.

"Archie," the General said calmly, sitting down beside him, "How is you son doing? Still in captivity in Singapore?"

"I don't know and yes, he is still in Singapore I guess."

"Do you think the Japanese are up to their same tactics? Have they figured out that he is your son?"

"Uh huh, where is this going General?"

Admiral Jameson could sense the tension was getting high. He poured ice water into two glasses and slid them towards Martin and Archie.

"You know, they say that Dunkirk was our finest hour in the war so far."

"We were horribly defeated but the way we rallied together to get our boys home was seen as a heroic victory. That was some fight, but we fought, and we fought with honour."

"Yeah," Archie said, taking a sip of water and leaning back, relaxing in his chair.

"And you fought in Dunkirk didn't you Martin? Asked General Watlington.

Martin nodded. "Yes, I was there."

"You got a promotion after that and in fact it led to you getting the Singapore command didn't it?"

"Sure did, but what of it?"

In the silence that followed Martin's question both Archie and Martin intuitively knew what was happening. The men had been in battle together and could sense when danger was near. They looked at each other, their eyes said it all. Britain had seen its worst defeat of the war and heads needed to roll for this one. Their heads!

With their exchange of looks General Watlington knew that he had brought Archie and Martin into the zone where he needed them. He too sat back, sipped his water and then slowly wiped his hands across his lips. He looked them both square in the eyes.

"Yes, that's right. We think you were arrogant and negligent. That your poor leadership led to the fall of one of our strongest outposts, and set back our offensive in Asia. And by you I mean both of you.

"Yes! we're going for your heads.

"You are both going to spend the rest of this war, and maybe years after, in the stockades."

"Horrible news, eh?" Air Marshall Smith said.

"Yeah, horrible," echoed the Admiral.

"Well that is not going to happen, we did nothing wrong." Martin and Archie said almost in unison.

The duel was set. The General, Admiral, and Air Marshall had laid down the gauntlet. Martin and Archie had picked it up. Whitehall was the location, and the stakes were high. In the eyes of the trio, the interrogators, the possible outcomes of battle were: the stockades, an honourable discharge, a dishonourable discharge, or a return to active duty. For Martin the battle held another possible outcome that was somewhat different.

Martin's days were spent, with Archie close by, under the bright light of interrogation. For weeks Martin found himself in captivity again as he, and Archie, where remanded to the Wellington barracks when they were not being debriefed. All the while he was forced to relive the events of his most demoralising days in the armed forces. Events that triggered emotions, triggered the darkest days of his captivity, triggered panic and terror in every ounce of his being.

There were days his head just didn't work, when it was like trying to run through water. Days he tried hard to focus. Days his brain would fog up and his thoughts would go nowhere. Maybe it was nature's anaesthesia, maybe not, but the fog numbed the pain, wiped out the trauma, and eased his pain.

Then there were days of absolute clarity, moments when he could see every detail and feel every feeling.

Martin's nights were spent alone and confused. At night in his viscera, muscles, and nerves there was terror. The self-doubt about his command in Singapore, the fear and flashbacks of the torture he endured at the hands of the Japanese would wake an incendiary terror. It was unnatural for his organisms to endure and survive these things. Night after night the panic attacks came, each time his brain would send messages of fear to the upper brain. His thoughts would become scattered, and normal functioning would be impossible. Whispering words of comfort to himself was his only refuge. He would say, "I am okay. I am strong. These fears will pass." These whispered words slowed those messages of fear that his brain received. It gave his higher brain a chance to become focused and functional once more. It put him back in the driver's seat of his own brain.

As the briefings continued Martin outwardly remained stoic and calm. Inwardly a whirlwind rose out of his body day after day, night after night, and blinded his eyes. Deafened his ears. Then as suddenly as it began, it was over. Both men were allowed to return to active duty. They were vindicated and given a week of leave. Archie returned to his family in Braemar, Martin to his family in Mayfair. However, Martin was not a whole man. He was broken. He no longer wanted to be out of the army, but instead, he now needed to be out of the army, as his inner panic and fear continued. Panic and fear that would be there until the army was in his rear view.

In matters of the heart and head Martin turned to his mother. Throughout his childhood Martin's mother, Jennifer Frost, was his task master, mission maker, and decider of everyone's general direction in life. She organised the chores, the school work, and the fun, like a caring and nurturing army drill sergeant. Martin's father did nothing but work; work at his job, work at being a leader in the armed forces, and work at building his network of influence. Once in a while he would smile or laugh - and when he did the world brightened for those precious moments - then he would sink back down into his world. In matters of war and work Martin turned to his father. As he did when anger about the Nazis attacks in the Atlantic and the skies made the war look all but lost and he wanted to do more.

Together his mother and father were an unstoppable force. They each had their separate roles in Martin's life. However, on this occasion flashbacks and fear about war troubled his heart and head. On this occasion Martin needed both is mother and father. So on the night of his vindication he brought them both together.

Surrounded by the tall walls, and ancient volumes, of the library in the Frost family manor Martin poured his heart out. He told his parents about what he endured in captivity, how he now questioned himself. The flashbacks to war and captivity were so real and vivid for him as he spoke. At first he was strong, unemotional, but then there was sadness, anger and fear as he spoke. As he shed layers of pain in waves of emotions. Little waves at first, then emotions that were so strong that he felt swept away. His eyes watered from the moment he spoke, but as he endured wave after wave of emotion the tears slowly began to flow. Before long he had given way to all out crying, and his parents buttressed him both physically and emotionally. It was a bound that he had not shared with his parents as a man, a bound that he had longed for over the years. With this support Martin had renewed vigour. The household, including even his sister Anne, returned to normalcy and the family flew into action.

His father had used his influence in the legal circles to get Martin a hearing in front of the panel that heard applications for medical discharge from the army. While Anne and his mother prepared Martin. Two days into his leave he was able to fight again. Although his struggles were not fully settled, he stood in front of that military panel strong, certain, and without fear as he convinced them to grant him an honourable discharge for medical reasons. The outcome that he always knew was a possibility. The outcome that the interrogation trio did not consider.

With that appearance before the panel Martin had not only renewed his zest for the law but also transported his mind to that night in Bletchley Park when he found the plan in Donovan's memoirs plan, and revived his interest in bringing to justice those behind the war. Those behind the trauma and tragedy experienced by millions around the world. Trauma and tragedy such as what he had and his family had experienced. Unnecessary trauma and tragedy. For Martin his struggles, and his search for these unscrupulous people, had aligned. The search had become deeply personal.

On the third day of his leave, the first day of his new life outside of the army, Martin awoke after one of the best sleeps he had had in years. Outside the Frost Mayfair manor the ground was still very much an obstacle course of rubble from the Nazis air rails, but inside, inside Martin, there was calm, clarity, but with a sense of urgency. Martin was ready to return to Bletchley to see Clara and Francis, to get to the bottom of that document, that plan. But first he needed to get to Oxford.

There wasn't a cloud in the grey and gloomy sky when Martin arrived in Oxford. To his liking, though, the rain had subsided from the day before and, but for a bit of a chill in the air, it was a good day to return to his alma mater. Moving about the city was like stepping back in time, before the war had begun. Before the streets of many towns had become obstacle courses with rumble from bomb blasted buildings everywhere. Not in Oxford though as Oxford was one of the few areas in Britain that had been spared from the bombs that rained over the country at the outset of the war, and even thereafter. Some said that Oxford was being spared as this city was where Hitler intended to have his headquarters once he had completed his invasion of Britain. Whatever the reason it was a good day as Martin made his way through the rumble free streets and directly to the Frewin Hall debating chambers.

It had been almost a decade since he was last inside the hall, but he knew if he was to find his brother Thomas then this would be the place. Thomas was a mathematics major and a keen debater who joined the Oxford Union on his arrival and never looked back. Sure enough from the second-story balcony of the chambers he saw his brother below engrossed in the back and forth of hotly contested the debate about the value of the war. On one side of the debate was the argument that millions ought not to be subjected to living in fear of tyranny. On the other side of the debate was the argument that if millions are sent to their death to save millions from tyranny, then what was the value of the war. At the conclusion of the debate Thomas' intellectual stimuli were in full throttle.

Martin saw the shock register on Thomas' face before he could hide it. In the surprised encounter that he expected Martin met Thomas outside of Frewin Hall. Thomas and Martin embraced. Thomas was glad to see his brother had returned from war alive and well. A small smile played on his lips and there was richness in his tones – luxurious and warm. A tone that remain as the two men ate supper together. It wasn't until Martin mysteriously insisted that he not go to America as a part of the exchange programme with Yale University that Thomas' tone changed. They mystery and seriousness of Martin words unnerved him. With a crackle in his voice, not more of a low-pitched whisper Thomas assured his brother that he would not go to America.

Later that night Martin arrived in Bletchley and once again took up residence in the Bull Commercial Hotel. Sure that the Oxford-Yale exchange of the brightest students was a part of the plan in Donovan's memoirs he took comfort in knowing that Thomas would be safe. With his comfort he was now ready to hunt.

29

The hours before the dawn-light brings a special kind of blackness, the kind that wants only to hold the stars and help them shine all the brighter. A warm black that hugs you ever so gently. A black that brings about an endearing desire to reflect on one's world, while also creating an atmosphere that conceals our deepest secrets.

Within the safety of this blackness, on a tiny airstrip somewhere in the wilderness north of Berlin, a single small wooden shack, just a silhouette in the darkness, adorned the airstrip. Trees also adorned the airstrip for as far as the eyes could see, giving complete cover from the sky, day or night, for miles around the airstrip. A two-seater, dual engine Fh 104, sat on a dirt runway not far from the shack. The Fh 104 planes were used to transport senior officers and officials of Nazi Germany. These planes were often called executive planes, and generally flew in areas occupied by the Axis forces, areas out of the way of any harm. However, this flight, the one Goebbels was about to take under the cover of darkness, would be different.

It was February 12, 1942 three days before the fall of Singapore and the start of Martin's captivity. Inside the shack burned a dim fire that had been lit for hours as Goebbels waited for the cover of darkness. He finally decided that it was safe to leave the security, and warmth, of the shack to make his way towards the plane. Goebbels moved slowly, and deliberately, towards the Fh 104 before the crackle of a shoe snapping a twig on the ground behind him alerted him to the fact that he was not alone. Swiftly turning, with his hand on his gun, he confronted his follower and the business end of a Karabiner 98 kurz - the standard German infantry rifle. A burly blonde Goliath of a man stood squarely at the ready behind him. A finger on the trigger of his rifle made it clear that he meant business and was ready to take decisive action.

"Put that damn thing away," Goebbels demanded.

Unaware that Goebbels had arrived before him Shultz had stood outside the shack awaiting the General's arrival.

"Sorry General, I didn't know you had arrived already and in the dark could not tell it was you," replied Private Shultz - a young, fiery, blue eyed, blonde-haired, muscular fella.

"Is the plane fuelled and ready?" Asked Goebbels.

"Yes sir, exactly as you instructed." Replied Shultz.

"And our cargo?"

"Safely on Board." Shultz answered.

"Let's get going then."

The war in Western Europe was quiet and most of the region was under German control. With other areas being controlled by Germany's allies or independent States, like Switzerland and Vichy France, who followed German policies. So the two men, Goebbels and Schulz, felt safe making their journey from Berlin to Switzerland. The two men had made this journey across German territory many times; always with a plane laden with stolen art and valuables. Goebbels would sell their ill-got artefacts, The Commission would grow their wealth, and the men would return to Germany.

With Shultz close behind, Goebbels walked to the plane, around the tail, and to the left-side door just in front of the wing. He climbed inside, fastened the seatbelt and shoulder harnesses. Shultz climbed into the other side of the cockpit and strapped himself into the seat. A wall of instruments and gauges sat in front of the men who now sat with their shoulders only inches apart.

"Have you flown one of these planes before," Shultz asked.

"Never before," replied Goebbels.

"As long as you are not too claustrophobic, you will be okay. It is really tight quarters in the cockpit of these little girls. You can take over and land when we are closer. You will be flying her before sunrise." Shultz said with a smile.

"We will see. Although it would be an excellent skill to have in these times." Replied Goebbels.

"Here put these on. It will get loud in here, and we will talk through them," Shultz said as he arranged his headset and handed one to Goebbels.

"Can you hear me?" Asked Shultz. Goebbels nodded confirming the headsets were working.

By February 12, 1942 the German attack on Russia was nearly nine months old and, with Hitler's main focus was on the war in the east with Russia, the Western allies were sending heavy bombers into Germany on precision bombing missions of military and industrial targets. The British Royal Air Force had also begun bombing German cities.

Goebbels and Shultz had been travelling in silence for nearly an hour when from the night came a sound as if thunder could be stretched. They tilted their heads upwards in search of the sound. Both men wondering if it was a friendly or enemy plane.

"Do you recognise that sound?" Said Goebbels.

"It's not one of ours." Shultz replied.

"Let's hope that they keep going and are not up to engaging us."

"I hope so General." Replied Shultz.

High above the two men, John "JJ" Jones could hardly believe his eyes as he piloted his R.A.F. Spitfire fighter plane through the clouds. Below him was what he knew to be an Executive plane that was no doubt carrying a high level command officer in the German armed forces.

In the corner of his eye, way below him, JJ could see the Fh 104 banking left away from his line of travel. JJ – flying one of only two Spitfires providing protection for a Bomber on its way back to Britain after a successful raid – had to make a split-second decision. The rest of the squadron had gone ahead, and the Bomber was a precious asset as, after a few repairs, it would be back the following night to bomb another German city.

Realising he had caught an enemy plane off guard JJ dived sharply, passing under the Fh 104's wheels and holding there directly below. He figured the Fh 104 wouldn't dare fire on him and risk more Allied air crafts joining in a fight.

In the other Spitfire accompanying the bomber was Lester, a young hotshot pilot with several kills to his name, and he had only been flying for less than a year.

Neither of the two pilots wanted to neither break radio silence nor risk a German attack if they fired on the Fh 104. Lester followed JJ's steep dive and settled his plane directly above the Fh 104 carrying Goebbels, Shultz, and the artefacts.

For several tense minutes the planes flew in unison, JJ at the lowest altitude, Lester at the highest, and Goebbels in the Fh 104 with Shultz in between the two. Goebbels and Shultz breathed a sigh of relief when JJ and Lester turned around to pick up their bomber escort duties. With the British planes now heading north the Fh 104 continued its journey south deeper into German-controlled territory. As they reached Lake Constance, on their approach to the Swiss border, Goebbels took control of the plane and with the ease of what seemed to be an experienced pilot, at the break of dawn; he landed smoothly on a small airstrip near Zurich, Switzerland.

Although the Swiss had resisted Germany as much as they could, they eventually had to choose between some compromises and complete surrender. As such, by 1942, Switzerland had settled into its role in the war. Switzerland had become Europe's money laundering capital. There was hundreds of millions of dollars in stolen assets, including gold taken from the central banks of German-occupied Europe, being laundered in Switzerland. Even the Jewish, that could, had smuggled their capital out of Nazi Germany, and the states Germany threatened, into Switzerland for safe keeping. Large amounts of the stolen assets and laundered money ended up in the hands of The Commission.

***

Hard on the heels of the inaugural meeting of The Commission, on December 23, 1933, in Paris, Junior had set in motion his own plan. He had told The Commission, at that inaugural meeting that the first aim was to bring back a single centre of power and control to the world. Everyone present at that meeting had thought that would be the reformed League of Nations. However, Junior had a different plan. Junior planned to make America the centre of control and he needed money to make this happen.

In America the Great War, followed by the Great Depression, coupled with isolationist policies left the country with a small standing military of barely one hundred thousand men across all branches. The American military had been depleted and Junior knew that military might was needed to be the centre of control for the world, and that money was needed to obtain military might.

Junior began his efforts to expand the military when the American army's weapons were obsolete, and the military was attempting to mechanise and modernise while facing low budgets, crushing compartmentalisation as well as economic ruin. Public opinion was vehemently against the expansion of the military until the late 1930s and Junior needed to gain public support for the expansion as well as the funds to expand.

The military needed to purchase thousands of ships, tens of thousands of airplanes, hundreds of thousands of vehicles, millions of guns, and hundreds of millions of rounds of ammunition. The military needed to recruit, train, and deploy millions of soldiers to theatres of action. Accomplishing these tasks meant paying entrepreneurs, inventors, and firms so that they, in turn, could purchase supplies, pay workers, and produce the weapons with which America's soldiers and sailors would defeat its enemies.

Junior shrewdly convinced Roosevelt, whose ear he still commanded, to appoint Henry Morgenthau to head the Treasury. Morgenthau he knew he could control, and convince, to take the direction he needed towards financing America's upcoming war effort. Through a stroke of luck, the ill fortune, and untimely death of Eugene Robert Black I created the opportunity for Junior to put his man in control of the Federal Reserve. In November of 1934 Marriner Stoddard Eccles took over at the Fed giving Junior the control he needed.

Under Junior's influence plans for financing the war were devised by the Treasury and the Federal Reserve. These organisations met frequently to determine how to finance the war and organise machinery for gaining public support of government securities. The plan was to finance the war through taxation, domestic borrowing, and government securities.

It wasn't long after the financing plans were put in place that Junior began funnelling money, taken from unsuspecting souls in Europe, and laundered by his Swiss banking friends, into the American military expansion. Even the other Commission members were unaware of Junior's financing of the American military.

***

Once in Switzerland Goebbels and Shultz quickly made their way to the Union Bank of Switzerland with their artefacts and gold in tow. In the dawn light the charcoal sky, of the eerily quiet streets of Zurich, had become a wispy silver, as if it was determined to become its own treasure. A sky that Goebbels had seen on many occasions, yet he still thought it to magical. Maybe this sky is magical, or maybe it was the treasure that I am carrying heightening my dopamine levels, thought Goebbels. A side gate to the Bank's building slid slowly open as Goebbels' convoy rolled towards the bank. Joseph Weinberg, a drawn elderly man with a champagne rose complexion and even rosier cheeks, awaited their arrival below the bank.

Joseph's wizened face peered out from under a fedora which was, except for a sparse fringe of white, the only thing on his otherwise bald and mottled scalp. His bright eyes, and jovial ways, and razor sharp mind, made him the perfect salesman. Seeing the arrival of Goebbels' convoy Joseph flew into action. Having been through the routine several times before he, with the precision of a Swiss watch, began spouting commands to his underlings. Take this here, that there, and so on. Shultz, who was expecting the croak of an old aged man when he saw Joseph was astonished that Joseph's voice was more like a sergeant major, strong and distinctly upper class. However, out of fear for his life he dared not to comment on anything he had seen nor heard. Within minutes the treasures were unloaded, negotiations completed, and Goebbels was on his way - with Shultz at the helm.

Not long after, at the airstrip, two F.B.I. agents awaited Goebbels' arrival. While not far away, on the shores of the Rhine, Joseph, having kept his share of the loot, stashed away millions into secrets bank accounts for The Commission - and Goebbels was already feverishly personally overseeing the loading of gold, and artefacts, onto a U-Boat bound for America.

Like the God of War herself, and still reeling from the euphoria of his meeting with Joseph, Goebbels strode over to the two F.B.I. agents. With each step he seemed to strike a deeper fear into the hearts of the two men. Why? They were working together after all. However, the men had heard stories of Goebbels' ruthlessness and betrayal. They knew it would only take one wrong move, the utterance of a single unexpected word, for things to turn ugly. They could be executed in the blink of an eye.

The men's eyes scorer Goebbels from head to toe, watching each step he took, as he approached. Their palms became uncontrollably wet as they shuffled from side to side. The men were nervous and wanted to get this encounter over quickly.

"Good morning General," said one of the agents with a stutter as Goebbels approached.

"What information do you have for me?" Barked Goebbels in reply.

Apprehension is the most natural of emotions when people see something or someone that has the potential to bring destruction into their lives. What's more, the emotion was mirrored in the soul. It is a real moment, significant and potent enough to be confident in the words that then flowed from their mouths.

Goebbels could tell the agents were a little apprehensive, and he liked to see that in people.

With a nervous stutter one of the agents began to speak. He told Goebbels of the travels of Martin, how he had met with someone, his brother in London, and that he had now returned to the war, taking up a command in Asia.

"And what of the other two," asked Goebbels.

"Nothing to report there. They have not made any progress with breaking the code. The man, Francis, is smart but without the key he will not break the code." Said the other agent is a jittery but strong voice.

"Anything else."

"Yes, Francis has a flaw that may become an asset to us later."

"A flaw? What flaw?"

"We have discovered that Francis frequents homosexual locales."

"Okay, return to Bletchley and keep an eye on those two. Wait for further contact in the usual manner." Goebbels said as he turned away from the agents.

Shultz seeing the exchange with the agents, and the earlier meeting with Joseph, could not help but to reflect on a younger Goebbels. A different Goebbels. What ever happened to him he thought. Goebbels as a young military officer had signed on to become a hero, to make sacrifices that could return the pride and better existence that Germany once enjoyed. But instead he has become a greedy tyrant. What happened was all that Shultz could think before he was snapped into action by the bark of a tyrant, by the bark of Goebbels.

"The machine," was the command he barked at Shultz.

Shultz rushed to the plane and quickly returned with a case. A small black metal case with polished silver hinges, latches, and locks - two of them. In it was a German enigma coding machine. Goebbels pulled out a set of keys, opened the case, and then began to type out a message which he sent before boarding the Fh 104 back to Germany.

Alfred was a tall stringy man that was dressed immaculately. It was evident from his grooming that he was a well-kept man, but not a rich man. A lifelong butler, a gentleman's gentleman, who had served Rockefeller junior from the day Junior, was born.

Attending to an enigma Alfred wasted no time in translating the message.

30

F orest Hill was once the sweeping estate of Rockefeller Senior, who had a large Victorian mansion built on a hilltop overlooking Cleveland and Lake Erie. The mansion served as the Rockefeller family's summer home until the mansion burned down under mysterious circumstances. By this time Senior's wife had died and he sold Forest Hills to his son, Rockefeller Junior. Little did anyone know that the site of the mansion held a secret. Rockefeller senior, well known to be a con man, had been obsessed with the day that he was found out and the law came knocking. To cure his obsession, he had built and elaborate network of tunnels on Forest Hills and a mansion beneath the earth. It was in this underground mansion that Alfred received the enigma message and hurried to pass it on to Junior, who was in Cleveland for the opening of the recreational park at Forrest Hills.

Gathered in a smoke-filled room, beneath the earth, of the Forest Hills mansion were the American members of The Commission and their guest. Three men sat in the armchairs, drinking scotch, smoking fine cigars, and plotting the fate of the world as they saw it. Wild Bill Donavon code name "Architect" and John D. Rockefeller Junior code name "Chowder", both members of The Commission, were meeting with J. Edgar Hoover the head of the F.B.I.

The room was dimly lit by lamps that cast a golden glow of rays spreading like petals upon the walls. In the centre of the room sat a large dining table, a remnant from the days when Rockefeller senior held extravagant dinners in the mansion. Those were the days when the Rockefeller's spread their new-money around and bought both power and influence. Junior was just a boy then, but he had always looked on in amazement, dreaming of the day when he would be in command like his father. The grain of the table flowed as if once it had had a pulse, as if a heart had taken in those brushed brown grains and then sent them on their way.

To one end of the expansive room a fire raged in a well-used fireplace. The fire was cracking loudly, but not so much to distract from the silenced seriousness that the room held. On the richly carved fireplace mantel stood an exquisite plate-glass clock, the chimes of which were just striking nine, and, keeping it company to right and left, were two dainty candelabras, each holding four candles. From the wicks of that candles glowed a warm and thoughtful light that enhanced the seriousness of what was about to follow that evening. A reclaimed oak drinks table, on top which sat a fine brandy, and exquisite crystal glasses, together with cushioned and contoured arms, adorned the fireplace.

Donovan was now the head of special intelligence operations for America, but Junior needed Hoover's help as The plan in Donovan's memoirs needed to be brought to a close. Junior's needed to convince his American cohorts on the whys and hows to shutting down the Operation.

"What is the status of Operation Checkmate?" Junior asked Wild Bill Donovan.

"I think everything is going to plan," replied Wild Bill.

"Think isn't good enough," Junior shouted.

"We have to be one hundred percent certain that we remain in the shadows, but achieve our objectives." Continued Junior as Hoover watched in silence, wondering why he had been called to this meeting.

"Tell me where we are on each aspect of the plan, and don't leave anything out." Said Junior.

Donovan took a deep breath, stood up, and began pacing the room in a slow and steady pace. Obviously in deep thought as he told the two gentlemen about the status of Operation Checkmate.

"When we met in Paris during the Great Depression, we decided on a three-pronged plan: one of people, one of science, and another for process. We have some problems but the plan is working." Bill said as he began to speak.

Bill continued to speak slowly and deliberately, Junior and Hoover were hanging on his every word.

"What we set out to do with the people part of the plan was to capture, entice, trick, or by any means necessary get the smartest people in the world. This part of the plan is going well. Getting that Carrie Buck case before the Supreme Court really gave us a lot of momentum.

Justice Holmes did his job superbly, and the public support that we got for the Eugenics initiative after his affirmation not only helped to get Davenport moving into Germany to push that forward, but also helped to get Hitler riled up to push his own programme. Hitler, though, has gone one step further than sterilisation, he is enforcing extermination. That should all help us with capturing the best people and winning the race for the best scientist. The money that we sent into Germany through the Rockefeller Foundation, Kelloggs, and others was a big help."

Donovan was calm and anchored in self-confidence as he spoke. However, his posture said so much more. His posture was that of a defeated and uncertain man. He did not stand tall as one would expect of someone that was speaking with such confidence. It could be that the expanse of the human atrocities that he was presiding over was taking its toll on him. With another deep sigh preceded by an awkward silence Wild Bill continued to speak of the next prong of the plan.

"With the science this isn't going as well."

"What is not going well with the science prong," asked Junior.

"With science we knew we wanted to get control of the best ideals and inventions from the countries around the world. One of these ideas was the code breaking technique of the British, but that isn't going so well. It is highly secretive and secure. We can't get close enough to it and we can't get a spy to help us."

"Any other problems with the science?"

"No the other areas are going well. Einstein and the other scientists are now over America and helping. Plus with the Nazis pushing our eugenics constructs in Germany many of the Jewish scientists are rushing to come over to America."

"So it's just the British code breakers that are the problem?"

"Yes"

"And what of the Manhattan Project?" Junior asked.

For the first time since he began to speak Wild Bill's composure was lost. He did not know about the Manhattan Project and quizzically asked, "Manhattan Project?"

Hoover was known for his arrogance, and while he had sat quietly by as Wild Bill spoke about Operation Checkmate, this was his time to shine and he jumped right into form.

"The Brit's had started to develop a super bomb but with Einstein over here, and the other scientists that you're The plan in Donovan's memoirs managed to get here, we were easily able to convince them that we should take it over. We told them that they were too close to the war and being bombed. The Brit's bought into that story and gave us control of developing the super bomb. They have stopped their project which they called Tube Alloys for some reason. We're calling our effort The Manhattan Project, and it's been secretly running since the start of the war." Hoover said with such smug arrogance that brought both Wild Bill's and Junior's blood to a boil.

Containing his desire to tell Hoover a few things Wild Bill asked Hoover, "So how do you know about this Project and not me?"

"My guys' have an intelligence role in the Manhattan Project. We're in a race with the Germans and Russians to get this damn bomb developed. The Russians are even trying to gather as many scientists as they can from out of Europe. Gathering as much counter intelligence as we can will help us to slow the Germans and Russians down, but also we can steal their work to advance our efforts. We might need to get help from the Brit's at some point, but on the plus side it will keep them quiet while we move forward with our plans." Replied Hoover.

"The Manhattan Project is going well. We are ahead in the race to this super bomb." Continued Hoover.

"That's good," Junior said.

"The Process prong is a little difficult as we are so reliant on the other Commission members, but it's moving along slowly. The Atlantic Charter wasn't easy to get done but we got there in the end. Disarmament of Europeans and other nations will help America to maintain control, and of course we can control America. However, we will need to fix the failed League of Nations thing next. Without that we might not be able to covertly mange the affairs of the world." Continued Junior.

The conversation was finally at the point where Junior wanted-ed. He was ready to begin to talk about the need to shut down Operation Checkmate. He began by asking Wild Bill and Hoover, "Do we need The plan in Donovan's memoirs any longer?"

"We seem to be in good shape with things, but there are some loose ends with that lawyer, spy, and code Breaker over in England." Junior said.

It was at this point that Alfred entered the room on cue. A truly gentleman's gentleman in every way, tall, immaculately groomed, almost too immaculate; were it not for his scraggly salt and pepper beard he could be called perfect. The men immediately went silent when Alfred entered the room breathing heavily, hands flailing about, and rushed in manner as instructed by Junior. Hoover and Wild Bill watched intently as Alfred whispered to Junior and gave him a piece of paper with the decoded enigma message.

"Is everything okay," asked Hoover.

"The message was from Goebbels. It is an update from your men in Europe that have been keeping an eye on the lawyer, the spy, and the code-breaker in Bletchley." Junior said in a cold and calculating but sincere voice that he could muster.

"Your men have reported that the lawyer has now returned to action in Asia, but the spy and the code-breaker are making progress with that copy of the Operation Checkpoint plan." Continued Junior after a pause for dramatisation of the moment.

Junior and Alfred's theatre worked perfectly as he drew Wild Bill into the fray.

"I don't know how I let them get hold of a copy of the plan." Wild Bill chimed in.

Junior, who was expecting the message from Goebbels, and had cued up Alfred's dramatic entry into the room, used Wild Bill's regret to begin his true agenda for the meeting - shutting down Operation Checkpoint.

He was always able to tune in to a person's inner feelings and use these feelings to bend, and mould, people to his liking Junior was sensing that Wild Bill was running low on will power. This ability to tap into inner, unspoken, feelings is not only a weapon that Junior deploys at will but also what has led to his insatiable appetite for power and control. In this case he knew that Wild Bill's regret had been burning inside of him for some time. With will power to fight such regret being a finite resource Junior knew that now was a perfect time to light the final fuse that will drain the remains will power of Wild Bill and deliver his continued servitude into Junior's hands. As a perfect manipulator does Junior used Bill's code name, to warm Bill's resolve, as he began to speak in the most monotone, and controlled voice he could command.

"Master Chowday, often we have to make choices that we regret. Then regret leads to self-judgement, and self-judgment to even poorer choices. But we must see our choices for what they are and harbour no regret, no self-judgment, as for the most part our choices are actions of practicality to protect ourselves or others." Junior said.

"Plus to judge you need to see all perspectives of a decision or situation through the lens of a man who is perfect in heart, perfect in soul, and all knowing - and that is why such matters are left to God." Hoover arrogantly added to the conversation.

With a brief smile, followed by a complete lack of acknowledgment of Hoover, Junior continued to speak.

"We are in a war gentleman. Not the war that the world sees being waged in Europe, but a war against those people and things that would change our way of life forever. We must not only improve our race by inducing young people to fall in love intelligently, and make more reasonable selections of marriage partners; but we must also ensure that we continue to be in control of their actions in the future. They must not know who is influencing them, or even why, but they must conform and we must succeed." Junior said.

"Well this war has brought together an odd combination of a lawyer, a spy, a code breaker, and our plan in the English country town of Bletchley. These three could bring us all out of the shadows." Interjected Wild Bill.

"This is a real mess!" Hoover shouted.

"What do you want to do Junior," asked Wild Bill.

Both Hoover and Wild Bill looked at Junior. The eyes of the three men locked for a few seconds, but it felt like eternity to Bill whose whole existence, since he was cajoled into servitude to The Commission, has hung on Junior's every word. Hoover, well, he simply wanted to read the mood in the room as he waited for Junior's wisdom to be bestowed. Junior didn't see the two other men at all, his eyes were intently focused on them, but his brain was elsewhere as he plotted his next words.

As a seasoned manipulator Junior knew his next words were critical to his plans. This would be a defining moment he thought. However, to make this moment work he needed to dig deep within himself. Conjuring up a fear that has been with him for many years. His fear of a world in which undesirables, the sub-class of humans, had multiplied to a point that they not only consumed his worldly surroundings, but were also rendering his kind to a minority. A fear that threatened his control, his power, and in his eyes his very existence. The fear that Junior conjured turned to an anger induced rage, a hot burning anger that drove him to seek to harm. His rage built like deep water currents. His anger could be seen in his eyes, which were now squinted as his face turned a flush pink, but his brain was in a different mode.

"We did everything right and there is no way this mess can continue." He shouted while drawing on but one of the bevvy of emotions that he had conjured. Anger.

"Firstly our Bletchley trio have to be stopped," he continued.

"Will you take care the trio Edgar," asked Junior.

"Yes, I have a few thoughts on how as well."

"It can't be linked to us though, okay?"

"It won't."

"What next then?" Asked Wild Bill.

Now able to move from emotion to emotional at will, Junior, within no time at all, switched gears from anger, brought on by telling his brain to sense a threat, to cold emotional indifference. To heighten the tension of the moment, Junior drew deep and long on his cigar, letting the smoke from his lungs out in massive circles, before lingering in the air and drawing the attention of the others. Not wanting to get on with conversation too quickly, out of fear of letting his associates known he had planned every little detail of their meeting, Junior sipped his scotch swirling it in his mouth to savour its rich flavour. Time passed in silence, as the tension built, before Junior spoke.

"Our friends in Germany and Japan have served their purpose. Hitler is operating on his own steam now, as is the Japanese military." He said.

"Mr. Hoover, have someone keep an eye on Mr. Goebbels. When the time is right silence him for good would you." Instructed Junior.

"As for General Tōjō, now that the Japanese have attacked on American soil there is an inevitable end to his reign in sight. The public will rally to have America enter this war, and Japan will be squarely in the cross hairs. We just have to bide or time and diplomatically close him out. Donovan, please ensure that the appropriate military support and action is taken in Japan when the time is right." Junior continued.

Wild Bill, and Hoover, simply nodded in agreement. With their nods the stage was now set, the actors were in their places, and the play was about to begin.

Both men then disappeared into the tunnels beneath Forest Hills, leaving Junior to savour yet another milestone.

31

It's a strange and scary sensation to wake disoriented and unfamiliar with your surroundings. Everything is hazy. Your brain is foggy, your eyes are glazed, and you struggle to find your footing. This is what happened to Martin the morning after his return to Bletchley following his captivity. That first morning back, in a jolt, Martin awoke disoriented. As the haze cleared from Martin's mind he not only realised that he was back in Bletchley, but was also comforted by being able to sleep. After many months the sleepless nights had dissipated. The fears and flashbacks were also subsiding. He glanced at his watch and groaned as he realised that he had overslept, but there was still time if he rushed.

Moments later he stepped through the doors of the expansive dining hall of the Bull Commercial Hotel. The usual breakfast place for Francis, Clara, and himself before his return to war. It was a Monday, the 15th March, a day after Francis had returned from America. If the other two-thirds of his search party were going to be anywhere it would be here, thought Martin. The usual place at the usual time. It was time for the Bletchley sleuths to return to exposing the truth. To obtain justice for so many that had already lost their lives.

At the door itself the aroma of burning bread, greasy bacon, and frying eggs greeted his nose, promising a whole range of pleasures and a full belly. Two smartly dressed elderly women from the Women's Voluntary Service welcomed him with toothy smiles. Their distinctive dark green uniforms were everywhere as they kept cleanliness and order. In addition to the warm welcome, the haunting Yorkshire accent of Pickles, the radio announcer, reverberated in the perimeter of the restaurant keeping all in ear shot updated on the essentials of the war. Excitement reigned as people ran hither and thither, and others engrossed themselves in conversation.

Something wasn't right though. Through the night the town had been overrun with soldiers. They were everywhere! Inside the restaurant and in the streets outside the hotel. A sight that instantly caused Martin's heart to race. Had the country been overrun by Nazis through the night, was a fair and natural thought that ran through his mind. However, as he was familiar with the uniforms of the men from all the different factions of the allies, Martin quickly recognised the uniforms as those of the Canadian Armed Forces, and with that his heart rate subsided as he continued to scan the room for Francis and Clara.

Martin was so angry with himself, he could scream. He was never late for anything. He grumbled to himself as he tried to keep his composure. He needed the rest but was still angry with himself as he was now in jeopardy of missing Francis and Clara. He dare not go to Clara's home unannounced - she might have a spy there and his life would be jeopardy. If he missed them here, then Francis would be inside Bletchley Park, and that was a no-go zone. He glanced at his watch, he had five minutes before they would normally leave. However they were nowhere in sight. Yet Martin continued to crane his neck in different directions, while shifting his weight from side to side, as he carelessly wandered and search. Then something odd happened. He bumped into a strange man, well, the man bumped into him. Actually, they bumped into each other. The man could've easily walked around Martin, but he didn't. It was Delaney, one of the F.B.I. agents that pursued Francis in New York, he too was back in Bletchley. Martin paid little mind to Delaney who just smiled at Martin and kept walking. If only Martin had known that Delaney was scouting him, making sure that it was indeed Martin, and that he too was back in Bletchley. However, Martin's focus was elsewhere and the man that bumped him to get a closer look at him did not take away from his focus. Martin was frantic, focused, and determined when the second man bumped into him. A soldier this time. The uniform startled Martin who instantly became fully aware of his surroundings. He opened his eyes wide and apologised for bumping into the soldier, a captain in the Canadian Armed Forces. The soldier seemed frustrated by the strange bump, but when Martin apologised he didn't seem to mind. Realising he was a soldier Martin didn't only apologise; he went on to strike up a conversation.

"Excuse me Captain, has the country been invaded?" Martin asked with a smile that said I know we haven't been invaded, I just want to know what is going on.

"You are worried about seeing so many of us Canadians, eh?" Rhetorically replied the captain with a grin.

"We just completed a training exercise in the south, and some of our troops are shipping out from Liverpool. So just a stop over here on our way up north." Continued the captain.

Even though his army days were behind him, he couldn't help but to be curious when he heard about a training exercise with this many soldiers. "Training exercise? Is there a big operation in the works?" Asked Martin.

"They don't tell us about the planned operations. We follow orders and be ready to go when they call on us."

"But if a name means anything we are preparing for a heroic battle. They choose to call it Exercise Spartan, and you know about the Spartans don't you?"

"Yes, well good luck when the day comes." Martin said before moving further into the dining hall in search of Francis and Clara.

Casting his eyes on a table at the back of the room, away from windows, and almost obscured, Martin saw a familiar face. It was Clara. There were two soldiers standing in front of the table preparing to leave which made the table hard to find. On seeing Clara, Martin tightened his focus on the table and could see that she was with Francis. He smiled.

As he walked slowly, and nervously, towards the table, Martin felt a stir in his loins that he hadn't experienced since he was last in Bletchley. He knew that a public display of affection was not possible. That he would have to bury that stir, that desire, deep inside him on this occasion. Jubilantly both Francis and Clara stood and broadly smiled as they saw Martin approaching. Clara was the first to move towards Martin, while Francis stood reservedly like a statue, watching, maybe hoping and wishing. On contact Clara gave Martin an embrace that went beyond the norms of public displays of affection, but as there was war raging most onlookers did not mind. They didn't even look. Clara's embrace was strong, she held onto Martin as if he was a treasure that had been returned to her unexpected. To some extent that was the case as they, Francis and Clara, had feared the worst for so long. Little did Martin, nor Francis, know that Clara to felt that same stir in her loins as she held onto Martin.

For the next hour the three sleuths spoke aimless about their time apart. They were careful not to speak of the memoirs, Francis' discovery, and any of the exploits that would be harmful to their mission if overheard. It was a joyful reunion that ended in a promise to meet for dinner that night at Clara's. Diner being code for let's meet and get back to work.

Black outs were still enforced and there were no street lights as Martin and Francis made their way to Clara's house. Separate and alone in their own rights, both men strolled comfortably under a moonless, star filled, sky. Both unaware of their accompanying travellers, Davis and Delaney, the F.B.I. agents.

Outside Clara's house the agents, still reeling from the scalding Wild Bill gave them in New York, took up a space in the shadows. Inside Martin and the others spoke of their time apart for hours. Both men knew they had to take out Francis and his cohorts discreetly, which meant finding that perfect moment - and exact method. They could patiently bide their time, watching and waiting, they thought.

Inside Clara's house, as their emotions rolled along like the seasons, the trio talked for hours about what they had been through over the past year. Much of the conversation was the mundane who did what catch up. However their emotions first began to show shoots of growth, spring growth, when they heard of Martin's capture and escape from the Japanese. They were rewardingly enlightened, as one might be by the breath of autumn colours, when Francis told them of his chased and escape in New York. Clara's chase across America and escape brought laughter to the trio. They must all have nine lives they joked.

What they all agreed on was that for certain the man called Rockefeller in New York was the same man in the plan. Plus both Clara and Francis had seen Davis and Delaney in Bletchley so they knew that they had the F.B.I. watching. Which meant that they were on the right path, albeit a colourful path.

Then Francis told the others that, when he saw Rockefeller in New York it came to him that Rockefeller senior had his Standard Oil men communicate in code. He used the nicknamed 'Club' for the company, and he was referred to as

'Chowder,' which was one of the code names in the memoirs. That meant that Rockefeller junior was 'Chowder.' That he knew that Goebbels, who was linked to Donovan by the two of them, was sometimes referred to as the Doctor because he had a doctorate in philology. The way Donovan wrote about the Architect it became clear that his code name was 'Architect'. That left me with the code name 'Razor', and after some research of major people in different countries I discovered that Hideki Tōjō was called 'Razor' because of his extreme use of razor sharp katana swords. "That was it, that's how I cracked the code names." Francis said as the trios clarity of things became vividly clear, as clear as the daylight on bright summers day.

However, their emotions took a turn and sank to their lowest, as low as emotions might reach on the coldest darkest day of winter, when Martin moved the conversation on again.

In as serious of a voice as he could muster, with a gaze at each of the other two that would bring a freight train to a halt, Martin said, "I am going to share something with the two of you that is confidential. You understand what that means? I am no longer in the army but it's still not something I should say, but it's important that you know."

"The reason I am telling you this is because it sickens me, and I think it's an unintended consequence of the actions of those men that put this war in motion." Martin continued.

"What is it Martin? You know we won't tell anyone." Both Clara and Francis said almost in unison.

"Army intelligence is that Hitler has started to exterminate Jews. They started over in Poland. A place they are calling Belzec. Over a half million just murdered already, and there is no end in sight. It's just horrific." Martin replied.

"Damn it!" Francis shouted.

"That's those Americans again, isn't it?" Continued Francis

"How so? What do mean? This was done by the Germans." Clara chimed.

"No! Remember the section in the plan that talked about capturing, enticing, tricking, or by any means necessary getting the smartest people in the world to America." Francis said as Martin continued to listen in with his eyes wide open in shock.

"Yes, how is this related?" Clara asked.

"Well, it wasn't just about getting the best people. It was some sought of master race thing, I think."

"That Rockefeller chap that was in New York with those two that chased me was also talking to a man from two American corporations - IBM and Kelloggs - those companies have spent a lot of money on eugenics. Rockefeller's Foundation also has put a lot of money into that as well."

"Eugenics? What is that?"

"Rockefeller, IBM, and Kelloggs are all also connected to this fella Charles Davenport."

"You know who he is don't you?"

"No!"

"Davenport is the American chap that has been pushing extermination of the weaker or defective members of the human race. Leaving a single stronger gene pool of humans."

"His work started in America, but a few years back he has been working with the Germans. IBM and Kellogg's have been funded him in Germany too. That's where I think Hitler got all of this cruelty.

"It's all a part of that plan that we found."

With those words said the room went quiet as the trio dealt with the lowest of the emotions they experienced that night. A sickening nausea developed in their guts. It was as if butterflies were fluttering around in their stomach, stirring up everything - mostly anger! Each of the three fought back tears as they digested the magnitude of the deception that they had uncovered.

"That makes sense because army intelligence also has a list of German scientists that they are trying to smuggle back to America. They are some of the smartest people in Europe, lots of Germans, some that don't want to go to America, but they are being enticed or kidnapped." Martin said, breaking the uncomfortable silence.

"Us Brits seem to be just going along with it. The yanks have us convinced that these scientists will be safer in America. They have even said they will share with us on anything that they invent. Bombs mainly. But there is more to this than we know." Continued Martin.

"So what do we do now with what we know?" asked Clara.

"Human suffering on the scale that the world is seeing now demands that someone pay. It will be Hitler, the Nazis, and the Japs if we can't expose the real culprits. We need to ensure justice is served." Francis added.

"That's right but we have to agree that we will not get too emotionally involved in whatever we do. Otherwise we will make mistakes. We have to agree to do this without passion or prejudice, okay?" Martin added.

Francis and Clara both signalled their agreement at the same time.

"I think we have to take this to Churchill directly. Rockefeller and the others may even have some Brits working with them so we can't trust anyone. It has to be Churchill directly." Francis said.

"I went to him when I needed more money for the code breaking. He was really supportive. I think he will help.

"But I am not sure how we get to him without those around him suspecting something - he is so protected."

With a satisfying smile of the cat that ate the canary Clara, who had a secret of her own, said: "We don't have to get to him directly."

"Churchill's closest confidant is the former Prime Minister of South Africa - Jan Smuts.

"Smuts moved to Britain when his party lost the government in his country. He has been in Churchill's circle ever since.

"But that's not the best part. Smuts has a mistress who is a German spy.

She has been secretly sending information back to Germany.

"We can get her help to get a meeting with Churchill.

"She wouldn't know why. Just that it's important, she will likely think that it an order from Germany. An assassination attempt."

"Okay, you take can of that Clara and let us know." Martin said.

"I had better get going then. I don't want the chaps at Bletchley Park asking me too many questions about my whereabouts." said Francis.

"I will walk you out." replied Martin.

At the threshold to Clara's Martin pulled the door shut with one hand and Francis to him with the other. It had been a long time since he had hell him in his arms. If truth be told though war and captivity had erased all such thoughts from his mind. Not tonight though. Martin had been watching and waiting for an opportunity for the two to embrace. All evening he had yearned for him. He realised he missed his face. He missed the cute way he moved, the way he would cuddle up with him and make him feel like everything in the world was alright.

There, outside of Clara's, in the doorway, Martin's face was so close to Francis' that he could smell the sweet ropy fragrance of the sherry he had been drinking, and then his tongue was in Martin's mouth. In all honesty Martin had not invited such passion, he merely wished to see Francis' face, hear his voice, and digest all that there had been. However, the kiss was so instantaneous; he didn't even catch a glimpse of Francis' face.

Francis' tongue plunged with such urgency, it all but overpowered Martin's senses as it sought something deep within his mouth; it wiggled, it pulsated, and made contorted sweeps. The kiss had the power in itself to force Martin, or somehow get him back, against the doorjamb, where he stood helpless with his eyes clenched shut.

In the emotion of that kiss a volume of passion was spoken that transcended reality. Martin was in a trance induced by Francis' tongue. In that kiss Francis too was in a trance.

After their kiss there was a delicious moment where Martin's face washed blank with confusion, like his brain cogs couldn't turn fast enough to take in the sensations he was experiencing. Every muscle of his body just froze before a grin crept onto his face, it soon stretched from one side to the other showing every single tooth, as did Francis'. Little did they know that, in those moments, standing silently in the shadows, was Davis and Delaney. They had seen it all.

Still, for Martin, there was more to come this evening. When he returned to Clara, there was something different about her. She had an endearing saunter about her as she approached him. Martin had never seen this side of her. Yes, she had been vulnerable with him, but mostly he saw the serious Clara - spy Clara. Her saunter was accompanied by a seductive smile. Her dress from the curves of her hips to tops of her knees swayed gracefully, and caught his attention on this occasion.

The transition had Martin's head spinning. One moment he was an accomplice, background at best, to anything he thought she might be feeling, and then next she appeared set on seducing him. He couldn't say which he preferred.

As Clara reached to put her arms around him, to pull him into her, Martin instinctively pulled away.

"Where is this coming from?" He asked her.

"You are very brilliant in multiple ways and when that is summed to make your entire self, well, that has me so impressed." She replied.

"I have wanted you from the time we first met at David and Peggy's."

"Does this have anything to do with the marriage thing again? Or the kiss that we shared before my return to the front?" Martin asked.

"That too, I do fear that one day I will be called before a tribunal, found to be a spy, then put to death.

"You are a lawyer, my papers are false, and I want to marry a British lawyer who can help me escape my past.

"But more than that, You are one amazing person, I want you." replied Clara.

"Off course I will marry you." replied Martin.

"You are an amazing person too, and I would never want any harm to reach you."

Martin and Clara shared an awkward embrace, and an even more uncomfortable kiss, before he returned to the Bull Commercial Hotel to ponder that evening even more.

32

The Hither Green Cemetery, in London, was the final resting place of thirty-eight children and six teachers who recently perished in a daytime bombing of the Sandhurst Road School. At the onset of the Nazi bombings of London many children had been evacuated, but in time they returned. Then, on 20th January 1943, with a distant air-raid siren blasting a Luftwaffe pilot circled the school, waved at the children on the ground, and unleashed his fury. A one-ton bomb transformed from neatly dressed school girls into ghastly frightening creatures, choking, covered in dust, and bleeding. Some dead, some dying, some in terrible pain. That was only six months before Clara set foot on the grounds of their final resting place.

The Hither Green Cemetery also sat on a plot of land that was once farmland which, in part, was purchased by the financing of slave owning operations, as well as, direct ownership on enslaved people in Jamaica.

Walking through the graveyard, on her way to arrange a meeting with Churchill, Clara couldn't shake the feeling that she was being watched. It was an eerie landscape of misery and suffering. Eeriness that was seeping into her bones, into her every being with each step.

It may have been the suffering of those enslaved people that gave birth to the eeriness that Clara was feeling. Or maybe it was the undead souls of those from the Sandhurst Road School bombing recently laid to rest that gave rise to her eeriness. Or maybe it was the silhouettes of the gothic chapels against the dark sky. Whatever the cause of her eeriness, it didn't matter, it was here now, and she had to deal with it, as this was the place that Doris had chosen to meet.

The cemetery had two identical Gothic chapels, except one was for Anglicans, the other four, Protestant Christians. The Anglican chapel was Clara's destination, and she was in deed being watched. Not by dead souls, no, her watchers were very much alive.

From the bell tower of the dissenters' chapel Clara saw the mysterious outlines of a person in the bell tower of the Anglican chapel. Damn it, she thought as she assumed she had entered the wrong chapel. As she turned another person stepped out of the shadows and was instantly in front of her. Clara stood as still as a statute, it was as if she had retreated inside herself; instead of being there in that moment. All of her senses where on full alert but it was as if what she felt, heard, smelt, were far, far, away and somehow disconnected. She was scared. Then the voice of the person repeated. "Clara, are you Clara?"

Finally she knew that the person in the other bell tower was her watcher. She had been under surveillance from the moment she entered the cemetery. She also knew that the person in front of her was not Doris.

Doris, Smuts' mistress, was a London socialite. She was well known to Churchill, and once had an affair with Goebbels who recruited her as a German spy shortly after the start of the war. Other affairs that she had were with Churchill's son Randolph. She even had her portrait painted by Churchill senior. Doris was able to move about the circles of London's high society and had become an invaluable German accomplice in London. She was in frequent contact with Clara, especially when German spies needed assistance in Britain. The last time Clara had seen Doris was in New York when she was on the run from the F.B.I. However, Doris had responded in the usual way when she asked to meet in London.

"Who are you?" A shocked, and surprised, Clara asked.

"You may call me Krystyna."

Krystyna Skarbek, the daughter of Polish aristocracy, was a real charmer of men who craved danger. She was also an eager supporter of the allied war efforts, and a member of the Armia Krajowa (Home Army) - the largest of the Polish resistance groups. Last year she had been smuggling intelligence out of Poland, to the allies, when she came in contact with Doris - a German spy captured by the resistance.

Doris was trying to infiltrate the Polish government officials, who were in exile in London, when she was captured. Under torture Doris told the resistance about Clara, who she was, as well as how contact was made and verified. When she was of no more use to them the resistance killed Doris, leaving her to be found in her London flat, in what appeared to the outside world as a suicide.

Now Krystyna was standing in front of Clara with her men ready to pounce at the slightest provocation. What followed next was a very cold, abrupt, intense, unnerving conversation.

"Where is Doris?" Clara asked.

"Dead."

"Did you kill her?"

"Yes, and we know that you are a spy for Germany."

Clara's heart was racing, as it once did when she was on the run in America. This time though she was certain that she was about to meet her end.

"I am, well I was a spy, but now I bring information to help the allies."

"You are Polish resistance, yes?" asked Clara.

"I am."

"Then you must hear me out. It is of vital importance."

"How do we trust you? You bring more lies and propaganda, don't you?"

"I am working with a decorated British soldier, and another man. Both men have Churchill's trust. They trust me, you can trust me too."

"What do you want?"

"We want to meet with the Prime Minister in person. But we cannot risk one of those close to him knowing about us, or what we have to tell him. That is why we have taken the approach of contacting Doris. We couldn't use the connections that we had already."

"Doris, if she were alive, could have spoken with Jan Smuts. We knew she was his mistress, and that he was close to Churchill.

"Are you able to secretly get us this meeting?" Clara asked.

"Yes, we will do this. We will be in contact."

***

In the intervening months, between Clara's eerie walk through the Hither Green Cemetery, and news reaching the trio of Churchill's agreement to meet, Junior had a meeting of his own. As much as Junior had tried to ignore it, he couldn't deny it any longer - the people section of his plan was not working, and he needed to do something about it.

The men, well Junior and Wild Bill, gathered in what Junior was now calling "the bunker. He chose the name because of its connection to the war in Europe and its role as his secret headquarters. In actuality, it was the dining room of his underground mansion located in Forest Hills.

"Bill, a year ago, in this very room, we thought the people section of the plan was on track." Began Junior as the conversation started.

"We had Davenport in place and riding the world of the undesirables was happening. But if we plan to secretly control the world after this war we are going to need to get ahead of what Hitler and those Japs are doing. If the reports are true then they are moving too quickly and have been reckless."

"We don't want the blame making its way back to America. Junior said as he paced back and forth around the table.

"Do you know of any evidence of what Hitler is doing over there? I have only heard reports but nothing confirm." Asked Junior.

"Yes, last year, I met with a member of the Polish resistance about this same thing. Her name was Krystyna Skarbek. The resistance had smuggled a report out of Germany that detailed the Nazis plans for the annihilation of the European Jews. It mentioned a Nazi killing centre at Chelmno. There was also the use of gas vans. They, the resistance, estimated that 700,000 people had already been killed by June last year." Replied Wild Bill.

"Now the politicians are wrestling over increasing the immigration quotas we have on that type - Jews." Continued Wild Bill.

Junior eyebrows raised as he paused almost mid-step. He wasn't shocked at all though. Junior was calculating his next move.

"Davenport and his people worked hard back in twenty four to get the Immigration Act passed with quotas that worked for us. Now they are talking about changing that, making it easier for the Jews, Asians, and others to just come over here and pollute our gene pool?" Asked Junior.

"Yes, in thirty-nine when the war had just started Congress refused to increase the quotas, but with these new killing camps who knows. We can't get to all of them politicians." Replied Wild Bill.

"So how do you think we should get ahead of this now?" Wild Bill asked.

With a calm but clearly frustrated voice Junior responded. "We can't stop what's going on over in Europe now. That's grown out of control. I guess that's what happens when you release those Hitler types on the world."

"But we can keep them undesirables out of America. Let's get Harrison, the new Immigration Commissioner, on this, okay?" Continued Junior.

"I know Earl Harrison, he would be supportive. I was at a cocktail party with him recently and his wife's remarks where interesting." Wild Bill said chiming in again.

"When the whole European immigration topic came up, and there was concern about the refugee children, his wife's retort was '20,000 children would all too soon grow up to be 20,000 ugly adults'. So I don't think it will take much to get Harrison on board.

In the months following Junior's meeting the American Congress didn't relax immigration quotas, and there was immense pressure on Latin American countries and Great Britain to admit Jewish refugees. With the pressure building on him Churchill decided to meet with the soldier that might have information to help him.

***

It was sometime in November 1943 when news reached Clara that Churchill had agreed to meet. He insisted that the soldier met with him alone. He also insisted that he bring proof of their vital information.

On receiving the news Martin and his cohorts quickly put in place a plan to travel to London. They were finally going to get the help they needed to bring those behind the plan in Donovan's memoirs - to justice. Excited, but unaware that they were under surveillance the whole time, the trio decided that they would travel separately. They also travelled on different days to avoid being seen leaving Bletchley together. In Bletchley, three friends being together was not suspicious, but in war times three friends travelling to London together might attract attention. It would be best to play it safe, they thought.

Over the course of three days they would travel to London and on to Mayfair, Martin's parents' home. Martin arrived at the Frost's Mayfair residence first and, after a bit of explaining, the Frost family was ready for the arrival of Francis and Clara.

With a sense of unease, Clara, the second of the trio to leave, boarded the train to Bletchley. She was uneasy as she was certain that she had seen Davis, the F.B.I. agent they chased her in New York, board the same train. However, in London there was no sight of him, so she made her way to Mayfair. The next day Francis had a similar experience, but in London Francis came face to face with Delaney, the other F.B.I. agent. He lost Delaney, as he did in New York, and made his way to Mayfair as. With the trio safely in Mayfair, Sarah, Martin's sister, did the scouting and quickly confirmed that there were two men watching the front of the house.

The meeting with Churchill, that would bring their nightmares to an end, was only hours away, but the trio was trapped. Frantically, they devised a plan. Moments later Martin Sr, Sarah, and Thomas, Martin's brother left the Frost's home and quickly scoured away in the opposition directly to where the agents laid in wait. True to form Davis and Delaney followed hotly behind, anxious to know what the trio where up doing in London. As the agents turn the corner Martin, Clara, and Francs, who had been keeping watch from the shadows of the Frost residence, made their way out of the house and in the opposite direction. It was nearly an hour before the agents realised that they had been tricked. By this time Martin and company were entering the gates of the Hither Green Cemetery. The most unlikely place for Churchill to have a meeting.

Martin's mother, the task master, had always told him that fortune favoured the brave. And for a longest time, until those dreadful days held in captivity, in Singapore, he believed her. But there was no being brave then, no, not at all, as with time he had been broken, demoralised, and traumatised. Images of being tortured, of being afraid, rippled through him as he, Francis, and Clara approached the chapel. The same chapel that Clara found herself in a few months early.

There was nothing eerie about her visit to the chapel this time though. There were men everywhere. Trusted men of the

Polish resistance and a few men Churchill trusted to protect him.

Only Martin was allowed to enter the chapel, and only Churchill was inside. In a pew near the altar the men sat for almost and hour as Martin told Churchill the whole story. From the day that the two of them met, and he was sent to Bletchley, to finding the document, befriending and turning a German spy, breaking the code, Francis' life-threatening night in New York, and the men now following them. Churchill sat steely eyed and outwardly unemotional as Martin showed Churchill the memoirs and recounted the trios' activities.

Inwardly though a shrewd Churchill, on the one hand, shocked, and was on the other hand already calculating his next moves. He now had the leverage he needed on the Americans and his wheels were already turning on how he would use it. The pressure to take immigrants would be seize immediately. Britain will become an equal partner in this, this whatever it is. But there was more that he needed to know before he could act.

"Does any of this tie to Roosevelt?" Churchill asked.

"We only know for certain that the secret society, The Commission, is led by this Rockefeller person. That there is high level German and Japanese involvement, and of course Donovan." Martin said leaving out naming Goebbels and Tōjō as a precaution until he knew more about Churchill's intentions.

"The Commission is extremely well connected to all of the seats of power in the world.

"Quite frankly Sir, they may even be connected to, and influencing, those close to you. Those that you trust."

Churchill told Martin about the news coming out of Germany of death camps, and that he was certain now that the Americans had planted this seed of human destruction in Germany.

However, he did not tell Martin of his time as a Vice President of the International Eugenics Congress, or that eugenics movement began in Britain before it spread to America and now Germany. He was either embarrassed about his involvement, or had his own ulterior motives.

Instead told Martin to do nothing more wait for his instructions. He also told Martin to keep what he knows to himself, tell no one else. That if he and his friends found any connection of the plan to Roosevelt to let him know. That Krystyna would be his contact. That she can be trusted. Most of all, he told Martin, to keep his wits about as his life and those around him is probably in danger.

"I will hold onto the memoirs for now." Martin said and the two men went their separate ways.

Later that month Churchill began his onslaught at a conference in Cairo, codenamed "Sextant", between Roosevelt, the Chinese President Chiang Kai-shek, and himself. Once the three leaders had finished their talks about ways to defeat Japan in the Pacific War, he met separately with Roosevelt. In a brief exchange Churchill began to use the information that Martin provided to his advantage.

"FDR, we have intelligence that suggests that after the Great War a few American business men began to orchestrate a second war."

"I have seen their plan, and it's a clever long game of strategic positions aimed at making America the strongest, and richest, nation in the world. Naturally they get super rich in the process."

"Have you heard of such a plan?"

"No, who is behind it? What's in this plan?"

"I will get to that, but first I am going to need some assurances.
"I am listening."

"One: Everything advancement is shared between our countries?" and Two: Our agreement can't go beyond the two us
but is must survive our time as leaders."

"If the plan is workable, and beneficial, then you have my
agreement. Now tell me about this plan." Said Roosevelt.

"The plan has a eugenics component that they call the people
section, which Hitler has taken too far. We both have our
fingers in that pie so we to give the world someone to blame
and get out. Immigration is an alternative but you're not going
to stick us Brits with those you don't want."

"There is a science component trying to get the brightest to
your country. We have our own but we can share here.

"Then there is the process component. Remember that Atlantic Charter, and the old League of Nations? Well we have
to revisit that and get something in place for us to control the
others."

"I know there is more to the plan, but first who is behind it?"

"Rockefeller and a few other business leaders in America. Do
you think you can get them in line?"

"Yes."

"Okay, you have my agreement, let's put some meat on this
later." Said Roosevelt as their pact was indelibly formed.

33

It was February 1944, and it had been months since Martin's return from his meeting with Churchill. Still the trio had not seen any activity from Churchill. Loyally they waited in hope that he would bring Rockefeller to justice. That one day there would be this grand news of the uncovering of an international conspiracy.

Private Woodhouse dreaded his treacherous journey into the mountains of the Scottish Highlands. The Private's Morris C4 lorry might have well been an open cabin transport as it offered very little comfort from the chilling and numbing air. Dread as he may it was a journey that he was ordered to make.

This time of year the mountains of the Scottish Highlands were vampire-white and stabbed the sky with trepidation and beauty. Their peaks were like harpoon tips shrouded in ghost-grey mist. A wave of white snow meandered down their sides. Over time crumpled piles of snow had rumbled to a stop at the enormously wide legs at the base mountains. The icy slick peaks and valleys of the roads weaved between scattered, barely visible, fog houses and the odd sighting of a buck.

Yet, the biggest fear that the Private had was returning to the base of the mountain after he had completed his high altitude mission. The devil's elbow might be passable on the way up, but coming back down on icy slick roads would surely be his death, he feared. The double hair-pin steeply elevated road was infamous in these parts. It's no wonder these folks stay in the mountains all winter long, constantly ran through his mind as he made the journey.

Half way up the mountain, in Braemar, a groggy Archie swaggered to his cabin door, a loose grin played somewhere in the shrub of his rust-coloured beard, as his hands took part in an internal conversation where he was, as usual, the victor and whomever is at his door this early in the day was the looser. The door has barely swung open when his face set like stone, and his mouth turned to a grim line. His eyes were barely open, and his head was still spinning after a late night in the pub, when he barked at the Private.

"What are you doing here?"

If the fear of the devil's elbow was a ten, on a ten point scale, then the young Private Woodhouse reached an eleven when Archie barked at him. On collecting himself he managed to mumble. "The General needs you back."

Despite the fail in Singapore, and Archie's ordeal at the hands of the Japanese, Archie was still cunning and ferocious in battle. The Scottish Gordon Highlanders were also a highly respected regiment and the allies where gaining momentum on the axis forces.

"What General?" Archie asked as he downed a large swig of whiskey.

"It's a bit early for that isn't it lieutenant colonel?"

"Listen, just get on with it, so I can say no then get back to bed."

"General Eisenhower Sir. He personally requested that you return to action.

The allied forces have been gaining momentum since he was given control over all the allied troops. There is some big offensive coming, and he wants everyone back."

"Any word of Major-General Martin Frost? Is he going to reenlist?"

"I know you fought with the Major-General in Singapore. General Eisenhower did send me to get him as well. But he is not going to return."

"Did Major-General Frost say why?"

"Just that he was working on a top secret mission that was more important than the battles themselves. He seemed in good spirits, but was awfully secretive. Somehow even Eisenhower doesn't know about his secret mission."

"That's too bad, he is a good man that I would gladly follow into battle."

"Eisenhower? Isn't he in command of the Mediterranean Theatre? Is that where they want our Gordans?"

"No, Eisenhower has moved over to become the Supreme Allied Commander in Europe. The Gordans could be deployed anywhere in Europe."

"Well if they need me back I will be there."

A few hours later Private Woodhouse, with Archie at the wheel of his Morris C4 easily navigated the Devil's Elbow as they made their way to London - to General Eisenhower.

***

Eisenhower's move to Supreme Allied Commander in Europe was one of the early strategic decisions agreed upon by Roosevelt and Churchill, after their pact was formed. It was an easy choice to agree. Eisenhower's star was rising, and he was known for his diplomacy. Auchinleck and Montgomery, the British choices, were both very stubborn and difficult. It was not known what the General's might run into out on the field of battle. Perhaps another copy of this plan, thought Roosevelt and Churchill as they agreed to Eisenhower's appointment to Supreme Allied Commander in Europe.

However, it was the Tehran Conference that truly tested the strength of the pact that they had formed. Weeks before the appointment of Eisenhower, and less than two weeks after their pact was formed, Roosevelt and Churchill, met with Joseph Stalin, the Soviet Leader. The meeting was to discuss war strategy. The plans had been in progress long before Martin met with Churchill.

Before their meeting with Stalin, Roosevelt and Churchill agreed that Stalin would be excluded from the pact. All that was left to be done was to carve up Europe, and to make sure the world never knew how this whole thing really got started.

With the knowledge of the plan that Martin gave them, the shape of what the world could be after the war, and their pact, Roosevelt and Churchill were now anxious to bring the war to a conclusion. Stalin was also anxiously waiting for the allies to begin their offensive in the west and south of Europe. He would attack from the north and east and they would meet in the middle.

The post war carve up of Europe was agreed at the Tehran Conference, and Roosevelt agreed to get Rockefeller and his bunch under control.

✳✳✳

Also in February 1944 Hoover walked through the doors of the "bunker" in Forest Hills - Junior's bunker. Something he did every third Tuesday of the month, at precisely 9:00pm. But Tuesday, was different. Hoover arrived late and distraught. He was visibly frustrated. He looked as though he was about to explode. His face was a flush and pink at his blood boiled over, and he took deep breaths to control himself. Ready to just shout at the top of his lungs, he banged his hands on the table like a toddler having a tantrum, before opening his mouth to speak.

"Where is the good scotch, Junior?" He asked with complete control.

"The cabinet to the left, on the top shelf. Now come down and tell me what has you this way."

"I want you to be patient with this, Junior. But we have a problem with the Bletchley three," Hoover said as he downed a large amount of the good scotch in a single gulp.

"Davis and Delaney were on them as they travelled to London, but they managed to elude them. It's looks like they are meeting with people and talking about the plan they found. But what's got me really frustrated is that they are on to us now."

"That explains things. I have been summoned to the Oval Office. Roosevelt must be on to us. Which means they probably met with Churchill."

"That's not good, but it may work in our favour."

"How so?"

"Well, Roosevelt hasn't contacted you to deal with me. That means that he and Churchill must be trying to make something of what we started. We just have to figure out how to survive this now."

Hoover was now settling down. The calmness of Junior was starting to clear his head.

"What next, Junior?"

"Next I meet with Roosevelt. I find out what he knows and what he wants to do. Then we can decide our next step."

Junior was no stranger to the Oval Office. He strode through the White House and was greeted as if was the President himself. As he made his way, his mind flashed through all the possibilities of where Roosevelt might go with the conversation. He thought he had covered every possible scenario. But as soon as Roosevelt began to speak he realised that there was one scenario he had not considered. After a few pleasantries Roosevelt got to the point.

"The reason I have asked you here is that Harry, in reference to Harry Truman his Vice President, doesn't want the Vice Presidency anymore. Truth be told I really don't think he ever wanted to be the Vice President. He wanted my job; he is a leader and a decision maker. He is frustrated being my second."

"That has been obvious, but has that got to do with me," asked a surprised Junior.

The bound of secrecy that came with the Vice Presidency would secure Junior's life long silence. It was a shrewd strategic decision on Roosevelt's behalf, as anything else was unthinkable. Junior's philanthropy and ties to the community made him indispensable.

"I want you to consider taking the job, Junior." Replied Roosevelt.

"I am honoured, Mister President. It's an incredible responsibility at a critical time. Let me mull it over for a bit and get back to you, though."

"Okay, but don't take too long."

The next day Junior declined the Vice President job that Roosevelt offered. He didn't spend a second of time mulling it over. Politeness led him to say he needed time to mull it over. However, he instantaneously knew that the moment he stepped into the Vice Presidency role he would lose the power, the influence, and control over the world, that he had.

Junior knew that real power is silent, invisible, and all-consuming. He knew he had the power to set global wars in motion, to steer countries, to repatriate the brightest minds in the world, to control the gene pool of the world, and to kill indiscriminately when needed. He knew he had real power; power beyond a meagre Vice Presidency role.

However, losing power was the reason Junior gave Roosevelt when he declined the Vice Presidency. Shrewd as he was he used the opportunity to further the objectives of the plan in Donovan's memoirs Plan. The process peg of the plan called for being in control of the mechanisms that ran the world. He had once, through his Foundation, controlled The League of Nations. Having first helped to get it setup. Now the President was looking to him, America was firmly in the world as planned, and the order of the world about to change. Now was the time, he concluded. The time was right for him to set in motion capturing control of the process mechanism that will run the run after this war.

"Mr. President," he began.

"There is much to do to set the world back on a level once or enemies are defeated. As you know I am honoured that you have offered me the Vice Presidency at such a critical time.

"However, Mr. President I must decline as my work with the Foundation would suffer, and it is all too important to me.

"The Vice Presidency will need a man that has fewer distractions and commitments than myself."

"But perhaps I may be of service to our country in a different capacity?" Continued Junior.

"Such as?" Roosevelt queried.

"We are going to need to come together as nations after this war. We must ensure something of this nature does not happen again." Junior said with as much sincerity as he could muster, having been the architect that set the war in motion in the first place.

"The League did not perform as it should have after the Great War. But it was a good idea. I would like to support the creation of a new league. A League of United Nations where we are all committed. My foundation will provide the funding. I even have some property in New York were we could build a world headquarters for the United Nations to meet.

"What do you think, Mr. President?"

"I like the idea. I think America can get behind it this time. Pearl Harbour made that abundantly clear. Plus the Brits are already calling for some kind of the Commission to Investigate War Crimes committed by Germany and that lot. It could be the start of something greater."

"Getting it headquartered in New York would also make America symbolic with the seat of world power."

"There is talk of a group of countries coming together to investigate what the Nazis and the Axis powers have been doing to civilians and prisoners. They are calling it the United Nations Commission for the Investigation of War Crimes. A bit of a mouth full, but perhaps this might be a catalyst for something bigger.

"I would very much like your involvement. Keep doing what you're doing with what is left of the League, and let's work together to get something bigger done. It will need your financial backing and network, as it must not be seen as backed by any one Government." Roosevelt said as the two men stood eye-eye shaking hands.

***

One month later the war rooms of Whitehall were buzzing with activity. It was March1944, the Americans were in full engagement mode, the allies were gaining on the axis forces, and there were several plans underway to see the end of the war. Whitehall was also the place that Churchill choose to meet with Martin again. Nothing clandestine or secretive about this meeting. No, he needed to neutralise the Bletchley three, and giving more credence to them with a secret meeting was not the way to go, thought Churchill. Instead he would bring Martin in and, in plain sight of all, they would hide their secret activities.

As Martin made his entrance Churchill glanced up from a table covered in maps. The room which was filled with Generals of every ilk, Eisenhower included, that looked on quizzically. With the hazy mist of grey smoke Martin couldn't distinguish one General from the other. He didn't seem too much care either. He was laser focused and desperate to hear what Churchill had to say. Churchill took a long drag on his cigar. A Cuban cigar. A La Aroma de Cuba, one of his favourite brands. With a glance around the room and a nod to Martin the room emptied. Churchill and Martin were alone. A bit less smoke with the Generals gone, but the stench of cigar and tobacco was still strong.

For his meeting with Churchill Martin had dressed in his fatigues. He was no longer on active duty but wanted to blend in, something that impressed Churchill.

"It's good to see you in that uniform chap," Churchill said as smoke poured out of his mouth.

"Come in, this won't take long."

Martin was focused more on the maps than on Churchill. The army curiosity must have got the better of him for a moment.

"On don't worry about that son, we have them on the run. It won't be long now." Churchill said when he noticed Martin's focus.

"Listen hear. I had the plan you gave investigated. Don't worry though, I didn't give anyone a copy and no one knows you steered me in that direction."

"But son there is nothing to the plan. Just a bit of wishful thinking by a few overzealous business types.

"There is no way they got anything moving on the plan." Churchill told Martin.

It had been so vivid and clearly etched in Martin's head that there was more to the war than the world knew that he was shocked and devastated when Churchill gave him the news.

"But ... but, Sir we have been followed by two chaps. They came done from Bletchley but we eluded them. They have been staying in Bletchley for some time watching us it seems. They're American chaps, and they seem dangerous."

"How can we explain that they? They must be after what we know about that plan."

"They are probably our folks keeping an eye on that Clara lady that first met with Krystyna. I hear she use to be a German spy but is helping our side now. Don't worry about them I will get them removed from watching her."

"Sorry Major-General that it wasn't the news you thought. But there isn't anything to the whole thing. You did the right thing though bring it to me. Our country is in the fight of its life, and we need chaps like you looking out for us.

"If you ever want to get back in the action just say so. We are working on a few offensives now and need every man capable of fighting." Churchill said before giving a nod to the Generals who had returned and was anxiously waiting outside the glass door.

With that a confused and distraught Martin took his leave.

However, there was a silver lining to Martin's visit to Whitehall. As he turned the corner in the winding corridors of Whitehall, he couldn't believe his eyes. There in front of him was his old friend Archie - Archibald Mackenzie of the Gordon highlanders. The last he had seen Archie, the two of them where being whisked away by the Red Cross as returning heroes. A stardom that didn't last long as they were quickly dragged into Whitehall for "debriefing" - in reality they were being interrogated, while the army hunted for a scapegoat.

"Archie, fancy seeing you here. What's going on with you?"

"They came looking for me, and I couldn't refuse. I heard that you did refuse. Some kind of top secret mission. How is that going?"

"Not so good my friend, I just received unexpected news on that front. It doesn't at up for me yet, but maybe it will. I might even join you before the war is over."

"Where are you shipping out to?" Martin asked.

"I was hoping to get back in action in Singapore, but maybe later. For now the Gordons with be pushing the Nazis back in North Africa."

The two men reminisced about the good times they shared. From the night they first met on that transport ship in Liverpool to the last time that had seen each other. Neither spoke of the dark moments in their journey.

***

Archie left for North Africa the next day, where the Allies, and the Gordons, had success. Archie's Gordons then moved on to take the island off to take Sicily. Archie's Battalion bravely fought their way into the village of Sferro. With the Germans now on the run they were becoming desperate to hold any ground that they could. In Sferro Sherbrooke the Gordons encountered a ferocious bombardment from German troops. As strong as they are courageous the Gordons, pinned down from the hills, withstood intense fire, but from the valleys they held their gains against tanks and infantry counter-attack. After a week of fighting, the Germans withdrew to Messina, then eventually away from the island of Sicily.

After victory in Sicily, Archie was hoping the Gordons would then be transferred back to Singapore but instead, after three months hard fighting, the Gordons were recalled to Britain to prepare for a major Allied offensive.

***

On leaving Whitehall Martin went to his parents' home in London. He knew he should've rushed back to Clara and Francis with the news from Churchill, but at first he was too distraught to deal with them. Then he became confused as things didn't seem to make sense. It was all too real to be just a few overzealous business men. Why did Francis get chased in New York? Surely he hadn't been considered a German spy. Why would a soldier like Donovan "Wild Bill" have the plan noted in his memoirs if it were just business men. Then there was discussion of a secret society - The Commission. He wasn't sure if Churchill was misleading him, or if it was as Churchill sad, nothing. Way too much wasn't adding up.

Martin's arrived back in Bletchley a few days later. Francis and Clara were also flabbergasted by the news. It just simply could not be the trio both thought. However, after hours of reviewing everything that they knew, the trio came to the conclusion that it could all be circumstantial. That indeed Churchill had to be right, he had access to greater resources than they did so could easily verify everything. They reluctantly agreed to let it all go and move on with their lives.

In the months that followed Francis buried his head into his code breaking, and returned to work on his theory of a machine that could think like a man. Clara and Martin did indeed get married. Clara did not have any family at the wedding as would be expected. Martin's family, Francis, and a minister were all who were present when the two intertwined their lives even further.

It was a simple wedding held, in Robin Hood sort of fashion, in a natural woodland setting. They wanted their wedding to honour how they came to meet. It was a simple chance meeting on a train that began their friendship, and now a simple wedding in the woods to begin their life together. Oh, what a life it will be, Martin thought as he awkwardly kissed his bride, then glanced at Francis.

As news of their marriage spread throughout Bletchley, Davis and Delaney questioned what they had seen that night outside of Clara's. Was it Martin and Clara, or Martin and Francis, that shared a kiss. But Francis walked away from the house. Maybe it was Francis and Clara. They muddled this over, debated it, and grew confused about it more and more. Then they got the call from America summoning them to abandon their work in Bletchley and return to Washington D.C. At that point, who kissed who, really didn't matter much anymore.

34

Martin hardly ever showed emotion beyond his disdain for the atrocities of the war, and all those that have condoned those atrocities. He showed a concern for the lives of his family, and a polite interest in the lives of those he served with in the army, but otherwise he was stoic. However, today was different. It was the first night of their honeymoon. Everything Clara was saying was perfect. When she voiced her happiness, every word was the right word, her emotions gushed out of her like an erupting volcano. They plunged deep into Martin's heart, invoking emotions that he had long buried, and others that he had never experienced. He felt as if he knew her better than anyone, if this wasn't love then he didn't know what it was, she had truly grown on him.

They had shared so much together in their pursuit for the authors of the plan that he had truly come to know her. He knew her weak spots, her desires, and those things that pained her - yet he had never seen her in the way that he did in these moments. She had changed right in front of him, from the strong focused spy to a soft wonderfully sensual woman. From a marriage of convenience love was truly blossoming. In those moments she was everything, there were no others, his attraction to her grew with each twirl she made, with each smile, and with each sensual touch. Their feelings were mutual, and it wasn't long before Clara was in bed waiting, wanting.

She tried to make out like she wasn't a wet, steamy, pile of desire where she nakedly laid in the bed. But she was lusting for him as she thought about the slick patch of hair, neatly nestled between, the two big swells of his breast muscles. She placed her hands on the curves of his breast as she turned towards him, being careful not to open her legs. She wanted him to open them for her. He did, and she was soft and wet where his fingers strongly caressed. He was hard, and she was as soft as she has ever been before. She was now putty in his hands, as every inch of her body quivered and ached for him.

Martin eased further onto the bed, and on top of her, as Clara stretch her legs open. Then after what seemed like an eternity of caresses, Martin entered her, like sliding into a velvet passageway. He slid deep, then even deeper, as she wrapped her long legs around his back. Her arms and legs pulling him closer and deeper, with every thrust of his manhood. They moved, they paused, they moved again, in a silent dance of love that neither wanted to end. Their face side by side, his tongue gliding, swirling and reaching into the depths of her mouth. The creek of the bedsprings, the moan of her desire, filled the air around them as he grew inside of her. He put his fingers in hers and stretched their arms out. Clara knew then that he wanted her to come first. But she couldn't, she wouldn't, until she could feel all of him, until he was so deep inside of her that she knew that her flesh was all that he desired. That he couldn't stop even if he wanted. She could feel him inside her, enjoying her. A feeling that she had not felt before. She knew then that she wouldn't come until he did.

With a loud moan, a manly moan, Martin let go of all he had, he had given himself to her. Instantly Clara felt his power, she to felt strong, pretty, desired. She took her fingers out of his hands, placed them behind her head. Her legs dropped back onto the bed and her moans went up and octave. With her eyes closed the colours of the world grew brighter, a rainbow of effervescent reds, purples, green, blues and yellows streaked across her eyes. Her moans went up another octave, then another. She could feel her excitement between her legs circling, circling, growing, growing, with each cycle, each swirl, her moan would increase and octave, the cycles of excitement grew shorter and shorter, faster and faster. She knew she was going to come. Then she did. The excitement between her legs, the colours, the moans, all got mixed together, as her body convulsed, and she milked every ounce of its intensity.

Their bodies merged into a white-hot ball of pleasure, flowing together until the last spasm subsided and they were spent in each other's arms, gasping, hearts pounding, unable to speak.

After a few minutes of recovery, Martin then asked her if she was okay. She was, he squeezed her tightly, got off of her and lied down beside her. Clara wanted to say more, but didn't, as she continued to milk the sensation, the ecstasy that she was feeling.

Finally, as her world slowly began to return to normal, Clara spoke again. "Martin! I have never felt what I felt with you just then! I can't find the words to describe it - there just aren't any!"

Martin kissed her gently. "Clara, to be fair, I have never had a woman who wanted me like you did. I have never before had - made love to - a woman like I did with you."

"I do love you Martin, with all of my heart." Replied Clara, as she snuggled into his arms again.

Over the course of the night, and into the next morning he enjoyed her, again, and again. By mid-afternoon they decided to turn on the radio for music but heard news of the war instead.

The long-awaited Allied landing in northern Europe had begun. Clara and Martin knew this day would come when they set their wedding date for 5th June 1944, but little did they know that they Allies would invade Europe the morning after their wedding. When American troops began arriving in Great Britain Martin felt they excited, more than once he considered re-enlisting but never did.

With the radio blasting Martin and Clara sat on the edge of the bed glued to the radio as a blow by blow account was given. There were close to one and a half million Americans that had joined the Brits, Canadian, and other Allied nations in the attack. Under General Eisenhower's command the Allied forces stormed the beaches in Normandy. Neptune, the naval component and assault phase, had moved tens of thousands of troops across the Channel and landed them on the beaches code named: Sword, Juno, Gold, Omaha, and Utah. While British and American paratrooper and glider forces landed inland.

Over the course of the next month the news that Martin and Clara heard brought a mixture of emotions: Excitement, Sadness, Pride, Hope, Anger surfaced as they were taken on an emotional roller coaster.

At first there was excitement as they came to understand the magnitude of the assault. Certainly this would end the war, they thought.

Then there was the sadness on hearing of the loss of life. Nearly all the first wave of men that attacked the beaches had died. Martin's heart sank as he knew if Archie had his way then the Gordons would be in the first wave. Sure enough as time passed Martin did receive news of Archie's death. The Gordon's were at the tip of the spear that attacked Gold beach; Archie led his men to victory that day, but died weeks later when mortar fire hit the Gordons' camp on the Germany - France border.

Pride and Hope surfaced as the troops, despite massive losses continued to advance on the heart of Germany. The Nazis were in retreat when their anger surfaced at the thought of the lives lost as well as with the nagging, haunting, feeling that this war was orchestrated for ulterior purposes. They knew what Churchill had told them, but too many questions remained unanswered for them.

In the months that followed the Axis forces continued to lose ground. Hitler sensing the end was near started to kill undesirables at an alarming rate. Even Davenport started to question Hitler's underlying motives for the war. Was it to gain territories or was it a war of annihilation? Roosevelt and Churchill met again with Stalin to continue to carve up the territories post war. Though, little did Stalin know that it was two against one at the time. By early April 1945 it was all but over for the Axis forces. The western Allies had crossed the Rhine on one side, and the Soviet Union had moved ever closer to the heart of Germany from the other side. It was now a race to see who would get to the centre of Germany, Berlin, first.

***

In America as the war neared its end Junior's problems grew more intense with the possibility of Goebbels being captured. He needed to get to Goebbels before the Soviets, but he could only do that if he had the support of the Generals — which he knew he wouldn't get. Therefore, Junior decided to elevate his position of control and turned to his most reliable friend - Wild Bill. In November 1944 he instructed Wild Bill, as the head of the Office of Strategic Services, to write to Roosevelt and convince him of the need for America to use both overt and covert methods to procure intelligence, and outcomes, on foreign soil. However, once covert was mentioned by Roosevelt to those around him, American agencies seemed to be coming out of the woodwork. Each jockeying for centralised control of intelligence — and the most lethal of weapons. Junior's adversaries were the State Department, the War Department, strangely the Post Office, but even his ally Hoover was trying to break away and take control for himself. The prize to be won was power. However, Junior had that power and he was not going to relinquish it without a fight. As the war in Europe, and the Pacific Theatre, drew closer and closer to an end, the battle for control of intelligence in America was also being intensely fought, Then it all came apart!

On 12th April 1945 Roosevelt died suddenly a brain haemorrhage was the cause of death. Vice President Truman finally got his chance to come out of the shadows. Unfortunately for Junior, Truman had been kept in the dark about nearly everything. Junior was caught off guard and the plan to have one of Wild Bill's men placed behind the lines was suddenly in trouble. Truman hardly saw President Roosevelt. He did not know about the secret plan and the pact with Churchill, nor Project Manhattan. In addition, only weeks after Roosevelt's death, Soviet troops stormed and captured Berlin. In Italy, German forces surrendered, as a beginning of the end of Nazi Germany.

The Italian surrender, though thought to be good by most, only added to the challenges facing Truman. The Blitz, the Battle of the Atlantic, and an everyday struggle for food, had left Britain in ruins, as was most of Europe, so Churchill, calling on a pact between the two countries pressured Truman into taking the lead in the post-war changes while he concentrated on healing his country. An obviously 'shell shocked' man, with so much going on around him at the time, Truman did not ask for details about how the pact came about. Truman knew nothing about the pact but he complied, he led, and the American leadership that Junior's plan had strived for was achieved. Covertly, and unintentionally in the end, but achieved nonetheless.

Allied forces, coming from the south and west, quickly followed the Soviets into Berlin. Along the way they liberated Italy and oversaw the death of Mussolini at the hands of his own countrymen. With the allies and the Soviets closing in on his headquarters Hitler relinquished control of Germany to his closest supporters. Karl Dönitz, who had led the military operations and Joseph Goebbels his friend and the man that helped his rise to power, took control.

By this time Agent One had embedded himself deep into the circle of guards and secretaries at Hitler's compound. Dressed in a German SS uniform, speaking fluent German, and with a message for Hitler from Rommel, was enough to get him through the doors. The Soviet artillery and the need for more guards at the compound was enough to keep him around. Although not fully trusted, by Hitler and Goebbels, Agent One was able to move freely about the compound. However, from the day that Agent One walked up to the compound doors to this day, 30th April 1945, he had befriended the secretaries more than the guards. He had a plan and today it was going to come together.

Agent One was often invited to have tea with the secretaries. They thought he was charming and sincere. They enjoyed his company, but little did they know that they were caught in his web, and like a spider with its prey he was reeling them in a little at a time. Today though, he would strike. There were four secretaries, all polite, but naïve. For months they had had zero contact with the outside world. Now they could hear the artillery shelling nearby and knew something was not right. Brunhilde was the elder of the secretaries and commanded their full respect as well as loyalty. She had been Agent One's primary target. Brunhilde was always careful not to involve herself in matters of the State, as she called it. But today was different. Today she and the other secretaries were scared.

"What is all the shelling about? Are we being invaded?" Brunhilde asked Agent One as she prepared tea for them.

Agent One knew that time was running out. He would not have another opportunity like this one to engage his plan. There was no way he was going to get close to either Hitler or Goebbels. It had to be the secretaries that did the deed. They were loyal, but it was apparent to him that Brunhilde, who was Goebbels' personal secretary, did not like him much. She thought he was unapproachable. He has never asked me a personal question, and probably has no idea of my name. Brunhilde had said to Agent One on many occasions. The other secretaries were different. Most worked for Hitler and admired him. But still they were in the dark about his activities, and this was Agent One's only hope.

"We are losing the war and this compound will likely be overrun any day now." Agent One replied.

"Hitler and Goebbels have an escape route, but we will be stuck, captured. Did you not know that was the case?" He continued as he watched the look of horror form on the faces of the secretaries.

"No, will we be killed?"

"Probably not killed, but you will have to answer to the world for what has been done by those two."

"There have been horrific killing camps setup by Hitler. Tens of millions have simply been exterminated, gassed, shot, you name it. Even more millions in valuables have been taken from them.

"This has been a terrible, terrible, time, and now these two men will simply slip away into the night. They will likely start up somewhere else and do this all over again." Continued Agent One.

Brunhilde's eyes went wide, and she stared at Agent One as if she were looking right through him. She appeared to be instantly ashen, as if all her blood had drained. As she continued to prepare the tea her limbs moved as if some inexperienced person was controlling them remotely. She was shocked, but most of all she was scared. The other secretaries, loyal as they were, also became scared and shocked.

"We didn't know!" A few of them said speaking at the same time.

This was Agent One's time to act. He too was scared, if this did not go well he would surely be put to death. Either as a spy or as a traitor, but his fate would be sealed. Cautiously but in a steady voice he said, "Now that you do know you can do something about it."

"What can we do?" They asked.

This was it. He was about to take the final step that he had been building to since that day when he parachuted into Poland.

"You can make sure that they do not escape. That they are not able to continue their business someplace else, at another time."

"Why do we have to do?"

"Tonight when you serve their tea, you must kill them all. Here is the cyanide just put it in their tea and it will all be over."

It was 3:17pm on the 30th April 1945 and things didn't quite go to plan.

The secretaries did prepare and take Hitler and his wife their tea, but Hitler, keen as he was about assassination attempts, smelt the burnt almond smell of cyanide and went berserk. It was then that Brunhilde moved swiftly. As if possessed she quickly grabbed Hitler's gun, a 7.65 mm Walther PP. A heavily engraved and embellished gun made specifically for him and presented to him by Carl Walther himself. It was a gift for his 50th birthday, and now the gift that would end him. A gift as it was miraculously lying right there in front of Brun-hilde when needed. A quick, grab and release, and he was dead. She had shot Hitler through the temple in what could easily be explained as suicide. Eva Braun, Hitler's wife of one day, on seeing his death, committed suicide by drinking the cyanide laced tea.

On hearing the gun shot the guards, Agent One included, and Goebbels, rushed into Hitler's quarters. The suicide of his wife and then Hitler's own suicide was explained to the guards. After some questioning and suspiciousness the story was accepted. Shortly thereafter, as per Hitler's last words on a written document his body was burnt.

With his plans gone wrong, Goebbels still alive, and the Soviets closing in fast Agent One had to think quickly. One thing for certain the new führer, Goebbels, was on high alert. There would be no getting to him now. But now what? Abandon the mission? Rush Goebbels' quarters in a 'kamikaze' like attack? The first thing to do though was to get the secretaries to safety, thought Agent One.

So he brought the ladies together 'for tea' again, but once the topic of leaving came up the Brunhilde was adamant that she will not leave. Staying and facing the conse-quences would be better than a life on the run. Plus they had done nothing wrong they thought. They were all made to serve Hitler and Goebbels anyway, they said. The other ladies followed Brunhilde's lead.

Almost twenty-four hours had now passed since Hitler's death. The secretaries were on edge. They tried to go about their duties as normal. The Soviet artillery was even closer now. Everyone's nerves were frayed, even the guards. The rustling of footsteps outside the bunker was the final sign that the Soviets had arrived. Two of the guards had given up, cyanide over a bullet. Finally Agent One decided. He would rush Goebbels quarters. A deep breath. One guard at the door, no problem.

As he eased his way past the open, two foot thick concrete and steel, door, a stroke of luck besieged him. Goebbels, who had now taken over supreme leadership, knew that there was no way out for him. Junior would be of no use to him now. His Plan B was to tell all, and claim to have been forced by Hitler. But he could not turn on a dead man. He thought to escape as Hitler had planned, but he would be hunted, found, and killed. So would his family. In those final moments, in a complete panic, Goebbels, a cowardly man, committed suicide rather than risk torture. His wife then poisoned the children, all six of them, before taking her own life.

Agent One surveyed the scene, collected his thoughts, and then quickly riffled through the room. Once he found what he was searching for, he scampered through Hitler's escape tunnel and out of Berlin. By morning he was safely in Poland and on his way back with Goebbels' notes of the plan in Donovan's memoirs plan.

35

In the Pacific recapturing the Philippine Islands was proving to be an impossible task. The battle for Japan also wasn't going well. In strategic cities, the Allies were hitting Japan with everything in an effort to destroy the Japanese war industry, and civilian morale. But this was not breaking the morale of the Japanese people, nor their military that lived by bushido.

Bushido was an ethical system by which ancient warriors, that were trained to fight, lived their life. The core values of bushido were honour and loyalty, but their values also included frugality, righteousness, courage, benevolence, respect, sincerity, and self-control. Those that followed bushido were immune from the fear of death. They were only motivated by the fear of dishonour and loyalty. If they felt that they had lost their honour, or was about to lose it, then according to the rules of bushido, they could regain their standing by committing a rather painful form of ritual suicide, called seppuku. Many of the Japanese kamikaze pilots, that were creating problems for the Allies, linked their deaths to seppuku. The Japanese spirit, their Bushido ways, and their culture were not only baffling to the Allies but to Junior as well.

However baffling as it was Junior still knew that it was only a matter of time after Germany fell to the Allies that Japan would fall as well. He was as unsure of his next steps as he was of the Japanese. In his mind Europeans the superior gene pool, this was why they were the ones brought to America when he began his eugenics repatriations before the war began. Now, he was surprised at the resilience of the Japanese. Was there something to their gene pool that he had overlooked? If he had, it was too late, Junior thought. Once Japan surrender, he could not be sure what Tōjō Hideki would do to preserve his honour. Seppuku? Tell all about The Commission? It was too much of a risk for him to take, and he was not about to let the last copy of the plan in Donovan's memoirs plan get out into the open. Agent One, who had gallantly performed in Berlin, was his only hope. But how? When? Could their bushido ways be helpful?

As Junior pondered how to secure the Hideki's notes about the plan, the process part of his plan was starting to take shape. While Wild Bill, and Hoover, pursued the Bletchley three, or influenced high-ranking officials in America. While Goebbels worked to bring about the war in Germany. While Hideki Tojo riled up Japan. Junior, through his Rockefeller Foundation, was quietly working to transition from the League of Nations.

First, he funded and kept alive The Economic, Financial and Transit Department (EFTD) of the League of Nations. By financing the EFTD's move to America, and all of its work during the Second World War, Junior had the power to control the EFTD and the reorganisation of the world's economic order after the war.

Second, he provided the United Nations Relief and Rehabilitation Administration (UNRRA) arm of the League, with staff, working methods, and a network of contacts around the world. By doing this Junior had the power and control to redefine the overall structure of the world's system of international organisations.

Now with an end to the war in sight the Allies, and friends of the Allies, began to create the master process document by which world order and economic control will be managed. They even met on his home soil at the United Nations Conference on International Organisation in San Francisco. The process that they created, the United Nations chapter, was the corner stone of the process peg of Junior's The plan in Donovan's memoirs plan.

By June 1945 the League of Nations was reborn as the United Nations, and the process part of Junior's The plan in Donovan's memoirs plan was complete. As 'icing on the cake' in July 1945 Churchill lost his re-election bid. Even though Junior never knew that Roosevelt and Churchill knew about his plan, or that Churchill had seen a copy of the plan, it was convenient for him as Churchill never talked of this plan with his successor - Charles Attlee. Yet the pact between America and Britain remained firmly intact, with neither country knowing its true origin.

In the pursuing months Junior's opportunity to get to Tōjō Hideki presented itself.

Despite the capture of Germany the work of the Manhattan Project had continued with urgency. An urgency that was there to avert the Germans getting a super bomb first had now become an urgency to end war. As it would only be a super bomb that would break the Japanese spirt at this point. And break the Japanese spirit it did. In August 1945, following a similar successful test, brilliant flashes of white light filled the sky above Hiroshima and then Nagasaki. While lights that morphed into rapidly billowing orange fireballs, tinged in violet and black, dissolved skyward above these unsuspecting cities. Then a tremendous explosion of sound, followed by thunderous echoes for miles around followed. The bombs had unleashed their terrifying power. The world had crossed the nuclear threshold. The spirit of the Japanese people was shattered. With dishonour and embarrassment they surrendered within a few days. Singapore and the rest of the Pacific Islands were swiftly recaptured, and the war was over.

With the war over the United Nations Commission for the Investigation of War Crimes flew into action. There were trials of those suspected of war crimes held in Nuremberg, Germany and in Tokyo, Japan. It was these trials that created Junior's opportunity.

***

There was silence. Utter silence as Hideki Tōjō sat at the altar of his shrine. Germany had fallen, Japan had fallen, and Tōjō had retreated to his home in Yonago. Maybe looking for divine intervention, maybe to repent for his dishonour, or simply to await whatever fate was to be bestowed upon him. Whatever the reason, as a devolved Shinto, he turned to the kami for guidance, for strength.

In Japan Shinto was the oldest faith. Referred to as the way of the gods. Shinto was not preached and deemed to be free of propaganda as it was deeply rooted in the Japanese people and traditions. There was also no founder of Shinto, and no sacred scriptures like the sutras or the Bible. In Shinto gods are called kami, and are sacred spirits which take the form of things and concepts important to life, such as wind, rain, mountains, trees, rivers and fertility.

Tōjō's Shinto shrine, to the rear of his Yonago castle, held a special meaning to him. In was sacred. Not sacred for the time he would spend there, nor for the gods that he would pray to in his shrine. His shrine was sacred as it was said to have been originally built by Takeminakata the god of wind, water, agriculture, and a patron of hunting and. Tōjō now prayed to Takeminakata for guidance and strength. It was Tōjō's plan to continue to pray and seek guidance until kannazuki, October, the month without gods. The month that the Shinto gods visited the shrine Izumo Taisha, the oldest Shinto shrine in Japan, for their annual celebration. The gods would soon be in residence, and not available to him at his home, so it was now, September, that Tōjō had to seek their guidance.

The Japanese Imperial soldiers no longer stood guard at his castle. This duty now fell to his sons, three of them, Hidetake, Teruo, and Toshio. Like hawks the boys stood watch over their father, mother, and four sisters Mitsue, Makie, Sachie and Kimie. They were expecting the inevitable, American soldiers. Instead he arrived, a lone messenger from Tokyo. At least so they thought.

An American showing up, even with a harmless message, would surely be shot. So, from the shadows Agent One watched as the messenger delivered his message to the Hidetake. Knowing that the trials were going on in Germany meant that his father would soon be arrested so, as Junior had expected, Hidetake swiftly took the message to his father. At the altar to his shrine Tōjō received the message. He read the message carefully, not once, but several times.

"By the time you read this you will be in immediate danger. American soldiers will be on their way to your home. They know nothing. You must not let them find anything. We need you to keep your mouth shut, and not let them know of our plans. How the war was started, nothing at all. If you have any evidence at your house destroy everything. Run and don't look back."

Junior expected that Tōjō would be honourable. That he would act swiftly and would know exactly what needed to be done. Junior was right, Tōjō was bushido after all. Moments after reading the message Tōjō watched as his only copy of his notes about the plan in Donovan's memoirs, along with the message he just read, disintegrated into ashes. Agent One, who had been lurking in the shadows of the castle, also watched on before silently making his escape. With only seconds to spare, Agent One slipped into the wooded area behind Tōjō's shrine and disappeared from Japan. Junior breathed a sigh of relief when he heard that Tōjō had done the honourable thing and removed any trace of their deception.

As the last visible piece of evidence was destroyed Tōjō did not run! Instead he greeted a pack of journalists and American soldiers at the door to his castle.

"I am Tōjō!" he told the reporters. He then turned, walked calmly to his study. Barricaded the door, and fired a gun into his chest.

At the sound of the gunshot, from inside, a dozen Americans crowded into his home wondering if he would survive.

Armed with pistols, they kicked open the door to Tōjō's study, which was barricaded with a piece of furniture; and yelled to Tōjō, who was holding a gun, "Don't shoot!"

Tōjō stood before them with a smoking pistol and a wound where he had just shot himself in the chest. But the gods did not intend for this day to be Tōjō's last. He survived, was transferred to Sugamo Prison, stood trial, and was hung without breathing a word of the nefarious plan that set in motion a cataclysmic series of destructive and deceitful events.

***

In America, Junior and Wild Bill, as the only remaining members of The Commission, moved on to phase two of their plan — creating what they needed to control the world from the shadows, and dismantling any links to their past deceit. Phase two had the same three sections as the first phase - process, people, and science.

The process section of phase two was largely complete though. Junior had successfully transitioned the League of Nations into the new United Nations. His last, and defining, actions were to secure his influence over the United Nations, and to ensure the seat of world power was in America. To accomplish these final actions, Junior donated land in New York City for United Nations headquarters. Once headquarters building was complete, so was the process section of the plan in Donovan's memoirs Plan.

The people section of the plan was to capture, entice, trick, or by any means necessary get the smartest people in the world. Immigration to America was under control. There were quotas and intense scrutiny of those who could come to America. However, the race, creed, ethnicity, and basically intelligence of those immigrating were substandard. Junior and wished for so much more.

In the fall of 1944 he took matters into his own hands.

"We are not seeing the smartest people coming over to America." Junior said to Wild Bill during one of their regular meetings in the bunker.

"They fear for their lives, and are under constant watch by Hitler's men."

"If we want them in America we will have to go get them and bring them back.

"It won't be easy though. The Soviets want them too.

"We might be able to get a few from other parts of the world a bit easier. But the German scientists ate the best." Replied Wild Bill.

"What will it take?"

"Intelligence and a special military force for this mission. I can get the intelligence arranged. But can you help with the military?"

"The Provost Marshall handles the military side of the immigrants coming over. They do the background checks and investigations. Those guys will have the military to help get the German scientists over." Junior replied.

"Don't they work with Hoover's F.B.I. team? He hasn't been with us ever since Truman agreed to reduce the OSS, and set up another intelligence agency of civilians that operate of foreign soil." Asked Wild Bill.

"Yes, but leave that with me."

It wasn't long before Junior had convinced Truman of the need for an operation to bring these scientists to America. Once Truman had agreed the operation took shape. It was given a name, Operation Paperclip, and an agency was created primarily for the purpose of bringing German scientists to America. The Joint Intelligence Objectives Agency (JIOA) made a difference to Junior's plan of getting the smartest people to America. In the pursuing years the JIOA brought hundreds of German scientists to America, they even brought some from other countries. Many of these scientists - physicists, engineers, architects - and those with knowledge that included biological weaponry and advances in rocketry were smuggled out of their countries under the cover of darkness.

To Junior's advantage Operation Paperclip repatriated billions of dollars in patents to America and further fuelled his wealth, Watson's wealth, and the American economic supremacy.

The people section of the plan also meant ridding America of those that were not suited. However, after the Nazis and the Japs had taken the 'ridding' too far, in phase two the plan in Donovan's memoirs plan, it became necessary to focus quickly on dismantling any links to their past deceit, instead of 'ridding' America of those unsuited. It helped that Kellogg had died along the way. Kellogg, although a close friend of Junior's, was a staunch supporter of eugenics - the 'ridding'. In the words of Kellogg,

"Long before the race reaches the state of universal incompetency, the impending danger will be appreciated, the cause sought for and eliminated, and, through eugenics and euthenics, the mental soundness of the race will be saved."

Kellogg was a useful ally when all this eugenics first began, but now, with everything out of control, his chirping in Junior's ears wouldn't be missed. Especially with what Junior needed to do to cover up his past deeds. Kellogg certainly would not take Junior's reversal in this area lightly.

In an about face, a reversal of everything that he had stood for in the past, Junior used his influence over the United Nations to progress and secure what they eventually called - a Convention for the Prevention and Punishment of the Crime of Genocide. A Convention that forbade all of those things that Junior once promoted: Killing members of the group; Causing serious bodily or mental harm to members of the group; Deliberately inflicting on the group conditions of life calculated to bring about its physical destruction in whole or in part; Imposing measures intended to prevent births with the group; and forcibly transferring children of the group to another group.

The Genocide Convention was ratified on the 12th January 1951. In the preceding years the United Nations expanded on the seed planted by Junior to create a in December 1948. With Junior's support of the Genocide Convention he had aptly removed all suspicion from himself, and The Commission, of their previous deceitful acts in the realm of eugenics and euthenics. The wheels of Human Rights were turning, Junior was above suspicion, but there was still work to be done on the people section of his plan.

The science section was still to steal the best ideas and inventions from the countries around the world. With the war over and the best scientists pouring into America inventions and ideas were flowing. Von Brun and others were using bomb making to advance a space race. Watson and others were using code breaking to create machinery that not only helped Von Brun but made them, and Junior, lots of money. Watson had expanded, no stolen, what he was able to get from Francis and Claude about machines that could think like humans. International Business Machines (IBM), Watson's company's advance in this area - computers - where enormous. The American economic engine was roaring forward and so was their world dominance.

The plan in Donovan's memoirs was a success and Junior was elated. A bonus weapon in the arsenal of shadowy world control had even materialised for Junior.

Shortly after Agent One returned to America, Truman began to dismantle those parts of the military that were established only for the war. The Office of Strategic Services was first reduced in size, and significance, and in time it was dissolved and a new agency formed. The Central Intelligence Agency (CIA), the new agency, was created on September 18, 1947, when Truman signed the National Security Act into law. This act not only allowed Agent One to continue to work for Junior in the shadows, but also legitimised his operations. Additionally it set the machinery in place for America's worldwide covert operations on foreign soil. A weapon that Junior would eventually need again.

However, successful the plan in Donovan's memoirs had been Junior was still not completely satisfied. He never was really, but this was different. What continued to nag at him now was the whereabouts of Donovan's memoirs that the Bletchley three found. It has never surfaced and he could not confirm that it had been destroyed.

36

Captain O'Cora, Frederick, went into battle as a conscientious objector, and returned as a hero. After Martin had fought for his right to fight for his country on equal terms, like any white man, Captain O'Cora joined the Royal Air Force. He trained as a navigator and went on to join the 139 Squadron. He became an expert in precision bombing and joined the elite Pathfinder Force. Many of his bombing missions were flown at just fifty feet instead of the normal 25,000 feet. When he had completed fifty missions, the time came for Captain O'Cora to rest, but he refused and volunteered to fly another thirty missions, many of those also at fifty feet. When the war ended Captain O'Cora had flown more than eighty missions over Germany and occupied Europe. He had earned the nickname 'The Dark Knight', and was awarded the Distinguished Flying Cross as well as the Distinguished Service Order.

On his return to Britain, after the war, Frederick settled back into his normal life as an engineer. With the war things pretty much returned to pre-war conditions for people of colour. The only difference was that there was starting to be more people of colour in Britain.

With the fighting over, most people returned to their normal life, but the legacy of the war could be seen everywhere in Briton. In the major cities, particularly in London, there were vacant bomb-sites, un-repaired houses, temporary prefabs, and gardens turned into allotments. The countryside was littered with wartime abandoned military bases. The combination of war damage and a scarcity of manpower, and materials, had created a serious urban housing problem. Nearly half the population lived in private rented accommodation, often in dingy rooms or bedsits with little privacy, comfort, or warmth.

The population, of roughly fifty million, mainly white, had overwhelmingly been born in Britain. But with the war came immigrants. Yes, Churchill gave in to the Americans' push for Britain to take some immigrants that they did not want — the undesirables as labelled by Junior and his staunch eugenicist. Most of the immigrants were white and European, many from Ireland as well.

However, to rebuild a post-war Briton, the Government also invited workers from the Caribbean, especially Jamaica, to fill job vacancies. They were offered jobs, such as labourers and transport workers. Many of the Caribbean immigrants were skilled workers, but because of racism and discrimination, they were forced into semi or unskilled work. They were sometimes derided as 'wogs' and — like many white immigrants, mainly Irish — suffered discrimination in employment and housing. As the rise in immigration continued, so too did the rise in racial violence in cities such as London, Birmingham, and Nottingham. Racial discrimination in Britain during the post-war period became rife.

Frederick was no stranger to race discrimination. He faced it head on with Martin when he sought to fight in the war. While he did not seek confrontation then, now as a decorated war hero, he did not shy away from it either.

On his return to Britain, Frederick settled in Manchester. There was plenty of work, and it wasn't long before he could get a regular pay cheque. When he was expecting his second child, Frederick decided it was time to get a bigger home. It was standard to see signs saying, 'No Blacks, No Dogs, No Irish', when looking for homes, but he found a suitable home in the Chorltonville Estate. The estate was close to his employer's transport routes and had all the amenities for his family.

He arranged an appointment and everyone, his parents, brother, wife and children, went along. They did not find any problems at all with the house; a spacious three-bedroom detached, and wanted to make an offer. He rang the agent, Anthony Smith & Sons, and had a conversation that went something like...

"Are you the coloured family who had a look around earlier?" The person who answered the phone asked.

"Yes." Replied Frederick.

"Our policy is not to sell to coloured people because that will jeopardise the sales of our other properties." Frederick heard in response.

It was a statement that was spoken so casually that Frederick was stunned. This can't be. I have risked my life alongside every other white English pilot. How can this now be happening? As much as he didn't want to jeopardise his employment, or his family's prospects, he also wanted justice. This was when he contacted Martin. He had stood beside me before and I am sure he will again, thought Frederick.

***

After the war, the Bletchley three pursued other interests as they got on with their lives. The plan in Donovan's memoirs plan became a distant memory. Sometimes they would meet up and laugh about their pursuit of the writers of the plan - two of whom they now knew to be dead. They would even, just for a faintly passing moment, wonder if they were misled by Churchill. The chasing the two Americans, who they have assumed over the years were F.B.I. agents, the coding of the authors names, all of that ... Was it really just their minds working overtime?

Francis remained keenly interested in machines that could think like humans. He moved to London where he continued much of the work that he and Claude had only talked about being possible. Although he did have some idea that it was from his secret code breaking work at Bletchley Park. In London, while working for the National Physical Laboratory, he designed a machine that could store instructions and carry them out automatically. However, he soon left London for Manchester and continued to improve upon his work. Francis, was enjoying his work but was never completely at rest. He had his secrets which protecting had become a daily job, and at times, a stressful way of life. More so than his relationship with Martin which benefited from both the wartime distraction, and Clara's frequent presence as one of the Bletchley three.

Martin and Clara remained in Bletchley and enjoyed a normal life in post-war times. Although he often struggled with his intimate relationship yearnings. Martin very much enjoyed being married to Clara, but he also would from time to admire a man. He knew that he liked both men and women, but did not know what to make of it. Once the war was over Martin also returned to the law, and had taken up a permanent job at Dunham and Associates. His cases were largely routine. People fighting with the Government to get their properties repaired the odd drunkenness case, and theft. There were very few divorces in Bletchley, but when they were, he would get those as well. It was Martin's legal practice that brought him back together with one of his first clients - Captain Fredrick O'Cora.

***

Martin arrived in Manchester the next day after Frederick contacted him. After the men caught up about their time in the war, they turned to Frederick's current predicament. Frederick was right. Martin was infuriated.

Breaking the bad news to Frederick, Martin told him that as much as he did not like it, it was a difficult thing to do anything about legally. There wasn't a law in Britain that says what was done to you was illegal. Plus there has been a case of this nature as yet. But yours could be the first.

Martin then explained the "The one I am thinking about is the European Convention on Human Rights." Martin said.

The United Nations declaration that came about after the war inspired the European Human Rights Convention, and that has been signed by Briton. Article 14 of the European Human Rights forbids discrimination on the basis of race and colour.

"We could take your case to the European Human Rights court." Martin told Frederick as his own mind flashed back to the plan in Donovan's memoirs Plan. For a moment Martin froze in time. He had made a connection between the war and what appears to be a positive outcome - Human Rights laws had got better. It was one of those moments when he questioned himself. Did Churchill deceive him or was the plan not only genuine, but was also acted upon? Now though, as he could see a positive outcome, he smiled to himself as he snapped out of his stasis.

"No, no, that won't be good for me and my family," were the words he heard Frederick saying as he returned to being present in the moment.

"Okay, let's go and have a quiet talk with them first. Maybe they will change their minds."

Martin thought as long as he was going to be in Manchester he may as well catch up with his old friend Francis. But he didn't trust himself so he asked Clara to meet him in Manchester for a bit of a reunion with Francis.

****

Three days later Martin, with Frederick in proximity, glanced across the desk of a young lady, Vicky, to find a face of arrogance staring at him. A privileged face. A too familiar face in Britain, these days. Racism. They glared at each other, sizing each other up. It was the first time Vicky had been in front of a lawyer, and a client. She was aggressive and forthright. Society was on her side of these things so why be concerned, were her thoughts.

"How can I help you Mr. Frost?" Sharon said making eye contact with Martin, and speaking as if Frederick was not even in the room.

"I will get straight to the point then. Mr. O'Cora here viewed one of your properties, and would like to purchase." Replied Martin.

"As I told Mr. O'Cora our policy is not to sell to coloured people because that will jeopardise the sales of our other properties. There isn't anything more that I can tell you."

Frederick maintained his composure as he heard those words for a second time. He wanted so much to scream, to tell

Vicky exactly what he was thinking. Tell her that he was better educated; more refined, and had a better job than most of the white people that they had sold to in Chorltonville Estate. However, Martin had told him to keep his composure, that to lose his composure would mean that they would win. They would label you and the words, 'See, see what I mean will quickly follow.' Martin also maintained his composure as he calmly asked Vicky to go and bring her manager out so that he could have a word with him. Vicky abruptly left.

As the men watched the sassy young lady briskly leave the room, Martin whispered those familiar words to Frederick once again, "Keep your composure, keep your composure. It doesn't matter who you are, keeping your composure when faced with adversity is always best. You're levelling the playing field when you do, and giving yourself a chance to be heard, to improve the outcome. It may not be exactly what you want, but it will be better, and you will feel better too." He said.

A few minutes later Martin, and Frederick, were joined by Vicky and another man. On Frederick seeing the man he thought that the man resembled an angry bulldog. This is going to go well was his immediate reaction.

In Britain class divisions were clearly reflected in how people spoke and dressed. Working-class men wore caps and clothes appropriate for manual labour, while middle-class men had white collars, suits and hats. Upper-class was different again. There was a similar, but less rigid, division between working women who wore scarves on their heads and middle-class women who wore hats. There were also class divisions in the education system. State schools for the vast majority, and private schools for the wealthy minority.

Vicky was working-class, and the man with her was a middle-class man, who attended state school. He was a short, burly, un-kept, white man. He wore a white dress shirt, a tie, and a rusty, well wore, grey tweed jacket that contrasted with his sandy coloured hair. But, the most noticeable thing about the man was his extensively protruding midsection. He walked as if his body was a little too wide for his legs, almost as if he needed to be taller to off-set his girth. He had a squashed-looking face that was beet red. A cigarette drooped from his lips on one side, and drool on the other.

The men stood opposite each other, Martin and Fredrick on one side of the desk, and Vicky's manager on the other side. Vicky stood with her manager. On each side of the table there were seemingly immovable forces ready to push against each other for control.

For such a large man Martin and Frederick was expecting the bark of a Rottweiler when Vicky's manager spoke — deep and rough around the edges, a manly voice. Instead he was as smooth as silk, with the bark of a chiwawa.

"Hiya, my name is Anthony Smith and I own this agency. I run it with my sons, but I make all the big decisions. Vicky has told me what has happened. There isn't a law telling us we must sell to your man so we are within our rights. But it's just about business, not your man here."

"I thought this might be just a misunderstanding Mr. Smith. That's why I told Mr. O'Cora, who is not my man that it would be best to just go over there and get things cleared up."

"You are right; there isn't a law in Britain that says you are doing anything wrong. But maybe you didn't know, it was recent, there is an international law that does. Britain has agreed to it and legal action could be taken against people in Britain based on this law.

"It's called the European Convention on Human Rights, and Article 14 of it covers discrimination, prohibits discrimination race. This isn't enforced as yet, but it will be soon. Where do you want to be on this matter when it happens? Think how your business may flourish as a result."

Hoping that what Martin said was official sounding enough to move Mr Smith's position, but expecting that immovable force, Martin and Francis braced themselves for the worst. While Sharon stood scared, and flush, as if she was waiting for the floodgates to hell to open.

To the surprise of everyone, and probably Anthony Smith himself, he smiled, chuckled, and in that smooth, silky, chiwawa voice said: "Hell I never liked that policy of ours anyway. Sharon let's get Mr. O'Cora setup to purchase that property."

"Mr. O'Cora you tell your friends that we are open for business. Lots of it, okay?

With Frederick's case behind him Martin was finally on his way to meet with Clara and Francis. Nervous and confused his heart pounded at the thought of seeing Francis again. His mind wandered from thought to thought as his made his way.

One thought that he had was when he was first with man, Francis. As a boy, teenager, and a young man, Martin was attracted to girls. He had curious thoughts of boys for years, but thought it was just him wanting to be friends with them. However, during his days at Oxford, playing rugby, he became attracted to a man. The second he laid eyes on Sean, the captain of the team, a lightning bolt went through him. He started not only fantasising about kissing him, but asking Sean on a date. Doing things with him - romantic things - that he had only associated with women. That was the first time that Martin could really imagine being with a man.

After Sean there was Emma. His attraction to her was instant. There was something about her that excited him and calmed him at the same time, as if they were best friends on a life journey enjoying one another's company. He fell in love and had a relationship that he thought would last forever. Conscription, and the army, changed that though. The army also allowed him to find who out who he was. He had had months to stew on his thoughts but strangely, while in Dunkirk, as the Nazis closed in on him, with life seemingly about to end, images of both Sean and Emma flashed before him. It wasn't a snap decision at all, but this was when he agreed with himself that he liked both men and women. This was when he knew who he was, when he truly wanted to be able to explore life as he wanted. Now he was thankful to have survived Dunkirk.

Another thought that he had was about the post war British society. Public attitudes towards sex and marriage were strongly conservative. There was still a social stigma attached to single mothers and their offspring, and sex between men was unlawful. Nevertheless the attraction of sex was openly apparent both in advertising, films, books, etc., in the clothes wore, and on the streets where female prostitutes openly solicited for business. Male as well in certain corners and under the cover of darkness. Those, like Martin, whose sexual behaviour deviated from the heterosexual norm adopted a low profile for fear of legal prosecution or social persecution. In the years before Francis and Clara, it was unnerving for him when he admired a man, and other times he felt safe when he would admire a woman.

Today though, with Frederick's case in mind, Martin also thought about the extent to which the European Human Rights Convention would cover his attraction to men and women. In Britain there wasn't anything specific and gross indecency, boys with boys, was illegal.

He pondered these thoughts until he arrived at Mr Thomas' Chophouse, a beautifully decorated pub with hand-cast terracotta blocks, Accrington brick, Victorian tile finishes, interior tiled arches and an intense green lustre. Francis and Clara were waiting for him.

37

Earlier that year Davis and Delaney had thought their days of keeping watch on the Bletchley three were a thing of the past. Just a war time requirement. Then news of Francis' arrest reached them, triggering a night of reflection on their war time exploits. They talked about seeing the Polish resistance and wondering who the trio had met that night in the graveyard. They laughed, they joked, and they reminisced. However, it wasn't long before their laughs turned to curiosity, and Delaney asked that had been on both of their minds over the years.

"What do you think all that was about?" Delaney asked.

"The following, the reporting back to Hoover, trying to capture that code breaker, Francis, in New York." Delaney continued.

"All of it seemed strange to me at the time. Hoover was working with someone. But who why?" Replied Davis.

"Now our code breaker from back then is in the news. I knew something was up when we saw him kiss that man."

"Yes, and we told Hoover about that as well. Do you think there is more to Francis' arrest? Could Hoover be involved?"

The men were not only left with many unanswered questions, but were also now curious enough to try to find out more. The next night they checked into Manhattan's Biltmore Hotel. They requested a suite in the south tower, suite 223. This suite was the one with a clear view of the suite that Hoover and his travelling companion, Clyde, had checked into earlier that day. Davis and Delaney watched from the south tower of the twin tower hotel as Hoover and Clyde prepared to go out for dinner. A dinner that they enjoyed with Junior and his associates at the Yale Club whenever Hoover was in New York.

In public Hoover was a serious and ferocious man. In private, particularly in the presence of Clyde, he was a jolly and playful man. After hours it was rare to see Hoover without Clyde and tonight was no different. As Davis and Delaney waited for their opportunity, Hoover and Clyde playfully bounced around their suite at the Biltmore. To pass the time Davis aimlessly asked Delaney, "Do you think there is any truth to Hoover being a homosexual?"

"Hoover is no fan of homosexuals. But it's possible. He is always with Clyde, they dine together daily, and vacation together, you never know." Replied Delaney.

"There was also that magazine article that talked about how dainty Hoover is, and the sweet smelling perfume. I think he wears ladies perfume. Sounds pretty homosexual like to me." Davis replied.

"But Hoover went on a rant about the fella that wrote that magazine article. I bet he wishes he hadn't written a thing about now. Anyway let's keep our eyes open, and try to figure out what's going on here."

"Yes, let's do, I think there has definitely been a lot going on that we didn't know about. Maybe now we can find out a bit more."

The time felt as though it passed as slow as molasses flowing uphill, but eventually Hoover and Clyde were leaving. Davis agreed to keep up the surveillance on Hoover, Delaney went in for a search of Hoover's quarters.

Hoover and Clyde made their way to the upscale, exclusive membership, Yale Club which was directly opposite Grand Central. On seeing their destination, and its proximity to Grand Central, Davis realised that he had an ideal escape route should it be needed. As an F.B.I. agent trained in counter-surveillance he was used to thinking ahead, and preparing for different eventualities.

After alerting Delaney to his location, and the Grand Central exit plan, Davis entered the Yale Club through the staff entrance. Slipped into the lounge where he found Hoover, Junior, and Wild Bill enjoying pre-dinner drinks. The smoke filled lounge was dark, the windows where covered in heavy drapes, and the lights were dim.

The three men sat in large, high-back chairs, Junior and Wild Bill had their chairs facing a third chair in the corner. Hoover sat in the third chair and had a perfect view of the room. He also had a perfect view of Agent One who had now become a permanent attachment to Wild Bill, it seemed.

The Yale Club had long been their refuge, a place where they felt as though they had risen above the mere mortals of society. At the tables are where their friends in an affluent community. There was a social bond amongst all who were present, yet trust was not a given. The tables were placed in such a way to give privacy to each. Inside the Yale Club, among the muted noises of people, their scent, and their occasional glances, you could speak freely. At least that was what the men thought, and expected, as they discussed all manner of secrecies.

The three men enjoyed their drinks, and their usual update on their exploits. Despite their earlier battle, at the end of the war, for control of the future of American covert operations they had remained close. They shared secrets and their loyalties to those secrets were an unbreakable bond. After the usual banter the conversation turned to Francis' arrest.

Davis, who was now sat within earshot of the men, perked up. But the tables were too far apart for him to hear anything clearly. He stood, as if he was leaving, keeping his back to Junior's table as much as possible, he walked closer to Junior's table and began to fumble with his coat. Then he quietly called the waiter over to fill his water glass. On doing so there was sufficient of a distraction for Davis to leave his jacket, and a listening device inside of it, near Junior's table. It was modern technology and Davis just hoped that it was working. Recording everything.

Over the course of the next hour Junior, Hoover with Clyde in tow, and Wild Bill discussed the setup of Francis, the secret pack, how they started the whole war, and how successful their The plan in Donovan's memoirs Plan has been. It was only fragments of the whole story, but Davis would later be able to piece it together enough to know the truth. Proud as peacocks the men were arrogantly talking, unaware of Davis' presence until he decided to leave.

As the discussions began to wane at Junior's table Davis thought that he perhaps had recorded as much as he was going to get that night and got up to leave. In doing so he knocked over the vase on his table. His water spilled over his trousers. An accident that proved to be detrimental. His secret presence was blown. Hoover turned, recognised Davis instantly, and nodded to Agent One. Aware of his having been discovered Davis grabbed his jacket, with the listening device, and dipped into the bathroom hoping to disappear from sight, before making his way out of the Yale Club. But on seeing Agent One enter the bathroom he knew his escape plan had failed. Davis had never seen Agent One before, but the agent had that look. That ex-airborne ranger haircut, the dark suit, and the solemn look was a giveaway. The M3 fighting knife that Agent One drew sealed the deal for Davis. His life was in danger, and this bathroom could be his final moments alive if he didn't act quickly.

Davis griped the wrist of Agent One. He jerked the agent's arm. Slammed it against the bathroom cubicle. The knife did not drop from the agent's hand. A kick to Davis' chest flung him back across the bathroom. Agent One lunged at Davis with the knife. Davis deflected the knife point with the cubicle door. He breathed a sigh of relief. Then, to gain a brief respite, Davis pushed the agent into the cubicle, and pulled the door shut.

Agent One grappled vainly to escape but with one swift stroke Davis shoved the door into the face of the agent. The force of the door knocked the agent to the floor. Hitting his head he is stunned but conscious. Agent One raised his hands, but before he could strike, Davis had slammed the door again. Still stunned the agent struggled like a landed fish as Davis quickly made his escape.

Grand Central was busy this time of day. There were commuters heading in every direction. The end of day traffic could be a nightmare, but on this occasion it was Davis' refuge. Davis stood in the centre of the main passenger hall, with one eye straining to catch sight of Agent One or anyone else following. He was also scanning the room for his escape route. Blood dripped from the wound on his arm. The agent's knife had cut him during their fight. But now he knew he had won; Delaney was right; he would be able to learn what had been going on all these years. He would be able to escape with his life. "Davis,

Davis, over here," a whispered voice called out from the south exit to the hall. It was Delaney. It was also the escape route.

Agent One bursted into the hall as Davis and Delaney made their escape. His scanning, searching, and frantically moving through the hall was in vain. His escapee had vanished.

The fight, the escape, was three weeks ago. Now Davis and Delaney were in Manchester. Martin, Francis, and Clara were also in Manchester.

Agent One was also in Manchester. When he lost track of Davis in New York, he was sure that Davis would head for Manchester. It was the scene of the latest news about the trio. Sure enough Davis did. So did Delaney.

In Manchester, Agent One awoke in the wee hours to get ready for his mission that day. The day's mission for the former airborne sniper was to gun down the rouge F.B.I. agents before they could make contact with the Bletchley trio. He stalked his prey watching and waiting for the ideal time. He knew Wild Bill would not be forgiving if he missed.

Davis and Delaney began their day at the one location where they could get to the trio. Francis' workplace. They followed Francis to the Chophouse where he met with Clara. Little did Francis and Clara know what was to come.

Also at the Chophouse was Agent One. He finished getting ready and stepped onto the roof of the building across the street. He hunched down and began to crawl up to the edge of the roof where he continued to wait. He eagerly awaited Davis and Delaney to get into the right spot for his shot. He would take them before they entered the building. The moment was near. The Agent then saw a woman and a man walk onto the street. It was Clara and Francis. The couple approach the Chophouse and swiftly went inside. He knew that he needed to act before they could speak with the F.B.I. agents. But he didn't expect what came next.

Davis and Delaney had entered the Chophouse through the rear of the building. They were now sitting with the couple, and a third man that he recognised as Martin.

Inside the Chophouse the trio were apprehensive at first. But quickly came around to listening to the men. Davis and Delaney told them the whole story, as they knew it from their exploits, and the recording of the conversation from the Yale Club. The trio filled in some of the blanks with what they had been through. From finding the plan in Donovan's memoirs plan, to meeting with Churchill, and being told by Churchill to ignore it - that the plan was not real. Before long the truth had unfolded, and the recording of Junior, Hoover, and Wild Bill was in plain sight.

Agent One noticed that they were talking, and that there was a tape recorder. He repositioned himself for the shot. He aimed, steadied himself, slowly squeezed on the trigger. The bullet pierced Delaney's flesh, ripping a hole in his heart, blood gushed everywhere. As Delaney laid in a foetal position on the ground, the others scampered about to safety. A second shot at the unprotected Davis, and he too was dead.

Martin, who had seen death on many occasions, was still severely traumatised. Only moments earlier he had developed a trust, a confidence in Davis and Delaney, and now they were gone. He had watched as they transitioned from human to corpse. Death on the battle field was expected but to have someone unexpectedly, and ruthlessly, gunned down as he sat inches away was traumatic, different. Although brief, it was a very eerie, soul searching, experience for him. There was a moment of grief, as if there was something in these men, their souls, reaching out to him for help - but he could offer no such help. Their cadavers, their corpses, their bodies without their souls, laid therein a way that was difficult for Martin to transmit to his subconscious. In those moments he gained an understanding why they have open coffin funerals. But for the brevity of it all, it was a surreal moment of reflection.

Snapping out of his shock, the armed forces man in Martin, jumped into action. He quickly grabbed the recording with the evidence. Then nearly on all fours he ushered Francis and Clara into the kitchen of the Chophouse, then out the staff entrance. Quickly slipping onto a now hectic street of scared onlookers, police, and armed forces personnel the trio slipped into a taxi and were whisked away.

The next day the Bletchley trio drove along the winding Lake District roads of Cumbria, in the north of England. It was a sunny, peaceful day, and the calm lake sparkled. It was an amazing time of year. Such beauty though was lost on the trio who had spent the night scared and moving from place to place. It wasn't until Francis made the bold decision to ask Arnold, one of his students at the University, if it would be okay for the trio to stay at his parents lake house for a bit. Arnold and Francis had recently become friendly, so it was a bit of a long shot, but one that paid off for the trio. They were finally nearing a place where they could be safe while they planned their next steps.

However, days would pass before the trio would get around to talking about what they had experienced or what to do next. They were traumatised and agreed one thing and one thing only. They agreed no talking about the shooting nor the plan in Donovan's memoirs Plan for two days. They agreed that they needed time to decompress before getting back around to their lives, and the problems of the world as they saw it. The peace and quiet was welcomed, and enjoyed by the trio.

In the afternoon of the second day, as Francis and Clara sat inside the lake house playing board games, Martin sat on the pier to read and clear his head. Birds chirped all around him as the lake waters swayed peacefully. As the sun began to set, the sky became entrancing. The purples, the blues, the shades of organelle and yellow took Martin's mind to another place. A place of solitude. A place where he could see clearly. In this moment he knew what needed to be done. As the air began to chill he decided to go inside. However, as he walked towards the house he noticed something odd in the water. He squinted; he strained his eyes, but couldn't quite make out what was so strange about what he was seeing.

Panic and fear set in as he rushed to get Francis and Clara. Before long the trio was sitting on the pier watching, waiting to see what was so weird. It couldn't be danger. No one knew where they were. What could be this strange object approaching them? Eventually, as the object came close enough for them to see, they couldn't believe their eyes. It was a kayak. Across the bow of the kayak laid a huge red deer, it's antlers trailed in the water on either side, and its centre mass obscured a man. Obviously a hunter on his return from a successful hunt. The trio began to laugh hysterically as the man and the deer passed. They laughed, and they laughed, until they could no more. In the moments after that, when the laughter had settled, they again came to understand that no fear, no stress, no worry was worth them remaining in hiding. It was good to laugh they thought, but now, now the time for them to act. It was time to return to the public eye. With these thoughts in mind, they carefully began to plot their next steps. This time they will be careful. This time they will expose those behind the horrors of the war that the world had just experienced. This time they will obtain justice for everyone harmed by the war.

***

When Wild Bill, Hoover, and Junior were told about the Chophouse scene they were not at all pleased. Davis and Delaney being out of the picture was a plus that perhaps saved Agent One the chastising that he feared. Now though, the Bletchley trio not only knew the truth, they also had proof and were nowhere to be found.

"What now?" Asked Agent One of the men.

"We need to finally silence the Bletchley trio." Junior said.

"It can't be as messy as Delaney and Davis, though."

"It won't be too bad, I can cover what happened at the Chop-house up with the Brits. They are both American so the Brits will be glad for us to take this one off their hands." said Hoover.

Agent One was then given his instructions. Do nothing, bide your time, strike silently, recover everything.

38

Francis was annoyed with himself. Oversleeping, running two blocks while a storm threatened overhead was not the way he expected this day starting. He was meticulous, organised, and always on time for everything. He grumbled to himself as he tried to place himself into the day's proceedings. How he overslept and was now in danger of being late on such an important day, was so frustrating for him. He had known that this was always a possibility, but had hoped that public opinion would have changed by now. That he would never truly be in this place.

He quick stepped up the steps, taking them three at a time, then rush inside the imposing building as the first angry drops of what was to be torrential rain began to fall. A quick glance at his watch showed that he had four minutes to spare. His perfect record of being on time would be kept intact if they could get to their designated room in less than three minutes.

"Good morning, I am so sorry," he called out as he half jogged, toward them. There in front of him was Martin and Clara. They had only spent the previous night apart since returning to Manchester after fleeing to the country. "Thank God, we thought something had happened to you," replied Martin.

Luckily, for the trio their court room was on the ground floor, and only a minute or two walk away. They rushed and arrived in the nick of time. Dressed in his 'patented' old sports coat and rather un-pressed worsted trousers Francis stepped inside. Finally, a small amount of luck, he thought as he took his seat.

The war years were a comfortable time for Francis, and others that were looking for same-sex partners. There was a need for women in the workplace, due to the lack of men. Children had been removed from cities and the family structures, with all their expectations, had been altered. Plus, the blackouts created the perfect environment for cruising and quick entanglements. There was also protection in the darkness of the blackouts for those looking for same-sex partners. Added to that was the constant nearness of death creating an urgency that encouraged impulsive couplings. After the war though, the men and children returned, and women were encouraged to become homemakers again. The lights came back on at night, and conservatism returned. Queer people, especially men, were seen as a threat to the upstanding British way of life. Francis returned to being very cautious.

He had not had a sexual relationship since the war ended. Until one day, a little more than seven weeks ago, when he was walking along Manchester's Oxford Street and passed a young man sitting on a bench. The young man was Arnold Murray, an out of work petty criminal that was estranged from his well-to-do family. A troubled young man who also made a small income from male prostitution. Francis glanced at Arnold as he passed, smiled, and then heard the brash voice of the young man say, "Got a fag?" Francis shyly went over, sat on the bench beside the young man. A few awkward minutes followed before Francis was brave enough to invite Arnold to lunch. "Beggars can't be choosers," Arnold said before heading off to lunch.

A few days later, at Francis' flat in Hollymeade, Wilmslow the two had sex. Afterwards Francis gave Arnold a penknife as a gift, but Arnold was unemployed and wanted cash instead. So the next time the two were together he stole cash from Francis. Arnold's friends also burgled Francis' flat a few days later. Sure that Arnold had robbed him Francis still had sex with him again, then in the morning the two men went to the police station. It was here, at the police station, that Francis' luck got even worse. During questioning, in the course of reporting the burglary, Francis admitted to having had sex with Arnold three times. Each occasion of sex counted as two separate crimes one of gross indecency with another male person, and the reciprocal crime of being party to the commission of an act of gross indecency. So Francis had committed six criminal acts. Still, after Francis made his statement, he asked the police officer: "What is going to happen about all this? Isn't there a Royal Commission sitting to legalise it?" He thought he would not be charged. However, the police ignored the burglary and charged Francis with gross indecency. All six criminal offences.

It had been seven weeks since his bad luck began when he first met Arnold. In that time, he had been arrested, chased, almost killed, and forced to hide out for weeks. Now, after a shaky start to his day, with Martin, his lawyer, at his side and Clara, his friend, in the stands for support, Francis, and his co-accused, finally stood in front of a judge for their acts. His honour Judge J Frazer Harrison was hearing of the case of Regina v. Lambert and Murray, and the trio were confident of a very positive outcome. After all Francis had an excellent man in his corner, a good support network, and he was a hero.

Even though he couldn't speak of what he had done, the world knew it was something and surely that would do him well, Francis mumbled under his breath. Maybe this will also be an opportunity of a lifetime as well. Maybe it will change things for everyone, he thought. However, that was not the case. It was a quick trial, and the court was not lenient on Francis.

Both men pleaded guilty on all six counts. Francis had impressive character witnesses, but Arnold's lawyer successfully shifted the blame onto Francis for approaching Arnold. "If Arnold had not met Francis he would not have indulged in that practice or stolen the cash," the barrister argued. Despite previous criminal convictions Arnold was only given a twelve month conditional discharge. The condition? Good behaviour.

Martin, saw what was coming and managed to steer the court away from sending Francis to prison. "There is treatment which could be given to my client. I ask you to think that the public interest would not be better served if he is not taken away from the very important work he is doing." Martin asked the judge. The judge followed Martin's lead. Francis was sentenced to twelve months' probation and was ordered to submit for anaphrodisiac treatment, to reduce his libido and sexual activity, at the Manchester Royal Infirmary. Although Francis thought that this, chemical castration at the infirmary, was better than prison he was also scared. Before leaving Martin and Clara at the court house he told them, "No doubt I shall emerge from all of this a different man, but quite who I do not know."

Francis' had lost control of life. What happened next was clearly in the hands of others - doctors, the courts. But Francis was not alone in his troubles. The American trio - Junior, Hoover, and Wild Bill - were also struggling for control of their lives. With Roosevelt, Wild Bill's friend from University and a vigorous supporter of Junior's, no longer in the Oval Office, Post-war America was not being kind to the trio.

It was the Red Channels, a pamphlet, that Davis, Delaney, and another former F.B.I. agent began publishing a few years earlier that started the troubles for the American trio. The pamphlet listed the names of over one hundred and fifty writers, directors and performers who the agents claimed were members of subversive organisations before the war but had not so far been blacklisted. The names had been compiled from F.B.I. files and information from a newspaper published by the American Communist Party. The Red Channels didn't mention the American trio directly, but it turned a big spotlight on pre-war subversive activities, making life difficult for the American trio in different ways.

Junior's problems had begun some months earlier. When he first found out he slammed the newspaper onto the table. He had just read what the politicians had started this time, and his emotions went haywire. It only he had intervened sooner, but he never thought it would go this far and now it was already too late. The House of Representatives had created a committee to investigate educational and foundations and other comparable organisations which are exempt from federal taxes. That would include the Rockefeller Foundation in their investigation, he thought.

This could prove to be disastrous. Officially the investigation is to determine whether these companies that can fly under the radar were using their resources for the purposes for which they were established. They were mainly concerned with organisations that may be funding communism, calling it the use of their company resources for un-American, subversive, or any activity not in the interest or tradition of the United States. That's not our organisation, but we do have some skeletons in our closet, and that was a wide mandate. How far will they go back? Will they uncover the source of some of our funding? What about Operation Checkmate, and The Commission, will this all be unravelled? Thought a furious Junior.

Months later, in the fall of 1952, Junior received the questionnaire. A document sent to all foundations with assets of ten million dollars or more. His blood boiled as he started to glance at the questions. Virtually every aspect of his Foundation's operations was being probed. Plus he was on his own, and the Bletchley trio could be the lynchpin in the noose that was tightening around his neck. Junior had very little influence over the men heading up the Committee doing the investigation. It was looking dire for Junior. Plus Wild Bill could be of no help, neither could Hoover, they both had their hands full with their own issues.

For Hoover, ironically, it was homosexuality that was consuming his life. The American Psychiatric Association had earlier that year classified homosexuality as a kind of madness, an illness. Shortly afterwards homosexuality became a political football. Republican senators quickly jumped into the fray and charged that there was homosexuality in the Truman administration, and that having homosexuality in the White House was a national security threat. The Republicans turned to Hoover, who was known to be a compulsively bureaucratic and controlling personality, who had an intricate system of files on people of influence. Files that were personal and confidential, official and unofficial, and all full of dirt. There were volumes of files on famous actors, syndicated columnists, senators, governors, business moguls, and members of the Roman Catholic Church all labelled as sex deviants.

The file that helped the Republicans was the file that Hoover had on Adlai E. Stevenson, the Democratic nominee for president, and one of the two best-known homosexuals in the state. Stevenson was nicknamed Adeline in some circles. Hoover, who had also exposed other homosexuals along the way, began a smear campaign against Stevenson. But in doing so the spotlight also turned on Hoover himself, who was thought to be a closeted homosexual. Hoover was in a battle for his own public survival. The last thing he needed was for yet another scandal if the Bletchley trio had found someone to talk too, and there would be plenty willing to listen.

Wild Bill had a different set of troubles. After the war Wild Bill travelled the world continuously to observe his organisation in action and to encourage the members of his organisation.

He was often nearby when Agent One was in action. But what was most important to Wild Bill was finding out about the shape of the post world order. Wild Bill had become convinced that a struggle between America and the Soviets was inevitable. He had earlier persuaded Roosevelt that, after the war, the America would require a civilian intelligence agency to provide information on emerging threats, especially Soviet threats. As a result of Wild Bill's efforts the Central Intelligence Agency (CIA) was built, but Wild Bill did not get what he wanted. He was not appointed to the head of the new organisation. Largely due to Hoover's campaign to head it himself. That was 1947.

Now with the 1952 presidential election in full swing, and Hoover, his nemesis from his first bid at becoming the head of the CIA, distracted with the smear campaign he was running, Wild Bill saw an opportunity. He campaigned for Eisenhower hoping to be named the head of the CIA if Eisenhower won. All the while though, Wild Bill's bigger worry was the Bletchley trio. They had information that would put him in a bad light and ruin his chances at heading the CIA. This nagged at him even more after the death of Davis and Delaney, followed by the disappearance of the Bletchley trio.

Each one of the American trio needed to get their house in order, which meant tying off any loose ends like the Bletchley trio. Fortunately for them, with Francis' quite public trial, the Bletchley trio had just resurfaced. Francis' trial had brought not only the conclusion to a horrific period of bad luck for Francis, but also the re-emergence of Agent One. After the Chophouse killing of Davis and Delaney Agent One had searched high and low for the trio. When his efforts to find the Bletchley trio proved fruitless he placed his hopes, faintly, into Francis attending his trial. He was pleasantly surprised to see the Bletchley trio in Knutsford when he arrived. The Bletchley trio had not seen Agent One before so it was easy for him to slip into the shadows of the public gallery inside the classical courthouse to watch the proceedings.

Soon the lives of the American and Bletchley trio's would collide yet again, and it would be Agent One to bring them together. At the conclusion of the trial, with Francis' fate sealed, Agent One and the American trio devised their new plan. A plan to keep their divisive past silenced, as they struggled to hold on to power in post-war America.

An upbeat and rejuvenated Francis emerged from the Manchester Royal Infirmary. His treatment had been deemed a success, and it was time to start his new life. The jovial Francis arrived at his flat in Hollymeade. His hands laden with shopping. In one hand he carried a basket of fruit, and in the other he clutched a small bag of essentials against his crumpled attire. His body was exhausted from his stint in the infirmary followed by his visit to the market. He entered his dusty flat. Unpacked his shopping. Turned on the heating. It wasn't long before the hum of the boiler bounced off the strips of walls and doors of his tiny flat. In time he took a shower. Made some tea and grabbed some fruit, an apple. To help him settle in for his nap, he picked a book from his laden collection. Further Arithmetic Progress Papers, by H. H. Thomas, would both stimulate his mind and relax him at the same, he decided. Little did he know that he not only had a shadow since his release from the infirmary, but that his shadow had also slipped in and out of his flat while he was in the shower.

Before long Francis was engrossed in his book. He reached for the cup of tea on his side table with one hand. His other hand was being used as a bookmark for the book he was reading. He took a sip of the tea, which was no longer piping hot like when he made it. He had been so so engrossed in his book that he had hardly paid any attention to the tea in the last hour. He was oblivious of the real world, oblivious of the wooden armchair he was sitting in, and oblivious of the now hard splashing raindrops on his window. For the past hour he had spent his time in a different, more interesting and more eventful world – a world he often fantasised about, a world where mathematics reigned supreme and machines could think.

The cold tea jolted him back to the world he lived in and his surroundings. On the table beside him was the fruit - the apple - which he had set aside for himself. He picked up the apple and sank his teeth into it. Immediately he knew something wasn't right. He stood, stumbled to his bed, and then, then it began. The beginning of the end. He drifted into the most peaceful hallucination.

All around him, lonely crickets were calling for his company. In his chest his heartbeat slowed to a steady beat. Even though his mind was working overtime everything was in slow motion and there was the brightest of lights that he had ever seen. After a while a voice spoke to him, a distant voice, like it was travelling wave of wind. An echoing angelic voice.

"Come to me my darling. I've been waiting for you." the voice said.

With a strongly functioning mind Francis was convinced that no one was really talking to him. But he could not resist the voice as it called to him. Succumbing to the pull of the voice he had to ask a question. Although he didn't really expect an answer, he asked.

"Who are you?"

"I am your past and your future."

"My past and my future? Do you mean to say that you are...?" A quickly fading Francis replied as his voice trailed off.

This time the only answer he received was a faint sound of a distant howling wind.

"Of course", Francis murmured, "I must be dying. But how? Who?" We're the thoughts in his mind before his body warmed and a peacefulness that he had longed for started to overtake him.

All of a sudden, a mysterious light appeared in the distance. A blue light. The light was faint but luring. Francis was being called to something he could not yet see. The echoing voice was emanating from the blue light, and Francis couldn't help but feel, somewhere deep in his gut, that he had been there before.

"Francis?" the voice called from within the blue light.

An exhausted and barely conscious Francis answered: "Yes?"

"Come here, Francis."

Francis turned in every direction, searching for the owner of the voice. Could it possibly be, he thought. It can't be. Was it Christopher calling to him from beyond?

Francis really didn't picture death to feel this way. "Where are you?" He asked.

"Come closer, come sit with me." The voice replied.

Following the echo of the voice, Francis looked up and saw a silvery blue light emerging from around a distant English oak. It was the most majestic oak that he had ever seen. The oak rose, and rose high into the cloud, way above the blue light, its lanky branches, covered in the brightest of bright sea form white leaves, spread widely as if they were welcoming arms ready to embrace him.

As he stood with his one hand cupped over his eyes, trying to see more clearly, he heard the sound of the voice riding on the winds of serenity once more. It was Christopher, his first love, his one and only true love, calling to him. Francis knew then that it was time. He peacefully gave into the cyanide that had been place in his fruit. A single bite of the fruit returned him to Christopher.

39

S hortly after Francis' death became public Junior received a telephone call.

"One down," the voice said.

"Was it quiet?" Asked Junior.

"It will look like a suicide. Nothing that can trace back to you."

"Did he have it?"

"No."

"Okay, Donovan's memoirs are still in the wind. We need to find them." With that Junior hung up the phone.

Junior then made another call. It was a short call, and only a few words were spoken.

"We are almost there." Junior said to the person on the other end of the call. Nothing more was said, and the call was over.

Elsewhere, on hearing the news of Francis' death, Martin was devastated. He didn't believe that he had committed suicide. Francis would not do that he thought. Why go through the infirmary ordeal to come out and commit suicide. The worst was surely behind him, were Martin's thoughts.

At the funeral Martin stood in front of Francis' lifeless corpse for what seemed like an eternity. He could not believe what he was seeing. Not long ago he had said his goodbyes to Francis as he went into the infirmary. He visited from time to time and was angry with himself for not being there when Francis was finally released. What might he have been through, was eating at Martin in each of his waken moments?

After a while a burly, clean shaving, man slowly eased his way over to Martin and whispered in his ear. "It is time." As Martin looked around he saw everyone around him in tears, crying and wailing over the body. They must have cared for him deeply. They were mostly co-workers as he had little a family to speak about. Still though he reconciled with the lost and was strong for Francis' family at the funeral. Well there was only his mother, but still he remained strong for her.

"I am so sorry Mrs. Lambert he cared for you so much!" Martin said as he fought back tears and embraced Francis mother in a hug. The body in the coffin was her son, but she wasn't quite sure what she was feeling. After Francis' father had died, the two of them had become even more estranged than they were before. Then there was the trial, the family embarrassment, as she thought, and now this, his funeral. She felt something, what? She wasn't at all sure. It wasn't sadness, and it wasn't relief either. She was feeling a bit curious, perhaps. What had made him that way? Was his shame the cause of his death? She honestly didn't know, but went along with the sadness and sorrow of those attending her son's funeral. He must have been a good person for so many to care so much about him.

The priest presided over a very inspirational ceremony, and his closest work associate, from the University, read a touching eulogy that they all worked to write. Then they put him in the ground and buried him. The rest of the day went by with people talking about how loving and caring Francis was to others.

As things began to wind down Francis' mother said goodbye to everyone that came to the funeral, and was escorted away by Francis' uncle. The only other relative to attend the funeral. Martin, Clara and a few others remained at the hall for a bit longer before taking their leave. To Martin's surprise there were no strangers, no one lurking about that he could see, and no reason for neither him nor Clara to be fearful. But he knew this couldn't be over, and there was something on the horizon.

The drive from London to Bletchley that evening seemed tense to Martin. Clara was not her usual self. She was preoccupied with something. Maybe she was scared.

"Is everything okay?" Martin asked.

"What do you think really happened with Francis?" Replied Clara.

"There has been so much going on that it is hard to believe that there wasn't some kind of foul play with his death."

"Does that mean that we are in danger too?

"What are we going to do about this? We can't just wait for them to get to us?" Clara quibbled.

You could tell from the tone of her voice that she was afraid, or she was a very good actress that played the role of damsel in distress very well. However, Martin saw no reason she would be acting, so to him she was afraid. That explained the strangeness that he was feeling from her. Clara had never feared anything in front of Martin, so this was all new to him.

"As long as we have the copy of the plan then we should be safe."

"They would have to know what we know about them, and where that copy of the plan is before they get rid of us."

"But they are not going to get to us anytime soon. So don't be afraid." Replied Martin in the most reassuring voice that he could muster.

"Why, what are we going to do?"

"I have a friend in MI 5. We can trust him. Tomorrow I will contact him and arrange to meet. He will know what to do."

The two then rode in silence for several miles. Martin was lost in his thoughts about how he had arrived at this point in his life. What could he have done differently? If only he had never brought Francis into this mess. His friend, and once lover, would probably still be alive. Not angry with himself, but disappointed, and inquisitive was how he was feeling. Clara was thinking about the ordeal as well. But her perspective was different. She was not thinking about what had happened. She was more concerned with what was going to happen. What needed to be done, was how she phrased it in her mind.

Martin broke the silence when he asked Clara, "Do you ever wonder where we would be had we not met on the train that day?"

"I don't really, because I know in my heart that it was our destiny to meet."

"Do you mean that the commotion on the train that sent me into your cabin, and the gentleman sitting beside you, who left as I arrived, was all a part of our destiny? All meant to happen?"

"Yes, I think that was the case. We were meant to meet. That is what my mother would say. Everything in life is destined to happen. Divinely constructed. She is so thoughtful in that way."

"Well divinely constructed or not, I was so glad that you said yes to having tea with me when our train stopped in Bletchley."

"But I was wondering would Francis still be alive if we hadn't met. If the whole thing with that plan that we had found never started.

"What do you think?" Martin asked.

Clara, whose mind was more on what was going to happen than the past, simply replied, "I don't know Martin, but I was drawn to you from the moment I first saw you." That twinkle of love that had always been in her eyes, slowly peaked through her stoic focus. She loved Martin, and it was obvious. He had been a love at first sight, and her love had grown since.

"Remember that first time that I came over to your house for dinner?" Martin asked.

"That red dress you wore still lingers in my mind," continued Martin.

"Yes, that was the night we shared our first kiss," replied Clara.

"It was also when you told me that you were a German spy. I was so surprised that you trusted me with that information. We hardly knew each other."

"I knew enough Martin. You are a good man and it showed. I knew I could trust you. I still do. Do you trust me, Martin?"

"Of course I do Clara. We have been through so much together. Why would you ask that now?"

"No reason, I was just wondering," Clara replied. He voice trailing off as the words she was saying were not matching what she was thinking.

The two arrived back in Bletchley to a solemn setting. There was so much that reminded them of Francis, and the happy times that they had shared in their home with him.

"I will call my friend from MI 5 in the morning. Let's try and rest now."

"Don't you think he will want proof of what you are telling him?"

"Maybe you should take the plan that we found and Francis' decryption notes with you. Where are they anyway? I thought Francis had them, but with his flat being a crime scene, and nothing being said by the authorities about the documents, I guess he didn't have them."

"No, I have been keeping those documents in a safe place, and I am glad that I have. With all that has happened recently you just can't be too careful." Martin said.

"But you are right. My friend will want proof. I will get the documents before I go to see him."

In the morning Martin gently opened the front door to their house. The rickety sound of the long-unused hinges sent a shiver up his spine and antagonised his jittery nerves. He trusted Clara completely but for her sake it was best that she didn't know the whereabouts of the plan, and Francis' notes.

Grateful to have finally pulled the door all the way open, he slowly stepped out into the dawn of a new day. It was early still. The sun had not yet risen. He paused for a moment, gathered his strength, gently shut the door and began his journey. The sparkle of frozen dew glittered caught his eye as he made his way. He was off to London, and would not drive, that would only alert Clara to his leaving. Let her rest and he will be back soon were his thoughts.

The first train to London was at 7:00am. By the time Martin would reach London the sun would be peaking through the clouds, and the chill would be slowly dissipating. Martin had made the trip many times before. However today was different. He was nervous, jittery, and checking over his shoulder on every turn. Being followed could not be the case today. He could see no one following him, yet there were eyes, and ears, all around him. At the train station Martin called his MI 5 friend who agreed to meet him for morning tea.

In London, Martin, who was now reaching a point of paranoia, walked briskly, always looking over his shoulder. Shortly after he arrived at Euston train station and was on the way. Martin made the turn from Hampstead Road onto Warren Street and was certain that he had spotted an unusual man following him. He recognised the man from the train, and then there he was again. Warren Street wasn't a busy street, so Martin slowed his pace down to allow the man to catch up. At first the man slowed as well. Martin's fear and paranoia was reaching new heights when he noticed that the man had only slowed to check directions. Maybe he was not following me, he thought as his paranoia dropped an octave. Then the man began to move briskly again, and Martin got a clear look at the man. It was the same man from the train. He was a young muscular man, clad in a dark suit, a charcoal grey suit that made him look much older. He was not carrying anything, this Martin found odd. Most men off to work in London carried either a briefcase of a saccule of some kind.

Perhaps the checking of directions was a ruse, and he was indeed after me, thought Martin, as he began to walk briskly again. Not taking any chances, Martin weaved through the streets of London. He would pause inside a shop and wait for anyone following. He even circled back over the streets he had travelled. After many evasive movements, Martin now one hundred percent certain he was not being followed, made his way to the Hither Green Cemetery, it was here that he had hidden Donovan's memoirs after his meeting with Churchill.

There was no-one in the cemetery, but near the entrance, sat an old gent who appeared to be reading a newspaper. Martin paused at the gate, the scenery was gloomy and two dimensional. The grey pathway melted into the still of the morning. He shivered. It was cold. But the shivers were not from the temperature, it was the uneasiness of the moment. He pulled his jacket about him and hastily made his way.

Across the cemetery, nearly ten minutes from the entrance, was the gravestone of Melton Prior, a former war correspondent, that went into battle with Martin's father when he was just a young man. Martin Sr. often credited Melton for his sons very existence, because Melton had saved Martin Sr's life during the Boer war. Melton Prior a name that Martin Jr. would never forget.

The gravestone had sunk into the soft soil giving it the appearance of shrinking. The words engraved on it were weathered the years of rain, could barely be seen, they sat just above ground level and were partially covered with vines that sprawled over the dirt.

After removing the vines, and dirt, behind the gravestone Martin revealed a case, inside of which were the plan and documents. Martin breathe a sigh of relief once the case was secured and wiped clean. He turned, looked at his watch, then church. "What awful creatures," he mumbled. Angels would be a better adornment for a church than the twisted gargoyles that were perched high on the building, "Why would anyone place a monster upon a house of God?" He thought.

Still, he made his way to the building. Martin had decided to spend the time, before he had to meet with his MI 5 friend, here. Francis had died, and he had not shed a tear. This time would be a time to grieve, a time to cry, a time to release the demons inside of him.

Still, he made his way towards the two identical Gothic chapels inside the cemetery. Martin had decided to spend the time, before he had to meet with his MI 5 friend, there. Francis had died, and he had not shed a tear. This time would be a time to grieve, a time to cry, a time to release the demons inside of him.

Returning to the same building where he had once met Churchill strangely had an extraordinarily surreal feeling. Grieving the loss of his friend, fearing what might come next with the whole plan and exposing the Americans, sensing the end of the ordeal was near, all weighed heavily on his mind as he opened the door to the chapel.

Although the building was now a place of worship for Anglicans, it was originally Catholic, the Church's history was closely related to Catholicism. Everything in the chapel had slept a while under a silken dust. Beneath the dust was a history that could only ever have been brought to life at the hands of struggle and triumph. A British history.

Inside the chapel Martin, who was raised a Roman Catholic, and often attended Mass in this same building, instantly felt at ease. As he looked around the structure, each part of the chapel had a symbolic meaning for Catholics, and childhood memories for Martin. From the vestibule he could see the baptism pool to the left of him. The paschal candle stands brought back memories of Easter services when the candles where lit and immersed in the pool as a sign of Christ come to life. He looked at the Holy oil near the pool and smiled as he recalled the Baptism of his younger brother Thomas. Turning to the small wall-mounted holy water fonts near the interior doors he blessed himself as he thought about his baptismal promises. Being here, at this time in his life, made him feel secure. The weight, if but for the moments that he would be here, were lifting. The Nave still had the pictures depicting the Stations of the Cross, an illustration of the story of Christ's crucifixion. Actually nothing had changed, but the use of the building as a place of worship for Anglicans rather than Catholics. The Sanctuary, the Altar, Tabernacle, all the same. Truly surreal for Martin who had not been inside the chapel in over a decade.

The morning was awakening and the light of the day had begun to beam through the Stained Glass windows, as if to raise the statues from the dead. Martin entered the nave, took a seat in a pew, and then knelt. He turned her head towards the ceiling and whispered a payer:

"Lord, I am grateful for all that you have done."

"The struggles I have borne, I know Lord, have been your way of preparing me for new challenges, and new heights in my life.

"Should I falter in my quest to finally expose the truth? Should I not be able to obtain justice? Should my fate be to be brought closer to you Lord, then I pray that you will continue to watch over Clara, and my family.

"We have all been humbled by your gift of life. We have done our best to only move our lips to say good words, to open our minds to friendship, and love, in every form and of all people.

"We have understood that your creation is divine and is to be cherished. Although with struggles, and triumphs, we have worked every day to bring your Heaven on Earth.

"Now though Lord, more than ever before, as I am about to face my greatest challenge, I pray for guidance that I may see my way through the turbulence of those who have harmed so many.

"That such evil is exposed and that the world that you have given us becomes a fairer, and must just, place for all.

"Oh, and Lord, tell Francis I love him, and miss him dearly. Knowing he is with you brings peace to my earthly soul.

"Amen"

Martin then sat in silence. He cried, and reflected on his life, his struggles, and his triumphs.

When his pain was processed, when his thoughts were done, when the ghosts had gone, Martin felt a sense of tranquillity. It was a sense much like the calm of an ocean at peace. An ocean that is not anchored to anything other than itself, yet it was vast and stable. He was finally ready to face whatever came next in this journey that began with his chance mission to help in Bletchley many years earlier.

With that he stood, pulled his jacket around him, and slowly, and carefully, wrapped his scarfed tighter. As he savoured the moments before he would step outside the chapel into a bitter wind that had begun to blew. His hopes on leaving the chapel were that his multiyear ordeal would finally be coming to an end. That his MI 5 friend would relieve him of his worries, and that the truth about the catastrophic war would finally be known.

As he exited the chapel in was over. A large dagger plunged into his back.

The blade viscously invaded his vital organs. Martin let out a loud shrilled cry that echoed in the mist. A second thrush of the blade through his back. His body fell to the ground, as the warmth of life was drawn from him by the coldness of death. Laying there, with blood gushing from his wounds, Martin saw the unclad ankles, heels of the bright red pumps, and sway of the dress of his attacker as she hurried away with the plan and the decryption documents.

***

Later that night. In America. At the Forest Hill's bunker. The phone rang. Junior answered the phone, listened for a brief few seconds, and then hung up. The voice on the other end of the phone call had simply said, "It is done. I have it."

Junior then turned to the room. Sat at the table was Wild Bill, Agent One, and Hoover. He then repeated what he had heard. "It is done. We have it," he said.

40

As for Clara, life was not as she had hoped. She had her family, and riches, but deeply missed her friends. Some days it was very difficult for her to cope. Over the months that followed her brutal stabbing of Martin she would often visited the Hitler Green Cemetery. Somehow returning there, to the scene of her crime, was an endorphin raising experience. An experience that allowed her to self-medicate. It had become her coping strategy until one day, not more than a year later, she mysteriously died from an unknown cause. Most thought it to be some kind of poison.

Clara died never knowing that on the night of her betrayal a backup plan was in motion. That night as soon as she disappeared into the darkness Martin Sr. sprang into action. He rushed to his son's side. In the distance the wailing of sirens could be heard. Blood was everywhere. While applying pressure to the wounds he told his son, "Hang in there son. Help is on the way." He connected a makeshift IV drip that he carried with him just in case of this, eventually. Then he waited.

This was Martin's backup plan, put into motion on his return to London from the Cumbria Lake District roads in the north of England. Fearing the worst he, and his father, devised the plan. The backup plan that his father insisted on. The same backup plan that has now saved his son's life.

The ambulance was a welcome sight, its flashing lights beneath the black sky were calming. In a huff of urgency Martin was carded away. Not long after, taking precautions, Martin disappeared into safety and anonymity.

***

One year later, in Maghiana, a small village on the Moroccan border with French Algeria, Martin sat at his usual table in the corner cafe. The place was filled with people always so close and so far apart. Each in a world of their own. In this place the brown hues, and dark aromatic scents, also stoked Martin's sense of nostalgia.

Martin wasn't sure if he was no longer thought to be a threat. The memoirs were taken from him, but he is the only person in the Bletchley trio still alive. So in this cafe, among the noises of people, their scent, and their occasional glances he had found his refuge. A safe place where he could give his brain the silence, and clam, it needed to understand.

Today, with a calm head, he understood that his prayers had been answered. Not by exposing those behind the plan in Donovan's memoirs, but instead in the unintended consequences of their actions. As the U.N. Charter of Human Rights, and all of its offspring, had cast the future in an even brighter light than he ever imagined. The bright light of the justice that he had fought to achieve had begun. Unintentional justice but justice after all, he thought as Marie walked into the cafe.

Marie was the other reason Martin would come to this corner cafe pretending to be there of convenience. Marie was pied-noir of French descent. In the coffee shop they were awkward lovers, afraid of their desire to connect to one another, they would pass each other daily without admitting the truth — passing like ships in the night. Not a word would be said.

With each stride the strands of her silky dark brunette hair would tumble. She had a sculpted yet simple frame. Her waist was tapered, and she had a beautifully tanned olive complexion. Each day her enticing, steel-blue eyes would gaze over at Martin, then her heart-shaped, strawberry, lips would slowly part as she drew him in with the mystery and beauty of her smile. Today, she smiled at him again. He smiled back. Then opened the card from his father. They were here checking, the card said.

41

That same night, in London, Clara hung up the phone and in a low whisper, that only she could hear, repeated the words, 'It is done.' Afterwards ... She sat. She closed her eyes. She began to reflect. Her mind first flittered on the times that she had met Junior, each time becoming vividly clear and flowing seamlessly from one encounter to the next.

The first encounter was Christmas Eve 1933. Clara had just left the Christmas Market with mulled wine for the holidays. He just appeared before her as she was passing the Christmas Tree in the town centre. A man she had never seen before, an odd man that she thought to be nervous at first, but later understood to be cryptic in his ways. It was near the Christmas tree where Junior made his approach. With his scarf wrapped partially around his face, and his hat tipped to cover his eyes partially, Clara could barely see his face. However, it was the gold and silver that adorned the tree that not only made it a fitting place for her first encounter with Junior, but also an encounter she would never forget.

"Salzburg, is a beautiful place is it not?" Junior blurted out.

Startled, but not afraid, Clara replied, "Yes, it is."

"Are you from here?" Junior asked.

With the second question Clara became suspicious. She began to walk off when Junior blurted out a name. A name that stopped her in her tracks and drew her back to him.

"Joseph Jakobs," he had said.

"What of him?" asked Clara.

"Joseph is a friend of a friend. Don't worry he is okay. This isn't about him.

It's about you." Replied Junior.

"Me?"

"Yes. I have something for you." Junior said as he showed her an envelope with more money than she had seen in her lifetime. It would take her parents, and her, more than a decade to earn that much money.

"What is that for?"

"It's a gift. But how would you like to have more money than you could spend in a lifetime?"

"What would I have to do?"

"Nothing right now. However, one day I may come to you and ask you to do something. You won't say no. You will do it, and when you do, you will be enriched beyond your dreams."

"But if you take this envelope. You cannot say anything, to anyone, anyone, about our meeting today, nor the money." Continued Junior.

Clara took the envelope and didn't think much of the encounter. Perhaps an unstable person who had her confused with someone else, she thought. But he knows Joseph's name, and she needed the money. So, she took the money and agreed to do what was asked of her at a later date - more to get rid of Junior than she was actually planning to do anything.

For Junior, though, it was a pivotal move in his strategy. He didn't have a clue when he might need Clara, nor if he ever would, but she was trusted by Joseph, and Joseph was trusted by Goebbels. That was enough for him. There may come a day when her lack of loyalty to the cause' may in fact become useful. He knew now that her loyalty, her compliance, could be purchased, and that was all that he needed. She was now a tool in his arsenal to be called upon if needed. Sure, enough the day did come when Clara would be called upon.

The last encounter was in the moments before Davis and Delaney met their untimely end. Over the years Clara had questioned Junior's motives and even his existence. She had never heard from him since that Christmas Eve in 1933. That day, near the Chophouse in Manchester, as she bounced along with a soft smile and a calmness to her that approached nirvana, she was possibly the happiest she had ever been. Then, all of a sudden, there he was standing in front of her. Junior was back. This time though she could see his face clearly. It was him. The man they Martin, Francis, and her, had been hunting. Fearing for her life she scanned the surroundings to see who else might be with Junior. To see where the sniper might be perched with her in his scope. But no one was there. Junior was alone.

"Why are you here? What do you want?!" She asked angrily. Her voice was raised so loud that it attracted the attention of onlookers. In response Junior casually turned his face away from anyone's eyes, and in the calmest of voices replied.

"It is time Clara. That favour you promised in the Christmas Market? It's time to do this one thing for me. It's time to be rich beyond your dreams."

"What do I have to do?"

"Kill them both. Destroy the memoirs." Replied Junior.

"Who?" Asked Clara.

"Your two travelling companions." Replied Junior as he walked away. Disappearing into the crowds outside the Chophouse like a ghost in the night.

Clara's brain floundered for a moment. Her eyes were taking in light beyond what her brain could handle. Every part of her went on pause while her thoughts caught up with what had just happened. It took all the courage that she could summon to exit the state in which she had entered. To reengage with the world and her surroundings.

She had grown to care deeply for both Francis and Martin. She could not fathom how she was going to have the strength to kill them both. But as hard as it was, she eventually dusted of her bruised emotions and went inside the Chophouse. Ready to meet Francis and Martin. Ready to do whatever it took to return to her family with the much needed, and earned, riches that they all deserved. Davis and Delaney's untimely death inside the Chophouse frightened beyond any state of fear she had ever experienced, and deepened her resolve. She knew then that the consequences of not doing as Junior had asked would be dire. It would be her death!

As her mind was returning to the present day, and to the realisation that she had indeed killed her dear friends, there was a sudden knock on the door of Clara's Vienna hotel room. The thumping on the door jolted Clara, completed her journey back to where she was, and what she had done. At the door a messenger, said nothing, just handed her a case. Junior had fulfilled his end of the bargain too. Clara was as promised rich beyond her dreams.

***

In America, several months later, with Clara now back in Salzburg with her family, on a brisk winters' day in January 1954, Junior, as was usually the case, awoke really slow and relaxed, allowing the day to come softly into focus. His troubles, of the being exposed for his past deeds of orchestrating the war where behind him, and life was good to him.

However, Junior was getting old. That morning he stood in front of the mirror for far longer than his vanity had demanded in the past. That morning observed more than a successful life. He observed and old man. There was a story, and incredibly richly exciting story, that he could see in every wrinkle on his face. In his eyes he could see even more. The lines of his eyes told of laughter, love, affection, and warm smiles that he had never truly experienced. Most of all though his eyes, his wrinkles, his face told a story of a man, and old man, that had journeyed through nearly eight decades to this moment when he stood here a weary, and somewhat dismayed man. He knew that age and wisdom were two separate things, and that one could arrive before the other. In his case, as a boy, he had been blessed with wisdom beyond his years. Now, though, the years, age, had caught up to him.

Hoover, had managed to silence all that had spoken of his homosexual tendencies with ferocious attacks on the individuals that dared to speak, and all that was precious to them. It had reached the point where his troubles had seemed in vain as none would dare to open their mouths to utter a single word that was not favourable to Hoover. However, Hoover, with a feeling of untouchability would create new troubles and confrontations for himself. He truly enjoyed the combat. Often much of what he would go to battle over was so far-reaching that he would not gain Presidential support for his plans. The creation of a World-Wide Intelligence service that he would leave. The suspension of the rights of people not to be unlawfully detained, was another plan that he advanced, that President Truman quickly dismissed. With Hoover being who he was and so often in the light of the public Junior was all too happy that his association with Hoover had drifted apart. This was not what he had envisaged ever when setting plans in motion to covertly control the world.

Wild Bill's troubles had also come to an end. He was never given the role to lead the new intelligence unit - The Central Intelligence Agency. None too pleased about the outcome of his failure to turn his intelligence efforts, and loyalty, over the years into a lead role Wild Bill eventually settled what was on offer at the time. He settled for the post of Ambassador to Thailand. He justified his settlement, not a failure, but an important post in a country was important to the ongoing Cold War. Wild Bill's transfer to Thailand was applauded by Junior as Wild Bill was also seeking too much of a spot light for Junior's modus operandi.

As such Junior had drifted further and further apart from both Hoover, and Wild Bill, creating an ever-increasing feeling of isolation and loneliness in his aging. A loneliness and isolation that brought him to his decision that morning as he lost himself in thought while his mirror stared back at him.

His decision? It is time!

Breakfast that morning was being served in the sun room of Junior's mansion. Not that there was much in the way of sun late January in Manhattan. But Foley, Junior's personal chef, had always insisted that he serve breakfast in the daylight of that room. Even if it is gloomy, now filled day, as it was this day. Abigail, his wife, and Junior duly made their way to the sun room and enjoyed yet another of Foley's five-star creations.

After breakfast, Junior summoned his children to the bunker. Their first visit, and inside look at the man, Junior, was about to happen. Junior had until this point been careful to shield his children from anything that he was doing. Anything that may not go well and harm them or their upstanding view of him as a father. However, this was about to change.

The boys, Nelson, Laurence, Winthrop, and David arrived together. Abigail, the only girl child, arrived an hour later.

With the arrival of Abby Junior began to speak. He told his children of his connections to the war. The creation of The Commission back in 1933. The fostering of the war through surrogates such as Goebbels, and Tojo, as well as the contents of the plan in Donovan's memoirs plan. He explained that the plan had been devised to ensure that the world would not return to the state it was after the first world war. That it was only this plan, and this way forward, that would ensure the future of the world. He was forthright and adamant that he had done the right thing. We could not leave the world to the politicians, he said. In a rambling thirty-minute monologue Junior unloaded everything he had on his children. He concluded with a desperate plea for them to pick up the mantle. It was their time now, he said.

Each of his children listened intently. The two older siblings, Abigail and John III were silent, but their support could be seen in their actions. Nelson and Winthrop, Junior's third and fifth children, both held political ambitions and were apprehensive. When it was their turn to speak, they let the family know that politics had its place. Laurence, Junior's fourth child, who not known to be an activist, but was a staunch supporter of the family, agree he would do his part but he was all too happy to allow one of his siblings to take the lead. It was David, the youngest of them all, that took up the mantle. As the eyes in the room turned to him David, a studious individual with a great attitude, and a sense of humour said, with the broadest of grins on his face, "So this is what the bunker looks like."

"I have always wondered what you were getting up to in this hideaway.

"Interesting stuff and all I'm all in." David continued.

Nelson then chimed in saying, "We must include the politicians."

But it was Abigail, with John III in unison and full agreement, that gave Junior reason to pause when Abigail, speaking directly to her father, said: "If this is going to happen, and we are going to include politicians and the like, then we cannot operate from the shadows as you once."

Junior had always thought that the best and only way was to operate from the shadows. It had worked for him with The Commission. Plus, there have been many successful organisations that worked from the shadows: The Illuminati, Black Dragon, Skull and Bones Society, and the Franklin Society he thought.

"How else will it work?" Junior asked. Open to anything that his children had to say. After all it was up to them as the mantle was being passed.

"We hide in plain sight," David said.

"We invite all of the most influential people in the world to meet at the same time. As long as we can get them all in one place, we can influence the outcomes and control the world in plain sight." Continued David.

With everyone in agreement, and David at the helm, the family gathering concluded in the usual way with the finest of brandy and best cigars.

Four months later, on the 29th of June 1954, their plan came to fruition. Calling it a conference, and not taking the lead themselves, for obvious reasons, the Rockefellers brought together a group of the most influential business leaders and politicians in America and Europe. They all gathered in the Scandic Hotel in Helsinki, Finland. At this inaugural meeting they decided to call themselves the Scandic Group.

Epilogue

The Great War (World War I), followed by the Great Depression, and with isolationist political policies left America barely able to defend itself, and economically suffering. By 1939 they had a small standing military of barely 100,000 men across all branches and were in no position to wage war.

In Britain, by the time World War I ended in 1918, the economy was on its knees. The war had cost over £3 billion and Britain's trade and industry was devastated. To pay for the huge war debts, taxes and sovereign debt was significantly increased. By 1920, Britain not only faced its worst economic situation in history, but had also been on the cusp of Britain's decline as the world's biggest economic power.

Many other countries found themselves in similar circumstances. None more so than Germany. Following the 1919 Treaty of Versailles Germany was forced to accept the blame for starting the war. They had to pay vast sums of money back to the Allies for the damage caused by the war. Germany also had their overseas empire taken away. The German army was reduced from two million men to 100,000 men, and the country was not allowed an air force, not allowed submarines, and could only have six ships. The German people were furious and ripe for the picking.

Then came World War II and the fates of many countries changed. Fortunes were looted from across Europe, and there was an unfathomable human tragedy. Yet, when the dust settled from World War II a new world order emerged and there were clear leaders.

However, what if World War II was a covert operation, an international conspiracy? What if there were unintended consequences?

We may never know.

What we do know is that over the years covert operations, corporate espionage, back channels, and secret societies have been used to accomplish many things. Some would say that these tactics and societies have been invaluable resources in the arsenal of politicians, and the business elite. Others would also say that secret societies have been of an invaluable aid to the orderly affairs of towns, cities, regions, countries, and the world for many years. Some would also question the morality of these covert like tactics and the existence of such societies. But there would be no denying that covert dealings, back channels, and secret societies all inspire curiosity, fascination and distrust.

Distrust being the operative word, as it is likely the distrust, born within secret societies and covert operations possibly intended for good, that has brought about the global state of affairs as we see it today.

Were secret societies the birth place of distrust? Was the disinformation campaign of Nazi Germany the birth of the information warfare in the world as we now know it to be? For that matter was World War II a covert operation, a staged insurrection, or some other form of secrecy to obtain global control? The answer to these questions may be debated and discussed forever, as, in its purest form, the distrust, born out of past secrecies, will reign.

Nevertheless, there is one thing that is certain. In every action there will be unintended consequences.

The social sciences teach us that unintended, unanticipated, or unforeseen consequences are deemed to be the outcomes of a deliberate action that were not expected or foreseen. Unintended consequences may lead to benefits greater than what was foreseen; or drawbacks such as some positives and some negatives at the same-time; or an outcome that is all negative and completely contrary to what was originally fore-seen.

An unintended, but welcomed, consequence of World War II was the start of the Human Rights movement of today.

In TURNING POINT Junior (J. D. Rockefeller Jr.), through a secret society and a covert operation, had set out to control the world from the shadows. A corner stone to his plan was the resurrection of the League of Nations, an organisation that he had funded and subversively controlled. On the heels of the end of World War II Junior was able to resurrect the League of Nations in the form of the United Nations that we know of today. However, owing to the human atrocities of WWII, which, in TURNING POINT, Junior had a hand in, one of the early actions of the United Nations was to put in place a Charter of Human Rights. The United Nations Charter of Human Rights was an unintended consequence for Junior, but an outcome that was greatly beneficial to the world.

Also, in TURNING POINT, Martin Frost (our protagonist) lives in the shadows of his own sexuality, while defending his clients against racially and sexuality motivated injustices. Had the seeds, planted by the UN Charter of Human Rights blossomed before Martin's cases, neither he nor his clients would have endured the struggles that they did.

If there can be any benefit from WWII, then it has to be the advancements in Human Rights born out of the UN Charter for Human Rights - a post WWII construct, and an unintended consequence.

About the author

John Wellington is an accomplished historical fiction writer based in the English Midlands. With a love for storytelling and a passion for history, Wellington's work is a captivating blend of suspense, romance, and mystery. His writing harnesses the personal challenges faced by his characters, weaving their experiences and struggles seamlessly into the rich tapestry of historical events.

When not writing, he enjoys exploring the outdoors through hiking and meeting new people from different cultures - feeding his innate curiosity and quest for knowledge. His experiences and observations provide fresh insights and perspectives on his writing.

Drawing on his love for hiking and travelling, Wellington brings a depth of understanding and a keen eye for detail to his novels. His meticulous research and dedication to authenticity brings history to life in a way that is both enthralling and enlightening.

Wellington's writing is also heavily influenced by his own personal challenges, and his ability to face adversity head-on has inspired the compelling characters that populate his novels. His novels offer an immersive experience for readers, transporting them to different eras and allowing them to witness the trials and triumphs of the past.

John Wellington has proven himself as a masterful storyteller, captivating readers with his meticulously crafted historical fiction.

His novels are a testament to his dedication to the craft and his unwavering commitment to bringing the past to life.